ZERO WORLD

BY JASON M. HOUGH

ZERO WORLD

THE DIRE EARTH CYCLE

NOVELS
THE DARWIN ELEVATOR
THE EXODUS TOWERS
THE PLAGUE FORGE

NOVELLA
THE DIRE EARTH

ZERO WORLD

JASON M. HOUGH

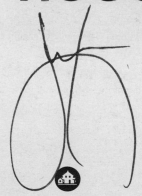

DEL REY NEW YORK

For Nancy

2016 Del Rey Mass Market Edition

Published in the United States by Del Rey, an imprint of Random House, a division of Penguin Random House LLC, New York.

DEL REY and the HOUSE colophon are registered trademarks of Penguin Random House LLC.

Originally published in hardcover in the United States by Del Rey, an imprint of Random House, a division of Penguin Random House LLC, in 2015.

The Dire Earth by Jason M. Hough was originally published in digital form by Del Rey, an imprint of Random House, a division of Penguin Random House LLC, in 2014.

ISBN: 978-0-553-39128-2
ebook ISBN: 978-0-553-39127-5

randomhousebooks.com

9 8 7 6 5 4 3 2 1

Del Rey mass market edition: June 2016

EDITOR'S NOTE

Keep reading after *Zero World* ends for the entirety of Jason M. Hough's thrilling novella, *The Dire Earth*. This exciting story serves as a prequel to his *New York Times* bestselling debut, *The Darwin Elevator*. . . .

The end.
That's where it started.
Or so they thought.

PART 1
INTEGRITY ASSURED

1

IN A LUXURIOUS FLAT overlooking Hyde Park the assassin's mind reverted.

He lay on a stiff mattress in a dark room, naked between silk sheets, cool conditioned air gentle against his face, when the rewind occurred.

Time had just been taken from him. He knew this because he'd been exhaling, a slow, measured breath that suddenly and quite inhumanly changed to a sharp inhale. He'd prepared for this, but even with all his measures to reduce the effect, the moment of reversion always left him disoriented and more than a little nauseous.

The routine he'd developed over the last dozen years involved a careful arrangement of his environment and physical state so that when his mind suddenly lurched backward to the trigger moment, the similarities would far outweigh the changes. He always used the company flat. The same bed, the same sheets, the same pillow. Set the thermostat to exactly 20 degrees Celsius. Kill the lights, draw the curtains, and send his handler, Monique Pendleton, the message: *I'm ready.*

Then he'd lie down, face up, hands at his sides. As agent Peter Caswell waited for her to trigger the implant, he would silently recite an old song lyric. Not aloud, just in his head. It was his secret anchor. His bridge across time.

Speak the word
The word is all of us

Again and again he would recite the words until the reversion moment arrived. It never took long.

This ritual was key. Days ago had been the trigger moment. Monique would activate the implant from her perch a few hundred miles above, and he'd get up and dress and go off on some clandestine job. He'd conduct his particular business, and then return here, to this same exact room, and put everything back just the way it had been. Once again he'd send *I'm ready*. He'd lie down in the same position, and he would wait for reversion.

And so here he was. Mission over, brain chemically reverted to that same trigger instant despite the days that had passed. The first half of the lyric—*Speak the word*—front and center in his mind. A bridge over the memory gap. He crossed it, silently. *The word is all of us.*

Three or four days deleted. That was the average duration, and so a safe assumption. All memory of his deeds wiped away. Conscience cleared.

To jump ahead in time like this, as any drunk would know, can really fuck with the head. To trigger in a London office and revert in an alley in Cairo produced a sensation of disorientation and vertigo that bordered dangerously on the unbearable. Even to go from day to night, or one meal to something totally different, could leave one a vomiting wreck for hours.

Caswell had learned all this the hard way, years ago. Gone from a beach cottage in Mexico, belly full of beer and fish tacos, to drifting in null gravity on an Archon Corporation ore processor with nothing in his gut but nutrition paste. That experience had nearly killed him. It had certainly made a mess of the Archon orbital. More important, the event had forced him to do the thing he detested most in this bizarre life: plan. So he invented the ritual.

Yet preparation went only so far. In four lost days there were thousands of minute differences both to the body and his surroundings, no matter how carefully controlled. Each tiny variation was quite easy to overlook viewed individually, but added together all at once the effect could crush an unprepared mind.

Here now, in this room, the differences began to fall inside his head like sudden rain on dry pavement. A relaxed heartbeat had shifted to a racing one, the rhythm slightly off. One instant he'd been exhaling, then abruptly breathing *in*. Such things made the mind want to react, and react he did. A sputtering cough racked his body. He let it pass and forced himself to focus, to continue the catalog of differences that allowed him to acclimate.

Before the trigger he'd been relaxed and ready, and was now out of breath. Okay, he could deal with that. He must have rushed to get here in time. Not so strange. What else?

A new ache in his left shoulder. Another on his ribs, though less intense.

Stubble on his chin that itched. That was odd; he'd shaved beforehand like always. Why hadn't he had time to shave again before reversion? Because he'd been in a hurry. Right. *Focus, Peter*. He filed that and moved on.

He opened his eyes. The room was pitch black, but that was expected. A sudden shift from day to night could really disorient him, so he always pulled the thick drapes fully closed. Slowly he lifted the blackout curtain beside his left hand. Just a hair, enough to get a sense of things. Gray daylight spilled in. Raindrops on the window. The Thames winding off into the distance between a forest of skyscrapers. London in the fall. That was good.

He let the curtain go, sat up, then stood. Muscles across his body were sore. He felt tired and hungry, yet seconds ago he hadn't been. There was something else, too: a faint antiseptic odor that reminded him of a hospital. Caswell felt his way to the bathroom and switched on the nightlight. He stared at himself in the mirror. A square patch of white gauze was taped to his left shoulder. There were sutures visible on the left side of his torso. Six stitches, recently administered. That explained the hospital smell. The stubble on his face was barely visible, representing perhaps four days' growth, thanks to the curse of Korean genes. What could he infer from a four-day beard? He'd gone somewhere where shaving had not been an option. Somewhere remote. A battlefield, maybe? There was no shortage of those around the world. Or had his cover required a disheveled appearance? His unkempt black hair said yes, maybe so.

Where'd you go this time? he asked the lithe form in the mirror. Not aloud; they'd be monitoring the room. *Do the injuries mean you screwed up? That you're losing your edge? Did you fail?*

For a minute he stared at himself, as if looking into his own eyes might reveal some hint as to what exactly he'd done in the last four days. This burning need swept through him every time, but he always battled it back. Not knowing was the whole point. And truthfully he didn't want to know.

A clear conscience was his greatest asset, the reason for his extraordinary success.

Caswell showered. First scalding hot, then ice cold. He toweled off, shaved, and dressed. Dark slacks, a maroon polo, light gray casual coat. Comfortable Italian shoes. A tungsten biometric bracelet he slipped onto his right wrist. The band performed all the usual functions but also interfaced with the implant, automatically regulating certain aspects of his brain chemistry according to his personal desire.

Phone, wallet, passport. This last he thumbed through quickly, looking for new stamps. There were hundreds of stamps inside, but none were new. No surprise there. Wherever Archon had sent him, they would have provided the required documents. This passport was his, and he had a few more pages yet to fill.

Now came the moment of truth. Clear conscience or not, there was one thing he simply had to know. He went to the kitchenette and gripped the handle of the fridge. Steeling himself against what lay within, he pulled the door open. White light bathed him from inside, along with a rush of frigid air that brought goose bumps to his skin.

The space was completely empty save for the one thing he always made sure they stocked for him: exactly twelve bottles of Sapporo beer. They were in a neat row across the top shelf, from one side to the other. Each had its famous label facing him, save for the last three on the end. Those three were turned to face away.

Peter Caswell felt his stomach tighten. Over the last few days, under the Integrity-Assured status his implant provided, he'd killed three people. All memory of this had just been deleted. Since he'd come up with this way to keep track a decade ago, he'd now assassinated a total of 206 human beings, and the only thing he knew about any of it was the number. That's all he wanted to know.

He could have tried to learn more: taken clandestine pictures, scrawled a secret coded diary, left himself a voice mail on some personal unlisted number. There were a thousand ways to drop such hints that fell outside the safeguards already built into the implant. But part of the reason for his top-ranked status in this career was that he'd never attempted to tell himself these things. The beer bottles were his one allowance. If Monique or anyone else at Archon knew about this, they'd never mentioned it.

Caswell removed the three backward bottles, set them on the counter, opened them, and poured each into the sink. A silent memorial to the three lives he'd taken and the widows or orphans he'd left behind. Then he took a fourth bottle out and opened it with that satisfying *tsuk*. The cap rattled in the sink.

"May someone remember you," he said for his victims, and drank.

On the elevator down he summoned an autonomous limousine on his phone. The sleek black vehicle waited for him outside the doors of the corporate-owned building. No one said a word to him as he exited. No one ever did. Friends, even acquaintances, did not suit him. Relationships were . . . difficult. Memories, the goddamn past, were not for him. He had only Monique Pendleton, the one person in the world who could understand his life, who knew what it was like to have bits of your memories stolen away for security's sake. And though he'd never met her in person, she was enough. Besides, she had the power to remove from his mind the horrors of what he'd done out there. She was the reason he could live with himself.

Peter entered the car and immediately barked, "Turn that off." The BBC news anchor on the seatback screen vanished. "Radio as well," he added. Silence enveloped him as the car slid into traffic. He stopped on the way and bought a scone and coffee, diligently avoiding the magazines and newspapers on display just outside the café door. News was poisonous. To glimpse some headline like THREE TOP MALAY DIPLOMATS ASSASSINATED IN BALI, or something along those lines, would fill his mind with questions. *Had it been me? Was I really capable of that? What if they were the good guys?*

He didn't want to know. He wanted to stay one step ahead of his past, his own version of Mr. Hyde.

But he also wanted to give himself every chance at success. He may have killed 206 people but he gained no benefit of experience from that. To him, they'd all been the first. And the next one to fall would be no different. The perpetual rookie, that's what he was.

"Heathrow, terminal one," he said to the car. His mouthful of scone mangled the words, but the vehicle obeyed without hesitation.

Caswell parked himself on a stool at Wetherspoons, the only pre-security pub in the terminal. He'd chosen the spot, and his mark, after several careful minutes of observation. Someone roughly his size, age, and build. A weary-looking Asian businessman fit the bill this time. Caswell ordered a brandy and ginger ale, plus a burger with crisps. He made small talk with the man next to him.

To be good at his job he had to keep certain skills honed. This was the only gift he could give his professional self: training. Practice. He had no memory of past missions to guide his actions in the field, so he lived his personal life in such a way as to best prepare himself for his next first assassination.

Oddly, it was not knowledge of weapons or martial arts that he prioritized. It was travel. The ability to go anywhere, under a hastily assumed identity, and survive. Not just survive, but thrive. Play the role via total improvisation. Adapt to the surroundings. Live in the moment with only his wits to guide him.

Reversion meant he had five days, give or take, of cooldown time. It was physically impossible for Monique to trigger his implant again before then. Doing so would drive him insane, or worse. So after each mission came the mini-holiday, and with his rather obscene bank account balance, Caswell could literally go anywhere and do anything. That's precisely what he did.

At the bar he ate and drank and made conversation with the mark he'd chosen. One Wei-Lin from Shanghai, a factory manager on his way to a conference in Brighton. Nice enough chap with a strong accent that Peter listened to carefully.

I am Wei-Lin, a Shanghai factory manager. That would do nicely. Caswell paid his bill and said his goodbyes. "I wish you all success in Brighton," he said to Wei-Lin, with a slight bow. The man blinked in surprise, for the voice he heard nearly matched his own.

Caswell walked across the hall, past a crowded simkit parlor, and into the nearly empty bookshop. He meandered to the travel section. In the center of the bottom shelf was a book titled *300 Thrills in 300 Pages: The Adventure Traveler's Guide to the World's Most Exciting Destinations.* Peter Caswell thumbed to page 206, one for each kill he didn't have weighing on his blissfully empty mind.

Page 206. Inland Patagonia, Chile.

"Right," he said to himself. Then he pulled his phone from his pocket and purchased a first-class ticket on the next flight to Santiago, plus a room at a five-star hotel. Wei-Lin had worn a Rolex and fine shoes, so it seemed appropriate for this borrowed persona. Clothes and luggage Peter would get on-site. Adapt and improvise. He'd introduce himself to everyone as Wei-Lin, just in from Shanghai, and strike up dinner conversation about his life as a factory manager. Make up lies on the spot about why he was in Chile, and anything else that came up. Perhaps even have an affair. Should he ever be sent there to remove someone from this world, he'd have a little firsthand knowledge of the place.

He'd *practice,* and hope it helped. After all, 206 bottles of Sapporo facing away from him might tell him his body count, but they implied something else, too: He was brilliant at his job. Whatever he was doing, it was working.

* * *

Peter Caswell was sitting in the concourse waiting for his flight when a little chime in his ear broke the monotony.

"Status, Mr. Caswell?"

"Hello, Ms. Pendleton," he said. "I'm fine, though the shoulder and ribs are sore. But other than that, all good. I'm at Heathrow, just off for holiday, you know?"

She knew of his post-mission activities: trips taken at random to dangerous, thrilling places. She approved with open jealousy, her office being in orbit at Archon headquarters. "Well, cancel your plans. Something urgent has come up."

"Urgent?" He sat up a little. Urgent had promise, but the timing made him skeptical. "What is it?"

"Are you familiar with the *Venturi*?"

For a second he thought he'd misheard. "You mean *the Venturi*?"

"I'll take that as an emphatic yes."

Dusty memories swam through Caswell's mind. Everyone knew at least something about the *Venturi*. A spacecraft where, allegedly, banned weapons research had been conducted. The whole thing had vanished about twelve years ago, leaving behind no shortage of conspiracy theories as to what had happened. Caswell figured the ESA had been up to something truly terrifying and, given UN rulings on how international laws apply to off-Earth activities, they'd scuttled the whole operation before any penalty might arise. "Okay, you've got my attention. What's happened? Details about their research finally leak?" he asked.

"Not exactly. Not yet, anyway. Someone found the damn ship."

Caswell closed his eyes and waited for the other shoe to drop. It was the nature of the job. Archon had obviously learned of this discovery early. Maybe Monique had been asked to eliminate whoever had spotted the thing. Perhaps she had a drone rifle for him to place, pointed at the front door of some astronomer's flat in Cambridge. It couldn't be much more than that. Caswell wasn't used for trivial tasks. He was a hammer, and a hammer drove nails. In his entire career she'd sent him on only a few missions that didn't rate the Integrity-Assured status his implant provided, and they'd almost always been gimmes. Right place, right time sort of stuff, never anything sensitive. And if the rumors were true, you couldn't get much more sensitive than the *Venturi*. "Fuck," he managed to say.

"Indeed. Now listen, I might have figured out a way to get you a seat on the salvage boat."

"What do you mean? What salvage boat?"

"The one that's going to try to reach her before the wreck falls into the Sun." She let that settle in for a few seconds. She always knew when to do that. "There's a flight leaving for Mysore in one hour. Be on it. I'll have papers waiting at our drop there. Full ident kit, plus a few other goodies the team is working on. Use the travel time to get familiar with the *Venturi,* because your cover requires you to know all about it."

"You realize I've just reverted, right? This is a lot of detail you're giving me, Mo." He felt uncomfortable knowing anything at all. It defeated the purpose.

"It can't wait five days, Peter," she said. "That salvage boat is our only shot. And anyway it's a long ride out there. I can activate your implant remotely before you reach the destination. This is, by the way, assuming they take you on as crew, which they had better, if you take my meaning."

So much for ritual, he thought bitterly. No posh flat above London, no comfortable bed, no silk sheets. No row of Sapporo in the fridge. He'd trigger somewhere off-planet on a damned spacecraft. And reversion? Who knew where the fuck he'd be. It was going to hurt.

"Triple pay," Monique added, as if reading his mind.

He snorted. "Throw in four weeks off and you've got a deal."

"Done."

Caswell puffed his cheeks and let out the breath. He glanced at the gate where his flight to Santiago had started to board. "Hell. Okay, Mo. I'm on my way."

The money didn't matter so much as the time to spend it. But it was the chance to remember, at least a little, that left his gut twisting with equal portions of excitement and trepidation.

2

THE DEAD SHIP TUMBLED through space toward the fiery surface of the Sun.

Peter Caswell studied the wreck that had been the *Venturi*. A spherical bulk constituted the largest piece, rolling end over end. Jutting from this was a severed portion of the truss that had once led out to the cargo bays and, behind those, the fuel and engines, all of which was now not much more than a cloud of debris trailing along like a comet's tail. Mentally he reassembled the research craft from the schematics he'd reviewed on the flight out. Everything seemed to be here, just shattered.

"Still holding air?" the mission commander, Angelina, asked, her deep, gritty voice thick with a Central African accent that left little doubt as to who was in charge.

Her question was directed to the man she floated next to, who went by the name Iceberg. He pulled back from his scope and glanced at his superior. "There's holes in it big enough to fly through."

Angelina smacked the back of his head. "Answer without being a jackass for once. What about power?"

Iceberg shrugged and pressed his eyes against the black rubber hood. "No way to tell, Angel. But it's not transmitting shit. Not even an SOS, and the lights are all off."

The captain hovered in silence. Caswell tried to imagine the mental deliberation going on behind her eyes.

The stated goal was simple enough: recover the black box. Someone wanted the *Venturi*'s data and was willing to pay a fantastic sum for it. Angelina and her crappy little independent salvage boat, the *Pawn Takes Bishop,* had known—and possibly paid—the right person at the right time, and won the contract.

Outside the *Venturi* grew larger.

"How the fuck did they lose track of something that big?" Caswell had asked Monique, reviewing the mission dossier in his bunk on the first night out from Earth. The ship dwarfed most space stations.

"My guess," she'd replied, "is deliberate forgetfulness to hide a rather embarrassing cock-up."

He could appreciate that. "Deliberate Forgetfulness" could be the title of his life story.

For the hundredth time he let his gaze casually flick across the other members of the salvage team. They were all older than his thirty-two years, rejects from the corporate asteroid mining operations that no doubt brought them off-planet in the first place. A tough and jaded bunch.

Their ship, *Pawn Takes Bishop,* constituted a pretty typical salvage boat—a corporate discard deemed unfit for work in the Gefion asteroid fields.

Another crewman, Klaus, cleared his throat. "Why's it up here, anyway?" He was looking at Caswell.

Angelina replied without turning her head. "What do you mean?"

"Up here. *Above* the Sun. There's nothing around, so what were they doing?"

"Classified," she replied with more than a little irony. She kept her gaze firmly on the display before her. "Ask the geek."

Caswell offered an apologetic smile, not really looking at any of them. "I was never privy to that—don't have the clearance, I'm afraid. But feel free to speculate. I'm curious myself."

The crew shifted uncomfortably.

Now the captain glared at him. "At some point it would be nice if you earned the air you're breathing, Dr. Nells."

Caswell raised his hands in defense. "You wanted a subject matter expert, so here I am."

"Tell me this, then: What are we going to find in there?"

"A black box," Caswell said simply. Then he nodded toward the wreckage on the display. "If you're lucky."

Pawn Takes Bishop docked with *Venturi* three hours later.

Everything had to be done manually given the lack of even backup power on the other side, but once the rings were secure a tap linked the two crafts' grids and some emergency lighting came on. Faint red light spilled in from the porthole. Iceberg studied the readouts. "Vacuum. Told ya."

Expecting this, Angelina had made everyone suit up an hour ago, save for Iceberg and the mousy engineer, Bridgette, who would remain at the *Pawn*'s controls.

To Caswell the suit felt like being wrapped in tape. The smart fabric allowed for a full range of movement, loosening just enough to let muscles flex, constricting again the instant they relaxed. It all added up to a sort of permanent state of evenly applied pressure, which his brain refused to translate as anything other than stiff-as-cardboard.

The round hatch swung inward and Caswell fell in line just behind Angelina. The big son of a bitch Klaus drifted inside without preamble, headlamp sweeping across a chamber lined on all sides with labeled storage lockers. Two other *Pawn* crew members followed behind Caswell, carrying the tools of their trade.

"IA6," came a voice in his ear. Monique Pendleton, transmitting from Earth a good nine minutes away. *"We've been studying the data from that scanner you're carrying, and only six of the* Venturi *crew are accounted for. One is missing. It's possible her transponder was damaged. Details inbound."* Seconds later a private message indicator blipped on the inside of his visor. *"Once you've installed the tap, your next objective is accounting for this person."*

Caswell turned off his local transmission option and sent a reply. "Understood. If she's here, I'll find her."

Monique's message contained a brief dossier on a scientist named Alice Vale. He scanned it with practiced efficiency, absorbing the important details. The motion pic showed a thin woman with short, stylish brown hair. Her eyes, close together, were large and brimming with intelligence. She hadn't smiled during the ID scan. Her gaze had a mixture of both intensity and distance that suggested someone who lived to multitask.

Caswell's eyes flicked across the details as the portrait spun around. A tall woman at nearly 180 centimeters, and rail thin. She'd been twenty-eight years old at the time of the *Venturi*'s disappearance. Parents, deceased. No husband. No children. Born in Chicago, educated at Dartmouth, tested out early straight into a graduate program at Cambridge. Studied biology and cognitive science. Accepted into the ESA at twenty-six, joined the crew of the *Venturi* just one year later. And then, a year into the mission, it had all ended.

"Sad," he muttered. A promising scientist, lost in her prime.

The team continued forward to the inner airlock door, which lay ajar and showed signs of fire damage around the lip and on the surrounding wall. Debris floated about. Angelina swatted aside a clump of charred fabric and moved up to help Klaus pry the damaged door aside. Together they wrestled its bent shape until a gap wide enough to pass through had opened.

A junction waited within, each wall scorched black by the same explosion or impact that had blown open the airlock door. Compartments led off in all directions.

Angelina and Klaus stopped in the center, letting the rest of the salvage team catch up. Caswell moved aside and steadied himself in the junction, letting the last two in behind him.

"C-and-C is that way," Caswell offered, pointing.

"He's useful after all!" Angelina cried. She turned to face the team. "Okay, the geek is with me. Klaus, you, too. Douglas, check the landers. Harai, see if any of the reactor vessels are intact."

"I thought you were just here for the black box?" Caswell asked.

"You don't know shit about salvage, so just keep quiet unless we ask you something, okay? Okay." She turned and drifted toward the command room. Klaus followed her. The other two turned and went in the opposite direction. Caswell soon found himself alone.

Exercise equipment adorned the surfaces of the room straight ahead. A treadmill. Some handles attached to pulleys embedded in the wall. A used water bulb floated lazily across his view. At the far end a hatch led to the medical bay. It appeared to be fully sealed. Looking at it triggered something in him: a sudden irrational unease, like a child staring down a basement stairwell into blackness. He shook the feeling away.

Satisfied the others were gone, Caswell floated to a blackened panel on the wall. From a pack on his midsection he removed an orange torque wrench, then used one finger to wipe away soot on the locking nuts. The magnetized wrench connected easily, and despite sitting out here for a dozen years, each bolt turned easily. He nudged the panel away from the wall and let it float next to his head.

"Captain?" one of the crew said. Douglas, it sounded like.

"Go ahead," came Angelina's reply.

"Lander zero-one is missing."

Silence. Caswell listened. He marked his audio recording minus ten seconds, just in case.

"Missing as in ripped away in the explosion?"

"Uh. Not sure. Zero-two is still here, looks intact."

"Copy that. Keep me posted."

The radio went silent. Caswell marked the exchange as interesting and sent it off to Monique, then returned his focus to the section of wall he'd just exposed. Within, neatly bundled cables in a variety of colors ran in every direction. In the center, a grid of gold indentations gleamed under the light from his headlamp. From another pocket on his torso he produced a small dark green plastic box with ridged edges. He powered the box on and waited a few seconds for the tiny LED on it to wink from red to a flashing green. Caswell flipped the device around and pressed it against the gold grid within the wall, then fetched the hovering panel.

He activated his private Archon channel. "Mo, the keg is tapped. You should be receiving data now. IA6, out."

Around him, rows of white lights flickered on, so bright

that his visor darkened to compensate. He switched back to the standard channel. "How's it going in there, Captain?"

"Thought you were with us," Angelina replied, her voice curt in his ear.

"Just, you know, soaking it in. Surreal to actually set foot in such a famous—"

"Get the hell up here, Doctor. We're on a schedule."

While she spoke he reinstalled the access panel. "Any . . . uh, any sign of the original crew?"

"Negative."

"And the black box?"

"I'm staring at it right now. Which means I need you here, right now."

"Sorry. On my way."

His gaze went to the exercise compartment again, however, and that round hatch beyond adorned with medical signage. The sight tickled something in his mind. Memories just beyond reach.

A thought began to worm into his mind—the inevitable conclusion whenever something like this happened to him. Déjà vu, or an infuriatingly familiar face. His particular skill set, his augmentation, made all such phenomena candidates for something else entirely: the remnants of a reality forcibly removed.

He willed the thought away. Down that path lay madness. Ignorance, he reminded himself, was bliss.

Yet he couldn't resist the pull. There was . . . something. Despite his better judgment he found himself floating in front of the round hatch marked MED BAY. He wheeled the lever to the open position and pulled. Something pushed against his suit. Air, rushing out. His visor fogged before sensors could compensate. Dry air hissed through fans in his helmet and then condensation retreated.

A monster rushed toward him, arms flung wide as if to grapple. Caswell's heart lurched before his brain fully understood: A male corpse was moving on the current of air that had just been sucked from the room. Caswell shoved the hatch back just in time to feel the limp body flop against it and repel away.

With a deep breath he opened the door again, a few centimeters at a time.

Six bodies floated about within. They were remarkably well preserved, considering the room had still held air. Air, he realized, that would have been stagnant for twelve years.

None of the bodies looked like Alice Vale, so he slipped the hatch closed and sealed it again. If Monique needed to know cause of death he'd explore further, but for the time being he felt no desire to mingle with the dead. He fired off another report to Archon. "Found the six crew you mentioned. They're all in the medical bay—no comments on the irony there, all right? I only glanced but given the room still held air, I'm going to guess sudden and very rapid acceleration did them in." Then he added, "No sign of our missing seventh. Continuing my search."

Caswell drifted into the C&C to find Angelina in the pilot's chair, tapping away at a foldout computer. Klaus knelt beside an open panel at the far end, fiddling with some gear he'd hauled in.

The room had the basic size and shape of all mass-produced station compartments. Five meters on a side, fifteen long, studded with attach points to serve virtually any purpose.

"How's it going?" he asked.

"Waiting for you," Klaus replied.

"Computers are up, huh?" he asked, more reproach in his voice than he'd intended.

Angelina's fingers paused for the briefest instant. "Nothing in the contract about not accessing them."

"If you say so. Find anything interesting?"

"Just—"

An urgent override from Monique clipped the captain's response. *"Agent IA6, this mission will continue under Integrity-Assured protocol. Sorry, Caswell, with the time delay there's no chance to offer opt-in. This came from the very top."*

His pulse swelled to a steady war drum on his temples. Integrity-Assured protocol, or IA, meant nasty business lay ahead.

Monique went on. *"Time critical, I'm afraid. I'm sending*

the remote command to enable your implant in exactly twenty seconds."

Peter Caswell swore. His ritual may be impossible here, but she could at least wait for consent. She'd always given him that much. Time to be relaxed. Opted in. Having fucking *agreed*. Caswell glanced about, feeling the clock tick away like a time bomb. He did the only thing he could think to do and slipped his free hand and both feet into the nearest stabilizer handles on the *Venturi*'s wall.

Ten seconds.

What was so damn important that they couldn't allow twenty minutes for him to opt in? Of course, Monique had answered that: *time critical*. If he were to decline it would take weeks to get someone else out here. By then the crippled station would have fallen into the Sun. He told himself not to worry. Monique had opted in, obviously. For him to be activated meant she had been, too. They were paired. Agent and handler, experts in their respective roles, recruited and linked because their bodies happened to be the rare sort that wouldn't reject the IA-class implant.

Caswell shut his eyes. He took two deep breaths and started to chant the lyric. He could do that much, at least. She couldn't take that away.

This mental anchor had not been part of the training. He'd simply thought it wise to have something familiar on the tip of his tongue when he eventually made the mental leap back across the reversion gap. Sometime, in the next four days or so, he would forget everything that happened from here to that moment. He wondered where he'd be when the time came. Could he get close to this exact set of circumstances? Unlikely in the extreme. But he could do one thing.

Microphone in his suit safely off, he used the seconds left to recite the old song lyric over and over, aloud in case that would help. "Speak the word, the word is all of us. Speak the word, the word is all of us. Speak the word, the—"

At the base of his neck an artificial gland received the specially crafted trigger message sent by Monique from more than 160 million kilometers away. The gland flooded his brain with a biochemical marker.

He lost track of the song lyric, wincing as engineered

chemicals sought out every last neuron like a creeping poison. A hot tingling sensation unfolded from somewhere in the back of his head, thorny pressure that started from the bottom of his skull and pushed up and out until his very scalp felt as if it were being prodded by a million tiny needles from the inside.

And then, quick as it had come on, the sensation subsided. Caswell fought to get his breathing under control and carefully opened his eyes. His vision swam, distorted by tears that would not fall away in the absence of gravity. He blinked rapidly to no avail and then gave up.

"I'm sorry to do that to you in the field, Peter."

You'd better be. He desperately wanted to speak with her, to have a real conversation. He bit his lip instead and waited to hear what task he had to perform.

"Your new mission is still being designed, I'm afraid. The reasons will become clear. For now, your new goal is as follows. . . ."

Caswell swallowed, waiting for the tears to dry and the pain in his head to abate. God, he missed the flat above Hyde Park. The ritual of it. "Never again, Mo." He growled the words, made all the more bitter by the knowledge that he'd forget them. He'd forget all of this.

"First," Monique Pendleton said in a flat, all-business tone that told him things had gotten very grim indeed, *"you are to eliminate the crew of the* Pawn Takes Bishop. *Immediately and with extreme prejudice."*

3

AGENT PETER CASWELL BOBBED against the wall, flexing his free hand and staring at the form of Angelina Monroe, captain of the *Pawn*. She flicked a finger across the display in front of her, reading about what had happened here, no doubt. Her curiosity and greed, that had caused this. Her mission had been to recover the black box, nothing more.

Nothing more.

She'd done it to herself, really. Signed her own death warrant along with the rest of her crew.

This was why Archon had inserted him on this mission. In case these people learned too much. Peter Caswell steeled himself to the task at hand. The murder he'd now perform. However much it might seem like the first, he reminded himself of the true tally: 206.

He found little comfort in that. It was the fact that he would forget everything that served to wind his pulse back to something manageable.

There was a dark red case about the size of a deck of cards on his left arm. Caswell opened the lid. Inside, nestled in a bed of custom-cut gray foam, was a gleaming black tube. He coaxed it free, taking care not to send the weapon floating away. With one quick shake of his left arm the case snapped closed.

Caswell flipped the object around in his hands. A "vossen" gun: Vacuum-Optimized Smart Needler. He'd trained with one, months ago. If he'd ever used it in the field he had no idea.

He gripped it and looked up.

Angelina was staring at him, her lips moving, one hand raised in a "What the fuck is wrong with you?" gesture. He pointed toward his ear and gave a shrug. The woman rolled her eyes and turned back to her work. If she'd noticed the object in his hand, paid it any thought at all, she gave no indication. Probably thought it a flashlight or screwdriver.

Caswell floated until he was beside her and aimed the vossen's business end at the glass of her face mask. Through the gland in his neck he communicated his intent to the weapon: a quick, quiet death that would leave zero mess.

One of the holes on the weapon puffed a tiny cloud of light gray smoke. Caswell caught the briefest hint of the missile's flight. Tiny flashes of yellow as the microscopically small thrusters propelled the toothpick-size projectile through the vacuum.

It hit her helmet and bored inside.

Resin burped out the back end, sealing the hole. Angelina's head snapped sideways. A puff of black sprayed across the inside of her visor, coating the surface from within. A blinded victim could hardly retaliate. Her body began to spasm.

Caswell listened on the open channel. Not even a yelp of surprise had come through because the needle had shorted the electronics in the helmet. Angelina bucked in her chair, clawed uselessly at her now-opaque mask. In seconds her panic and terror turned into a thrashing as the needle's payload went to work on stopping her heart.

Finally she went still, her arms drifting out to either side.

He felt almost nothing for her. It wasn't a lack of compassion, either. That realization struck him as most peculiar. Caswell fully recognized that he'd just taken a life. Someone with friends, perhaps a family. A past and a future. But despite recognizing all that, he found he simply couldn't see this floating, limp body as that person anymore. It was just a corpse now, not something to be mourned. Any grief or regret for those slain would be something he'd deal with . . .

Later.

A chill coursed through him. This is why he was successful. He knew with total certainty as he stared at the body of
Angelina Monroe that he'd feel remorse for this later. Or he
would, except his memory of this would be taken away, his
conscience cleared.

Movement caught his eye. Across the room, Klaus still
faced the compartment where the black box waited. He
hadn't turned, hadn't noticed anything going on behind
him. He'd just stretched his arms, still waiting.

Caswell drifted past the dead captain and plugged him,
too.

The big man took longer to die. He thrashed as she had,
then suddenly kicked out from the wall and groped wildly in
the emptiness for his assailant. Perhaps he'd heard of a vossen, or perhaps he'd just made assumptions. Either way, his
fingers twitched and flailed for Caswell. But Caswell had
moved to rest beside the black box. Klaus's frantic motions
eventually found the prone form of Angelina and he just
managed to gather her in his arms before he, too, went still.

The embraced pair drifted free in the room, faces hidden
behind ink-stained glass.

Caswell let out a breath. *How can I feel nothing?* Delayed
mourning, was that really it? Really him?

Another theory presented itself. His implant might be
short-circuiting the emotional response automatically. It
could do things like that, if he didn't mind the fevers that
would follow. Force him to focus, even fire his neurons
faster, which made everything else seem to slow down.
Maybe it could also dampen whatever part of his brain felt
compassion. He wanted to believe that. The alternative was
too horrifying.

Monique had her reasons, he reminded himself again.
This wasn't in cold blood. These people, their captain at
least, must have accessed highly sensitive information in
the *Venturi*'s computer. She must have been about to transmit it to Earth when he'd plugged her. Monique had seen it
coming. She'd employed him to prevent it. Maybe he'd just
saved a million lives back on Earth. A fantasy, perhaps, but
he had to believe it. Above all he trusted Monique, without
reservation. This was just a job and he was the tool for it.

And, he thought, *I seem to be pretty good at this.*

Sliding into the rhythm of the task, he turned back toward the *Pawn.* He felt calm now, despite what his brain had been through only minutes earlier, despite the nasty business he'd just performed and the conclusions he'd drawn. He pushed back to the central junction, glanced at the *Pawn*—airlock still sealed—and drifted on toward the aft of the station.

The one called Harai rounded a corner ahead, directly in Caswell's path. Caswell ignored the man's puzzled glare. He floated straight to him and fired the needler at point-blank range.

Harai's reaction was different. He all but ignored his sudden blindness and took a vicious swing at Caswell with his right arm. In zero-g the punch had little behind it, and served only to send them both careening off each other. Caswell flopped into the wall and whirled. His target hit the opposite wall, pushed hard with both legs, and came rocketing back. Midway across, his whole body spasmed, then again, more violently. Caswell uncoiled himself and moved aside, letting the now-limp body bounce off the surface next to him and drift.

That's three, he thought. *Three more.*

He turned and stared straight into the wide, shocked eyes of Douglas. "What the fuck?" the man shouted. He had a toolbox in one hand and frantically groped through it with the other until he found what he wanted. A meaty, half-meter-long wrench.

"What's going on?" someone asked. Iceberg, back in the *Pawn.* "Report."

"That prick we brought on just killed Harai!" he shouted, swinging the wrench.

Caswell ducked under the metal bar. It rebounded off the wall, sending a jolt up Douglas's arm. Caswell fired the vossen gun at the same moment. He missed, the tiny missile rocketing into the distance. Caswell fired again, but Douglas was spinning now, his momentum all wrong. The second needle slid into his suit just under the left armpit, burrowing through the Kevlar fabric to worm in under the collarbone.

Payload delivered so close to the heart, Douglas's entire body jerked absolutely rigid. The man became a stick figure.

His face contorted, eyes bulging outward. Blood burst from his nostrils and mouth as the man began to spasm uncontrollably.

"Iceberg," Caswell said. "I don't know what Douglas is talking about. He's acting . . . strange. Bring a med kit."

"Where's Angelina?"

"Unknown. She came back to inspect the lander bays with him, and went silent. Klaus followed, same thing, so I came to see what was wrong."

"I didn't hear them discuss any of this."

"Neither did I," Caswell said.

A pause. *"Then how do you know why the captain left C-and-C?"*

"Can we talk about it later? Douglas is curled in a ball here hitting the sides of his helmet with his fists, and I think I can see one of the others down in the cargo bay, drifting limp. Harai maybe. Bring a stretcher while you're at it."

"Jesus," Iceberg said. *"Fuck. Okay. Bridgette, meet at the airlock."*

The waiflike engineer's voice came through in a rasp. *"You believe that guy over Doug? Have you ever known the float to get to him?"*

Iceberg said, *"No, that's why you're meeting me there. Bring—"*

Caswell tuned out the rest. He floated back to the main junction. A quick glance at the airlock door that led to the *Pawn* showed no one on the other side, yet. Good. He whirled and propelled himself to the eerily familiar MED BAY door and whirled it open, killing the lights via a panel beside it.

The *Venturi's* mummified crew bobbed about inside. Caswell grabbed the collar of the nearest man's suit and hauled him out. Corpse between him and the airlock door, Caswell braced his feet against the wall. He waited there, coiled, vossen gun in one hand and human shield in the other.

Motion at the airlock. Iceberg's sky-blue-tinted hair, then his beady eyes peering through the tiny window. If he saw Caswell or the corpse in the darkened room it didn't slow his entrance.

Good, Caswell thought, and braced for the attack.

The airlock door began to move. Caswell pushed off hard with both feet, propelling the limp body before him. Halfway to the door he shoved it ahead. The body lurched forward, arms flung wide. The effort slowed Caswell's own progress. As the gap widened he raised his needler and waited, drifting in behind his shield.

A blast of white fog hit the corpse at point-blank range. Fire extinguisher. It stalled the body and then pushed it backward, sending it cartwheeling. Caswell had streamlined himself to reduce his own target area and, somehow, managed to slide right past the flailing corpse. He flew past just as the extinguisher's blast let up. The girl, Bridgette, held the device. She saw him an instant too late. The microscopic missile hit her face mask and instantly clouded it black from the inside. Her fingers squeezed on the extinguisher reflexively, sending another cone of white that arced across the tiny airlock. Unable to stop himself, Caswell barreled right into her as her body began the death throes. He caught a glimpse of Iceberg behind her. The man held a med kit in both hands, his eyes wide with terror.

Caswell plugged him from a meter away and floated lamely in the middle of the room until both bodies grew still.

His pulse raced. His whole body felt cool with sweat. He wanted to scream, "I'm a monster!" so loud that he'd hear it himself on the other end of this. But he did not scream. As he drifted between the dead and his pulse began to slow, Peter Caswell decided that he would mourn these people, just as soon as the job was done. Before Monique took the memory away. Did he always do this? Yes, he must. He had to believe that.

He let a full minute pass before he signaled on the Archon channel. "The *Pawn*'s crew is retired. God damn, this vossen gun is a nasty bit of kit, Mo. Advise on next steps. IA6, out."

No handhold within reach, Caswell drifted for a while. He could do nothing but stare at his handiwork. "I'm a killer," he muttered. "A heartless fucking killer." For the length of the mission anyway. Then he'd go back to being a man merely trained to kill. The rookie.

He could hardly wait.

Finally a handhold came within reach. He secured himself to the wall and considered his situation. "Mo," he said finally, "that missing lander. Might be that our absent crew member, Alice Vale, tried to flee this disaster all those years ago. I'm investigating."

He left the dead to drift. Back inside the *Venturi* he weaved his way around bodies and debris and kept on toward the rear of the smashed vessel.

Inside he found a passage that bowed in from either side. Airlock doors faced one another at the center of the hourglass-shaped passage, one for each lander. He glanced through the porthole on the first and saw the white-blue ESA markings on the hull of the craft nestled within. Caswell spun to the opposite window.

The other bay was indeed empty.

"Right then," he said. He bookmarked the video feed recorded by his helmet and filed the clip for priority upload home. "Confirmed, Monique. One of the landing craft is missing, and it's too clean to have been ripped away in whatever calamity happened here. Nothing aft of this point save a debris cloud. Advise."

Had Alice Vale taken the boat? It would have been loaded with some supplies and fuel, though certainly not enough to survive a dozen years in the black. But then she wouldn't have needed to survive so long. Perhaps she'd flown it home. Sold the weapons research that had gone on here and was safely back on Earth, living under a false ident on an island somewhere. Sitting on a beach in Mexico, perhaps. Biting into a fish taco and watching the glitter of sunlight on jade waves.

More likely she'd simply been yanked out of one of these holes when the station was damaged, and even now her body tumbled through space toward the Sun. As for the missing lander . . . well, Monique and whoever was feeding her the mission parameters would know what to do about it. He waited.

* * *

"Well done, Caswell," Monique sent after a lengthy delay.

Her next set of orders was even more surprising than the first, and frustratingly vague.

Preparation took several hours. As instructed, he left all the bodies in the C&C, moving them to one wall and fixing them in place with nylon straps to ensure they'd go down with the ship. "This station is a bloody mess, Monique," he sent as he went about the grim business. A dozen bodies now rested in the doomed vessel. Six from the original crew, six fresh ones from the *Pawn*. The thirteenth, Alice Vale, probably drifted among the debris cloud that trailed the *Venturi* toward the Sun.

The grim task complete, Caswell shifted focus to the *Venturi*'s black box. He moved the device into the salvage ship. Following Monique's instructions he gathered all of the food and water he could find on the *Pawn* and transferred it into the *Venturi*'s lone remaining lander. Once done, Caswell boarded the supply-filled landing boat and sealed himself inside. He sent Monique another update, then waited. The cockpit was cramped, every seat save his holding packages of food and water. His own gear and clothing lay safely tucked within one of the storage compartments.

The lander, guided by remote instruction from Earth, detached from the *Venturi* and drifted to the aft docking ring on the *Pawn Takes Bishop*. Caswell watched from his tiny porthole as the *Pawn* then detached itself from the doomed research vessel.

This little ballet of spacecraft continued as the *Pawn,* with Caswell's lander attached, floated out to a safe distance and then powered up its engines. The thrust pushed him back into his chair and kept him pinned there as the salvage craft served as booster for the comparably small lander, powering the tiny craft onto its new trajectory. After eight hours of one-g burn the *Pawn* unceremoniously let him go. She fell away and, a few minutes later, turned to begin a long spiraling trek to Earth, empty of crew but carrying one tiny, and very valuable, black box.

In a few days Angelina and her salvage team would burn

up with the *Venturi*. Weeks later the *Pawn* would arrive back at Earth. Monique had something else in mind for Caswell and his tiny lander, something Archon wanted both of them to forget about in due course.

The operative sat back. He studied the three-dimensional map before him as the lander zipped along. Thanks to the *Pawn*'s boost he now drifted away from the Sun at a touch over 150 kilometers per second. A dotted arc marked his trajectory, stable now after eight hours of growth as the boat had gained velocity. To his surprise this path did not arc and spiral out toward Earth, like the faint blue line that marked the *Pawn,* but instead implied a journey to an empty swath of nothingness directly above the Sun.

"You're on a course to intercept the missing lander, where you will ascertain the fate of Alice Vale. This is all I can tell you for the moment."

He sent back, "Why not take the *Pawn*?" and waited twenty minutes for the reply.

"You'll find out," his handler said vaguely.

Caswell ate fried rice from a self-heating package, then napped for a few hours. When he woke another thought occurred to him. When Monique had ordered him to eliminate the *Pawn*'s crew she'd neglected to give him the regulation speech about thought-access orders. "What did you mean, 'that's all I can tell you for now'? We're under IA already, so what the hell's this about, Mo?"

Twenty minutes later she replied. *"All will become clear in due course, Peter. Trust me. This will be the most interesting mission you'll ever forget. I guarantee it."*

To pass the time he played the craft's computer in games of Go, chess, and several modern games that relied on stealth and patience. Between matches he studied Alice Vale's dossier, but it had so little information he'd memorized it after only a few hours.

On a whim he used her picture to represent the computer opponent in his games, though after a particularly nasty round of Knife and Coin he decided against this. No need to paint her as an adversary. She'd simply survived. Escaped that doomed station only to realize too late that the tiny landing boat had little on board in the way of fuel or supplies. Granted she'd flown silently. A curious detail, but one that could be the result of a simple equipment malfunction.

He studied her face one last time. She'd be forty now if she'd lived. "How far did you get, young lady? How many weeks or months did you last out here?"

The picture did not reply, of course. Caswell sighed. How many hours had passed for her inside a ship just like this before she'd regretted not simply staying with her crew? They would have been friends. Like family, even. And they'd died a quick death, from the look of it. Preferable, surely, to starving out here in the chilly void. Yet she'd fled, and transmitted not a single word about any of it back home. This fact he found most odd.

With a tap of his finger her image vanished. He played six more rounds of Knife and Coin before dining on a packet of vegetable korma—spicy and surprisingly good. Then he slept.

The faces of those he'd killed haunted his dreams.

He woke eager to forget.

4

"HEY, MONIQUE," he sent as his craft approached the destination marker on its navigation screen. "What's the bounce timer on this activation, anyway? Just occurred to me you never said, and we're already flirting with the record."

Any activation of his implant included an automatic reversion timer. If he were to run, or fall into enemy hands, this ensured there would be at least some hope of clearing his memory of any sensitive information before a potential disclosure—voluntary or otherwise—could occur. In his career he'd never gone more than one week under IA.

Her reply amounted to yet another disquieting detail of this entire affair: *"I haven't set it yet."*

Caswell shifted uneasily, a frown growing the more he thought about what she'd just said. A trigger without a reversion fail-safe? Was that even possible?

An hour later a blinking red message on the main screen caught his eye. He'd been locked out of manual control.

The short-range nav showed nothing other than a few tiny chunks of debris he'd been tracking for days now. In his six days flying it had barely changed. Zero sign of the other lander, or Alice Vale's body.

His little craft sped away from the Sun at a blistering clip, his distance to the star now roughly equal to Earth's, his position exactly perpendicular to her orbital plane.

Without warning the lander turned around to face the Sun. Her engines powered up, filling the cabin with a deep, unsettling hum. The sensation of gravity returned as if some invisible weighted blanket had been laid over him.

"I've turned about and am under thrust again, Mo. Hope that is expected. What's this about? Mission aborted, or . . . ?"

Something had been forgotten, perhaps. Surely it was too late to catch the *Venturi* again before she plummeted into the Sun.

He cursed the delay in Monique's response for the hundredth time. All he could do was watch his velocity decrease. Caswell didn't know much about astrodynamics, but this seemed like a horrendous waste of fuel. More disconcerting was the fact that he'd been locked out of manual control. It implied a lack of trust. That made him squirm in his chair. His trust in Monique, and hers in him, had always been absolute. It had to be.

Another thought struck him. "Mo, it's possible this craft has been compromised. I'm locked out, and will soon be headed back toward the Sun."

The calm, intelligent lines of Alice Vale's face came to him, unbidden. Had something more sinister happened to the *Venturi*? Was she still out here, after all this time, and had she now sent him to the same fate as that doomed station? He discarded this idea as sheer paranoia. Certainly the woman could not have survived for so long. Besides, the radar screen showed emptiness all around him. There was literally nothing out here.

He waited ten long minutes until Monique's welcome voice filled his ears.

"Relax, Peter. This is expected. Your course was carefully programmed. I'm sorry to trickle information to you like this, but rest assured it will all make sense soon. Very soon. In fact, keep an eye on your velocity relative to the Sun. When it hits zero, I will finally be able to explain."

Caswell settled back into the cushioned seat and waited, eyes never wavering from the tiny readout that marked his speed in relation to the Sun. What the hell did coming to a dead stop have to do with knowing his orders? He pondered this as the number dwindled, the lander's meager rockets burning through fuel at an alarming rate. Then, the moment the display reached zero, the thrust stopped. Everything went perfectly silent. He was sitting perfectly motionless above the Sun, exactly perpendicular to Earth's orbital plane.

"Godspeed, Peter," Monique Pendleton said.

"Meaning what?" he said aloud. Then, "Oh. Shit."

Outside the stars began to vanish.

5

THE STARS DID NOT vanish as if snuffed from existence. It was a gradual fade. Even the blazing Sun visibly dimmed. Baffled, Caswell reached to pull his helmet off, thinking visor malfunction. Only he wore no helmet.

The flight instruments began to flop about as all navigational markers faded. The craft switched to the crude secondary option—navigating by recognizable stars. This failed, too. Everything outside simply dwindled like the closing scene of a film.

Fade to black. The end.

His heart lurched. He would lose his link to Earth. To Monique. "What the hell is going on?" he shouted. "Monique! I've . . . everything . . ." Of course, shouting was pointless. He was nine light-minutes from any help.

An icon blipped on the communications screen, a new encoded message. He let the tiny camera above the screen scan his retina and waited, swallowing a growing sense of panic.

Monique's face appeared. He'd come to love her face. For security reasons they'd never met in person, and usually her transmissions were audio only, save for their twice-yearly joint assessment. She seemed to stare right at him. Her intense blue eyes gleamed with the reflection of displays. She'd cut her hair since the last time he'd seen her. The fine, dirty-blond strands were tucked behind her ears and falling away past her shoulders. The style accentuated her full lips and smooth, golden skin.

She smiled her conspiratorial half smile, her eyes slightly downcast as she did so, and then she began to speak in her rich, matter-of-fact way: "The following information is classified, and marked in memory as thought-accessible only. Say 'begin' to continue."

"Begin," he said.

Thought-access lock begins.

We could not tell you of the nature of this mission until now because there had to be zero risk that you might transmit any of what I'm about to tell you back home.

While you've been out there we've been very busy here, Peter. Busy reviewing the logs from the *Venturi*, busy studying the onboard video and audio the station captured before her destruction.

This message had to be prerecorded because I now have no way to contact you, nor you me. You've traveled, Peter. Entered something and come out the other side. We're not quite sure what that something is. Be assured another ship is being prepped to investigate but that will take time. Time we cannot afford.

You were close and had transportation, so we decided to send you . . . through.

I'm rambling.

She took a deep breath, then fixed her gaze on the camera. On him, her agent.

You may have heard the ESA was conducting secret weapons experiments out there. That is true, but they found something else, as well. Twelve years ago the *Venturi* discovered, for lack of a better term, a wormhole. Be it to another place or time or . . . dimension or whatever, we're not quite sure. Nobody is, and the ESA isn't talking or truly doesn't know. That's not important.

The important thing is the crew of the *Venturi* went through. The whole ship experienced what you likely are now. A transition. Everything has probably faded to black, if their reports are accurate.

Make no mistake, Peter, you're traveling some-where.

What you'll find there is something Alice Vale de-cided was worth the murder of her entire crew. She sabotaged that ship, Peter, and then she went back.

She went back, it would seem, to play God.

Outside the stars began to return. They were in different places now.

6

THE LANDER FLOATED, still and silent, above an unknown star.

Gradually the flashing errors and alarms on his myriad of screens returned to a stable, if somewhat abnormal, state. With nothing else to go on, the algorithms that guided his ship had apparently given up on finding the familiar and decided to lock on to this massive sphere of fusion for the simple fact that it was there.

The computer even gave the star a name: Unknown M-Class.

This did not help his frayed nerves.

Caswell did the only thing he could do and just sat there. A full-gamut frequency scan appeared on the main screen, searching for anything familiar. Nothing turned up. Another sweep began, specifically for the transponder from Alice Vale's landing craft. It concluded with no matches. The scan repeated and would continue to do so. He relegated it to a secondary display, idly wondering if Alice had fled the *Venturi* only to plunge into the star on this side.

He realized suddenly that Monique's recorded instructions had paused when the instruments went haywire. He tapped the screen and playback resumed.

This is without a doubt the greatest discovery in the history of mankind, and Alice Vale may well have ruined it. Not just with her knowledge of the ESA's weapons experiments, though that is our primary concern.

We've cobbled together some data from the *Venturi* to help guide your ship. Unless our friends in Sci messed things up, you should start moving any moment now.

On cue the craft's thrusters blipped and coughed, sending him into a harsh rotation on multiple axes. His stomach lurched. He suddenly became aware of a mild headache that, like a purple cloud on the horizon, threatened to become something much worse very soon. While Monique continued her explanation he set about finding medication and a meal.

A course has been set for the second planet in this system. As you may have already noticed, the planet orbits its star at roughly 1AU, same as Earth, and the similarities don't end there.

Caswell felt silly. Overwhelmed and silly. He hadn't noticed any of this. In fact he could barely form a coherent thought. He paused Monique's message manually this time and shoveled a spoonful of soba noodles into his mouth. The simple movement of his jaw as he chewed served to ground him somehow, and with a few more bites inside him his unease began to abate.

Sipping a bulb of green tea he took stock of his situation.

First and foremost, he told himself, listen to Monique. Really listen. Latch on to her voice and devour every word. Memorize it, even though he'd eventually forget. Ground himself in her as his ship had just done with the star below. He could only imagine how she'd maintained such a calm demeanor through this. Certainly it all must seem as amazing—God, not just amazing, but absurd—to her. He simply had to trust his handler. He put himself in her shoes. Sending her "other half" through, of all things, a wormhole or whatever the hell it was, unable to converse with him or even to know his fate.

"This will be the most interesting mission you'll ever forget," he said aloud, echoing her words. He nodded at her picture. "You certainly had that bit right, Mo. Understatement of the century, more like."

Caswell put the drink bulb aside. He tuned out all distractions: the ship, rattling at maximum burn; the lingering warnings on his screens and the near-total lack of recognizable names. He let it all become just background noise and tapped PLAY.

The similarities between this world and Earth are, in fact, astonishing. And they're apparently why Alice Vale returned here.

For reasons that will become imminently clear, the planet to which you now approach was dubbed "Duplica" by the crew of the *Venturi*. Here's a picture taken from just a few thousand kilometers altitude.

He drew an involuntary sharp breath as the image appeared.

Because he was looking at Earth.

The blue oceans and wispy white clouds, the familiar shorelines of her continents. It was all there. "Duplica," he whispered. "Indeed."

From orbit the planet would fool anyone. And yet it was not Earth. The planet was second out from its star. It had two moons, both rocky and with darker complexions than Earth's. One was larger and orbited slightly farther out. The other was barely more than an asteroid.

According to the computer there was not a single artificial satellite in orbit.

His astonishment gave way to confusion and then simple curiosity. *What is this place? How does a perfect copy of Earth even come to be?* The implications of that made him shake his head, embarrassed at how quickly he'd leapt to such a conclusion.

I know what you're thinking right now, and believe me, we're as confused as you are. The folks in Sci have been working day and night since you sent the

data. Those with enough clearance, anyway. I'm sure
you can appreciate now the magnitude of this discovery.

"You're damn right I can," he growled. He could appreciate it very fucking much. Enough in fact to understand why
he'd been asked only days ago to slaughter six people in cold
blood. Angelina Monroe had dipped into the station's data-
store, perhaps even tried to copy or transmit the information. News like this required careful handling, surely. If
Archon could own it . . .

His thoughts turned to the original crew of the *Venturi,*
drifting lifeless in that medical bay. Had they met a similar
fate? A remote command sent from some ESA boss to jar
the station hard enough to kill all aboard?

No. It had been Alice Vale. "She went back to play God,"
Monique had said. Murdered the crew. Somehow that detail
hadn't quite registered when she'd first mentioned it. But
now . . .

We'll know more soon enough, but these details are
not the reason we sent you. They don't activate people like you and me to do a geological survey, now
do they?

"No, they do not." Caswell steeled himself. *Here it comes,*
he thought. *The point.* He could guess what she wanted him
to do, but gritted his teeth and waited all the same.

Before Monique went on, the image of Duplica and her
moons cross-faded to much closer footage, taken from low
orbit. Viewed like this, minor differences became apparent.
Most notable were the craters. A whole series of circular
wounds that weaved like a mottled snake from southern Europe, down to India, and up through the Koreas. Though
British raised, Caswell had been adopted from Korea. The
sight of his homeland thrashed by impact depressions shook
loose latent feelings of anger and sadness in him.

What he thought of as the Pacific Ocean drifted by, and
the California coast came into view. The string of craters
continued, all the way to the coast of Florida.

Thoughts came to him faster than he could process even their basic nature, much less any deeper ramifications. Should he think of these places in such terms? Was there an actual California or United Kingdom here, in the political sense? Hell, were there people at all? It could simply be a copy of Earth at the landmass level, a feat of terraforming never dreamed of before.

But the very fact that he saw so much green here meant plant life, at least, and that in and of itself was quite possibly the most important discovery in human history. Life existed here, something never found before despite all the effort made in that regard. Alice Vale and her crewmates had found extraterrestrial life.

She went back to play God. . . .

A chill ran up his spine and settled across his scalp. "What did you find here, Alice?"

When England came into view the image zoomed in again.

Caswell went perfectly still. There were roads and villages. A massive city, as big as London, though not in quite the same location. This metropolis straddled the Severn River, not the Thames. Curiously, it seemed to be surrounded by nature, not sprawl, and similarly hard-edged towns and cities were sprinkled across the landscape. Thin roads, or perhaps tracks, connected these places.

What the crew of the *Venturi* found here is nothing short of miraculous. A planet almost identical to Earth, populated by intelligent life. Human life, Peter. Whoever they are, however they got here or how this place came to be, they appear to be at a technological level similar to where we were in the 1950s. The *Venturi* even intercepted radio transmissions that sound an awful lot like English, believe it or not.

"English?" he blurted to the empty cabin, unable to stop himself. He'd yet to get his mind around the idea of life, human life, on another world, geographic similarities or not. But English? "How the hell is that even possible?"

The footage began to cut from one scene to the next. All

taken from orbit, grainy and unsteady, but what they showed was unmistakable. A train of sorts, powering along tracks. Boats with oddly curved sails bouncing along on white-caps. A vast square of something like concrete with dark diagonal forms moving about chaotically like insects. Caswell squinted, unsure what he was seeing, and then it clicked: the shadows of people, meandering, in the late afternoon or early morning.

After their visit, the *Venturi* returned to Earth's side of this wormhole and, from what we can gather, a huge debate began within the crew. They argued over what to do with this discovery, and who to tell about it.

At some point, Alice Vale formed ideas of her own. From the access logs you provided us, we know she spent the better part of a day in her bunk download-ing data. Patent databases, schematics, knowledge archives on almost every topic imaginable. Moun-tains of information related to every technological advancement humanity has ever achieved. Even things like culture, fashion, and art.

She took all this with her, Peter. She killed the rest of her crew and ran back to this place as the sole representative of Earth, armed with all our collective knowledge. We don't know why, but we can guess.

"To play God," Caswell said aloud.

We think she's going to give it to them, probably hoping they'll reward her with wealth and prestige beyond anyone's dreams. She'll be a curiosity, a ce-lebrity like no other. Perhaps even heralded as some kind of messiah.

"What a brilliant, crazy, ambitious play." Caswell grunted in admiration, and then he brought Alice Vale's image back to his screen. He found he could view her as an adversary now, and a formidable one at that. In her face now he saw the drive, the ambition, and perhaps a hint of the ruthless selfishness that drove her to take these actions. He'd mistaken it all before as pure intellectual intensity.

She must be stopped, Peter. I'm sure you can understand why, but let me make this very clear: She could ruin this place. Contaminate it in more ways than what is obvious. Perhaps she has already. Her weapons knowledge alone is very dangerous, but this goes way beyond that.

This is a sovereign world, full of unique cultures and intelligent human life. We should have done what the rest of her crew advocated: study them, make contact when the time was right, take every possible measure not to alter their course. This world is not yet spacefaring, and we should have waited until they were ready to meet us before introducing ourselves. We should have chosen what we told them very carefully. For all we know they're vicious and bloodthirsty, and perhaps Alice Vale has told them where we are. She has the information required to educate them on every major weapon program embarked upon by humanity in the last two centuries. The sorts of things we've taken great pains to remove from Earth, and prevent ever being built again. And there was the weapon she and the rest of the *Venturi* crew were working on, which goes far beyond anything that came before. If she gives it to them, the results could be catastrophic. For Duplica, and possibly even for Earth.

Your mission is to eliminate Alice Vale. Secondarily, destroy any artifacts of Earth she brought along, most especially that data trove.

With any luck she never even made landfall. Or if she did, they saw her as completely mental and threw her in an asylum. Whatever the case, do the job and get away with minimal impact. For all our sakes leave nothing behind.

Due to the circumstances of this mission, I've set up a delayed IA reversion trigger. Upon landing on

Duplica, you'll have fourteen days to complete your objectives.

A timer appeared on-screen below Monique's face and held steady at fourteen days, zero hours, zero minutes, zero seconds.

Be back aboard your ship in eight days, since it'll take you six to reach the wormhole again. If that is not possible, then at a minimum get off the ground before the timer hits zero. Log your results in the secure drop, lock in the reverse course, and sedate yourself. It should have just enough fuel to get you back to this side and we'll be waiting to pick you up.

I know this will test you to the very limit, Peter, but I have every confidence. It's not so unlike one of your holidays, right? You're the perfect man for the job.

Good luck, IA6.

~Monique Pendleton, IH6, out.

These details are classified per your contract with Archon Corporation. Any attempt to speak, write, or otherwise divulge your objectives will trigger immediate reversion. Thought-access lock ends.

He spent the days that followed studying video logs recorded aboard the station. As a nonscientist it helped him immensely to hear their discussions, their debates and hypotheses. Before the betrayal that would kill them, the crew of the *Venturi* had done a remarkable job during their brief visit to the world. At the time they had no idea if they would ever return home to share their discovery, making their efforts all the more impressive.

No matter. Whatever the tipping point had been, it had happened and Alice had embarked on this scheme.

She'd rigged a bomb. And a clever one at that. Killed the rest of her crew and departed with that data trove and, presumably, supplies to the planet below.

On a whim he checked for Lander One's transponder again. The scan showed negative. Of course nothing would come up. In his professional estimation Alice Vale was simply too smart for a mistake like that.

He'd have to track her down the old-fashioned way: detective work, spycraft.

"With 1950s technology." He collapsed back in his chair, overwhelmed as the enormity of the task ahead of him crashed down like an avalanche.

He must step onto this world with nothing but the clothing on his back, and even that he'd have to swap for local garments as quickly as possible. He didn't know their customs or, hell, know the first damn thing about the life-forms he would meet. Yet somehow in two weeks he needed to acclimate, find his target, perform the task, and leave? Monique had been right, he was the perfect man for the job. Every one of his adventure holidays had been in preparation for this mission. Only this was no holiday. A life would be taken. An entire world's course of history was potentially at stake.

Peter Caswell decided to follow the spirit of Monique's orders, if not the letter. A little extra risk of contaminating this place he could stomach if it meant his chances of success increased.

No matter what, he'd have to return to his ship before his implant released the biochemical agent in his brain. Every neuron, every synapse and dendrite in his brain that had changed since the moment his implant had first flooded them with the marker, would suddenly and irrevocably rewire itself back to that moment. Mentally he would find himself in that weightless instant staring at Angelina Monroe, only to emerge who knows where with a song lyric on his tongue.

The word is all of us . . .

The implant had other uses, though. And being hidden within his body it was perhaps the one technological marvel he could take with the confidence it would remain hidden.

Caswell closed his eyes and massaged his temples. He pressed his fingers hard into the skin there, savoring the slight pain that would signal his implant. A smartwatch he wore usually handled such tasks, regulating him automatically in subtle ways. This manual approach, by pressing the temples and thinking deliberate thoughts, he'd not done in years. He needed to be sure it still worked. The artificial gland in his neck released chemicals per his desire, calming him, sharpening his focus. He'd regret it soon, but for now he needed the edge. He had to get this right.

He turned to selecting a landing site.

It seemed likely that Alice would seek familiar ground. He studied her birthplace in the mountains of Colorado, but that area lay within the path of destruction. In one of the recordings Caswell had studied she'd mentioned a village in France called Olargues, some sort of childhood vacation spot, but it lay too in the wasteland of craters. He glanced at Alice's file on another screen. According to the dossier she'd lived the last few years of her time on Earth near the ESA's British headquarters in Lancaster, England. He scrolled there.

The culture on this world favored densely packed towns and cities, leaving much of the landscape wilderness; including the outskirts of Lancaster where Alice's flat on Earth had been. In the end he picked a clearing near a lake roughly eighty kilometers from there. High ground near plenty of fresh water, and no roads anywhere nearby. Curiously, the water levels of just about every lake and river he saw were lower than Earth's. The coastlines, too.

There seemed nothing else to do. His finger hovered over the landing sequence icon, though, as he tried to think of anything else he might have forgotten. He was no good at this sort of thing. Improvisation was his specialty.

The screen bleeped at him. The landing window was closing. He tapped the button and settled back, a shiver coursing through his body. Soon he would set foot on an alien world.

Within seconds the tiny ship began to reorient itself for atmospheric entry.

Flame roiled outside the tiny porthole. The craft bucked and hummed, every surface shaken to the verge of tearing apart. Then, as quickly as it had started, the flames gave way to blue sky. Clouds whipped past. A jarring lurch almost made him pass out as the landing rockets fired. The craft floated down the last hundred meters toward a blanket of snow.

On the screen in front of him, the IA timer turned yellow and ticked down by one second. Then another. Thirteen days, 23 hours, 59 minutes, 57 seconds.

Caswell started a timer on his wristwatch to match. His gaze lingered on the device. It was sleek, just a thin strip of titanium around his wrist inlaid with a curved, organic screen. A luxury smartwatch, packed with the latest tech. More powerful than all the world's computers combined a hundred years earlier. What about here? What would happen if someone in England circa 1956 found it lying on the ground?

Not much, he realized. Their biometrics would fail to activate it. To them it would probably resemble a rather modern bit of jewelry.

There seemed no debate. He needed a timer synced to the one Monique had started. On Earth time, not Duplican. Even a small difference in the planet's rotational speed could shave minutes each day off his window. He would leave it on, he decided. Absolutely worth the risk.

Get in, do the job, get out, forget. Ignorance is bliss; consequences require recollection. If Archon needed him to know anything about this place after the fact, they'd rebrief him.

PART 2
**STRANGER
ON THE
INSIDE**

7

EVEN A STIFF BREEZE off the ocean could not banish the smell of smoke and burned flesh.

Two state coroners emerged from the façade of the ruined laboratory, a white body bag held between them. The shiny fabric was sealed to hide the charred horror within. Then another pair of coroners came out, followed seconds later by a third.

Melni Tavan watched from the front row of a crowd of onlookers that dwindled rapidly. With the flames extinguished little remained to hold their attention, and anyway people had things to do. Only the youth and the retired stood their ground, huddled in a dozen quiet conversations as the dead were tucked away.

She'd gleaned next to nothing since her arrival. The chinups, so named from the way their helmet straps compressed and lifted their chins, made no special allowance for her reporter's credentials. They all recited the same birdshit line. "Accident, officially. All I can tell you, miss."

Of course the expected rumor of a bombing spread through the crowd. Those damned Southern insurgents, at it again. So easy to tack that card to anything bad. Melni couldn't really blame them. She would do the same when she wrote her article for the *Weekly*. She must or else risk becoming the target of rumors. Whispers that she sympathized, or worse.

She bit her lip, her eyes never leaving the three whitewrapped corpses now being slid into protective casings for the ride to the city morgue.

Was he among them? She shuddered despite the layers of clothing draped over her body. It had taken her an entire season to turn Onvel. All of her careful plans hinged on him and his position at the laboratory. To lose him now would set her back a year, a year the South didn't have. Worse, the situation presented immediate and dire risk to her cover. Onvel's office would be packed, his belongings sifted through. All that research, assigned to someone else. Had he been careful? Had he really taken all the precautions she'd urged, or only said as much?

A knot of fear began to fester within her. She had to know. She had to get to Onvel's office before anyone else, or at least know that the fire had cleansed it. Melni followed a narrow lane beside the blackened building until she came to an alley that ran along the back. There was a door there, but also a lot of people. Detectives milled about, flanked by representatives from Valix Corporation, the lab's owner. Some bore smudges of black ash on their otherwise impeccable corporate suits, but most looked fresh off the roller from the company's Upwest headquarters.

Three doors slammed in quick succession from around front. The coroner vans began to rattle away, tires crunching on bits of ash and ice in the road. Melni went back the way she'd come, before anyone saw her. The vans rolled by her, sleet crushing beneath their tires. A shopkeeper hosed the sidewalk in front of his business, his face as gloomy as the ash he washed away.

Melni tried to get answers from the Valix suits out front. They muttered scripted apologies and moved farther inside the police line. She peppered the ranking chin-up with zero success. She had to do these things. Her cover demanded it.

Conventional wisdom said to slip into a role where no one would notice you. Be someone who could move about without earning attention from the chins or the NRD. A nighttime delivery driver, that sort of thing. That's what her instructors back in Riverswidth trained the recruits for. It did not matter that these methods had never produced significant results. It was the way things were done, the only way they knew.

And then Melni came along. The student journalist, one

of many hired part-time to write news briefs for senior government officials. She'd been thorough, sifting through obscure sources and connecting things others failed to notice. And, despite being told not to, she'd analyzed and offered conclusions. She couldn't help it. Melni was a *desoa,* descended from refugees of the Desolation. Her pale skin, purple eyes, and golden hair marked her as such and made her a second-class citizen among the native peoples of both North and South. Her mother had taught her that to succeed in life she'd always have to do more than she'd been asked, or risk going unnoticed. So she had, in all things, including that government job. She feared they'd dismiss her for inserting her opinions in the news summaries. But instead her work had been noticed by the powers that be in Riverswidth, and she'd been recruited to the role of intelligence analyst. Her *desoa* looks were, for once, a benefit. Her people were the only kind rightfully found on either side of the great crater belt.

But she was young and untrained. She lacked confidence. They told her she'd never make a good field agent. Being *desoa* she'd faced that sort of discriminatory conclusion her whole life. Naturally she immediately applied for a field position. To her surprise, they'd accepted. They put her on a boat for South Valgarin before she really comprehended what it all meant. After barely a month of training on local customs of the region she was given fake papers and confusing instructions. She made the harrowing journey through Central Valgarin alone, across the vast wasteland that was the Desolation. The land of her ancestors. Finally she found herself in the North, and fell into her prearranged cover as a reporter for a small newsprint.

In truth she was nobody. An agent of the lowest rank and skill, shipped off to the other side of Gartien, where she could someday prove herself without risking too much damage. All they'd asked her to do is send back any information she might come across related to military deployments along the border there.

Something else had caught her attention, though. Locals were grumbling because of major changes in the mining industry, which was moving jobs and equipment east to

Tandiel. Melni investigated and uncovered something interesting: All these changes in the mining industry were due to demands made by Valix. There were orders for vast quantities of processed minerals with no known use. Originally her goal had been to send this information south, but a companion at the press happened to read her notes and thought it equally fascinating. The paper printed it. All this in her first week on the job. Things only spiraled from there, because that small press was owned by the *Weekly* in Combra, home of the North's leadership and the Valix Corporation as well. Her article made the rounds, and as it had in Riverswidth her aptitude gained instant notice. Melni soon found herself on a boat again, on her way to Combra, to join the team covering Valix at the source. Almost overnight she'd landed in a front-and-center position on the South's stage of covert assets. Their top agent, like it or not.

A familiar face snapped Melni back to the moment. One of the newly arrived detectives was a man she knew, a source within the department she'd used in the past and become friendly with, Boran Kulit. He shrugged at her probing questions but his eyes darted to and lingered on a small mealhouse across the street. She nodded understanding and moved on.

The crowd soon melted away entirely. Melni completed her show of asking questions, enough to warrant the birdshit story she would write that evening, and then hurried across the street to the café. She fetched ginger water and a curd biscuit from the counter, paid, and found a table by the window where she could see the door.

"What a blixxing mess," Boran said, sliding onto the bench across from her a few minutes later. He placed his blue tented hat on the table and flicked a bit of ash from it, then ran both hands through his long black hair. Dark bags of weariness hung under his eyes, marring his otherwise smooth Northerner's brown skin.

"Biscuit?" she asked him.

The detective declined. He ordered cham with a quick hand signal to the man behind the counter, then just sat there, eyes distant.

"I have questions," she said.

"Shitpipe Southern bastards," he muttered, not hearing her.

Melni gave the words time to settle. She chewed and swallowed some of the biscuit. "The chin-ups said it was an accident—"

"Of course they did!" He remembered himself and lowered his voice. "That is what the Valix people told us to say. 'Call it an accident and go about your patrols.' Like they own us."

They do, and you know it. She only thought this, though. Aloud she asked, "You really think it was insurgents?" There were a few cells operating in the area. Melni had no contact with them; she only knew this because her handler had said as much. She made a mental note to ask him if they had anything to do with it. She doubted it, though. They didn't make things look like accidents.

Boran grimaced. "All I know is something does not taste right. I would just prefer that we determined the truth on our own, not be handed it by Valix suits."

Melni sipped her drink thoughtfully. Too sweet for her taste. Not the spicy variety like they served back home. "Mmm . . ." she breathed, pretending to enjoy it. Boran took no notice. His focus remained on the lab across the street. She followed his gaze to black-scarred bricks around the windows and entrance. A thin waft of gray smoke drifted out from a hole in the roof. Beneath it all was the knowledge that three people had died here. Not just people, she reminded herself, but top researchers for Valix. Tantamount to an assault on the Triumvirate itself, these days.

"Boran," she said, taking care to keep her voice level. "Do you have the names of the dead? I would like to do them honor when I prepare my article."

"Hmm?" His gaze swung back to her. "Oh. Yeah." The heavyset man pulled a weathered paper pad from his pocket and thumbed the empty pages up front until he reached the first with scribbled writing. "Let me see. Crall, Harginns, and Dumon."

So there it was, just like that. She kept her hands on the cup and her face carefully blank. Inside her heart felt as if gripped by a fist. Onvel Harginns. Her insider, her informer, dead. The closest she and the South had come to unraveling the secrets behind the Valix Corporation's incredible string of technological marvels. To die like this, so soon after Onvel had told her of the critical work he'd recently become involved in, work he promised to provide to her in the form of a stack of stolen documents.

"Tomorrow they will clean this place and completely rebuild it. I guess they can afford to, eh?"

Melni only nodded. Her mind raced.

"As gratitude," Boran said, "for keeping our noses out of their shitpipes, Valix has invited all of the detectives to the returning ceremony."

"I would love to be there," she said, a little too quickly.

Boran waved a dismissive hand. "Take my place if you like. It would bore me to tears, but you . . . If you wish to honor the dead in your report, that is the place to go. This," he said, gesturing at the ruin across the street, "is no place for honor."

"Sure you do not mind?"

He shook his head. "I am too busy with the Hillstav incident."

"What Hillstav incident?"

He shot her a glance and snorted a single laugh. "So that news has not leaked yet. Well, believe me, you will hear of it soon enough."

"Is it related to this?"

The detective's eyes widened at the question, and she knew it was something he hadn't considered before. He thought about it for a moment and then shook his head.

Melni squeezed the detective's arm in gratitude, paid for their food, and left. She walked the entire way back to her flat, taking side streets and alleys. The complicated path gave her time to think.

There seemed only one conclusion that mattered: If Onvel had left anything behind that might implicate her, everything would end. All the careful cultivation of this persona, all the contacts she'd made under the guise of a reporter, would disintegrate. She would have to make sure that didn't happen. The South might never get a better chance to infiltrate the Valix machine. Melni's pace quickened. She had a lot of preparation to do.

At zero hour, when the streetlights outside dimmed ten times to signal the end of the day, Melni slipped out of her building via the service entrance. An earlier rain had gone, leaving the paved roads as imperfect mirrors of the city they served. She'd dressed like what one would expect of a young, attractive, unattached woman abroad in the middle of the night: for a party. A black long-sleeved shirt, brown skirt that ended mid-thigh, and matching boots that came just below the knee. She wore fake spectacles and a semi-clear, hooded plastic shawl—quite fashionable these days for the under-thirty set—over her close crop of blond hair.

It being a workday, pedestrians on the streets were few and far between. Only one pedicab pulled along beside her and offered a ride, halving the price at her initial decline, rattling away when she reiterated her desire to get a good walk in.

A few new low-slung ground cruisers rolled by, with their shiny wheels and quietly humming electric motors. They were a stark contrast to the cough and patter of the old compressed-air sort like you'd find all across the South. Melni thought these new cruisers obscene displays of wealth and laziness but could not discount the appeal of their curved forms and ease of use.

An old stone bridge led over a canal and into Loweast. Classic, weather-beaten homes and corner stores gave way to the gleaming modern storefronts and office blocks currently considered fashionable. There were advertisements, too, huge brightly lit tallframes promising luxury or convenience or the latest modern marvel. The monstrous advertisements were everywhere these days. Melni found them sort of fascinating. Not for the products on offer but in the interesting techniques employed to try to grab attention in only a single image and perhaps a few words. Few saw this brazen attempt at manipulation for the art form it clearly was. To Melni it was like acting, or lying. Yes, very much like lying.

She ducked into a public lav and, breathing through her mouth, traded her skirt for a pair of comfortable slacks, her plastic shawl for a more modest scarf. She ditched the costume spectacles, which were courtesy of the amateur theater she'd joined a year earlier. The props and costume room proved quite useful for her night work, as did the occasional bit of acting. She lived her life as an act and found that the extra practice and exposure to Northern accents and body language kept her at the top of her trade. As an added bonus she would then act badly in rehearsals, guaranteeing she'd never be put onstage, at least for any appreciable length. The theater only kept her around because she'd so enthusiastically offered to help catalog and maintain the props.

There were few people amid the Loweast office blocks at this hour. Those who were had their weary heads down, hurrying home, done with whatever task had kept them at their desks so late. Melni strode past the glass-walled frontages, under dimly lit signs for engineering, aerospace, and materials firms. All seemed built lasterday, all cut from the cloth of Valix Corporation. Partners, emulators, or hopeful competitors.

She walked taller, swung her backpurse from one shoulder now. The slacks implied she herself had just left the office. Danna, an advert designer, she decided.

As she walked her thoughts drifted to Onvel.

It would take years to replace him. To turn another with his kind of access, not to mention his talent and eagerness. Years the South most certainly could not afford, not at the rate the North was advancing thanks to their golden inventor.

Two chin-ups strolled by her. She favored the officers with a thin smile, one that spoke of a late night working, something they could relate to. One smiled back; the other didn't notice her. They both had the dark brown skin of true Northerners. Her pale skin and purple eyes marked her as the spawn of Desolation refugees from Central Valgarin. Many generations removed, yes, but still an outsider in either half of the world. If she had the coloration of a true Southerner, and those narrow ice-blue eyes, she would never have been sent here to spy on Valix. Southerners in the North were very rare and placed under constant scrutiny.

Three blocks later the charred building came into view. She found a shadowed redbrick alcove with a decent view of the burned lab and waited for the streetlights to dim hour one. Another hour fifty after that and Garta would rise. That was okay, she thought. No need to walk home again at that much more suspicious hour. No. Twenty minutes inside, tops, then a short walk to the safe house on Bandury Lane. It was a miserable little cave but it had a bed and bathroom and the rent was paid up the last time she checked. Then back to the *Weekly*'s office, bags beneath her eyes and in a skirt that spoke of another wild night with her actor friends. Nothing unusual.

It took her until the lights dimmed the hour to spot the duty guard. She or he stood under the awning of the lab's entrance, arms folded, leaning casually against the blackened doorframe. After a few minutes the woman—Melni could see no masculine drape of hair to the shoulders so it must be a she—began to circuit the perimeter, handheld electric lamp sweeping across the damp avenue and sleek corporate façades that lined the road.

Melni slipped off her oversize shoes. Underneath she'd worn dancer's slippers instead of socks. She pulled her backpurse around and secured it tight across her chest. With one last look around she sprinted, running on her toes, crossing the span in ten heartbeats. She leapt across the empty space where the front door had been and bounded to the far wall of the reception area with only two taps of her feet. Her slippers left smudges on the damp, ash-coated tiles. Nothing anyone would notice unless there was a reason to look.

She crept forward, navigating by nothing more than the memory of a crude map Onvel had once drawn for her, until the third bend in the hall. There, in the pitch black, she waited and listened. Other than the distant patter of runoff water, she heard nothing. Satisfied, Melni slipped a flashlight of her own from the small pack now strapped to her chest and thumbed the switch. A soft white beam flooded the interior hall. Bright, stable, and with a battery that would last until sunrise. She shook her head at the luck of the North and their genius benefactor. Would any industry be left untouched by the revolution Valix had started with their products? Semiconductors, microchips, supercapacitors . . . and who knew what else, lurking in underground labs out at the end of the dark tracks the rollers never took.

She came to a closed door and toed the foot latch, gently kicking out to open it halfway. No ash here. The door at the far end remained closed as well. Moonlight filtered in from high glazed windows on the outer wall, tinged yellow by the glass, alive with dust. Marble tiles of varying, creamy colors glowed softly in the moonbeams. Along the inner wall, to her right, a row of cherrywood doors presented themselves like firstwords gifts, only instead of ribbons they had brass-plated name tags across their middles.

Melni darted along the hall to the fifth door. Onvel's office. Ignoring the flutter in her stomach at the sight of his name etched in brass, she toed it open and slid inside.

The room smelled like him: spice and smokeleaf. Papers were stacked on every available surface. "Damn you, you disorganized curd," she muttered. She studied the sheets on top and tried to picture herself as him in here, working. She stood where he would have, for there was nowhere to sit. Onvel liked to roam when he worked, so he'd specifically requested a tall bench in his office instead of the usual desk and chair. This meant that he could work anywhere in this room. "Think, think," she whispered. There, a mug and pen. She padded over and glanced in, saw a shimmer of light reflect off the last few sips of cham, and grinned. She played her beam across the papers within arm's reach. The smallest stack proved most recently dated. Typed lines of text and equations marked up heavily with Onvel's neat handwriting. Were these the critical documents he'd spoken of? Were these what he'd planned to steal for her?

Light played on the far wall. In seconds a warm, shifting glow began to flood in from the hallway outside. Then came footsteps, and voices. Four or five people at least.

Melni plucked the top ten pages. Any more than that might be missed. She folded the crisp paper into a stiff envelope she'd packed for this purpose. Hopefully the poor researchers back at Riverswidth could make sense of what he'd been working on before the "accident." If he'd died for this project, perhaps it had been something truly worth dying for.

The footsteps grew closer. Melni glanced around. The office had only one door, and nothing in the way of furniture but the long U-shaped desk against the back wall. She went for the door, intent to kick it shut, but the newcomers were right outside. She did the only thing she could think to do: She let her momentum take her to the wall beside the door. There was no time to turn around. She inhaled and flattened herself as the office door swung inward.

The footsteps outside all stopped, save for one pair. Someone came a few halting steps into the dead man's workspace, then stopped.

Melni felt the door bounce gently off her shoulder blades and come to a stop. She held her breath in and cursed the inability to see.

"If only he'd been in here," a woman said.

A familiar voice. A famous voice, precise and hard and strangely accented. Words spoken so fast they often ran together, like "he'd" instead of "he had." Melni bit her lip. After all this time, all her work, her cover, her sneaking about, her turning of Onvel, to have this of all moments be the first time she'd stood in the same room as *her*.

"But then he loved the moment, didn't he?" the woman said. Alia Valix said. Alia the genius. The finest inventor in all Gartien's history. The most mysterious, too.

"The moment?" a man asked.

Alia Valix took a few more steps into the room. Melni heard a soft brushing sound. A hand across paper, perhaps. "The moment. The final test. The proof of concept. That moment. Why else would he have gone to the lab to see it turned on?"

"Ah, yes. Yes he did. Never missed a final run, not that I can recall, anyway." The man coughed. "I am sorry, Miss Valix. About the loss. The losses, I mean. We all are."

The famous woman sighed. When she spoke again Melni almost thought it a different person, so sudden and complete the change was. Sincerity and regret had vanished. Callousness, and that well-known inventor's drive, were filling in. "Bring all of these papers up to the mansion. I'll review his progress myself and try to work out the conclusions."

"Right away."

"Right away," Alia repeated, in a way that implied they had very different ideas of what that meant. "These papers should never have been left sitting out. We're lucky no water worked its way through the ceiling yet. You can already see it saturating up there, look. I won't have this research put at such risk. It's critically important. Does that resolve?"

"Perfectly, Miss Valix."

Low voices in the hall. Someone ran off the way they'd come.

A silence followed, disturbed only by the occasional drum of fingertips on stacked paper. "Can the building be saved? The lab?" Alia asked.

"We are not sure yet," the man replied.

"Guess."

"It is not really my place to—"

A new voice from farther out in the hall now. A young woman. "Our initial assessment is no, Miss Valix. Not the lab, at any rate. A report is already on its way to your office."

"I wish you'd brought it along."

"We did not know you were—"

"Obviously. I just wish you had, that's all." She took a long breath through her nose, as if trying to inhale patience like oxygen. "I look forward to the report. Let's go see the lab."

"This way," the man said.

The group departed, trailing behind the click-clack footfalls of their corporate leader. Onvel once said that talking to Alia was like talking to someone who already knew everything you were going to say, and the simple act of waiting for clumsy words to roll off your tongue was torture for her. Every single conversation the woman ever had was, for her, an exercise in patience akin to waiting for a child to draw a conclusion you'd known for years.

They would return, and soon, to carry the stacks of papers away for Alia to review. Her tone had implied the utmost urgency. Melni risked a glance out into the hall. They'd left no guard behind. There was no reason to, but she wanted to be sure.

One ear perked for returning footfalls, Melni moved back to the center of the room and tried to put herself behind Onvel's eyes once again. *Where would I hide things in here? Would I even do that?* There were stacks of papers on the desk surfaces and in the corners on the floor. A few shelves on the wall were similarly cluttered. All just like the man's flat. "It's not that I shun organization or cleanliness; it's that I'd rather not have to cross the room to find something," he'd said when she'd met with him there for the first time late one night a year ago.

She'd shuddered at the sight of the mess. It went against every instinct she had.

Footsteps outside, so close she couldn't believe she'd missed them.

Melni turned to see a demure woman of perhaps twenty walk into the office. She carried a stack of cardboard boxes, and was so preoccupied with not dropping these, she never saw Melni. Never saw the flat-handed strike that hit her windpipe.

The woman gasped at the sudden blow and fell backward. The boxes clattered to the floor. Her head smacked against the tiles with an audible crack and she went motionless.

Melni had acted without thinking and instantly regretted it. An attack would raise questions with obvious answers. An intruder had been inside. Searches would happen, revealing missing documents. Valix would tighten security, becoming even harder to spy on. *This is what happens when you act on instinct!* she screamed at herself.

Melni glanced around. She may have struck out in haste but she could still plan. Yet there was nowhere to hide the body, and she couldn't just leave it. The woman might remember something when she came around. Melni looked across the room and then up at the ceiling. Alia's words came back to her. No water had worked its way through the ceiling *yet.* In the center of the smooth surface Melni saw a large discolored section, slightly bowed from the weight of the liquid pooled on it above.

Her plan came together in an instant. She dragged the unconscious woman to the center of the room, then stood on the desk and began to punch at the waterlogged material above with one of Onvel's chewed pencils.

The tip punctured the saturated surface on the third try and filthy water began to trickle through. Melni hopped down and repositioned the body so the stream fell directly onto the woman's mouth and nose.

Within seconds the trickle turned into a steady pour, then a gush. Abruptly the woman coughed. She began to writhe under the deluge. Melni couldn't watch this person drown. She would not be able to live with herself. But she couldn't just flee. Not yet. So she clasped her hands over the woman's mouth and nose. "I'm sorry, I'm sorry," she whispered, her own eyes closed, as the writhing turned to a frantic spasm and then, ultimately, a weak flail. Then perfect stillness. Melni opened her eyes. The water continued to splash on the motionless body before her.

She fought back tears, though her grief was not for the life she'd just taken. The only life she'd ever taken, part of her mind noted with cold distance. The tears were for what this corpse represented. The death of control. Her careful plans and nurtured identity, slipping away.

Yet what could she do but try? Figure something out. She couldn't run away. There was no one to run to. Her handler? Melni wanted to laugh aloud at that idea. The old man had been waiting for something like this to happen ever since she'd stumbled into this position. He had made it very clear that there was no escape option for her, no team waiting to evacuate her south of the Desolation should her true identity be discovered. She was on her own. She had to try to put things back in order.

Melni closed the dead eyes with the brush of two fingers, rolled the body facedown, then slipped backward out of the room. Seconds later the ceiling in Onvel's office came crashing down in a sudden avalanche of soaked pressboard, insulation, and water. The liquid splashed down with raging force, toppling the tables and spilling papers everywhere. Everything, all his work, ruined. Except for the ten pages she'd tucked inside her envelope.

The rising water lifted the dead woman off the floor. She began to bob amid the soaked papers. It all looked like a very sad accident, Melni realized. She felt morbidly pleased at the luck, yet her pulse pounded and her stomach felt as if tied in knots. It would only be seen as an accident if she was long gone when they found the body.

Distant voices broke her state of semi-trance. She fled, running toward the back of the building, weaving through vacant hallways that smelled of smoke and water.

Eventually a tiny rectangle of light high on the wall indicated a way out. It was a ventilation window above an alley door. The door itself had been chained and locked from the outside. She climbed to the narrow window instead and found it swung outward to a forty-five-degree angle. Just enough to squeeze through.

Cold pavement met her hip. She grunted, stood, and hobbled across the street into the safety of a shadow.

The safe house on Bandury Lane had been recently used. Food in the cabinets, clean clothes in a variety of styles and sizes filled the bedroom benches, and of course the customary note on the table. Addressed to a fictitious Aunt Bezzy, it spoke of a fine time together—*love you, Auntie, see you soon!* It also told Melni which agent had stayed, for how long, and if there'd been any sign of other covert entry or curiosity from the neighbors. There hadn't.

Melni burned the note. She stripped and washed her clothes, taking care to scrub any ash from the soles of her dancing slippers. It was only two-past, dawn just tickling the Eastern skyline. She ate toast even though she despised the sweet Northern bread, drank a glass of water, and slept on the floor for an hour. To use the bed, inviting as it was, would mean another hour here cleaning sheets.

By third hour Garta shone brilliantly in a cloudless sky. The city had woken, come alive with the usual daily bustle as millions of Northerners took to their jobs. Melni watched from the safe house window, a mug of cham in hand. They went about like ants on the streets below, every man in a dark hat, every woman in a patterned scarf. The fashionable, happy, prosperous North. How quickly it would all collapse if Alia's influence vanished. Melni could have done it, right there in Onvel's office. Could have kicked the office door shut and strangled the woman while keeping her companions outside. Instead she'd killed some random Valix employee.

Melni sat and wrote a detailed report in substitution cipher. She left no detail out. She added it to the small cache of papers she'd lifted from Onvel's office and sealed the envelope, then set it aside.

Next she wrote her own little note to go on the table, thanking Auntie for the visit. She cleaned every surface she'd touched while inside, then set off.

Melni hailed a pedi and instructed the fresh-faced rider to an address across the bridge near Embassy Lane. She walked calmly against the tide of office workers to the building where Onvel lived. *Had lived,* she corrected herself. The gate to the inner courtyard stood open so she pushed through as if she lived there. A dozen steps before his door Melni stopped. There were people inside. She could hear crying, and low voices. His family, already gathered to mourn him.

Melni turned and left before anyone could see her.

She hurried a few blocks and boarded another cab, doubling back almost half the distance to Harborsedge. On foot again she strolled along the waterfront. The midday hour of fifth brought a bustle of foot traffic to the old stone roads as cargo hands sought a meal and some conversation before the second half of the day.

It had not always been so tranquil here. This stretch of coast had been a hopeless crime-ridden stain only a decade ago. Massive economic shifts since then had changed all that. There were still long cargo ships docked along the harbor, but their contents were imports, not manufactured here. Luxuries made cheap and far away, or the raw materials needed to fuel the booming technological sector so dominated by Valix.

The company's voracious appetites were already legendary.

Recently some questioned the impact of all this, thanks in some small part to questions Melni herself raised in her articles. Surely all this growth, all this exploitation, came at a cost? Alia Valix, true to her reputation, remained one step ahead. Pollution from one invention was solved by the next. Not just solved but turned into a benefit. Lack of jobs for all the hands idled by automation? Valix Education Centers were available for anyone made redundant; they'd even pay you to attend. In a decade the number of skilled designers, engineers, and scientists would double. Melni had never heard of anything like it, and she feared for what it meant to her beloved South. In Riverswidth they worried the North's progress would become unstoppable. Though Melni would never admit it, she'd come to feel that this moment already lay in the past.

She made her way to the interior display room of Croag & Daughters, an antiques shop known for a fine selection of writing tables and comfortable chairs. Melni went to a particular desk that would never sell. She pulled a drawer, reached inside and lifted the false bottom, then slipped her envelope beneath. There was no one else in the tiny store, save the owner, who did not even look up at her entrance. He was stooped over his worktable, eye pressed to a magnifier trained on a tiny, colorful jewelry box that looked pre-Desolation.

Melni reset the fake bottom and slid the drawer shut. "I am very interested in the desk," she said on her way out. She had left a drop. "Would someone be able to deliver it this evening, say around eight and fifty?"

Croag agreed. That evening someone would fetch the envelope and take it to the dockyard. At half-nine a boat would slip out to sea. Her meager prize would be aboard, bound for the South, where some analyst at Riverswidth would try to make sense of Onvel's last work for the Valix Corporation.

Her handler would be angry. Ten pages of possibly meaningless information did not even come close to accounting for the fact that she'd lost her Valix insider, her potential saboteur.

She'd have to start fresh now, find a new cog she could turn inside the mighty Valix machine. Assuming, of course, the powers that be back home would allow her to do so.

Viewed objectively the chances of continuing her mission

or being immediately recalled seemed equal. Everything depended on the response from Riverswidth in three days' time.

There was only one thing she could do: keep going as if her cover were intact. She still had a job to do, perhaps the most important job in all the world.

8

THE LAMPS OUTSIDE had barely dimmed third hour when Melni left for her office on Newberry Terrace, near the city center. A stiff wind off the ocean had sent temperatures plummeting overnight. She hugged herself as she walked, her treadmellow shoes all but silent on the cobbled backstreets.

She expected an empty building, save perhaps a few of the zone correspondents who kept careful vigil throughout the night for anything interesting coming in from points far to the east or west. What she found instead was a bustling den of activity. The sight of it made her breath catch in her throat.

"Ahey. What is it?" she asked the first person to pass by her, a reporter whose name she couldn't recall. "What has happened?"

The tall, thin woman cocked an eyebrow. "Four rassies, dead. Murdered."

Rassie. The North Rassle Department, or NRD. Elite state police. To accost them would earn a lifetime in prison. To kill? Four? She could scarcely imagine the punishment. No one in their right mind would dare take on the NRD. Except . . . Melni shivered. Another asset from the South, perhaps? Some botched mission? "Wh-Where?" she managed.

"Way up past Hillstav. Beaten to death with a spade, apparently." The woman stepped in close, dropped her voice conspiratorially. "Word is the killer dragged the bodies to a clearing and performed some kind of sick ritual. Stripped them. Covered them with dirt, if you can believe that. Keep that last bit to yourself, Mel. No one else has it. We have a friend in the rassies talking. Might even run a midweek about it. 'A madman in the hills.' The people will eat it up."

Melni glanced around at the buzz of activity in the wide, airy room. A dozen reporters were already in, probably all anxious to get the assignment. They'd be checking timetables for express rollers north and wondering who they could pass their existing stories to. Speed was of the essence now, lest she be dragged into this mess. She stood and walked purposefully to the wire room. The operator on duty rolled his eyes when she entered, then offered a strained smile. "A bit busy, Mel."

"It is not about the Hillstav thing."

His eyebrow cocked up. "Oh?"

"Yes. A local matter. Can you get me Boran over at the station?"

The operator grumbled a bit, then started plugging wires. "Everything is clogged. Give me a few, all right?"

She waited just outside the door. A couple of minutes later she plunked herself down in booth three and grabbed the handset. "Detective Boran?"

"Just a moment," the operator at the police station said. The line popped and hissed a few times in her ear.

"Ahey," a gruff voice said.

"Boran, it is Melni. From the *Weekly*?"

"Thought you would call. Look, about that Hillstav business. You are the third to—"

"This is not about that," she said.

He grunted. "What then?"

"The accident at the Valix lab," she started, "any new developments?"

"No."

She let out a long breath. "Nothing at all?"

"Well," he hesitated. "Look, do not report this. We had to sign something called a nondisclosure agreement. Some new legal birdshit Alia insisted on. Means we—"

"I can guess what it means. You have my silence, promise."

A few seconds passed as he evidently tried to decide how much trust he could put in her. She felt suddenly proud of the ethics she'd employed while working this cover. Just the right blend of probing questions and dogged patriotism.

He said, "They were testing a chemical mixture, a new coolant for some kind of engine. It all goes straight through my ears, of course, like most of what that *desoa* woman says . . . no offense meant, of course. The test led to an unexpected reaction, an explosion. She actually demonstrated it for us with a tiny sample. Gave quite a whump."

Her handlers would want to know about this. "Quite a whump" meant possible use as a weapon. "Interesting. But listen, about the memorial—"

"Yeah," Boran said, "held at her estate tomorrow. By Garta's light *do not* tell anyone I gave my invitation to you."

He said he'd leave the paper at the front desk under her name, and clicked off. Melni sat in the booth for several minutes, trying to decide if this was a stroke of luck or a horrible risk. Both, she concluded.

She stopped only to grab her backpurse, waving off several editors who claimed they needed to see her right away. "On to something big," she muttered to one with a wink. That was all it took. Half an hour later, just before the midday hour of five, she stepped into the station headquarters in Upwest and gave her name. The receptionist handed her an envelope without a second glance.

Melni took a pedicab to the fashion district. Most of the boutique windows were filled with the typical drab style of Combra—grays and browns like sky and soil. For a memorial, color would be required, the more the better, and she decided to spend extravagantly. She went to Blade's, one of the best tailors and a rising star in the trade after Alia Valix had selected them to produce garments based on her own designs.

Twenty minutes later and two months' salary lighter, Melni emerged. She spent the afternoon and evening alone in her flat, preparing. The spare bedroom she'd long ago converted for photoprint development. A dark blanket covered the only window. Tables lined the walls, covered with square metal basins under shelves of various chemicals.

Boxes of supplies were tucked underneath the tables, paper, lenses, and filter masks spilling out in unkempt fashion.

She knelt by the far table and pulled a box out from under it, revealing a small furnace vent behind. She removed the slotted grating and reached inside. The ventilation channel within bent ninety degrees, and she had to shove her arm all the way inside before her fingers brushed the end of a length of twine. Melni coaxed it out, and the parcel to which it was attached. She could have done this with her eyes closed, not that the dim red studio lamp was much better.

The canvas bundle weighed only a few pounds. She rolled it open on the floor of the room and considered the contents. Her hand went reflexively to the pistol. It was cool and satisfactorily weighty in her hand. Not the sort of thing to carry into the Valix house. The weapon went back into its cloth wrapping. She selected instead a good knife and a set of lockright's tools, packing them into loops of elastic fabric she'd sewn into the thigh straps of a pair of rather indecent stockings, high up and on the inner portion where the typical frisk was unlikely to probe.

Melni finished her ruse of film work and left the room. She had dinner in, and was midway through the meal when the door chime rang. A representative from Blade's stood in the hall, carrying a rectangular beige box.

"Your purchase, with gratitude," the woman said, handing it across the threshold. "Signature, please."

Melni signed, then expressed her own gratitude with a fourcoin from a jar beside the entrance.

An hour later she sat on her bed, sipping bad Cirdian wine and studying photographs she'd clipped of the Valix grounds from various sources. The memorial gathering would likely take place on the east lawn of the vast estate. Around the property's perimeter ran a high stone wall, broken only by three gates. All three, Melni knew from numerous scouting trips, were staffed full-time: ten hours a day, ten days a week. The guards were well trained, many recruited out of the NRD, lured by high salaries and the tantalizing prospect of working close to the paragon herself.

The space between the lawn and the building proper was

split between a vast hedge maze and an artificial lake. "What that must have cost," Melni whispered.

Her eyes were drawn to the house itself. The vast building had required almost a year to construct, and at least for a brief time had been utterly unique in architectural style. It was elegant and somehow even understated despite the enormous size. The walls were in a daring white, capped by overlapping red tiles that hid the usual mess of vents, pipes, and chimneys on the roof. Some of the walls were even curved, and there were windows everywhere. Any one of its marvelously fresh features might have failed on its own, but taken as a whole few could say that it didn't work. Quite the opposite. It was a masterpiece. The question few Northerners asked anymore, the question that drove every action Melni took in her covert occupation, was how a refugee orphan from the wastes could manifest such brilliance across so many fields. Engineering, physics, and mathematics all at least made a kind of sense. The disciplines went hand in hand. They could be learned. But Alia Valix excelled at anything she set her mind to: politics, fashion, law, commerce, architecture.

How? How did her mind work? Her company was decades ahead of any competitor, yet rather than trying to crush such foes, Alia showed a stunningly deft hand at business acumen as well. She licensed, she contracted, she forged unlikely partnerships across seemingly unrelated industries. As a result the North benefited at a pace matched only by the woman's net worth.

And it had all happened so blixxing fast. That's what Melni could not wrap her mind around, and what had the South so concerned. The Quiet War, started shortly after the Desolation had so neatly divided Gartien into North and South, had in all that time never veered far from a state of equilibrium. Valix had changed all that, and with terrifying speed. The North's rate of technological advancement grew exponentially each year now. At Riverswidth the analysts, if you could get them to talk candidly about such things, said another year or two of such unchecked progress would lead to weapons and countermeasures that would render the North unstoppable should they decide to escalate. Even pessimistic estimates had the North winning a military victory inside of ten years, should it come to that. The way things were going, Melni wondered if another scenario entirely might play out. Citizens of the Southern states might begin to eye the progress enjoyed by their Northern peers with a little too much envy. They might start to wonder why they shouldn't switch allegiances, geography be damned, and who could blame them?

The flat's thin walls creaked as a frigid ocean wind came in off the harbor and moaned through the streets outside, driving rain to clatter against the windows. Melni drained her wine. She shifted her attention to a schematic of the mansion proper, stolen from an electrician's office during the construction process. She reviewed the security systems and excessive plumbing for the hundredth time.

The drawing had vexed her from the moment she'd first cast her gaze upon it, for what it lacked rather than what it showed. In the center of the home, below the main rooms, was a gaping blank area marked simply "Think Tank."

For a long while Melni just stared at the empty section of paper, as if the act would produce the detail she so desperately wanted. Tomorrow she'd be on the grounds. Closer than ever before to the famed room where Alia pondered the problems of the North and how to profit from fixing them.

Even now this mysterious place seemed as far away as shining Garta herself.

9

SEVERAL HUNDRED MOURNERS SAT in tidy rows of red chairs on the emerald lawn.

Melni's vibrant dress from Blade's had turned heads since she'd stepped out of her pedicab and through the gates. Peach with white piping, the outfit ran to her knees in a form fit, accented by a tiny matching shawl and hat. Above her left breast she'd pinned a purple flower, and she'd left her backpurse home in favor of a small white evening case. All Valix-inspired styles, of course. Melni tugged the shawl tighter against the tenacious chill breeze.

On a white-clothed table in front of the chairs were four ornate spheres of brass and steel. Inscriptions covered the smooth surfaces between studded rivets. They were vessels of the highest quality to carry the remains below. In the old days, well before the Desolation, people believed the soul of the departed would continue down, all the way to the center of Gartien, the beating heart of the world where they believed a fragment of Garta gave heat and life from within while the star blazed above. In that molten core one's essence would dissipate and mingle with others from all over the planet, eventually recombining into a new soul and returning to the surface to enter the body of a newborn babe with its first words. Only then would a child be named.

A quaint view from a more superstitious time. Still, the tradition carried on for sentimental reasons, as did the first-words naming ritual.

Respects were paid for a full hour as Garta set behind

crimson clouds on the western horizon. One hundred full minutes of silent, serious introspection. Melni welcomed the bell signaling an end to the quiet and the start of the festivities. Alia Valix herself led the procession. She held an actual lit torch high above her head and walked confidently through the great hedge maze her property featured. The labyrinth being of her own design, Alia followed the optimal path to a clearing in the center. Here a wide, white pavilion sat invitingly in the glow of thousands of winking candles. The waitstaff, which seemed to outnumber the guests, swarmed in and began guiding people to tables of food and drink arrayed around the perimeter of the vast space. The families were taken up into the pavilion and guided to ornate couches and chairs where they could receive condolences in reasonable comfort.

A cup found its way into Melni's hand. She sipped at the sweet golden liquid, pleasantly warm in her throat and stomach on such a cool evening. Circling the periphery, avoiding conversation, she mingled and observed.

Whenever possible she deposited the contents of her cup into a potted plant and then took another from one of the staff's trays.

Eventually she made her way into the maze. Others wandered there, too. Mostly in pairs, they walked arm in arm and spoke with the kind of conspiratorial quiet that so often comes with unexpected death.

Having pretended to consume six glasses of wine, she stumbled her way toward the Valix house and climbed the immaculate white stone steps. A pair of waitstaff, no doubt security under the gray garb, pulled open wide glass doors for her without challenge.

"Lav?" she asked.

"We have facilities available by the pavilion, esteemed guest."

"Gratitude, but it needed to be cleaned. Someone had a spill. So they sent me here."

"Our regret. Up the steps, then, to either wing. Second door."

Drawing on her mental map of the house, Melni took the right passage from the top of the stepwell. Left would have led to a series of guest rooms and the staff quarters, among other more mundane places. To the right would be Alia's own apartments, workspaces, meeting areas, and—one floor below, near the very center of the house—the entrance to the Think Tank itself.

In the lav she locked the door and checked the time, then killed the light. The party would end soon. The families and close friends would follow Alia Valix to her yacht and sail off to return the remains of the dead, ten miles offshore. Everyone else would leave.

Except Melni.

She sat there in the plush lav for two hours, until even the sounds of cleaning faded and the house grew silent. After a good twenty minutes of quiet she got to her feet, stretched, and slipped out of the room into the dim hallway beyond.

"May I help you?"

The voice made Melni's stomach flutter. There was no mistaking who it belonged to.

She turned to face Alia Valix. The woman stood just a few paces behind her, statuesque under the wan light of a dimmed chandelier above. She'd chosen a light blue outfit with sand-colored trim, in a style almost identical to what Melni had chosen. The cut accentuated her unusual height and thin, rather bony frame. The similarity in outfits, and their pale midlands pallor, made Melni suddenly feel like one of the legions of young Valix wannabes. "I just . . ." she paused and collected herself. "Drank a little too much and dozed off. My regret."

For an instant Alia's gaze bored into her like the flare of a searchlight. Then she softened and stepped aside, pointing back toward the middle of the house and the doorway Melni had so innocently passed.

Melni mumbled her gratitude and shuffled by.

"Do I know you?" Valix asked.

Melni slowed, then stopped. Her mind raced, caught between wanting to leave no impression whatsoever with this woman lest she be wondered about later, and the very possible fact that she'd already crossed this line.

"It's just," Alia said, "I know all the families now, and of course my own people who worked closely with the . . ." She trailed off, allowed a brief silence. "Were you friends with one of the—"

"I have an invitation," Melni said, clicking open her evening case. "A friend could not attend and asked me to come in his place." She handed the paper across despite the fact that Alia had not reached for it.

An uncomfortable second passed before Alia reached out and took the offered slip. She studied it briefly and handed it back with a thin smile. "You're a friend of Detective Kulit?"

"Yes."

"Are you a detective as well?"

"No, no. I am a reporter with the *Weekly*. Boran is just a friend."

Alia studied her face, then briefly glanced at the rest of her. "I do know you! Melni Tavan, yes? It's okay, I make it a point to know all the press in Midstav. Alia Valix," she said, holding out a hand.

"I know who you are."

"You wrote a very nice piece about our partnership with the Tandiel mining conglomerate recently."

Flustered, astonished, Melni could do nothing except offer a meek smile. Despite her true purpose here, to receive recognition, even praise, from this woman of all people, left her speechless. And in a quandary. The last thing she wanted was to be known to the person she was here to spy on. Already she could feel her ability to blend in slipping away like water through cupped hands. And yet, where one door closed, another . . .

Alia's brow creased. "This is the moment where you, the ambitious young reporter, ask for an interview."

"Oh, I could never. Not here, not during a memorial. I would be tossed out on my ear."

"I'm giving you permission."

Melni swallowed. She shifted on her feet and felt the sheathed knife on her left thigh grate against the lockright implements on the right. "Surely you have guests to—"

"Everyone's gone. The families took my yacht but I decided . . . well, I didn't feel right going along. So I'm stuck here, I'm afraid, waiting for their return so I can close the event officially. Please, ask me. I could use a distraction."

"All right, then," Melni said. To her own ear she sounded like an uncomprehending child asked to apologize for some archaic slight. She cleared her throat and lifted her chin. "Miss Valix, may I ask you a few questions on behalf of the *Weekly*?"

Alia took Melni to a large den and left her sitting alone for several minutes. When she returned she'd shed her mourning dress for a simple dark blue blouse over black slacks. She took the seat behind the desk without a word and sat for a few moments studying a sleek beige cube emitting a harsh greenish glow from the front. In that light the woman looked cold, almost sickly. The box sat atop another, the lower one thin and rectangular in shape like the box that Blade's had delivered Melni's dress in. The front tapered down slightly and sported at least a hundred buttons in neat rows. A computer, Melni realized. She'd read about them but never seen one in person. Just a few years ago it would have taken up the entire room.

"Thirsty?" Alia asked without looking.

Melni shifted in the small, plush chair. "Gratitude, but I am fine."

Alia tapped a few buttons on her computer and the green glow of information winked off. Without the cold glare on her face she looked more like the polished businessperson the press was used to seeing. She didn't seem tired at all, despite the hour. "Well, I hope you have questions or this will be a short chat."

Melni fumbled with her pad of paper. She set it in her lap and pressed the cover open to the page she'd jotted notes on while Alia had changed clothes. "Gratitude for speaking with me," she started, lamely.

The woman across from her waved the comment aside with a tiny gesture and the flash of a smile at the corners of her mouth.

Melni glanced down at her notes, groping for the right strategy, torn between the need to learn answers and the desire to be forgotten by this person before the next setting of the Sun. The silence in the room became an oppressive, palpable thing. Alia began to tap her fingers together.

"Right," Melni said. "The Think Tank."

"Yes?" Alia asked, one eyebrow arched in slight amusement.

"How about a tour?"

Alia laughed brightly.

"Sorry," Melni said. "Had to try."

Another wave of the hand. A curt dismissal to an amusing question.

Melni tried a different tack, one she hoped would be unexpected. "Where are you from, Miss Valix? I mean, the Desolation obviously. We have that in common, at least," she said, pointing to the pale skin of her own cheek. "But most of us went north or south centuries ago. Your ancestors stayed. Where specifically?"

A flash of annoyance touched the woman's steady blue eyes. She puffed out her cheeks before answering, something Melni had seen her do in countless public appearances. "Given your profession," she said evenly, "I'm sure you know the answer to that as well."

"I know what most people know, probably. Raised in a remote cabin in one of the disputed regions. You have said you do not remember exactly where—"

"All true."

"This always surprised me," Melni said.

"Why?"

She leaned forward, pen poised above the paper. "Your astonishing intellect implies a rather exceptional education. And yet you never learned where your own home was?"

"So?"

"A bit odd."

"Not really."

Melni frowned. "Can you elaborate?"

"Look," Alia said. "If you're trying to find out where my parents are, forget it. They passed away. I stayed until the supplies ran out and wandered. North, as luck would have it. I've explained this many times and don't care to continue doing so."

"My regret, this is not what I sought. I wish to understand the education you received, given the mind it led to."

For a long pregnant second Alia stared right into her. Then she nodded, once. She was used to questions. Bored of them.

Melni went on. "You were schooled at home by parents of, it's fair to say, humble background." When Alia made no response Melni continued. "I am curious why they focused so absolutely on certain topics—physics, mathematics, chemistry—and shunned things like history and geography, as you have previously remarked. It is . . . well, at a minimum I am sure you can agree this is an unusual approach. The results dispel any argument, of course, but . . . well, I suppose what I want to know is what you think of it now. Should we raise our children with similar regimens? Are we wasting our time teaching our youth about history? About great works of art and literature?"

"Of course not," the woman said. She ran a finger along the lock of hair pressed diagonally across her forehead. "My parents were . . ." She paused, puffed out her cheeks again. "They weren't well educated themselves. And in my case, they simply made do with what they had, which wasn't much. Beyond the basics, once they'd taught me to read I was simply given full access to any book they had or could find. Some topics were simply underrepresented. And, as a result, I suppose, I was never really interested in those things. It's actually quite embarrassing, if you want to know the truth. I can't tell you how many times I've suggested an idea to my staff only to be told it was tried fifty years ago, or a hundred, sometimes a thousand! This is why I'm so grateful for the people I work with, and why I spend so many nights in the Think Tank simply reading old books. After all, those who don't study history are doomed to repeat it."

Melni's journalistic instinct took pen to paper at the remark. "Can I quote you on that? That is a lovely phrase."

Alia grinned at the request. "I surprise myself sometimes. By all means, quote away."

"Gratitude." She scribbled down the words.

There came a soft knock at the door. Unbidden, two armed private guards strode in, weapons drawn and aimed at the floor. Melni glanced back to Alia. The amused pride had gone, replaced by a sudden coolness.

Alia, eyes never leaving Melni, leaned to one side and opened a drawer. From within she pulled a single brown envelope. With calm deliberation she unwound the twine clasp and folded back the flap, revealing a stack of photoprints inside. Like a dealer of cards she fanned them out on the surface of the desk facing Melni. "Now," she said. "Perhaps I could ask some questions?" The woman steepled her fingers and pressed them to her lips. "How well did you know Onvel Harginns?"

The words crossed the space between them like an arrow in flight. Melni stared in horror at the images before her. They were all of the same thing. Onvel and Melni, together. On a park bench. Seated across from each other on a tram. At dinner, the night he'd expressed feelings for her that Melni did not exactly rebuff, though she felt nothing for him romantically. She'd needed him, nothing more. "I . . ." she started, lamely.

"I'll rephrase my original question," Alia said, all patience drained from her voice. "What was the nature of your relationship with Onvel Harginns?"

"Friends," Melni whispered.

Alia leaned over and tapped one picture in particular. It had been taken from directly above. They were seated on the floor of Onvel's small flat, huddled over the mess of papers he'd snuck out of his office.

Melni swallowed. *How much do they know? What could I say that would get me out of this room?* "He . . . he wanted to show me the sort of work he did. I understood none of it."

"Birdshit," Valix said. Another series of prints was pulled from the drawer. Melni, working under the light of a candle, making copies by hand of the pages Onvel had said were important. In the next she saw the safe house on Bandury Lane, Melni climbing the steps. Then another: Melni walking into Croag & Daughters, the antiques shop in Harborsedge. The image had been taken from a second-story window, somewhere across the street. They'd been waiting for her, watching the place. Did they know about the drop? Had her last message, and Onvel's final research, made it out? Garta's light, how long had they been watching her? Some of the images were from her earliest days with Onvel, after he'd confessed sympathy for *desoa,* and even the South.

She thought back through the events of the evening. Boran offering to let her be here in the first place. The time she'd spent hidden, so she thought, in the bathroom. The surprise invitation to this interview. She'd been lured here. She'd isolated herself, out of contact for hours. Melni could see NRD and Valix agents alike fanning out across the city, arresting everyone she'd been in contact with. She'd been expertly played.

"Search her," Alia said.

10

ONE OF THE GUARDS stepped in behind her. He grasped her by the upper arm and hauled her to her feet.

At that instant every lamp in the room flickered, then died. The computer's fan whirred to a stop.

Swallowed in absolute darkness, Melni froze. A terrible empty silence held the room for a fraction of a second. Across the desk, Alia emitted a thin, sharp breath, more frustrated than afraid. Melni heard her fingers probe around the surface in the dark, then fiddle with something. The intercom. "This is Alia. Someone give me a status report."

Nothing, not even static.

The guard holding Melni's arm let go of her, fumbling for his own radio or perhaps a flashlight.

Melni drove an elbow straight back into his gut. He grunted, fell. She dropped to the ground and lay flat on her back. Buttocks raised, knees at her chest, she reached up her own skirt and slid the knife from its hiding place against her thigh. She flicked it open as she rolled, expecting the lamps to bloom again any second.

Flight was not an option. She needed a hostage, the highest-value unarmed asset present. She came up to a crouch and, trailing one finger along the outer edge of the desk, worked her way behind it. She found Alia's chair and reached out, ready to hold knife against neck. Her hand brushed the fabric of the backrest. Empty.

The guard she'd hit groaned. The other made sounds of a frantic search through clothes. There was a thud and he cursed. A dropped lamp, or pistol? And where had Alia gone?

Melni's foot brushed against something solid. She knelt and found the tip of a shoe. The woman had hid below the desk. Melni reached for her but her fingers only found the walls of the empty space below. She felt for the shoe again and found it, and another, empty and resting on the floor.

A brilliant beam of a light swept frantically about the room. Melni pushed back from the desk and came up to a half crouch, then pretended to fling her knife toward the guard wielding the lamp. He flinched, dodged to one side. She used the distraction, vaulting the desk. Landing before him Melni kicked the man hard between the legs, followed by a punch to his throat, her fingers a flat, hard wedge. The combination sent him to the floor, desperate to cry out yet unable to get a breath. His light fell and rolled across the carpet, splaying long ugly shadows along the bookshelves.

Melni whirled back to the first guard. He'd dropped his pistol while trying to get a bulky handheld radio out of a holder on his belt. Trapped between gathering his weapon or defending himself, he could do neither effectively. She moved in and kicked him so hard in the face he fell again, his head smacking on the corner of a glass table. The surface shattered. The man screamed, writhed onto his side. Blood streamed from the back of his head.

On the far wall, opposite the door, a section of bookshelf had rotated aside, revealing a dark space behind. The concealed door was rotating back to its original position. On the other side of that wall, according to the house plans, the mysterious Think Tank waited. Melni vaulted the mess of glass. Three steps to cross the room, then she dove and tucked into a roll through the door a split second before it hissed shut.

Just inside she collided into the back wall of a narrow hallway. The door clicked as it closed, plunging her into absolute darkness. Faint footsteps came from somewhere to her right. Melni could see nothing at all. She rested a hand against one wall and began to walk slowly forward at a crouch, knife held in front of her at a right angle, edge instead of tip in case she ran into something solid.

A faint lamp winked on somewhere around a corner fifteen feet ahead. The light jerked about, cycled in intensity. Melni rushed to the corner and darted around, coming in low, blade held just below eye level.

She found herself in a huge cylinder-shaped room, thirty feet wide and just as tall. The air inside smelled of fresh flowers. Every surface was flawless white, meticulously clean, and almost luminous in the weak light from the lamp.

Alia did not hold the electric torch. She stood silhouetted, just two meters away, her back to Melni. She seemed paralyzed, frozen in the brilliant white beam of an electric torch held, Melni now realized, by someone else.

A third person inside the impenetrable Think Tank.

Melni leaned to one side. In the center of the room was a perfect circular column of softly glowing blue water. Fish of every size and color darted about within, circling a massive chunk of reef encrusted with gently swaying plants and tendrils. Pyramid fish clung to a rock near the base. A cloud of small silvery specks swarmed around near the very top, where a soft light lit the caps of waves on the surface of the installation. The whole thing seemed more sculpture than aquarium to Melni. She'd never seen anything like it.

In front of this spectacle stood a man. Melni could barely see him in the flaring gleam of his torch, but the shape of his profile gave the gender away. He held the beam rock steady just in front of his face.

If he'd noticed Melni, or cared, he gave no indication.

"Alia Valix," he said in a strangely accented voice. "You've done well for yourself."

A long, stark silence followed. Alia swallowed loudly enough for Melni to hear. She shifted in her stance. Finally she spoke, her voice a terrified whisper. "How did you get in here?"

"Trivial," he replied. "Three, four, twenty thirty-nine. Using your birthday for the entry code? Very sloppy. Who's your friend?" He flicked the beam ever so slightly toward Melni. "Come out where I can see you," the man ordered.

Melni complied, keeping her gaze at his feet and concealing the knife behind her leg. Her mind churned on the scenario unfolding before her. Who was this man? Stranger still, how did he know Alia's day of birth? Nobody knew the date of their own birth, much less someone else's. First-words, sure. Alia's firstwords was well known, given the lavish parties she'd thrown to celebrate the anniversary in recent years. She famously held the status of "all zeros." Zero minutes, zero hour, zero month, zero year if one abbreviated the latter.

The more important bit of intelligence in his comment became suddenly clear. If he knew the date of her birth, he must know specific details of her life before she'd stumbled out of the Desolation all those years ago. Despite herself, a tingle of excitement danced up the skin of Melni's arms and along her neck.

"That's far enough," the man said.

She'd only taken a step, putting her in plain sight but still close enough to Alia that he could keep them simultaneously illuminated in the beam. A tactically wise choice. He had, she now saw, a pistol held oddly in his right hand, not the normal left. Instead he used the left, which held the thin tube of the electric torch, as a means to steady his aim. Melni shifted her grip on the knife. She suddenly felt like third bird in the nest. A background player in something larger. Here she stood next to the wealthiest and most famous person alive, cowering in the bright beam of an armed . . . what, assassin? Burglar? Jilted lover?

A faint ticking sound rippled across the ceiling high above, followed by a dim but growing white light. In the huge cylindrical aquarium a stream of bubbles began to rise from the pebbles that filled the bottom. Somewhere behind the walls came the whir of fans moving air and pumps moving water.

The man turned off his light. Without wavering the aim of his gun he lowered the torch and slipped it into a loop on his belt.

Unable to resist, Melni took a quick glance about the room. She'd expected something like a library, with floor-to-ceiling shelves overflowing with volumes new, old, and perhaps even forgotten to time and the Desolation. A place to read, to contemplate. She'd expected giant blackboards filled with chalk lettering—equations, bubble maps, and the random scribbled insight. She'd expected beakers and glass spheres filled with strange chemicals bubbling over lit burners. Instead there was only the aquarium, and, off to one side, a simple desk with another of the beige computer systems resting atop its otherwise clean surface. Oddly the desk and its chair sat on a low circular dais.

The notion that Alia could generate all her amazing ideas from this simple, serene place made her all the more fascinating.

Training kicked in. Exits? None obvious, save where she'd come in, and that had closed behind her. Had it locked? Given its concealed nature, probably. And given Alia's obsessive secrecy around this chamber it seemed to Melni unlikely that anyone on her staff would be entering on their own.

She shifted her attention to the man. He wore plain, ill-fitting Northern garb. Versatile, simple stuff favored out in the forests near the ice sheet. A rare sort of outfit to see in the city, except maybe down by the docks or near the roller platforms of the industrial zones where lumber or other goods were unloaded. His boots did not match the rest of the getup. They looked like standard chin-up patroller issue, in fact.

His face surprised Melni most of all. That slightly beige skin, the narrow eyes, and thick black hair. He was a Southerner, a native rather than a crater-band refugee like herself. There were hardly any such people north of the Desolation, and they usually kept well away from the cities.

Peculiarities began to register the more she looked at him. Narrow eyes, yes, but not the usual Southern blue. His were a dark brown, almost black. And his hair, while black, was cut shorter even than Melni's, leaving his ears uncovered. Not a man's style at all.

How had he come to be here? Parachuted in to do the job she had presumably failed at? If so, why dress like this?

Did he have an escape plan? Or was he just some loner, driven mad by a life lived on the wrong side of the Desolation, his misfortunate ancestors trapped above the centerline? Was he here to take some kind of twisted vengeance?

None of that explained how he would know the date of Alia Valix's actual birth, though. He must be from Riverswidth.

"You," Alia rasped.

The word stiffened him. For the first time his aim wavered, if only for an instant.

"You," she said again. A whisper now, full of venom. When she spoke again her words were measured. "I'm surprised they'd send you, considering the mess you made. Atoning for past mistakes, are we? It took you long enough to figure out you'd missed one."

The man's brow furrowed. The gun lowered several inches as he stared, dumbstruck, into Alia's face. He opened his mouth as if to speak, then shut it.

"Are you here to take me back?" Alia asked.

Now the gun snapped back to its original position, dead set on the middle of her chest. "Where's the data you took? In there?" He nodded toward the desk, or perhaps the computer sitting upon it.

"Even if you torture me I won't tell you where I've hidden it."

The assassin shrugged. "Then I'll search for it on my own. Thanks for saving me the headache." He leaned his head in, sighting down the length of the pistol.

Alia held out her hands, surrendering to fate.

"Wait." The word came from Melni's own mouth before she knew she'd decided to speak.

The man kept his weapon trained on Alia, but his eyes slid between the thin slits to look at Melni. "Who the hell are you?" he asked.

"Melni Tavan. Station N. I have authority in regards to this asset." She moved in front of Alia, into the line of fire.

Again he shrugged. "No idea what you're talking about. Stand aside."

"This woman is my objective," she went on, letting her knife show, "and I need her alive. There are questions that must be answered."

"Yes, questions," Alia said to the man. "You must want to know why."

For the briefest moment Melni saw something in his face. He did indeed have questions. Refraining from asking them came from something more powerful than curiosity. It was training, and orders. "We already know why. It's obvious," the man replied.

"You're wrong. You'll ruin everything—"

"We'll take our time. Do it right. Or we would have," he added, suddenly thoughtful. "It's probably not even an option anymore. You've poisoned the well—"

"I'm *defending* the well, you son of a bitch. You have no idea what you've stumbled into here," Alia said. "But that's you, isn't it? The unwavering assassin. Cold-blooded murderer. Say any more, by the way, and you'll have to kill this woman, too."

He gave a casual shrug of his shoulders and renewed his aim.

"Wait," Melni said. *What in all of Garta's light were they talking about?* "Just . . . please—"

"Lights off!" Alia shouted, very loud and carefully clear.

Incredibly the lights obeyed her voice. Darkness swept back into the room, absolute save for the dimly glowing disk of the aquarium's surface, high above.

Four gunshots barked in rapid succession. The rounds zipped past Melni's ear and gave little *thawps* as they burrowed into the wall somewhere behind. She dropped to the ground, heard footsteps where Alia had been and a muttered curse from the assassin.

"Intrusion scenario!" Alia shouted.

A vibration coursed through the floor. The sound of grating metal mixed with snapping electrically activated locks. Another whipcrack from the gun. Sparks erupted from the wall to Melni's left, where Alia's voice had been. There was a heavy ringing thud from the direction of the small desk. Somewhere on the far side of the room she heard an almost imperceptible hydraulic hiss and then a deeper, heavier metallic clang.

The man had his flashlight back on and was frantically swinging it about the room. Melni rolled to her stomach and came up in a crouch, her knife held out despite the lack of opponent. The weapon felt suddenly pitiful.

Alia had vanished. Where the desk and chair had been there was now a metallic dome studded with rivets. Before

Melni could ponder the reason for this she heard a series of thin mechanical whirs from all around. The man heard it, too, and swung his beam across the circular wall of the chamber. At every compass point, up close to the ceiling, a panel had opened, each perhaps one foot on a side. Concealed within were circular openings: pipes, like cannons lurking behind their gun ports.

A queer noise filled the room. Behind the walls, above the ceiling, came the rattling of pipework and the gurgling, uneven sounds of rushing water.

Above this came Alia's voice, amplified and made tinny by a concealed sound system. "I'm sorry it has to end like this, but I cannot let you ruin what I've started here."

The pipes coughed, each spraying a fine mist of water.

"This way!" Melni shouted. Without looking she turned and ran for the secret hallway she and Alia had entered through. All around her the hidden pipes began to belch little blasts of water. Then the deluge came. Six massive streams poured into the room and began to pool on the floor. Before Melni could even reach the opening there was an inch of water on the floor. She slipped as she tried to take the corner, slammed into the hallway wall, and began to slide along it on the torrent of frigid liquid pouring into the Think Tank. The impact ripped her evening case from her shoulder. It splashed into the water and sank, gone. Without the benefit of the stranger's torch she found herself in near-total darkness, carried by the flood of water.

Panic filled her as the current slammed her bodily into the far end of the narrow passage. In the impact she lost her grip on the knife and it splashed near her feet. She imagined the razor-sharp blade swirling around violently in the vortex of current around her legs. *Forget it!* her mind screamed. *Get out, get away!*

Somewhere to her right would be the concealed bookshelf door she'd entered through. She came to a shaky stand, groped around in the inky blackness for any kind of handle. Nothing. The water came to her waist now. She took a gulp of air and dove, fumbling along the base of the door for a foot latch. Again, nothing. Melni stood again and heaved against the surface with her shoulder, to no avail. She pressed her back against the opposite wall and kicked. The door did not so much as budge. The water, now at her chest, gave no indication of slowing. No drainage. A perfect seal. In the chamber behind her, the dome over Alia's desk made a sudden and terrible sense. That tiny table and its computer were the only things in the room worth protecting.

The hallway turned from possible exit to virtually certain death trap. She kicked hard, cupped her hands, and pulled toward the vast chamber of the Think Tank, but against the torrent she made no progress. The water came on too fast, grinding in a violent maelstrom where the narrow hallway ended.

Less than a foot of air remained. Without an exit the water pressure would soon equalize, so she shifted focus to breathing, craning her neck out of the sloshing surface until her lips met the ceiling. One last swallow of air, then Melni pushed off and down. The pressure against her vanished as the hallway filled to capacity. She kicked off and kept kicking. Her arms were almost useless in the narrow passage so she pressed one to her side and held the other out to feel her way through the pitch black. She thrashed her feet, kicking hard. The frigid water bit into her skin. Her lungs burned for air.

A light swung through the darkness. There, the end of the tunnel. Melni kicked harder and reached out. Her fingertips brushed the end of the hallway and she turned, pressed her feet against the wall, and thrust her body back into the Think Tank. She kicked upward, pulled with her hands and arms. Her lungs demanded air, burned for it. Any second now her body would disobey the force of will.

With a splash her head broke the surface. Melni gulped fresh air and treaded water. Around her the pipes near the ceiling still spewed water at a colossal pace, the deafening streams churning the surface. Already half the room lay submerged. The cool blue column of the aquarium jutted from the center of the pool. Below, in the murky depth, she saw the beam of the stranger's electric torch swinging about. He was frantic. Drowning. Perhaps he didn't know how to swim.

Despite the pain in her lungs and the tremors running

through her cold body, Melni paddled toward the light and, once over it, dove and kicked downward. Near the bottom she spotted the blurred shape of the man. He was near the dome that had covered Alia's desk. She reached for him, grabbed him tight by the neck of his shirt. Feet against the bottom she thrust upward, letting bubbles stream from her mouth to guide the way. He struggled against her. A slap at her arm, then his fingers wrapped around her wrist and he pulled. Melni held on, fighting him, wanting to slap sense into the blixxing idiot.

Her face broke the turgid surface. The ceiling was only a few feet above now.

The man came up next to her. He gulped air and then whirled, mouth twisted into a snarl. He shouted over the crashing water. "What the hell's the matter with you?"

"You were drowning. I saved your life!"

"Save yourself, Melanie, or whatever your name is. I've got a job to do."

One foot of air space remained. The pipes had submerged, leaving only the sound of water lapping against the walls and the giant glass cylinder.

"We need to work together," Melni said. "Find a drainage point and force it open."

"Do as you like. I'm getting into that dome."

"Drain the water first! Think about it. You will only get one more chance to swim down there before we have no air left. Drain the water and you can hack at that steel ball all you like." The tumultuous water had them bobbing like toy boats. Melni's head bumped the ceiling. "Please, there is no time to argue."

The water reached his chin. They both pressed one hand against the ceiling now to keep their heads from smacking into it with each churning wave. He stared at her, weighing options, gauging her wisdom and, she sensed, her authority. "The fish tank," he said. "Any flesh eaters in there? Anything poisonous?"

The question surprised her. She glanced toward the ring of thick glass now just barely visible in the shrinking gap between water and ceiling.

"Think!" he shouted at her. "You saw it, right?"

Melni nodded vaguely. She hadn't paid attention to the species within. Ocean life had never been a subject of much interest to her. "I did not. I—"

"Ah, fuck it. It's a risk we'll have to take. Move to the tank and get ready to swim up. Get as much air as you can."

With that he plunked below the surface and kicked downward, his beam of light scanning the floor about twenty feet below.

Baffled, Melni did as he asked. Hands on the ceiling, she pawed and kicked over to the glass and pressed herself against it. A silvery fish with huge impassive eyes swam past her face.

There came a deep, muffled thud from below, followed by a second and then a third. Without warning the glass in front of her spidered with cracks and then shattered. The shards held for an instant and then, all at once, vanished, sucked downward into the dark water. Melni felt herself hauled under as the two bodies of fluid warred for equilibrium. The downward pull reversed a split second later. An invisible fist threw Melni into the ceiling. Turbulent water surged all around her. She hadn't taken the breath the man had advised. Now she swam, panicked yet again and hating herself for it. A ring of dim light marked the space where the glass had met ceiling. Something slid across her shin and with it came a searing pain. Another jagged bit of glass, thrown about by the swirling currents in the pool, ripped across her forearm. Melni bit back the urge to scream and powered to the circular opening. Her lungs burned. She groped around and found the rim, took hold of it, and heaved herself up.

A rippling surface loomed above. She kicked hard and pulled against the water with both hands, buoyed by the raging, swirling current. Her hands found air, then her face broke the surface and she inhaled. A metal grate ceiling greeted her. The dim light came from above it. Melni clawed at it with one hand to stabilize herself, then methodically went from panel to panel, pushing with what little strength she had left. There, near the center, a section budged. She shoved at it again and kept shoving, kicking despite the glass all around her feet and legs. The panel rotated up and over, smacking against the floor with a deep, reverberating clang. Melni gripped the edges and pulled herself through. She wanted to scream when her shin scraped along the edge. The cut bit deep. The water tinged red.

For a second she lay panting on the cold metal grate. A splash below brought her back to the moment. The man surfaced, tried to shout, gurgled instead.

"Here!" Melni yelled, reaching down through the open panel. A stream of blood ran from her arm down to her wrist. She bit her lip and shoved her hand into the cold reddish pool. A second passed, then another, then fingers brushed hers and she had him. She hauled, gripping his forearm with her other hand and heaving until his torso lay on the platform. For a heartbeat she thought he'd drowned. Then his mouth opened and he drew in a long, desperate breath.

His clothes had protected him from the glass. She grabbed two fistfuls of shirt and hauled him the rest of the way out. The man came to his knees and fought to control his breathing. Twice he coughed, spewing water onto and through the grated floor.

Finally he got his knees under him and sat upright, hands at his sides, breaths still coming in huge, anxious lungfuls.

"What now?" Melni asked.

11

PETER CASWELL STARED at the grated floor. In the murky depths below his feet he could see the dome. In his mind's eye he could see Alice Vale cowering beneath it.

She'd been ready for this. She could probably last days inside that iron dome. If only he'd had more time. If only he'd recognized the drainage pipes through which he'd entered for what they were. A thousand "if onlys" ran through his head, but none mattered. What happened in that room had already slipped away, like the water dripping from his chin through the grate in the floor. Just memories now, and memories were of no value to him.

"What now?" the native repeated, imparting more authority into her voice.

He glanced over at the sprite of a woman, seeing her clearly for the first time. Short and thin, with a pixie cut of light blond hair that served to offset unsettling purple eyes. Pale white skin a stark contrast to the chocolate brown of virtually everyone else he'd seen on this world. He'd learned early after landing that his Korean looks marked him as those of Gartien's South, what he thought of as Africa.

I have authority over this asset, she'd said. *From Station N.* The words of a spy. But for whom? Some corporate adversary of Vale? He'd heard about a rivalry between North and South but put little thought into it, preoccupied instead with the fact that he could understand about ninety percent of what was said around him. Had Alice taught them? Converted a whole world to a new language in a dozen years? Impossible, surely. So how, then? Everything else was different. Race, culture, politics, none matched Earth. Only the lay of the land and the language were similar, and no matter how hard Caswell tried, he could find no relationship between the two.

No matter. Whoever this woman was, she seemed to think they were on the same side. A useful misconception if he played it right.

Caswell shook away the thought. There was nothing here to play. He should ditch her, immediately. She represented complication and risk. She didn't even carry a weapon, her knife evidently lost in the water.

"What is your marker?" she asked. "To whom do you report?"

"Quiet," he said, more harshly than he'd intended. "I'm thinking."

The opportunity to complete the mission had come easily, then gone in catastrophic fashion. Annoyance welled up inside him. It would have been a work of art. Neat, tidy, and quick. To come this far having only landed five days ago? Idly he wondered if he was always so efficient. He willed focus and pain suppression from his implant. The gland responded in an instant, and then it started to tingle slightly, a signal that the chemical reservoirs were running low. He'd no way to replenish them, save the food on the lander eighty kilometers away. Everything he tried to eat or drink here came right back up, violently.

Survival became the immediate goal. Flee this fiasco, go to ground, and figure out a way to salvage the op. Complication or not, this girl had made it in here. A place, by all accounts, impregnable to outsiders. So maybe she could help him escape. Maybe she could help him find something, anything, his body could digest.

While he thought through this she removed her shawl and tore it into strips, tying one around her calf and the other her forearm. Red stains blossomed on the sopping wet fabric.

Peter checked his pistol, shook his head in dismay at what he saw inside, and tucked the weapon into his waistband. He walked a circuit around the tiny room, studying the walls and ceiling. There were two tables off to one side, each piled with containers of varying size and shape. In another corner, a green metallic box roughly one meter on a side stood. White pipes linked it to receptacles on the wall. Machinery hummed within. "This must be where they maintain the aquarium."

While the girl stood and watched he began to open the containers on the table, boxes first and then some of the bottles. He sniffed at them. Unidentifiable chemicals. *Fuck it,* he decided. He opened all of them and motioned for the girl to back away. She did, pressing herself against the opposite wall. She gasped when he heaved the first table and flipped it over. The containers tumbled off with a crash, their contents spilling through the grated floor and into the dark water just below. Powders of varying color, chemicals that stung the eyes and made the nose twitch. He toppled the second table over next, then stood back and admired his work.

"Why did you do that?" she asked.

He shrugged. "To buy time. Instead of simply draining the room, now they'll have all sorts of headaches to deal with. It's a chemical stew, full of razor-sharp glass and frenzied fish. If she's in that dome, and I suspect she is, it might be hours before they can safely get her out." *Maybe they never will,* he thought but did not say. Perhaps he'd accomplished his goal after all.

The burst of speech was the most he'd said in one go since landing. The people here spoke with precision, sounding each word. It was English, but strangely accented and sprinkled with many unfamiliar words and subtle differences. He'd avoided conversation almost entirely since landing for this reason. But this woman, Melanie or whatever her name was, she'd overheard some things in that room below. Perhaps simply ditching her would not be enough.

She stared at the water, her eyebrows raised. "But we need to swim out through that water."

"Not true," he said, pointing up.

In the center of the low ceiling there was a circular groove, perhaps a meter in diameter. Next to it was a second much smaller panel, square in shape. Caswell pressed on the square and it rotated open from a concealed hinge, revealing a red handle within. He pulled it. With a hiss of air the circular section rotated down. An access tube ran upward into darkness. From this a ladder slid down, stopping just above the grated floor.

"I should have noticed that," the woman said, quietly, for herself.

"Let's go," he replied, and climbed.

The rungs led up about two meters. Caswell reached the top and began to open the second hatch. He stopped himself and looked down. The native waited on the floor below, staring up at him. Caswell pressed his index finger to his lips, demanding silence. Her eyebrows raised expectantly for some reason. Not as if the need for silence confused her, but that she expected him to follow up with another sign. A confused second passed. Finally he turned away from her and, with slow, precise movements, pulled the lever.

Darkness beyond. He climbed out and found himself in a small, frigid room that featured only the hatch on the floor and a single door, a line of pale light marking its edge.

Seconds more passed and the woman did not appear at the hatch. He glanced down at her and she stood exactly where he'd left her, staring, waiting. For a moment Caswell considered closing the hatch. Jamming the mechanism somehow and ridding himself of her.

He knelt and whispered just loud enough for her to hear. "What the hell are you waiting for? Come on!"

"You said you had something to say."

"I didn't."

"You did!"

The confusion on his face must have matched hers. He shook his head. "I don't have time for this. Get up here, or find your own way out."

She climbed. He offered her a hand and she took it, wincing in pain when he hauled her up.

"You need to get those cuts looked at," he said.

"I plan to, if we get out of here alive."

She rubbed warmth into her arms while Peter closed the hatch. The metal disk came to rest with a loud, purposeful *boom*.

Sealing Alice Vale's tomb, if he was lucky. Peter crossed to the door and used his foot, in the curious fashion of this

world, to open it a few centimeters. Outside he saw only a
dark, overcast sky. Dawn had yet to break, but the clouds
above reflected enough light from the great city around the
house to illuminate the surroundings. The girl came to his
shoulder, peering out from behind him. Gently she placed a
hand on his arm and urged him to crouch. He complied, and
to his surprise she pushed the door open the rest of the way.

The dark, flat rooftop of Alice Vale's extravagant mansion came into view. Small puddles of rainwater dotted the
black surface. White pipes and vents jutted up through the
roof at seemingly random positions. None was large enough
for a person to climb in. The girl leaned out and glanced
quickly in every direction, then ducked back in. Next to him
now, he noted, not behind. She let the door rest almost
closed against the frame.

"Empty," she said. "There is a servant's stepwell at the
southwest corner. Eight sections to the bottom, then a hall
that leads out to the cruiser stable. What is your name?"

He blinked, surprised by the sudden question and simultaneously impressed with her knowledge of the house.
"Caswell," he managed.

"Caz-will," she said, trying it out. "An unusual name."

Between the speed at which he'd found his target and his
desire to avoid unnecessary contact on this world, he'd yet
to bother inventing a persona for himself. A mistake, in
hindsight. He tried for a casual shrug, as if he heard this all
the time. "Yes, I suppose it is. My parents were unusual."

"Your *parents* chose your name?"

He shrugged again, lamely, aware he'd made some blun-
der of tongue or custom yet beyond the desire to care. He
started out the door. He felt famished, and his throat was
painfully dry. Worse, he had the come-down from use of his
gland to look forward to soon.

"Unusual indeed," she agreed, gripping his arm. "Let me
go first, hmm?"

Caswell hesitated, then stood aside and made a sweeping
gesture with one arm.

The woman cracked the door open again. A light rain now
fell, pattering against the roof and bringing the stagnant
puddles to life with circular ripples. She hesitated only a

second and then sprinted off, barely making a noise. Caswell followed, once again impressed. Standing above the fish tank he'd thought her not much more than a frightened mouse, but now . . .

Her path weaved them around the jutting vents and the occasional skylight. She passed these on the side where their shadows would not fall on the hazy white surfaces. Very smart.

At the southwest corner she came to a door. She hiked her skirt up to her waist and knelt. Strapped high up on her thigh were a set of locksmith's tools. Lockright, Caswell corrected himself. He'd stolen a set just hours after landing, just before the police had come for him. Four bodies still lay up there, somewhere, buried in the snow. Another four bottles of Sapporo, that made ten already on this mission, a new personal record. The girl selected one of the tools, so sure in her movements that he could guess she'd done this many, many times. She practically attacked the lock on the door's handle. Within seconds the rather basic lock sprang and she toed the foot-high handle upward.

"Do you have a weapon?" he asked. They were halfway down the stairwell. Sounds of alarm and panic filtered in from the house, too muffled to carry more meaning beyond that.

"I lost my knife in the water," she said. "You?"

"It's spent. I suppose I could throw it at someone."

The steps ended at a pair of doors, one in front and one to the left. Melni listened at one and then opened it a crack. "Hold it open," she said.

He slipped a finger through, eyeing the space beyond. She knelt beside him and pulled tools from her hidden set of picks.

"What are you doing?" he asked. "It's open already."

Her fingers trembled from the cold as she attacked the fasteners, which held an iron bar that linked the latch mechanism to the foot lever, or "foot latch." The length of metal came free in seconds. She handed it to him and went to work on another.

"Good idea," he said, testing the weight of it.

"Better than a fist." She hiked her skirt again and secured

the tool. Caswell looked away when she glanced at him, embarrassed. If she'd noticed, or cared, she made no sign. Instead she hefted her iron rod and coiled herself at the door. "It is about thirty feet," she said, "then through the kitchen, then the stable, which has an exit at the back."

"Fine. Let's go." Days earlier, hiding in a bedroom above a rural tavern, he'd learned from an old book that their measurement of a foot was roughly equal to Earth's: a third of a meter. He'd learned a lot of things in that room, including the supposed life story of Alia Valix, genius inventor, savior of the North.

Melni pushed the door open and slipped into the long hallway beyond. Small doorless rooms lined either side, stocked with foodstuffs and other supplies. At the far end was the kitchen door. She sprinted for it, carpet softening her already catlike footfalls. Caswell followed just a step behind. Halfway there the handle on the far door lifted from the other side. The girl ran faster, raising her bar.

Caswell grabbed her by the back of her shirt and hauled her to one side, into a pantry piled with linens. He held his index finger up and pressed it to his lips. Her eyebrows slowly rose, just as they had above the Think Tank, but she said nothing.

He positioned himself in front of her. By the sound of it he estimated two people had entered the hall. They rushed along toward the stairs. He saw familiar black uniforms, just like the men he'd killed in that house in the North. He pounced, shoulder first, slamming the trailing officer off his feet. The surprised man tumbled into the storeroom opposite with a crash of flour crates. Puffs of white powder filled the air. Caswell did not pursue; instead he went after the lead man and hoped the girl would get the hint.

The man before him slowed, started to turn. Caswell swung with all the strength his implant could gift him. Iron met hard skull with a vicious crack and went on into the spongy matter below. The guard collapsed without so much as a grunt, lifeless.

Caswell whirled, blood pounding in his temples.

The girl stood over the limp body of the other guard. Already she rummaged through the dead man's belt for the still-holstered gun.

"Take their uniforms," he said.

"Their what?"

"Clothes. Outfits. Whatever."

"Outfits. And no, there is no time. We must hurry."

Caswell turned back to his victim, panting. Blood dripped from the iron bar in his own hand. He dropped it on the carpet beside the body. Eleven kills, now. He decided she could keep the other one on her own tally.

He snuck a glance at his watch, counting seconds, waiting for his gland to bring calm back to his world.

"We must hurry, Caswell," she said, with a reasonable pronunciation.

"Let's go then."

Two of the mansion staff huddled together in one corner of the kitchen. They stared wide-eyed at the pair of soaking wet strangers, too surprised to cry out an alarm. Peter ignored them, as did his companion. She burst through the far door and on through a small coatroom that linked kitchen to stable.

Luxury versions of their three-wheeled "cruisers" crowded the long room, pointed outward toward six rolling doors. The woman darted around the first vehicle and followed the back wall to the very end of the room, where a single narrow door led out the rear of the building and to the gardens beyond.

Caswell moved up right behind her, breathing hard. She turned to him. "Just so we have clarity, this," she said, holding a flattened hand perpendicular across her lips, "means 'be silent.' This," she said, holding her index finger up to her lips as he had, "means 'I have something to say.'"

"It's Melanie, right?"

"Melni." She exaggerated the pronunciation for his benefit.

"Duly noted, Melni. Now, what's beyond this door?"

"Something called the Zen Garden," Melni said. "I am not sure what that means."

Caswell nodded. "Rocks and gravel. Not much in the way of cover. And then what, the perimeter wall?"

She squinted at him. "How did you gain entry to the Think Tank if you do not know the basic layout of the mansion?"

"Stay focused. The garden, then the wall?"

"The perimeter wall is still distant. There is an artificial lake between. We could swim that and climb over. Or the hedge maze a bit farther on."

"I've had enough swimming for one day. The hedge maze, then, provided we don't get lost."

"That is no concern. I memorized it."

He grinned at her. "Of course you did. Lead on then, Melni."

Her knowledge of the grounds proved perfect. Beyond the door a rock garden waited, with even rows of manicured stones in varying shades of gray. In places the rows curved elegantly around large chunks of polished volcanic glass. A narrow path surrounded the space, with benches on three sides. The back of the stable formed the fourth edge, its entire height covered in climbing vines.

They stood in the open doorway, allowing their eyes to adjust to the darkness. Frantic voices could be heard in the distance, all from inside the house. The whole estate had drawn inward, toward the catastrophe. Out here the grounds were whisper quiet.

Melni darted out and raced along a narrow walkway lit by tiny footlights beside the neat gravel rows of the garden. She took the corner at speed and bolted straight into a gap in the long hedgerow beyond. Caswell raced to keep up. She moved like an apparition through the maze, so quiet that he almost lost her.

Eventually an exit presented itself. They emerged at a colorful pavilion that had an almost ceremonial look, wholly out of place in the modern Earth-styled gardens. A few white floodlights had been turned on, casting the tent in pools of blinding brightness and long shadows. The place seemed deserted, though Caswell noted the trampled grass all around, dotted with the occasional used napkin or dropped plate.

A shrill alarm began to wail. And below that, more dis-

tant, came the rhythmic bleating of what could only be police sirens.

"This way," Melni said, running low along the inner edge
of the maze to the next gap. She sprinted now, the way lit in
the reflected glow of the floodlights. Her route led to a long,
narrow lawn and the gravel drive beyond. Melni pulled
to a stop. Caswell, distracted by new sounds behind them,
bumped into her.

"What—" she started.

He threw a hand around her shoulder and pulled her to the
right. Six, maybe seven people jogged toward them from
the gravel drive. Gate security, maybe. They were still far
off and, unless they knew intruders were on the premises,
might simply be rushing to help with the flooded central
chamber and their trapped employer within.

Caswell rushed Melni to a grove of trees that served to
obscure the view of the high perimeter wall. He ducked behind a trunk as the security detail came into view. Four went
around the maze altogether, but two broke off and headed
straight into the gap Melni had just led him through. The
trailing guard pulled up at the edge, his gaze scanning the
ground. He studied the trail of fresh footprints. Then he was
staring directly at Caswell. He opened his mouth to shout.

A thunderclap shattered the air. The startled guard staggered backward, hands at his chest, and toppled to the grass.
Caswell held the alien pistol at arm's length, studying it.
Most of the guns he'd encountered on this world used compressed air to propel the bullets. This one used gunpowder,
or something like it. Another "invention" of Alice's?

The guard's companion reemerged from the maze a second later and Caswell shot him in the gut.

"Time to go," he growled, and dashed off without waiting
for the woman.

She followed him through the darkness. Weaving between the fragrant trees, legs burning, wet clothes like ice
on his skin, Caswell ran and ran. He found a portion of wall
where a tree had grown carelessly close and shimmied up
using the bony branches for support. At the top he hauled
himself over without care for what lay on the other side. His
feet slapped against the rocky luminescent concrete, send-

ing splintering pain up his shins. He staggered a few steps away, making room for the girl.

Melni mimicked his climb and crested the wall right where he had. She landed with far more grace than he'd managed, and stood facing him. Her posture, her expression, betrayed surprise that he'd waited for her.

"Which way?" he asked.

In answer she took his hand and started to run again, down the faintly glowing lane toward the sleeping city.

12

THE SAFE HOUSE on Bandury Lane was the only place Melni could think to take the stranger, despite her orders not to return there. So she ran that way, the man at her side. At first he matched her pace, but gradually he began to lag and she had to tug at his hand. His narrow Southern eyes were now thin slits, and the color had drained from his face and lips.

Garta, still half-concealed behind the eastern horizon, lit the upper floors of the city in a weak golden light that crept down the walls at a glacial pace. Frost clung to the lower windows where the light had yet to reach. Along the narrow streets shopkeepers swept the sidewalks, their breaths coming in little clouds with each push of the broom. The smell of brewing cham came and went on the wind, beckoning the citizens to rise and begin seventhday work before the final three days of the week—the days of rest—arrived.

Melni bustled along with her head down, shivering against the chill wind on her still-damp clothing. The man fell a pace behind her. He looked near collapse but refused her hand now. In a half hour the streets and alleys would be packed with people. Given his rural clothing, his strong Southern looks, and perhaps most of all his womanish short hair, she doubted anyone would fail to mark him. The pair of them together would be remembered.

"You're sure this is the right way?" he asked in a hushed, ragged voice.

He had a peculiar way of speaking, joining words together

as if it took too much effort to sound them properly. Melni knew only one other person who did that: Alia Valix. She filed that knowledge and forced her mind to focus on the moment.

"Somewhere safe. I hope."

"Not exactly confidence inspiring."

She glanced at him. "You are the one who came here with this"—she eyed him head to toe—"outfit. Honestly it is the trifecta of stupid disguises."

"It's got me this far."

With every word he spoke, every odd bit of body language, doubt grew in her that he was from Riverswidth. So where, then? Some Valix Corp. rival? An insurgent faction within the North? Or perhaps . . .

A buzz of dread and excitement flickered through her at the thought he might be one of the Hollow. She knew of the elite force only in the vaguest terms. Gossip and legend, really. Their existence would never be expressly admitted to or denied by the top tier of Riverswidth. They were shadows. Men and women trained far away in total secrecy, rumored to infiltrate friendly places as a matter of training. It made sense they'd have their own mannerisms, their own peculiar way of speaking. But then they should be able to mask that, too, and expertly so. If blending in was a skill they valued, Caswell seemed entirely inept in its practice. Everything else, however . . .

Melni turned into an alley barely wide enough to walk single file. A dozen paces in she whirled on him. "Time to explain yourself."

He pulled up a few feet away and glared at her. "Not going to happen," he said.

She folded her arms.

The man studied her. Above, Garta's light had reached the third-floor windows. Soon the streets would be bright and bustling. If he sensed this, or felt the urgency of their situation, he gave no sign. "I can't tell you—"

"Are you a Hollow Man?"

"I . . ." He trailed off, his eyes searching hers. Then he nodded, once.

A lie. He was lying. She couldn't see it in his face and

it terrified her because she could not imagine what sort of creature would attempt to use the ultra-secretive Hollow as a cover. They may have been after the same target, but she felt certain now he did not get his orders from Riverswidth. Yet for now she must let him pretend so.

"Can we keep moving?" he asked. He looked haggard now, as if descending into sudden illness.

Melni swallowed her doubts and the fear that lay just beyond. They were adrift and being hunted. Get to the safe house, then somehow force answers from him, that was what she must do. Because whatever else he was or claimed to be, this man knew, and was known to, Alia Valix. Melni may have lost her cover, everything she'd been working toward might have collapsed like bonfire kindling, but she did have *him*.

She turned and started walking again. Whenever circumstances allowed, she ran. Twice she slipped back into an alley to wait for patrolling chin-ups to pass by. The officers strolled in their usual lazy fashion, a very good sign. Perhaps Alia had yet to alert anyone beyond her house staff of what had transpired in the Think Tank. Her fame and stature might hinder such a move, in fact. If investors heard someone had penetrated the house and entered the Think Tank they might panic. Her ideas were of incalculable value, and if rumors started that they'd been stolen . . .

Freshly paved angular streets gave way to the cobbles of Old Center, with its dense clusters of weathered buildings, creeping tendrils of mold worming up gray stone walls and around the edges of wooden doors so old they looked painted black. Gaslamps, ornate iron things that craned out over the bumpy, winding lanes, dotted the sidewalks with little pools of golden light. Small piles of snow were everywhere, telling the story of where Garta's light fell and where it did not.

People began to emerge from those black doors. Melni slowed to a casual walk. She took her strange companion by the arm and tilted her head to rest on his shoulder. Just two lovers walking each other to work. Both pale and shivering, underdressed. One with an arm and leg bandaged with the bloody shreds of a funeral shawl. Nothing out of the ordinary. Not worth a second glance, surely.

It seemed an eternity before she stepped up to the BAN-DURY LANE marker brick on the sidewalk. "Not far now," she said through clattering teeth.

Every passerby gave them a sidelong glance, if not a wide berth. One old woman even crossed the street while still fifty feet away. Melni abandoned the lover's pose. She almost jogged the last block and absolutely did jog up the front steps to the building.

At the door she knelt and hiked up her skirt to pull the lockright implements from their concealed strap.

The lock sprang in seconds and she toed the door open without bothering to put away her tools. Three flights up she came to the safe house door and repeated the exercise. This lock took much longer. There were perhaps only three or four lockrights in all of Combra who could coax a mechanism such as this one open. And none of them would be able to guess why it proved so difficult, for they could not see the insides: six very delicate teeth instead of the usual three. It had in fact been smuggled in. She took great pride that she could spring it at all, and even more so that it took her less than a minute. The stranger watched her with mild curiosity. If her ability impressed him he again kept it professionally concealed.

One step inside, Melni froze, a gasp escaping her lips. Broken furniture littered the great room. Shattered glass and porcelain covered the kitchen floor. Every cabinet open, every drawer pulled out and lying on the ground, smashed. Great knife-carved lines ran vertically along the walls every foot or so.

She started to say something. His hand on her shoulder, very firm, silenced the words.

Sounds from the bedroom. A tearing of fabric. The rustling of papers.

Melni kept her gaze fixed on the open door to the bedroom. She reached back and pressed her hand flat on the man's leg, urging him out into the hallway. She stepped back after he did, and winced as the floorboard creaked. Outside she pressed herself against the wall and stared at her companion, who'd taken a similar position on the opposite side of the doorframe.

"Friends of yours?" he whispered.

She shook her head.

"What do we do?"

Melni wished she knew. Where else could she go? Valix knew about her flat, about Croag & Daughters. And here, too. Nothing was safe. All those photoprints Valix had splayed before her, like a catalog of everywhere she'd gone since arriving.

Except . . . there was one place not covered in that stack of images. "I have an alternative plan."

He looked dubious.

"Problem?" she asked.

"Yeah. Why are you helping me?"

"We are on the same side."

"I doubt that."

"You said you were a Hollow Man."

The corners of his mouth tightened. "Yeah, well, I may have lied about that particular detail."

"I know."

"Then the question remains."

She leaned into the open doorway and took in the scene inside once more. Whoever was in the bedroom remained there. She heard low voices. Someone laughed. Melni leaned back behind the wall and took a long look at the man. "Same side or not, we have the same target. I want to know how you got into the Think Tank. And I want to know why Alia Valix recognized you."

"And if—"

She held up a hand. Footsteps came from within. "Later," Melni said. Then she turned and jogged back the way they'd come. The stranger followed.

Outside she tucked him in a dark alley two corners away and went back to the street. The first pedicab to dawdle by was occupied. She waited, arms folded and teeth chattering, for another two minutes before the next came bouncing down the cobblestones. A young woman rode at the tiller. She seemed a bit dubious at the promise of payment upon arrival, but given the lack of other fares she finally relented.

Melni offered gratitude and ran to fetch the stranger. He'd pulled his jacket up to cover his hair and kept his head down, as she'd instructed.

"Wild night," Melni said to the driver. "He tried to dance on the offering pool and fell right through the ice! Like an idiot I tried to pull him out only to slip and go in myself. Can you believe the luck?"

The cabdriver scrunched her face at this but said nothing.

Beside her, Caswell pulled his jacket tight and closed his eyes. He rested his chin on his chest. His whole body shook, but not from cold, she thought. The beads of sweat on his brow, those pale lips—something else ailed him. Had he been shot? She wanted to ask, to search his clothes for stains of blood, but the tiller would probably force them from the cab if Melni started fussing about injuries and illness.

If felt good to ride, despite the jarring vibration from the old roads. As Bandury Lane fell away behind them Melni began to think about what lay ahead. Right now Valix agents or NRD goons were probably all over her flat. Would her hidden supplies still be there? Perhaps, but that would have to wait. She had a different destination in mind, one from a part of her life not documented in the photoprints Alia had shown her.

The cab rattled its way out of the city center and across the bridge into Loweast. Cobbles gave way to smooth pavement again, and with the rhythmic whir and grind of the cab, Melni found herself drifting on the edge of sleep. She needed rest, but then she needed a lot of things just then. Rest would have to wait.

"Stop here," she instructed the driver when they were still a block away.

The cab drifted halfway onto a sidewalk and Melni hopped out. She left her companion to wait with the driver until she could return with money.

A dingy alley served as cast and crew entrance to the theater, but it was early and nobody was around. Melni ran straight to the back door and set to work with her tools again. The lock was a good one, but she'd sprung it many times in the last year and could have done it blind. In seconds it clicked and she was in. She headed down the stairs to the prop room. She listened briefly at the door, then peered inside. Darkness and dust waited within, as always. Long wooden tables were heaped with half-finished costumes and props in various states of assembly. No one was there but her. At the back of the room she opened a drawer that held fake money in various currencies. Nothing that would fool a shopkeeper, but good enough for stage. However she'd always kept an envelope in the back with real currency inside. She plucked an eightcoin out and dashed back to the cab, half-expecting it to be gone or surrounded by chin-ups. But the cab was right where she'd left it, the stranger still sitting in back. He appeared to be asleep, but his eyes opened slightly as Melni paid the fare.

"Come with me," Melni said to him.

He nodded gravely and climbed out.

A minute later she led him into the prop room.

"What is this place?" he asked, his voice just more than a whispered croak.

"Supplies for stagecraft. I volunteer here most ninedays. It has proved quite useful."

"Very smart."

"Are you okay? You look ill."

"I'll be fine."

With his approval she selected a passable Combran businessman's outfit—secondhand stuff but it would do—and a fine black wig that would give him shoulder-length hair. He donned it with a wrinkled nose but it did the job. She added a smart pincher's hat just in case, and a pair of slightly tinted reading glasses that were in fashion. They hid the shape of his eyes reasonably well. His skin color she could do nothing about, however.

While he dressed she went to the lav to relieve herself. There was a medical kit beneath the sink behind bins of face paint. She took both and returned to find the man trying on various pairs of treadmellows.

"Are these," he asked, "appropriate? For men, I mean." He bounced on his toes. "They're damned comfortable."

Melni ignored the negative and positive combination of words, deciding from the pleased look on his face that he meant the latter. "Sure. But they are rarely worn with a suit like that." She selected a similar pair in a more neutral color for him, then set to work picking out clothes for herself.

She went for a typical office getup to match his, adding only a dark brown hooded shawl big enough to keep her face at least partially concealed if not entirely in shadow. Then she went to the opposite side of the room and climbed a wheeled scalesteps propped against the floor-to-ceiling shelves. She glided the steps until the bin marked WEAPONS was right in front of her. The contents were mostly fake swords and daggers, plus the odd ax or whip. She ignored these and pulled out the bag of pistols.

The stranger watched with a bemused smirk as she dumped the fake guns out onto a table. She shrugged at him. "All for stagecraft, but in a pinch brandishing one might buy you a few seconds."

Finally she stripped away last night's clothing, including the bloody strips of her shawl. Two months' salary that outfit had cost, and it was now just a tattered mess. She set to work bandaging the cuts from the shattered aquarium glass. The man turned and browsed the wall of prop bins. Repelled again by exposed flesh? Was he some kind of religious fanatic? There were some pre-Desolation sects that held bizarre, arbitrary beliefs about such things, but as far as she knew they'd all died out. Caswell walked the entire wall, picking up seemingly anything that caught his eye and studying each with intense curiosity.

Dressed, Melni hauled herself up to sit on the edge of a table and faced the stranger. He took several seconds to sense the scrutiny, and came to sit opposite from her by unspoken arrangement.

"It is time we talked," Melni said.

He stared at her, impassive, even harder to read now behind the tinted glasses. At least his color had returned. He looked focused again.

Melni sighed. Where to start? She decided their predicament trumped his eccentric nature. But first . . . "What is your real name?"

"Caswell."

"A name as unique as you are."

"If my name's a problem then call me whatever you like."

Melni waved him off. "There are plenty of odd names here. Caswell, then."

He inclined his head slightly, as if bowing to a parent. Another odd gesture. Another contradiction. What sort of spy is proud of his local clothing yet acts, talks, and names himself in a way that begs attention?

"You were at the mansion to assassinate Alia Valix," she said, careful not to make it a question.

Caswell just stared at her, his expression blank. "My, uh. Look, my training prevents me from revealing details of my mission. A mental block, if you will. I could not tell you if I wanted to."

She'd heard of such things. Mental tricks, often performed at street-side stalls to get adults to act like their children, or to mimic a wild bhar. Sometimes to forget their own name. "But you could deny it?"

He smirked. "I could."

"And if you do not deny, that would count as agreement?"

"You catch on fast."

"So you are here to assassinate Valix. On whose orders?"

He said nothing. A smile played at one corner of his mouth.

"Not Riverswidth?"

"Not Riverswidth," he agreed. He started to say more, thought better of it, and waited.

"Fair enough," she said. "What can you tell me?"

"Not much." He held up a hand to stay her response. "Trust me, the less I say, the better."

A silence opened between them, as wide as the Endless Sea.

"Look," Caswell said. "Thank you—I mean gratitude—for helping me." He tugged at the lapel of his trim coat. "I don't know who you are or why you were in that room tonight, but I'm guessing we've both already learned more about each other than we should have. It's best we go our separate ways now."

"Where will you go? What do you plan to do?"

"My mission hasn't changed. It's just going to be a lot more difficult now."

The slaying of Alia Valix had never been suggested to

Melni as an acceptable outcome to her mission. The South wanted her inventions, her ideas. Or, barring that, they wanted her in one of their interrogation rooms for a year or two. "Suppose we worked together."

Like a lazy snowflake the suggestion took its time to settle. Caswell once again glanced at the bracelet on his wrist. A nervous tic, perhaps. "How would that work?" he asked.

Melni pushed off the table and paced in front of it. "Our goals are somewhat aligned. You seek to kill Alia Valix, whereas I want to question her and learn the secrets of her prolific mind."

Caswell's face remained carefully blank.

Melni went on. "In both cases, we need to get close to her again. But she will be barricaded now, at least for a while. And she will have every NRD goon and suited chin-up on the glance for us. Impossible to get to her now. We must disappear, let the water drain, if you will pardon the expression. Regroup and plan."

"Hmmm . . ." he said.

"You are capable, this is obvious. You know about things that I would very much like to know, too. How you came to know Valix. How you entered her impenetrable Think Tank."

He waited, saying nothing.

"But you also obviously need help. You dress wrong. Your hair is wrong. You use words and mannerisms I have never encountered before. How you made it this far is beyond me. It is as if you were just thawed out of the ice sheet."

At that his face lit up and he barked a laugh. "That's a good enough explanation. Go with that."

She shook her head. "Let me help you."

"And in exchange?"

"In *trade,* when the time comes to eliminate your target, if there is opportunity to question her first you let me do so." She would have to hope she could stop him when that moment arrived.

"So you can find out where she gets her ideas?"

"Yes."

The stranger closed his eyes, hung his head until his chin rested on his chest.

Melni studied him. "Interesting."

"What is?"

"You know this already. I can see it in your face. You know how she does it."

Caswell didn't move. No denial came. But instead of saying nothing, this time he spoke. "The explanation you seek is incredibly dangerous, Melni. As in, end-of-the-world dangerous. Even if I could tell you, I would not."

He actually knows, Melni realized with a shiver. *He may not know the hand signal to compel someone to silence, or how to dress, but he knows this.* She swallowed, hard. She had to report this.

"So now what?" he asked suddenly. "What do you propose we do?"

"We need a safe place to lie prone for a while. They found Bandury Lane. I have to assume every other asset I have access to is compromised. So we flee. I shall update my handler and get revised orders. When Alia comes up for air, we try again."

"There may not be time for that," Caswell said carefully.

"Meaning what?"

He grimaced. "Meaning I have a window of opportunity to finish my task." The phrase *window of opportunity* tripped her for a second, but she found she quite liked it after the fact. His tone, however: That held a dangerous finality. The kind of certainty only the terminally ill could muster.

"Why?" Melni asked. "Is something going to happen? This 'window' will close?"

The man fell silent once again.

"Tell me," she urged. "Garta's light, are they going to mobilize? Is it to be war? That is what you seek to prevent?"

Caswell held up a hand. "I can't give you details, Melni. All I can tell you is that in . . . Christ, I don't even know what sort of calendar you keep."

"Who or what is Christ?"

"Never mind that." He let out a long sigh. "Bloody hell this is difficult. Okay, look. You already think me strange, so I suppose this can't make things any worse. Tell me about how you measure time here."

"You really do not know?"

"Just . . . please. I was thawed from the ice, remember?"

Melni started pacing again. "Well. All right. Where to start? One hundred seconds to a minute, one hundred minutes to an hour. Ten hours in a day. Ten days in a week. Ten weeks in a month. Three months per year. Is that what you mean?"

"That's perfect. The day, is it measured from the middle of one night to the middle of the next?"·

"Of course. How could you not know this?"

He glanced at his bracelet again, then up at the ceiling, his mouth working in silent translation. "Well, a day is a day, at least. Hold up your hands."

She did so, splaying her fingers at his insistence.

"Now fold one back."

Baffled, Melni curled one thumb up against her palm. Nine fingers remained. She looked up at him and waited, but he simply looked back at her. His eyes darted to her fingers and back, several times. He could not say what he was trying to tell her.

"Nine?" she asked. "Nine what? Hours?"

He shook his head.

"Nine days?" When he did not shake his head, Melni made the next conclusion. "You have nine days to achieve your goal?"

Again he kept his face carefully blank. His way of admission.

"All right, nine days. Or what? War?"

"I can't tell you that."

Melni balked. "If you fail will I still be able to complete my mission?"

"I won't fail," he said. And he meant it.

13

SHE WENT OUT after dark. Snow swirled about her for the entire walk to a public box, four intersections away. She slid inside and reached for the handset.

Melni punched in a number she'd never used before. One she'd memorized long ago. It would only work once.

A series of chirps followed, then irregular clicking sounds as switchboards in Combra, Tandiel, and who knows where else routed the call into suitable obscurity. Finally there came a single, stern pop, followed by the faint hiss of a successful link. Somewhere on the other side of Gartien, in some dim basement at Riverswidth, an analyst waited for her to speak.

"14772 adrift," she said. "Requesting guidance. Cover irreparably damaged."

Another click. The hiss died. She wound the handset's wire around her finger, unwound it, wound it again. Minutes passed before the click-hiss signaled another connection.

"14772," someone new said. A gruff woman's voice, full of authority and age. "Are you in immediate danger?"

"No."

"Report."

She laid it out in the barest terms possible. Her risky interview with Valix, the horror that Valix knew all about Melni and her clandestine efforts. Her entry into the Think Tank, and what had happened in that bizarre place. The man she had found already inside. "He was there to kill her, but

AV knew him. This fact seemed to surprise him, and she used that to evade his gun."

"What is her status now?"

"Unknown."

"Speculate."

Melni sucked in a nervous breath. "Alive. The room had a space for her to hide. She knows of me, and she knows this other assassin. They look for us, but I think they wish to keep the incursion quiet. There has been no public reaction as of yet. Oh, and you should know that B. Lane is compromised and should be immediately closed."

"Presume all assets in the city are closed to you."

Judgment, rebuke, there. "Understood," Melni said, barely a whisper, her gut twisting like a writhing snake. "What are my orders?"

"This man, where is he now?"

"Nearby. He works alone here, I think. Is he one of ours?"

"Speculate."

"I have no idea."

"Speculate."

"I do not know who he works for."

"Speculate, 14772."

Melni racked her mind. She still had no reasonable answer. "One of AV's competitors. Maybe. I really do not know."

"You said he was a Southerner."

"He is, but he's very . . . ignorant. Could he be one of the Hollow?"

"Speculate."

"He said he was."

"Then he is not."

Melni gripped the handset. "I know." Her orders would come next, and "jump from the nearest bridge" seemed a very real possibility.

Time passed. Snow fell outside the public box. The voice said, "He was able to penetrate the Think Tank. AV knew him. He knows things that may be useful. This is what I hear from you. As your cover is blown you are to immediately desist all efforts to reach AV. This man, the assassin, is your new objective."

Melni tightened her grip. "Kill him?"

"It may come to that. For now stay with him. Find out who he is working for. Find out the nature of his relationship to AV. Keep him out of enemy hands and, above all else, *prevent him from completing his mission.* At least until we've had a chance to assess the situation. Contact again in two days."

The woman rattled off a number, made Melni repeat it, then disconnected.

From a mealhouse she'd never visited before Melni bought spiced curd pies and a large flask of very strong cham. The streets bustled as the end-of-week nightlife began to build. Chin-ups walked along with their customary casual arrogance, but seemed in no greater number than usual. They paid no special attention to her, even when she walked right past them and offered greetings.

Melni half-expected Caswell to be gone when she returned to the prop room, but he remained where she'd left him, sleeping peacefully on the table, a pile of costume jerkins under his head for a pillow. No one else was about. The company was between productions just then, and it would be days yet before the next cycle of prop work began.

The smell of food and cham stirred him. He sat and stretched, then wandered off to the lav. She set the pastries out on the table and poured them each a full steaming cup of the delicious-smelling beverage.

Caswell returned, leaned on the table's edge, and ate pensively. He tasted each item as if fearing poison, before hunger finally got the better of him. In the end he devoured three pastries in as many bites. Once the cham cooled he guzzled it down. He glanced at the mug, a prop version of a pre-Desolation goblet, appreciatively. "What's this drink called?"

"Cham," she said, the gaps in his knowledge now more amusing than surprising.

"Not bad." He sipped the last few drops and set the goblet aside. "Look, uh, Melanie—"

"Melni."

"Sorry, yes. Melni. I have to go north. I have supplies cached there. Things that will make my task easier."

"What sort of things?" she asked.

Instead of answering he turned and rushed to the lav. A few seconds later she heard him gag and then vomit. When he returned a minute later, wiping his pale face with a hand-cloth, she offered him a sympathetic frown.

"Everything I eat here disagrees with me," he said.

"That is not good."

"My supply cache has the nutrients I need. Medicines, too."

The "nutrients." How odd. "Where in the North?"

"Got a map?"

It took only a few minutes to find one in the bin of wall adornments at the back of the prop room. The map was antique only in appearance, weathered by hand in this very room. In truth the details were only a decade old.

"Here," Caswell said, tapping the paper near a lake in the mountains.

A lake just north of Hillstav, where earlier that week four NRD agents had been slain and ritualistically buried. "Some bodies were found near there a few days ago," she said.

He said nothing for a time. Then, "You're wondering if that was me. The answer is yes. An unpleasant business but I had no other choice."

She wanted to ask about the ritual, what reason it had. Instead of placing the bodies in a nearby lake that would have allowed some semblance of a return to Gartien's heart, Caswell had dug shallow pits in the ground and placed them inside, covering them with dirt. Denying a return via the depths. Perhaps he thought the corpses would take longer to find this way. Melni decided it did not matter. Murder of state police is what mattered. She had killed, too, in the Valix house. That woman in Onvel's office. They'd both be put to death if captured.

"Well," she said with a sigh, "at least they will not expect you to return there."

"Good. I say we leave now then. We've already stayed here too long."

"We must define a plan, figure out—"

"No plan. I hate plans."

"A plan is what you need to reach this goal, Caswell."

He clamped his mouth shut as a shadow of anger fell across and then left his face. "Fine. You've got something in mind?"

"We will need warmer clothes. And, there is one more place we need to stop first."

By ninth hour the streets were alive with weekend revelers. Men in smart suits of dark blue or darker gray, grinning under square-brimmed hats of the latest fashion. Women in Valix-inspired outfits; slacks with wide belts, white shirts with oversize cuffs at the wrists, and shawls of muted color often clasped at the neck with a bit of gold or silver. They walked in merry groups, at this hour still composed of co-workers seeking to impress their supervisors without the constraints of the office. After midnight professional social duties would give way to the more relaxed company of friends and family. On any other night Melni would be strolling arm in arm with reporters and perhaps an editor from the *Weekly,* invading one upscale bar and then retreating to establishments more suited to their modest salaries. At midnight she'd be one of the first to beg off, and then it would be a brisk walk to one of the dives her friends from the theater enjoyed for a night of wine and slurred poetry. All to serve her cover, of course, though faced now with the death of her invented persona, Melni was surprised to find how much she would miss such nights and the company she shared them with.

"Is it always so crowded?" Caswell asked.

"It's seventhday. Work is done, officially, but an evening out with co-workers is an unwritten law. Hardly anyone ever skips, save for illness. To do so might mean lost favor in one's career."

"You'll be missed then?"

"I will, but not enough to raise concern. When I fail to appear at the *Weekly* on firstday, questions will be asked." She decided not to add that it was doubtful to take so long. Given the intelligence Alia Valix had so brashly shown her, agents would likely be at the *Weekly* even now, searching her desk and the file room. Her co-workers were in for a full day of questioning, no doubt, come firstday.

A thought returned to her, that Boran might have given her the invitation to Onvel's memorial with full knowledge of who she was and what Alia Valix intended to do, that the whole evening had been no more than a setup. That was very likely the case, given everything that had happened, she decided. The idea that she could not rely on Boran's help anymore felt strangely liberating. The man detested the South. Working with him had always been an act of self-constraint.

Melni led her improbable ally across the bridge into Old Uptown toward her meager flat. She took a circuitous route, in shadow whenever possible. The lights dimmed tenth hour just before they reached her building, plunging the streets into darkness ten times, each for the span of a heartbeat.

With the light outside her window gone, Melni saw back-lit shapes moving behind the drawn curtain of her window.

She pulled Caswell into an alcove and waited.

"What is it?" he asked.

Melni nodded toward her window. "Third up, one column from the edge. My home, and they are inside."

"So fuck it. We leave."

"I . . . can guess the meaning of that . . . And no. There is something I need inside." She glanced about. There were no out-of-place cruisers parked on the road. Whoever was inside had either walked here or been left to watch the place.

Caswell cleared his throat. "We're disguised. Why not just go up there and pretend to be friends of yours? Everyone's supposed to be out with their co-workers, and you didn't show. We were worried."

"Not bad," she admitted. "You had better take the lead, though. That might seem odd, the man taking lead, but if they recognize me . . ."

"Fine."

With her guidance Caswell strode across the street and into the foyer of her building. They ignored the callbox and went for the stepwell. He took no care to quiet his footfalls and even uttered a few mumbled bits of conversation to sell the ruse.

On her floor he stopped and removed the heavy overcoat she'd selected for him, laying it over the rail. "Does your door chain from the inside?"

"Chain?"

"Some kind of secondary lock. Or, maybe a peephole?"

"It is just a door."

He nodded and started down the hall, letting her tugs on his sleeve guide him to the right place. At her door he stopped and ushered her to one side. She set to pretending to fix her shawl's clasp, keeping her face carefully low and turned from the door.

Caswell raised his fist and rapped on the door with his knuckles, three times. Death's knock.

"What are you doing that for?" she rasped, baffled.

He glanced at her, confused, when the lever began to rattle from the other side.

The door cracked open an inch. "Who's—"

Melni groped for words that might buy time.

Caswell, however, kicked out. The door flung inward. With a heavy smack it propelled the man behind it backward. He yelped like a wounded cani. Caswell did not stop. His reactions were lightning quick, a warrior driven by pure instinct. And something else, too. Something she couldn't quite put her hand on. While she stood there trying to analyze the threats and map out a plan of attack, he was inside, fighting them. Someone roared in alarm, then came the jarring bang of pistol fire. One shot. Across the hall from Melni a bullet buried itself in the wall with a shower of dust.

She ducked beside the doorframe and chanced a glance in. A chin-up lay on the ground in front of Caswell, scrambling backward in abject surprise. Another, an NRD officer she thought, stood in her kitchen, pistol clasped between two hands, vapor curling from the barrel.

Caswell dove on the one that had fallen, simultaneously avoiding the aim of the shooter in the room beyond. The man in the kitchen held fire, and retrained his weapon—on her. She ducked to her left as another whipcrack sound shattered the air. Shards of wood exploded from the doorframe just inches from her right ear. The impact shifted something within her. She had to act. She'd die here if she didn't. Caswell, too. Melni swung herself around the door. She grabbed a heavy book from the table beside the door and flung it toward the kitchen. The volume spread open like a bird taking flight, pages flapping. The gun went off again, right through the thick mess of flying paper, throwing a plume of scraps outward like tossed snow. The book sailed on and hit the agent square in the face with more force than she'd dared hope. The man twisted as the impact came, slipped on the tile floor, and went down behind the serving counter.

Caswell and the chin-up grappled on the floor, fighting for another drawn pistol. Melni leapt over them and rounded the corner of the serving counter at a half crouch. She had to fight back her own mind, dash away her own screaming conscience that urged caution. Melni had trained in close-quarters combat; all Riverswidth agents did. But that had been almost two years ago, and she'd never once needed to use it. Some part of her suddenly understood the constant repetition of those sessions. Her actions happened before she could think. Indeed her own thoughts were contrary to what her body did. She came in fists raised just as the NRD agent managed to recover. He swung his weapon up. Melni slapped it aside with the palm of one hand as he fired. Compressed air exploded from the barrel, tore at the side of her cheek. The violent noise drowned her sense of hearing into a mess of muffled tones under a high-pitched ringing. She jabbed with her other hand, extended knuckles into his neck, hard. Her aim was off, hit the collarbone as the man's gun clattered across the countertop and over the other side. Now they were equal. He squared on her, fists up and ready. In his eyes she saw nothing but calm calculation, and fear coursed through her. An NRD agent, one of their elite. Against her, an analyst. The girl who could speculate.

He struck, his punch grazing her forehead as she leapt back. The kitchen was tiny, her back now inches from the wall. He advanced, his mouth curling into a snarl. Another punch, she blocked with her forearm. Pain exploded from wrist to elbow. Somehow she countered with a jab toward his abdomen. He'd expected it, took it with clenched teeth and a groan, then retaliated. A fierce swing, meaty left fist. Melni ducked under it, a mistake. His right was the real blow, and it came in a blur and crashed brutally against her jaw. Stars swam before her eyes. Her knees buckled. Melni tried to get her fists up in desperate defense for what was to come next.

A hiss-crack sound filled the air, loud despite her already stinging ears. The NRD agent's head snapped to the right, and suddenly the cabinet beside him was dotted with blood and clumps of brain matter. The man collapsed where he stood, his eyes on her the whole way down.

She glanced left, stupefied. Caswell stood there, holding the agent's own pistol in one hand. His other hand was covered in blood, and behind him the chin-up lay motionless on the floor, facedown.

"Whatever you needed to get here, you'd better do it fast," he said.

Melni blinked away her shock and the blinding pain in her jaw. "Watch . . . watch the door," she managed.

He nodded and moved out into the hallway, glanced in both directions, then came back inside and pushed the door closed. Melni left him there and went to the darkroom.

There was paper everywhere, scattered like the red leaves of return. Bottles of solvent lay in their own spilled contents on the floor. Her camera on the table had been smashed to pieces. The finality of what she'd just been through numbed the sight of all this. Her mission was over, there could be no doubt about that now. Her life here, everything she worked for, was gone. Worse, it would set back the South's efforts to unravel Alia Valix's genius for a year or more.

What now? Alone she would have no doubts about the next step: Go south, as quickly as possible. Contact no one, do not look back. Just . . . flee.

But the stranger changed everything. An assassin. A damned good one by all appearances, despite his strange mannerisms and . . . well, strange everything. She'd been ordered to bring him in. And he wanted her to take him farther north, away from the Desolation and the safety that lay beyond.

Melni opened the air duct under the table. It showed no

signs of being tampered with. Still, she held her breath as she reached inside, so far her shoulder pressed painfully against the opening in the wall. She gasped with relief when her fingers brushed the small piece of twine. Some gentle coaxing and she had it. Seconds later the bundle of fabric to which the twine was attached came sliding out. She took the whole thing under her arm and left the room.

Caswell had dragged both bodies behind the kitchen counter. He offered her one of their guns, but she declined. "I have my own in here," she said, patting the bundle.

He nodded at that and stuffed the extra weapon in the belt of his pants. She saw the glint of metal inside his coat, and a wooden handle. One of her carving knives, concealed with a makeshift harness of string from one of the cabinets. Resourceful, this one.

"We really must leave now," she said.

"Right. Lead on." His voice bore the hint of pain.

Melni glanced at him. Again she saw the pale skin, the sweat on the brow, and the colorless lips. He shivered despite the warmth in the room. "Do you become ill after every fight?" she asked.

He grunted a laugh at that. "Another mental trick," he said, as if that explained everything.

She wanted to ask more, but there were sirens outside. Distant but growing.

14

ON THE TRAIN—what they called a "roller" here—
Caswell slept. The urge to use his implant for a chemically
augmented rest came on strong the moment they'd reached
their cabin, but he'd fought down the craving. That form of
sleep, where portions of the brain were shut down in careful
sequence, and then brought back up so that the next could
rest, was useful in a pinch but no substitute for the real
thing. Besides, he was a wreck, and he knew it. No food or
drink in five days, and not for lack of trying. Everything he
tried his body rejected instantly, even boiled water. This had
left his chemical reserves low. Even if they weren't, though,
he didn't think he could handle another boost from the engineered organ on such an empty stomach. His reactions had
grown steadily worse. How Alice Vale had survived all this
time he had no idea.

He slept fitfully, distracted by a litany of fears. Would
they come for him and the girl? What if he talked in his
sleep, said things that would clue Melni into his true origin?
And beyond that, the reversion moment loomed. His watch
ticked slowly, irrevocably toward it. He had to get this business over with and be gone from this place, preferably well
before all memory of Gartien left him.

A porter brought a wheeled tray in. Complimentaries,
Melni had called them. Hot cham and cold pastries—and a
demand to see the two passengers' tickets. The outfit Melni
had picked for him had worked well, much better than the
farmer's garb he'd stolen the day after landing. No one paid

him much notice, and the ingrained social norm here seemed to be an assumption that the woman of any pair was the authority. Well, Caswell had no problem with that at all. He lay across one of the two bench seats, his back to the cabin, and listened as Melni provided their papers and accepted the snacks with a simple "Gratitude."

"Boarded where?" the porter asked.

"Mealhouse Row," Melni said. Then added, "In Midstav."

The porter clipped each ticket. Caswell listened as he handed the slips of paper back without further query, then proceeded to set the snack tray beside the window.

When the door slid shut Caswell rolled onto his back and sat up. She handed him a cup but he waved it off.

"Thanks— Gratitude, but no. My stomach," he said.

Melni nodded, concern plain on her face. How he must look. How confused she must be at the highs and lows his body moved through.

Outside, trees whipped by in rapid flashes of dark green and brown. Beyond, rolling plains hidden under white snow moved steadily from north to south as the train hummed along. Midday sunlight glinted off the blanket of ice on the ground.

She sipped in silence. He watched the scenery blur across the window.

"This is going to be a boring partnership if you will not speak," she said.

Caswell grinned. He glanced at her, saw the curls of steam rising from her drink. He offered a smile and hoped that would be enough.

But she tried again. "Can you tell me anything about yourself? This mental block only relates to your objective, yes?"

Caswell considered that for a moment. He settled back into his seat, rested his head against the suedelike red cushion. "Pretend for a moment that I've been away for a long time," he said. "Or . . . no, better yet, pretend I'm a child. A small child just learning of the world beyond my own isolated home."

"I . . . I shall try."

"Educate me."

She raised an eyebrow, confused.

He tried again. "Teach me. Start with this rift between North and South."

Melni leaned back in her seat and tucked her feet up underneath her legs. She cupped the mug in both hands and smiled warily at him. "A history lesson," she said.

"Yes. I'm someone who knows a lot about certain things, and virtually nothing about others. Strange, but true."

"Not so strange," she said.

"Oh?"

"I noted the same peculiar feature in Alia Valix, just before she tried to have me arrested for spying. So you are not the only one with such an upbringing. Odd that she seemed to know you, given that."

Caswell didn't like this line of thinking one bit. He said, "Just . . . table that for now, okay? I'm a child. Explain the world to me."

Melni considered this for a long minute. Evidently she didn't like the shift in focus back to her, but finally her face softened. "All right, then. We have an hour before we reach Hillstav. Where to begin . . ."

So she talked, and he hung on every word like, well, exactly like a curious child.

Melni started two centuries ago, with the single defining moment in this world's history: the Desolation. Before then Gartien had been made up of fifty or so nations, with dozens of small alliances and petty rivalries that produced only the occasional war. Then came the rocks from the sky. A string of fireballs that lasted a whole day. They rained down. Some as small as pebbles, some as big as cities, and as the planet turned they drew a wavy line of craters, annihilating everything they fell upon.

The Desolation, this area came to be known. An uninhabitable, charred wasteland strewn with smashed cities and millions of dead, never to be properly "returned," whatever that meant.

The meteor strikes neatly divided Gartien in two halves, North and South, and filled the atmosphere with ejecta from the impact events. The planet cooled, the coastlines changed. Survival became everyone's focus as the cold years went on and on. Nations began to band together out of mutual need, naturally separated by the swath of destruction. At first the people of Gartien had banded together, as best they could, in a spirit of overcoming this catastrophe. Somehow this degraded into suspicion and jealousy, even skirmishes at sea.

An equilibrium eventually came to exist. The nations of the North were allied and working together. The South was much the same. And between them was a vast disputed no-man's-land. Open hostilities were hampered by this gigantic divide, and anyway both sides were happy to focus on simple survival. It was as if Gartien had become two worlds. Interaction became the occasional diplomatic meeting surrounded by the Quiet War. Spying. Assassination. Secret plots. Both sides not wanting to invest in a vast military, given all their other worries, while simultaneously worrying the other would do just that.

Caswell marveled at both the similarities to Earth's own Cold War, and the differences. More than that, he began to see the potential ramifications of Alice Vale's influence here. Near as he could tell this world had no weapons capable of mass destruction. Nature had warned them away from such things with this Desolation event. Now Alice Vale, under the guise of Alia Valix the genius inventor, had embarked upon an exceedingly clever and careful plan to unleash inventions on this world that all seemed geared toward one eventual conclusion, ending the hostilities here in the same way the United States had brought World War II to its sudden, shocking finale.

"We had a balance so long as neither side gained some advantage," she said. "And I think, in a way, this balance is preferable to true war. Armies are expensive. Death is expensive, and we had had enough of death. This was better. Is better."

"But not as good as peace."

She shrugged. "There have been a few attempts at such, but they always crumble. The history of mistrust is too deep."

Caswell nodded, as thoughts of Berlin and Moscow, the Pentagon and Vauxhall Cross floated through his mind.

"You know all this," she said.

Caswell glanced up at her. He shook his head. "I know a similar . . . version, you might say. A story."

"How did it end? The story."

He grimaced. "One side had a better system than the other. Once this became obvious, the other side faced a choice: ditch their own system, or destroy the other."

"What did they choose?"

"They chose to change."

"And this worked?"

He shook his head. "It tore them apart from the inside."

She fell silent then. Her gaze shifted slowly to the landscape that smeared across their window. Ice began to form in the corners of the glass, and soon the view became murky as a heavy snow fell. Caswell decided to let her ponder what he'd said. He let the sway of the train lull him, along with the low hum of its long rows of rubber wheels against the half-pipe track in which it moved. He tried to take his mind off the smell of the food and "cham." It had tasted wonderful when he'd tried it in that prop room, until it had wreaked vengeance on his alien gut.

"Tell me what happened in Hillstav," she said after a time. "We left a lot of problems behind us. I should know about the ones ahead."

"Fair enough," Caswell replied. "I came upon a house. It was empty and I needed supplies, so I broke in. Used some, uh, lockright tools I'd stolen earlier. Then some men arrived, apparently searching for the person who'd robbed the lockright. They surprised me and I killed them. No choice in the matter."

"And then?"

"I stole one of their . . . um . . . the three-wheeled thing. . . ."

"A cruiser," she said.

"Cruiser, yes. I stole one and fled."

"But before that . . ."

He shrugged.

Melni squinted at him. "Four bodies were dragged away from the cottage and buried in a ditch."

"Ah, yeah. I didn't want anyone to find them."

"A ditch beside a lake," she said.

"That's right."

"You couldn't return them to the water?"

"Huh?"

"It was right there. They may have been your enemies but to deny a proper return, that—forgive my saying, but that is unnecessarily cruel. No one would have found them either way, yet you chose to keep them from—"

Caswell understood now the gravity of the mistake he'd made when he'd buried those four police officers the day after he'd landed. In truth he'd wanted to dump the bodies in the lake and leave, but something had stopped him: the guilt of taking innocent lives on a world he had no business being on. Killing them was not like killing the crew of the *Pawn*. These were utterly innocent, being in his way their only crime. He'd wanted to make things right, at least a little. Honor them somehow, not leave them in the pools of blood where they'd fallen. Instead, like a bumbling idiot abroad, he'd made mockery of their most sacred ritual. "I didn't know the custom. Forgive me."

"How could you not know that?"

Caswell fought to keep his face blank.

"Help me resolve," she tried. "How could you know so little? You and Alia, both. And yet for all that she knew *you*! There is a connection here, I know there is, and if you want my help—"

"The roller is slowing."

"What?"

Brakes squealed from beneath the car. Caswell leapt to the window and glanced in both directions.

"There are no platforms for miles," she said.

"Yeah, well, we're stopping."

"Wait here," she said. "I will go look."

He nodded and tried to watch through the frosty glass.

Seconds later he saw two uniformed soldiers moving along the tree line. They hunkered down about halfway along the train's length, almost parallel to the cabin Melni had picked. One raised a spyglass or binoculars to his face and began to scan the windows. Caswell ducked back and swore. This was no stop for an obstacle on the track.

Behind the roller, a cruiser streaked across the field of

snow, white spray kicking high from the single rear tire. It stopped twenty feet from the tail car. The two occupants hopped out. They high-stepped through snow that came up to their knees. One carried a rifle. The other gripped a folder between two gloved hands.

"Curd," Melni said, reentering the room. "NRD. They are searching the cars, starting at the back. Two of them inside already."

He heard the panic in her voice. "What can we do?"

She looked at the floor, jaw moving soundlessly, at a loss, a deer in headlights. For all her planning, she'd not anticipated this.

He grabbed her by the arm. "The situation, Melni. Describe it for me. You can do that, can't you?"

"Speculate," she whispered, monotone.

"Yes. Please!"

In an almost robotic voice she rattled off the details. "They have surrounded us, watching all the doors. No cover for a hundred feet in any direction."

"Is there a luggage car?" Caswell asked.

"No."

"Anywhere to hide?"

She glanced around. The tiny room had nothing but two benches that doubled as beds, and a closet too small for even a single person to conceal themselves in.

"That porter brought food," he said. "From where? A restaurant car?"

"I do not know 'restaurant,' but there is a porter car, two ahead. They store food there. Cleaning supplies, spare parts. It is behind the engine. But," she added, holding a hand up to stay his instant move toward the door, "it will be staffed. And they will search it soon enough."

"We have to run then. No other choice. Come on." He turned for the door.

"No, wait," she said. Her eyes met his. "I have a plan, I think."

She explained and he took in the details without comment or question.

"That," he said, "just might work."

Melni scattered the remnants of the cham and pastries on

the benches and floor. Then she flung the narrow window wide open. The roller's track was a curved ditch, so the snowbank was only centimeters below the window. Next she scooped handfuls of the white powder into the cabin and made sure it splayed violently across the thin carpet of the floor.

"Good enough," he said, impressed. On a whim he grabbed a small carving knife from the tray. "Let's move."

She went out first, moving one cabin over. It proved unlocked and she went in, closing the door behind him when he followed a second later.

Silence, then. Just his breaths, and hers.

Less than a minute later a door clacked open at the far end of the car. Footsteps in the hall, and low voices. They sounded bored. Good.

Melni glanced back at Peter and he nodded his readiness.

The NRD officers reached the adjacent cabin. One let out a startled gasp. The other rushed inside, heavy footsteps across the six feet of carpet and then at the window.

Melni burst into motion. The plan relied entirely on timing.

Caswell followed on her heels: left turn into the hall, left turn into the neighboring compartment. A male guard stood a step inside, his long black coat like a curtain drawn across the interior. Melni lowered a shoulder and drove into the center of his back, leaving her feet. The man yelped in surprise as he flew forward. He went face-first into the legs of his companion, a female. She'd half-turned from the window at the sound of Melni's entrance, her rifle too long to ready in the cramped quarters.

A cry of alarm died on her lips, the hilt of the carving knife protruding from her breast. Caswell had not expected much more than distraction from the small blade, much less a solid wound. He'd never been much of a knife man, as far as he remembered, at least. It had slid right through the uniform, though. All the way. The NRD officer glanced down at the hilt, a look of wonder and surprise on her face. Then the life drained from her features, and she collapsed.

On the floor, Melni fought to keep her prey pinned. The

man writhed wildly, spurned to terror at the sight of his dead comrade. Caswell stepped in to help, then held back when Melni raised one arm high, her pistol gripped like a baton. She smacked the back of the man's head with it. Three, five, eight blows. Bone crunched, and then came the spongy wet sound of brain being pulverized. The back of his head became a clump of long blond hair mixed with sticky, dark red blood before he finally, mercifully, went still.

Breathing in huge gulps of air, Melni staggered to her feet and studied the carnage before her. "Why would he not stop struggling?" she asked, her voice not for him. Just a whispered grasp at her own humanity. "Garta's light, what have I become?"

"At least he can't talk." He gripped her shoulder and urged her to be calm. "Focus now. The coats, right?"

"At least he can not talk? How can you say—"

"The coats, Melni. You made a plan, let's stick to it, eh?"

"Coats. Yes, coats," Melni agreed. The vacancy in her eyes faded. She blinked. "Coats."

Caswell hunched over the man on the floor and began to pull his heavy black coat off. Seeing him disrobing the officer, Melni returned completely to the moment. She knelt and grabbed the female agent by the lapels. The knife had to come out before she could remove the garment. Melni's face scrunched up as the blade pulled free. Caswell watched, ready for her to lapse into remorse again at the sight of the blood. He reminded himself—and not for the first time—that Melni would remember all this. She'd carry what she'd done here, what she'd been capable of, on her conscience for the rest of her life.

But by sheer force of will Melni maintained control. His mention of the plan seemed to work like a talisman on her. She set the weapon aside and started pulling arms from sleeves.

Caswell was a good six inches shorter than the NRD man and swam inside the huge overcoat. Worse, his hair and skin color were completely wrong. With any luck, distance and speed would obscure these inconsistencies.

Melni picked up the rifle and, as was the Gartien way,

took the lead. "Remember," she whispered, "we are arrogant rassies on state business."

The rearmost car was for "standers," she'd told him. Those who couldn't afford a seat. It smelled of sour sweat and old newspaper. Melni shouldered her way through the sullen passengers, a palpable air of superiority in her gait that Caswell mimicked.

A pale-faced porter stood at the back. If he noticed that the two agents coming toward him were different than those who boarded minutes earlier, he gave no sign. Melni jerked her chin toward the rear exit and he obediently opened it.

"What has happened? What is wrong?" the porter stammered as she strode by.

Melni did not so much as acknowledge him. She hopped down from the side of the car. Footprints marked the path the two officers had taken. She did not slow. Caswell, on her heels, kept pace and did not look back.

The NRD cruiser rested in fresh snow a hundred feet away, steam wafting off the motor's exposed heat sinks. Blue and yellow right-of-way lights flickered in their strangely mesmerizing pattern.

"You saw them get out?" Caswell asked.

"I did."

"Who was driving?"

She thought back. "The man."

"Better let me, then." He'd driven most of the way from his landing site to the city of Midstav, in a stolen cruiser not unlike this one. They seemed to have two types of vehicles here: the older, compressed-air style that looked like something out of a 1930s German vision of the future, and those like the one before them, sleek and new, powered by battery. Alice's influence? He thought very probably. This world was full of such signs of new and rapid technological advancement, and it all pointed back to the woman playing God. Exactly as Monique had assessed.

They'd crossed half the distance to the car. Melni angled herself toward the rear seat. Caswell aimed for the front. His body teetered on the verge of betraying him. He'd never been so hungry or thirsty in his life. Not that he could remember, at least. His breaths erupted in large puffs, his thighs ached from traversing the knee-deep snow. Ten meters now. Five.

A distant voice reached his ears. "Agent Tolis? What is the matter?"

Melni ran, legs lurching in the deep snowdrift. Caswell did his best to keep up. He felt dizzy. He wanted to force chemicals into his brain, consequences be damned. But that option no longer remained to him. The well had run dry.

"Halt!" the same voice shouted. "Halt!"

A vicious crack rang out and rolled across the landscape, sending birds to flight from the line of trees beyond the cruiser. Two more shots followed. Ahead of him something *thwapped* into the snow in a miniature white explosion. Melni twitched abruptly. She swatted at her left arm as if someone were trying to grab her there. Her hand came away red.

Fuck, he thought.

"Blix," Melni said, then fell face-first into the snow.

He threw her limp body into the cruiser. A bullet hissed past his car. Lots of people were shouting now, from behind. He didn't look back. He just jumped into the forward seat, found the switch that activated the motors, and roared away in a shower of white powder. Little eruptions of snow popped up all around. The crackle of gunfire. Engines whirring to life, then sirens.

"Melni?"

She said nothing.

Caswell put it all out of his mind and focused on driving. Back home hardly anyone ever drove a car anymore. Everything had been automated decades ago. But in some parts of the world, the third world most often, one occasionally had to manually operate a car. Caswell had visited such places on his post-mission "holidays." He'd even taken the occasional trip to the Nürburgring in Germany, where wealthy adrenaline junkies like him thrashed around twenty kilometers of twisting road in antique supercars. A keen sense of self-satisfaction went through him like a warm wave with the knowledge that his risky, expensive, spontaneous training adventures had truly paid off. He tossed the little "cruiser" along a snowy trail, shot through gaps in the trees, bounced over the uneven terrain. For a time he even forgot about the wounded girl in the backseat. A stupid smile had replaced his grim concern, and when he realized this he wanted to slap sense into himself. The lack of food, he decided. It was making him delirious. They both needed help, and soon. But he couldn't stop as long as there were lights in the mirrors. She might die before he found her medical help, but she'd most certainly be put to death if these fucking "rassies" caught them.

Time passed in a blur of trees and snow. The lights grew more distant but he knew he was leaving perfect tracks for them to follow. This couldn't go on.

Luck favored him in the form of a road, recently cleared. He bounded onto it, pointed the lithe vehicle toward what he hoped was north, and set the acceleration handle to maximum. The rear tire fought for purchase on the gravelly surface and then bit. The cruiser rocketed forward.

He drove for a long time. Twice he jerked awake, the car grinding against packed snow beside the narrow road. The mirror remained devoid of pursuers. Finally he eased back and let the car roll to a stop beside a frozen pond some twenty meters off the road. Snow fell in lazy, oversize flakes.

He hauled Melni from the backseat and laid her on his jacket. The cold bit, numbed his skin. His stomach felt like a stone. Caswell ignored all this and inspected the girl's wound. It looked bad. A lot of blood. He melted some snow in his hands and washed it with the bit of water that didn't slip through his shaking fingers. She let out a weak groan at this. Her eyes flittered, then closed again. Her lips were as blue as a summer sky.

Desperate, Caswell searched the car and found something akin to a first-aid kit. He had no idea what most of the contents were for, but the long strips of bandage were all he needed for now. He packed one against her wound and tied the other over it. Finally he stuffed some snow in her mouth, and put her back into the vehicle.

He drove on. A sudden overwhelming craving for chewing gum fell upon him. Something to keep his saliva flowing, and sleep from overtaking him.

Hours later Melni stirred. "What happened?" she asked, her voice like dry paper being crumpled.

"You were shot," he stated. "I think I've lost them but I have no idea where I'm going. We need a map or something."

Melni groaned. "How . . . long?"

"Maybe," he said, then paused. "Three hours by your, you know."

She coughed.

"The bullet only grazed you, gouged a line across the muscle and back out again. I packed the wound as best I could."

"Gratitude," she whispered. "Need . . . a doctor. It is worse than it looks."

"Can't do it."

She protested, tried to sit up, and groaned in agony.

"Hold tight, okay? I have a better idea. No surgeon required."

She said nothing.

"Melni?"

Caswell glanced back. She'd fallen unconscious again.

15

BRILLIANT LIGHT BLAZED from above, at once painful and pleasant, like Garta at the zenith of a Renewal-month sky. Yet no heat came from this light. Just the brilliant fingers of glare that stretched to the corners of her vision.

Melni blinked, and the light became more focused. She blinked again. Not Garta at all, but a lamp of some sort. It was circular, embedded into a recessed channel within a white ceiling made of square tiles.

Something tugged at her shoulder. She tried to turn and found her head had been strapped down. Her arms and legs as well. She tugged at the bonds with no effect. This must be an NRD interrogation room. She tried to test the strength of her bonds but her body would not yet cooperate. She heard a grunt of concentration, someone standing nearby.

"Where—" she croaked.

"Don't move." The voice was Caswell's. He was rummaging around beside her, probing her arm with something.

Her skin there felt warm and seemed to almost buzz. He'd numbed her. While he worked she tried to look around. Above her was a tiny round window, set inside an oval— a door? It had a wheel attached in the center, with four metallic bars sticking out to each edge.

"Sorry about this," Caswell said suddenly, and laid a soft strip of white fabric over her eyes.

Instinctively she shook her head. The fabric began to slide and fall.

He pulled it tight across her face. "Remain still, Melni.

I'm almost done and we'll be on our way. I cannot let you see this place."

If she glanced straight down past her nose she could see only a small strip of uninteresting wall now. "Where are we?"

"My landing craft."

"Some kind of submersible?"

He pressed something hard against her shoulder, then began to expertly wind bandage around the double wound. "Yes, very much like that. Drink."

Something tickled at her lips. She opened her mouth and felt a firm yet spongy tube slide between. She sucked timidly. The water tasted like nothing at all, blissfully cold. She drank eagerly until he pulled the tube away.

"That's enough for now. Can you eat?"

"I'll try," she said.

She heard the sound of paper, or something like it, tearing. Then another brush against her lips. She opened her mouth and felt the squared end of some sort of hard bread or biscuit slip in an inch. Melni bit down into a dry, crumbling bit of flavorless nothing. She did her best to chew while Caswell held the remainder against her closed mouth. The biscuit thing turned into mush in her mouth and left a slightly sour mineral aftertaste. "What is that? Besides awful, I mean."

"Nutrients," he said. "Sterilized and utterly bland, I'm afraid. Designed not to interfere with the painkillers. Hopefully you won't react to it as I do to the food here."

Melni took another few bites and shook her head at a fourth. The pain in her arm had vanished, and the flutters in her stomach were indeed much reduced. "What happened?"

"You were shot, lost a fair amount of blood."

"That part I recall. Vividly. I mean after that."

She heard metal clinking against a pan. Then a hiss of air.

"I drove," Caswell said. "Hard at first, on the glowing roads."

"They did not chase?"

"For a while, yeah. Until I left the road for a frozen river. I followed it most of the way here. No small feat with the lights off and without that glow. Didn't see a single light behind us after the first few miles."

She gradually became aware of a myriad of strange noises: soft chirps, the low constant breath of circulation fans. And a warmth, as well. He'd removed her coat and overshirt, yet the room felt like a hearth-side table in a meal-house.

He offered her another bite of the inoffensive biscuit. She shook her head. Her stomach felt on the verge of betrayal. "What happens now?"

Caswell leaned into her limited field of view where her nose held up the blinding fabric. He pressed something against her forehead and slid it down to her temple, then studied it. Next he removed a band she hadn't realized was there from her left forearm. It was white with a blue stripe, and had some words printed on it she couldn't quite read. To her surprise they changed when he ran his finger across them. He tossed the strange bracelet aside, out of her narrow view. "I've been thinking. It's best I work alone. Sorry, but each minute I spend with you is an enormous risk, however aligned our goals might be."

"That poses a bit of a problem."

"I know."

"If you succeed, I'll lose my chance to interrogate her."

"Nothing to be done about it. I'm running out of time, Melni, and my mission is too important."

"So you're going after her alone."

"Yes."

Melni swam inside her own head. Every coherent thought felt like a physical thing she had to grasp and yank free from the two-fisted clutch of fatigue and drugs. She needed time. Even an hour. "I may be ordered to stop you." It was an empty threat given her wound but she could think of nothing else.

"Possible. You'll note, however, that I have you strapped to a chair. I could just leave you this way, sedated, until I'm done. I could kill you, if it comes to that. Your people have no idea where you are."

"Would you?" she asked. Of course she had made contact with Riverswidth. And they had been very clear: Bring Caswell in. Keeping that from him now oddly felt more like a betrayal than prudent spycraft. Still, she felt sure he wouldn't heal her wound only to shoot her himself.

He took his time to respond. "You seem a decent person, but I'd be lying if I said your life is more important than my objective. Don't force me to make that choice."

"I . . ." She gritted her teeth. Damn the moons, whatever he had given her had extraordinary power. She felt as if floating in a warm bath. Her left arm felt fine, if numb, despite the bullet that had torn through her muscle and nerves. She had almost bled to death. She damn well should have. Had she stumbled into a Midstav doctor's office with a wound like that, she'd be in bed for weeks, at a minimum. "Caswell, listen. I do not know who you work for or what their ultimate objective is, but removing Alia Valix should be a last resort. The South could benefit more if we gain intelligence on her invention process. Surely you can see that?"

"You're wrong. I can't explain why, but you're wrong. And anyway I have strict orders." He sighed. Started to move.

Melni fought to concentrate, aware and embarrassed at how feeble and stammering her voice sounded. "Take me to the coast, at least? One of the logging towns? There's one called Portstav west of here. I can buy passage south from there." No need to tell him there was a listening post in that seaside town. She could make contact, report to Riverswidth. She'd suggest a new plan: Let him go but follow him. Let him lead her to Valix, then stop him before he can kill her.

Betray him, that is what you really mean.

The kinship she'd felt for him in their hasty flight from the Think Tank, from Midstav, felt suddenly like a chain of brittle links. So they'd both been in the Valix house. So what? Her duty to the South outweighed whatever power had sent him here. In that sense they were adversaries. She had to start acting that way. For all she knew he was lying about his intention to kill the woman. To let him go, to not do everything in her power to stop him, might be seen as treason back home.

He had moved out of sight again. She could hear him

rummaging through various unknown objects. Filling a travel pack, perhaps. Preparing to leave. "Right, okay. Fine," he said. "Rest for a bit while I get my kit sorted, and we'll be off. We'll part ways at Portstav."

Melni lay still—she had no other choice, really—and resisted the strong urge to sleep by concocting yet another plan: Get to the coast, figure out some way to delay Caswell there, make contact with Riverswidth via the agents at the listening post. They could provide her with supplies, papers.

Perhaps they'd know the scope of the hunt for her and the stranger. Fleeing south may already be impossible. Suddenly she could see herself, holed up in some dank room in Portstav with the local listening team for weeks, even a whole month, until the search abated.

After a time she felt the strip of fabric across her face shift, then tighten.

Caswell nudged her. "Lift your head." When she did he tied the strip in a quick knot and helped her sit upright.

"How do you feel?" he asked.

"The arm is fine. My stomach, however, is not happy with you."

"Sorry. I'm worried about giving you anything more complex. We'll get something proper for you to eat at the first opportunity."

"You sound better."

"A thousand times better," he agreed. "Chicken tikka masala."

"Huh?"

He hauled her by the right elbow off the . . . it wasn't a doctor's table, she decided. Just a reclined chair. Not unlike the formfitting style found in the NRD police cruiser, actually. Strange to have it in a larger space. She reached out her hands to feel for him and a second later his fingers brushed hers. He grasped her firmly but gently by the wrist of her good arm and guided her to a few paces from the chair.

Something above them ticked and then rattled. There was a hiss of air, and something plopped on the floor near her feet. Snow, she realized.

"I'll go up first," he said. "Clear any fresh snow, and get the cruiser ready."

"All right."

"Do I need to tie your hands behind your back or will you leave the blindfold in place?"

"I will behave."

He laid her coat gently over her shoulders, expecting a wince of pain and apparently pleased at the lack of one. "Gratitude," he said quietly. Before she could reply his boots were tapping against the rungs of what must be a scalesteps pulled down from the ceiling.

She heard a heavy mechanical whir and then a sharp rising hiss that ended in a pop. Cold air rushed inside, startling against the almost uncomfortable warmth of the . . . submersible, or whatever it was.

Next came the sound of boots crunching on snow. He didn't climb down anything, so this vehicle must be completely buried in a drift or even underground. This gave her a shiver. The noise abated as he moved away.

Melni could not help herself. She reached up and lifted the blindfold from her eyes.

She stood in an oblong room, like the inside of an egg. White walls, floor, and ceiling, all merged together to form one contiguous space. Above her head was a round door with an inlaid window, now open. Another identical door lay opposite it, at her feet. It had a circular window in the middle, damp soil pressing against it from beneath. The other walls consisted of rectangular tiles in varying size. Each had a small metal handle embedded in a circular depression in the center, and a label just above that. Many were studded with tiny circular lights glowing in green, though here and there a few showed red.

Melni turned around and her breath caught in her throat. The other side of the room was dominated by a sleek chair that reminded her vaguely of a teethright's office, only instead of cleaning instruments dangling before it there were display screens, similar to what she'd seen inside Alia's Think Tank, but impossibly thin. Each was full of vibrant-colored, fantastically sharp text and images.

"What in Garta's light—"

"Mel!"

The shout came from directly above her. She glanced up

in time to see Caswell's feet falling toward her and just barely moved out of the way before he crashed into her.

"You really shouldn't have done that," he growled.

"Regret, I—"

"Save it. We've got to go, now."

He shoved her toward the scalesteps and forced her to clamber up. She saw him kneel and grab a large white bag that he'd placed on the floor, then turned her focus to the patch of gray sky directly over her head. White flakes of snow drifted lazily across the circular view.

Outside she found herself standing atop the scarred outer part of an egg-shaped vessel. At least she thought it was egg shaped. Most of it was buried in ice.

The vessel lay in a pit about ten feet in diameter; slick shiny walls of ice about six feet high and steeply sloped were all around the portal through which she'd climbed. Water ran in rivulets down to the exposed surface of the ship. Had its internal heat carved this hole? She thought it must be so. A deep thrumming sound became evident, though it sounded far away. Melni whirled about for the source and saw instead a patch that had some regular snow piled like a ramp at the edge of the depression. Her companion's boot prints were all over it.

"Go! I'm right behind you," he hissed.

She darted up the icy slope in three steps, almost slipping, Caswell right on her heels. He pressed his hand into the small of her back and urged her onward, faster. One arm useless, Melni staggered awkwardly ahead to the NRD cruiser. The vehicle lay fifty feet away, in the middle of an undulating slope covered in snow. To her right she saw a frozen lake surrounded by hills. Patches of dark gray exposed rock jutted from an otherwise perfectly white landscape.

Melni chanced a look back, desperate for additional details to the supposed submersible buried in the ice, beside a lake rather than in it, on a mountain peak that must be a hundred miles or more from the ocean.

What she saw instead flooded her with all-consuming fear.

Three hundred feet upslope a gigantic dirigible drifted

along. She'd never seen one so big, though there'd been rumors of the North working on such things. The massive airship was fifty feet off the ground and moved as lazily as a whale. The thrumming noise she heard came from its lifters: four massive circular blurs mounted on boom arms that jutted from a central spine atop the bulbous monstrosity.

Slung on its underbelly was a cabin. Porthole windows dotted the length of it, but more concerning were the doors, three that she could see, and three more on the far side. Outfitted soldiers stood in each. And below, dangling from black ropes, were more. The first of them reached the ground even as she watched, and immediately unslung rifles from their shoulders.

"Down!" Caswell shouted, and then he was on her, diving, driving her to the snow, as bullets *thwapped* into the ice around them.

She had time only to register the sting of cold on her cheek before he hauled her to her feet and they were running again. He guided her by the collar of her shirt to one side of the stolen cruiser and thrust her behind it as more gunshots rang out. Something whistled over her head. Another round hammered into the fuselage of the little vehicle, cracking the front window.

Caswell flung himself to the ground next to her and immediately set to rummaging about in his oversize white bag. Despite the bullets sizzling through the air around her, and the renewed throb from her wound, she managed to glimpse the word ARCHON printed on the side of that bag. The word had no meaning to her, but stylized as it was she thought it must be a corporation or brand name. She filed that, something to look up later. A clue to his employer, perhaps.

He'd pulled a hard rectangular case from his bag and now leaned over the contents of it. He snapped two objects together and twisted in a third. Then he was up, leaning over the canopy of the cruiser and sighting down the barrel of a very strange-looking rifle. The barrel was unusually thick.

Melni managed to twist around and glance over the tail end of the vehicle as he fired. She expected a booming crack, perhaps followed by one of the eight approaching officers falling dead. Instead the sound produced was a flaring sigh. The projectile that emerged flew on a brilliant yellow flame that left a trail of thick smoke in its wake.

The missile rose above the heads of the oncoming soldiers and lanced straight into the nose of the gigantic airship. She braced herself for an explosion. None came. Instead she saw what looked like rolling lightning dance across the skin of the mechanical floating whale. At once all four rotors stopped spinning. Without the benefit of their lift, the craft nosed downward and began to fall. Whatever gas filled the huge body, it was not enough alone to support the weight of the thing. The dirigible plummeted faster and faster, the NRD soldiers already on the ground scattering, those still shimmying down the ropes dropping ten, twenty, even thirty feet into the snow just to get away.

The nose hit the ground with a grinding crash. The explosion came a split second later. Yellow-white flame erupted from the nose and then, faster than the eye could track, began to slice through the seams of the fabric hull. A blinding, white-hot light bloomed from the entire doomed ship, followed by a deep *whump* sound that she felt more than heard. The light roiled, transformed into a rising inferno that licked up from every gaping hole in the tattered skin. Fireballs rolled upward until consumed by their own smoke clouds.

A grating crash followed as the cabin slammed into the ice. She could not see it through the flames, but the noise said everything. Nobody could survive such a horrid, fiery impact.

Most of the operatives on the ground had fallen or flung themselves from the explosion. A few still moved.

Suddenly Caswell had her by the arm. He yanked her viciously to the open cruiser door and shoved her into the backseat. Without a word he tossed his large white bag across her legs and slammed the back canopy door shut around her. He took the tiller's chair and they were off in a violent spray of white, bounding down the mountainside, away from flames and death, away from his vehicle.

Caswell, she realized, was muttering a single nonsensical word, over and over.

"Fuck, fuck, fuck, fuck—"

16

THE CRUISER BOUNCED and lurched down the long slope.

Between spine-jarring impacts Caswell stole glances over his shoulder at the snowy hillside lit orange by the roiling skeleton of the blimp. "Should've told me they had aircraft."

"I did not . . . just rumors. Odd shapes floating high above the rolltowns of the Desolation. I have never seen—"

"Forget it," he said. "Keep quiet for now, will you?"

Caswell drove like an animal spooked and routed from its den. The cruiser leapt off each undulation on the long slope, crashing down an instant later with teeth-rattling force.

After an agonizing minute the slope eased. Wisps of tall grass poked through the heavy snowpack and scraped along the cruiser's body like probing, bony fingers.

"I see no one following," Melni said.

"They don't need to," Caswell replied.

"Why?"

"Have a look."

The tandem two-seater offered a fantastic panorama for the driver, but Melni had to lean and press her face close to his seat to see. She gasped.

He yanked hard on the V-shaped steering control. The cruiser lurched right in a huge spray of snow, and stopped.

At the base of the hill, along an imposing wall of trees, were lights, a dozen at least, evenly spaced at fifty meter intervals.

"Garta, they must have the whole mountain surrounded!"

As they watched, some of the lights burst from the tree line and surged onto the slope. NRD cruisers, spewing huge plumes of white powder from their rear tires.

"Maybe," he said. "Let's see how well they play chicken."

"Chicken?"

"Uh. A bird, about—"

Melni grunted. "I know what a chicken is, just not how to play it."

"Two opponents on a collision course, knowing the impact means certain death, both expecting the other to swerve."

"Ah. We call it who-flinch. Everyone calls it who-flinch, actually. Except you," she said, a bit more terror in her voice with each word as Caswell sped toward the approaching lights.

The gap closed. The cruiser directly ahead suddenly tilted to one side and vanished in a violent spray of snow. Caswell crashed through the icy wall and bounced off the ridge of snow the enemy's tires had left.

Melni fell back into her seat. She grunted in pain.

"Buckle in!" he shouted, hoping for once that his words made immediate sense.

The cruiser's motor strained to give the power he sought. Suddenly the vehicle bounced once, then again. Caswell saw the trees approaching and turned slightly to one side, aiming for a gap. The ground smoothed, and glowed dimly. A road, as he'd hoped. "They must have cleared it on the way up," Caswell said. "Bloody kind of them. Which way do we go?"

"I have no idea where we are."

Caswell reached into a pocket under his seat. He'd discovered it while looking for a first-aid kit. He pulled the folded paper from it and handed it over his shoulder.

"What is this?"

"You're navigating."

She fumbled about with the paper, then turned on an interior lamp. "This is practically useless. NRD patrol guidelines."

"Find something better, then. Once we lose them, we'll head to Portstaff, or whatever the hell."

"Portstav."

"That." In his rearview mirrors lights suddenly danced, close. "Shit. Hold on!"

He threw the vehicle into a turn toward a connecting road, tires shrieking with strain. Melni yelped as he applied the handbrake and sent them into a spin. The vehicle went backward off the road and settled into the snow between two trees. Caswell killed the lights, popped the canopy, and stood on his seat.

"What are you doing?" Melni asked.

He ignored her. Instead he focused on the intersection of the road, twenty meters away, and raised his hands. Gripped in his fingers was a vossen gun, one of four he'd left Earth with. One he'd used on the *Venturi*. Another, intended as a spare, just went up in the airship crash. The last was in his bag on Melni's lap.

The weapon felt good in his hand. The weight of it, the quality of the materials so unlike all the antiques they ran around with here, reminded him of home, of progress. Holding it filled him with a natural confidence his implant could never quite produce with chemicals. This tiny weapon likely dwarfed anything these people could wield against him. He kept his back to Melni, careful to hide the device from her. Best she not know its power.

He let the first car round the corner and come on. The NRD agent at the tiller veered to his right in a spray of snow.

Via his gland, Caswell gave the weapon its task and let it handle the rest. There was a thin sound like a snake's hiss. The projectile lanced from the tip of the weapon and across the stretch of road, riding its tiny rocket plume. It hit the enemy cruiser's window and half the canopy went black from the inside. Caswell fired again toward the backseat, then adjusted himself as the next vehicle came around. He repeated the process with infinite calm, only this cruiser skidded off to the other side, stopping virtually even with the first but on his right.

A third came. Caswell did not let this one get so far. Another pinpoint of light, as thin and brilliant as a shooting star, zinged across the road and vanished into the glass window of the oncoming cruiser, painting it from within. The panicked driver yanked hard, lost control. The vehicle flipped, throwing snow high into the air, and crashed down with a thunderous wrenching of metal, glass, and the jumbled contents within. It came to a rest with its rear wheel still spinning madly, engine wailing like a dying animal.

He shot the fourth car. The fifth. They could not see the calamity before them until they rounded those trees, and by then it was too late. Behind him Melni began to mumble, a mixture of a scream and something like delighted surprise. Caswell's weapon spat a pinpoint of deadly light each time a cruiser came into view. Zip, puncture, the *whoomp* of obscuring ink, then the inevitable crash. Eight cars met this fate until finally the intersection became so choked with disabled cruisers that the ninth stopped well short, just beyond the vossen's meager range when fired in gravity and atmosphere.

"Time to go," Peter Caswell said.

He fell back in his seat and slammed the canopy shut. The car lurched into action, tire spinning in place as he pushed the motors to their limit too quickly. Then the rear tire found traction, spitting snow and glow-in-the-dark gravel as the full force of acceleration took hold. The speed pressed him back into his seat. *Like a night run on the Nürburgring,* he thought, with juvenile satisfaction. Confidence built within him again. He'd eaten and drank, filled a duffel with extra food packets and water bulbs. He knew on a conscious level that he was more skilled in the art of killing than these relentless "rassies." All he had to do was find Vale, and use the vossen on her. If he could get close enough.

Then he could go home, and become a rookie again.

17

THE LITTLE NRD CRUISER tore down a rural road toward the coast. Snow whipped past like angry insects. Giant sentinel trees pressed in like canyon walls on both sides.

A cold fear had seeped into Melni's mind. Not the fear of enemies after them, nor even the fear of this man sitting a foot in front of her. No, her fear came from within. The sense that her own soul had cracked in the last two days, and might shatter if this went on. There must be twenty dead in her wake now. A whole squad, plus their cars and, Garta's light, that gigantic airship.

How many more would this man kill before his cool wrath finally found Alia Valix?

Speeding toward the west coast of Combra, she realized she knew the answer: quite a lot. She'd have blood up to her own elbows, too. So what? They were of the North, were they not?

The problem, she now realized, was that this insanity had crossed over into act-of-war territory. Snooping around the Think Tank was one thing, easily made to look like industrial espionage. Even assassinating Alia Valix herself could be made to appear a result of the same intra-Northern feuds, at least to the extent of plausible deniability.

None of that would be possible now. This had become a tactical strike, and not even very tactical at that. A lot of well-trained and well-equipped rassies had died up on that mountainside. The dirigible was not the type of thing the North would lose to such an action and stay quiet about.

The idea that what had just transpired might be the spark that ignites a war seemed suddenly very real to her.

"Caswell," she said.

"How's the wound?"

"Manageable."

"Look. I'm sorry about what happened back there. Couldn't be helped."

"About the . . . about that 'landing craft' you took me to."

He leaned them hard into a tight turn and then the road leveled out, cutting a narrow gouge through trees for miles ahead. In the far distance she could see the waters of the Endless Sea glimmering softly in the blue-gray light of two full moons. "It's best you forget what you saw there. I warned you to keep the blindfold on."

"I have to ask you a question."

"I'd prefer you didn't," he said.

Melni thrust the outdated map aside, heat rising in her cheeks. "This is not much of a partnership if you can ask me all manner of strange questions but I cannot ask you one simple thing."

"Our partnership ends at Portstav, remember?" he rasped. She saw his fingers clamp down on the tiller and then flex.

"I've gathered my supplies," he added. "You have my thanks—gratitude, whatever—for helping me get there, a debt I believe I've repaid. As for the rest of our deal, I'll drop you at this town on the coast as you requested and continue with my mission."

"Fine. I just want to know one thing—"

"No," he said, barely contained anger behind the single word. "I cannot tell you anything about me, or what you think you saw back there."

"Hmm," she said, looking down. "All right then. Can you tell me anything about the contents of this bag on my lap?"

His head jerked to try to see.

Melni pulled a random item out. A square of some kind of flexible foil with a spongy center and a little capped tube extending from the top. With some effort she sounded out the words printed across it. "Readi-Eat Meal Pack. Pork in Curry Rice with Carrots. I wonder what those things are."

"Put that away."

Melni did so. And then grabbed another item. A cylindrical tube. "Vac . . . Vac-um . . . Vacuum-Optimized Smart Needler."

"Knock it off! If you think I'm joking—"

"Property of Archon Corporation. Another strange word, Archon."

He swerved hard toward the side of the road, rear tire shifting under sudden heavy braking.

"Ibuproxin, five hundred em-gee? Am I saying that correctly? Plus—"

"ENOUGH!"

The car had stopped. He hauled the canopy open and snatched the tiny pill bottle from her hand. Then he grabbed the bag itself and, after a brief battle with her grip, pulled it from her lap. He almost fell backward into the snow when it came free.

Melni watched him carefully even as she tucked the "Smart Needler" tube under her right thigh.

"Get out," he said.

"What?"

"You heard. Out. Now. I'm leaving you here. I should have left you in that pool at Alice's house. At every opportunity you insist on ignoring the ground rules I laid out, and if this—"

"Alice?"

He stammered to a stop.

"You called her Alice."

"Alia," he corrected himself. "Slip of the tongue. Now, out. I mean it."

Melni thought of another approach. "Do you read much history, Caswell?"

"Come on, I'm losing patience."

"Because those who don't study history . . ."

He sighed. ". . . are doomed to repeat it. I know, I know. Enough stalling."

"Familiar with that phrase, are you?"

He rolled his eyes as if she were some petulant child, and

started to reach for her. Then he slowed, and stopped. His gaze was on her now, cold as the frigid air in which he stood.

Melni looked straight at him. "Alia used that phrase in my interview with her. I had never heard it before. I thought it so clever I asked if I could quote her, and she agreed. She seemed rather proud of it, actually."

He backed off a half step, his gaze now searching the space between them.

"So," Melni went on, "either you were listening, which is possible. But I don't think so. Or, you know this phrase as if it were absolutely common knowledge. Like the game of chicken, despite the fact that I, and everyone else I've ever met, calls it who-flinch."

The steam went out of him then. His gaze fell to the side of the car and then the snow at his feet. His shoulders slumped inward.

"What was that room you took me to, Caswell? No submersible gets buried in snow halfway up a mountain."

Silence wedged between them and grew.

"That," he said finally, "was my ride home."

She thought he would open up then, but the silence stretched on. He just drove. The little cruiser continued to wind toward the coast. Dark waters shimmering with diamond reflections of the moons, Gisla and Gilan.

Twice he killed their lights and pulled off the road. She'd start to ask why and then hear what he'd heard well before her: vehicles. Through the gaps between dark trees they watched caravans of vehicles—NRD, Fire Suppression, and Medical Emergency—thunder inland toward the site of the airship crash. Caswell would sit and watch until their flashing blue and white lights could no longer be seen in the distance, then he'd creep their vehicle back out onto the road and continue on.

Ten miles from the coast the cruiser sputtered and began to drift silently to a stop. She helped him push it off the road and behind a thick bramble. He found an emergency spade in one of the side compartments and used it to shovel snow atop the spent vehicle.

"According to the map there is a village about two miles away," she said. "We can borrow another cruiser there."

"Will they be watching for us?"

"I would be," she said. "But I do not see a better option."

"How's your arm?" he asked.

Melni tried for a casual shrug, but her expression must have said otherwise. Caswell immediately fished through his bag and handed her a pair of tiny white lozenges. Her forearm throbbed. A two-mile hike without some of his truly impressive medications was out of the question. She swallowed them without further hesitation.

"Did Valix invent these pills?" she asked.

"I'm sure she'd claim as much."

They walked along the softly glowing packgravel road, her in front of him. The sky had cleared and both moons hovered a finger's width apart at the zenith, full and bright. After a quarter mile she glanced back to ask him if he wanted to stop for water, only to find him staring up at the sky with unconcealed wonder written across his face. She held on to her question and turned her focus back to the road ahead.

"I've been thinking," Caswell said suddenly.

"Oh?"

"Deciding how much I can tell you."

"If you are worried about me divulging secrets—"

"It's not that," he said, a note of weariness in his voice. "Not exactly, anyway. It's hard enough that I can't directly reveal to you the specifics of my mission. It goes deeper than that, though. Because even sharing with you, generally, the truth about our mutual target could have dire consequences."

Melni grinned, glad he couldn't see her face. "So you do know where she is from."

He didn't say no.

"And," Melni probed, "you know the truth behind her genius? All the inventions?"

"She's smart, no question, but her genius is only in the manner, the precise sequence, in which she's doled them out. She possesses a collection of knowledge that is . . ." He hesitated. "Very advanced, Melni."

"Wait," Melni said. "So are you saying she found some writings on all these topics and she pretends it is all the product of her own mind?"

"That's not far from the truth."

"And," Melni went on, her mind racing from conclusion to conclusion faster than she could form the words, "you possess this knowledge, too? You both found it—"

"No," Caswell said sharply. Then, with patience, "No. I'm vaguely familiar with some of it. And no, she did not find it."

"So what then? She stole it?"

Silence.

"From where?"

"Can't say. Before you object, hear me out. To even answer you in the most general of terms could have repercussions."

Melni voiced a theory she'd come to before, but filed as insanity. "You came here from the future, did you?"

"Time travel is impossible, Melni," Caswell said.

Not a lie. Not exactly. But something in his tone told her she was close. She said it again. "You are from the future."

He smirked. "In a way I suppose I am."

The village was barely more than a cluster of tall dormitories that looked a hundred years old, huddled around a single mealhouse and central square. There were dozens like it all over the North, built to house seasonal workers who once flocked to this part of Combra to work the mills and fisheries. As the world continued to cool, such work pushed farther and farther south, and then across the ocean, where the labor came cheaper. Melni doubted this village would be at half capacity even at the peak of season. Now, in the frigid month, it was possible the only people living here were those who maintained the place. Of the hundreds of windows that soared above them along the faces of the eight buildings, only three were lit. The two intersecting streets were empty, piled with snow. She saw signs of foot traffic on them, to and from the shuttered mealhouse. Given the dinner hour, she had expected nothing else, but still she sat among the trees with Caswell for a good five minutes before approaching. If the NRD was watching this place they'd concealed themselves expertly. Melni thought it more likely they just hadn't fully pieced together what had happened on the mountain yet, and were probably too busy marveling at the remains of Caswell's "ride" than investigating the whereabouts of the two fugitives who'd been inside.

Of six public cruiser sheds on the edge of town, only one had a vehicle inside. Melni set to work coaxing the old thing to life. However long ago manufactured, the cruiser had been well maintained and recently prepped for travel, judging by the air tubes still dangling from the tanks on its haunches. Compared to the NRD's Valix-powered electric model, this one was pokey and loud, running on a compressed-air engine that rattled like a shallow drum.

She took the vee-tiller now and guided the creaky old thing around the perimeter road and then turned sharp left on the south exit road. Between the faintly glowing surface of the road and the bright dual-moonlit sky she left the lamps off. The aging cruiser squeaked and groaned on every little bump. Her eyes tracked the air gauge carefully. Not much there, but enough to reach Portstav.

The coastal town finally came into view eight minutes later. A sprawling clump of lights and smoking chimneys huddled around a rocky bay where perhaps two dozen ships of varying size were moored. In its heyday Portstav would have been home to perhaps fifty thousand grim-faced frontier folk, but now fewer than five thousand remained. The structures farthest from the center were almost all shuttered and pitch black.

Inside one of those abandoned, crumbling buildings was the listening post. Melni hoped so, anyway. She'd memorized a list of Southern assets active in Combra just before making her way across the Desolation, but that had been years ago. A reason to use that knowledge had never come up until now.

She prowled the empty, windswept streets for nearly an hour before a sign finally jogged her memory. Melni turned and rolled slowly down an unlit avenue lined with warehouses until she came to a four-story brick building with boarded-up doors and windows. A placard above the entrance read HINE LUMBER. Melni pulled the car to the side of the littered street and silenced the engine.

"We're here," she said.

Her companion made no reply. She turned and saw he'd fallen asleep, his bag of supplies clutched tight to his chest like an infant in need of comfort.

Melni turned back and studied the brick building. One boarded window, on the corner of the top floor, had a small symbol drawn on it. Two vertical lines with a single horizontal one bisecting them. A symbol for Riverswidth. She'd found the right place, and tried to envision the interior. A team of communications specialists. Cipher experts, engineers. Rows of equipment perhaps concealed in a basement or hidden central room.

She opened the canopy. Caswell did not stir, so she shut and locked the glass and walked as casually as one could in such a place to the other side of the street. The roads were utterly empty, so she took her time, making a circuit around the building. The only entrance seemed to be the front door, boarded with thick planks of sentinel wood nailed securely to a frame bolted into the bricks themselves. Beneath a first-floor window to the left of the entrance there was a large crack in the bricks. A section had fallen out, hit by an errant cruiser, perhaps. The filthy building was otherwise unmarred. She went to the window above the crack and turned to face the opposite direction. Directly across the road stood the dark pole of a dead streetlight. She crossed to it and stood at the base. Every other light on the street that she could see had an empty socket where a bulb had once been, but not this one. Melni knelt and examined a small square panel at the bottom. With some prying it came loose. She reached into the dark cavity within and probed about until her fingers brushed a switch. It clicked when she tugged at it, and the bulb above began to emit an ugly brown light that slowly grew to a murky yellow that barely reached her. She stood in the little pool of ruddy light and watched the brick building. Long, silent minutes passed.

The board across the first-floor window at the crack in the wall shifted and swung outward. A shadowed person loomed inside, one hand gesturing come-hither. Mclni flicked the light back off and jogged across the street. Using the crack as a foothold she vaulted herself into the dark interior.

Melni landed in a roll and would have come to a stand had she not forgotten about the wound. Her arm hit the hardwood floor and flared with fresh pain. She knelt there, clutching at it.

"Oh my, oh dear," the person within said. It was an elderly voice, a woman's. She helped Melni to unsteady feet and spoke in a matronly tone. "In from the cold, are we? And who might you be? A poor little runaway?"

"14772, traveling as Melni Tavan," she said, gently probing the wound.

The old woman shifted roles instantly. "Hmm. A one-four, are you? A long way from Midstav."

There came a dull click. Melni flinched, then a handheld lantern bloomed to life. It lit the craggy, lined face of a very old Northern woman. She had the robust form of a life lived on the frozen frontier. Flabby jowls hung from her cheeks and shook when she moved, matching the motion of great saggy unbound breasts under a loose blouse. "You are the first visitor in some time," she said with a kind smile that revealed two rows of uneven, yellow teeth.

"You are alone here?" Melni asked.

"I am hardly here at all," the woman said. "Come by twice in ten to check the reel, but there is all kinds of chatter tonight so I stayed. 19220 is the number they gave me but Anim Corda is what they called me on my firstwords. Pleased to know you."

"Pleased," Melni agreed. "Sorry to come in unannounced but I have an emergency report to file. Can you help with that?"

"I can."

"I also need to arrange passage on a boat to Tandiel. Is that possible?"

"It is possible. Not easy, but possible."

"No one can know."

"That is what I assumed. There are people at the port, sympathetic to us, who can help."

"Gratitude," Melni said earnestly. "I have a companion in the cruiser. A friend. He is not one of us, though."

"Use your judgment, dear. I will not tell anyone if you want to bring him in, too."

"Again, my gratitude."

"Yes, yes. Enough birdshitting about. Come up. I will make you something warm to drink and you can tell me what your business is."

Melni nodded and went back out the way she'd come. Caswell came alert the instant she cracked open the door of the cruiser. "Come with me," she said.

He followed without a word, clutching his overstuffed bag.

18

"THIS IS ANIM," Melni said, gesturing to the old woman inside. "She is going to help us."

Caswell nodded. He'd learned by now to speak as little as possible, his accent and strange phrasings an instant give-away of some intangible wrongness with him.

Anim led them up creaking stairs to a vast room on the fourth floor.

Fifteen meters on a side and dotted with a grid of square pillars, the room housed abandoned machines apparently for woodworking, concealed under greasy linen sheets. Paint peeled from the walls in great dingy white strips, crushed to powder where they'd fallen to the mottled hardwood floor.

In the center of the space, well away from boarded windows and the interior hallway doors, was a workspace made of four mismatched tables arranged around one of the square support pillars. A single work lamp cast a small pool of dim yellow light over heaped, crude electronics. A bulky ear-phone rested in the center of the light's focus, next to a thick sheaf of papers and a mug that bristled with writing implements.

"This have something to do with the explosion up on Law's Peak? Lots of chatter about it an hour ago, then some-one ordered all quiet and it has been just that ever since."

"We," Melni paused. "Uh . . ."

"If you cannot say, that is all right. I take no offense. Old Anim has little in the way of clearance."

"Gratitude. Where is the rest of your team?"

Anim chuckled dryly. "Just me here, regret to say."

Caswell saw Melni deflate somewhat at that. She'd expected much more, clearly. How well did she know her own "side" in this so-called Quiet War? When it came to Alice Vale's mansion she'd memorized every last detail. The only conclusion he could reach was that she'd been in deep cover for some time, isolated from the wider scope of Riverswidth's intelligence apparatus.

"Only one chair, I fear," Anim said. She gestured for Melni to take a seat in the rickety antique and then bustled off into the darkness. Seconds later another light winked groggily to life, on the far wall between two covered windows. Beneath it was a narrow counter. Anim set to work making cham and heating soup, or something like it, over a portable stove.

"What is this place?" Caswell asked under his breath.

Melni nodded toward the stacks of radio gear. "Listening post. Coded transmissions from up and down the west coast of Combra are transcribed and sent south for analysis."

"What sort of transmissions?"

Anim bustled over with two steaming mugs. "You name it," she said, cutting off Melni's thanks. "Shipping lines coming in from Tandiel. The Navy base up at Highstav. The NRD officers are our primary objective, though they went quiet last month. Not much to hear now, regret to say. That is why the others have left."

"Went quiet?"

The woman nodded apologetically. "Just a loud hiss where there used to be voices. Sometimes it abruptly ends, and when it starts back up you can hear birds chirping."

"Birds?" Melni asked.

"Yes, birds. But sort of mechanical, like a child's toy."

Caswell pondered this. "Can I hear some?"

The old crone seemed to notice his accent then. But she only shrugged at him. Perhaps she'd never been outside this secluded town. Maybe all accents were exotic to her. She leaned past Melni, plucked the earphone from the table, and took to wiping the cushioned oval on her shirt. Satisfied, she handed it to Caswell. As he put it on, she arranged dials on several of the machines.

He listened for a time, inhaling the scent of his cham without drinking any as he held the worn earphone to the side of his head.

When the chirping happened he knew it instantly. A sound of Earth. He knew this not from direct experience, but old films and television shows. More of Alice Vale's influence, clearly. Another stepping-stone toward whatever goal she sought here.

Monique's orders kept him from telling Melni or the old woman any of this, though. He pretended to listen for another minute, then gave a bored shrug and handed Melni the earpiece.

She listened intently, her eyes on him. Caswell turned away, studying one of the bundles of wires snaking up the pillar and along a beam on the ceiling. Anim wandered back to her pot of soup. It smelled wonderful, much better than the packets he'd stuffed into the bag.

"Caswell?" Melni asked, her voice carefully quiet.

"Hmm?"

"Do you know what it is?"

"Not really."

"But you know something."

He closed his eyes and inhaled the steam from his cham. The urge to sip the wonderful drink almost got the better of him. Caswell set the mug aside. "Just a guess." He debated giving her more, a hint, perhaps. The basics of an acoustic computer modem is what she needed, but that kind of influence is what he'd been ordered to avoid. Uncomfortable, feeling now more like he was betraying a friendship rather than being a loyal soldier, he wandered off to help Anim with the meal.

They sat on cushions on the dusty floor by the windows and ate in silence. The thick "estu," as Anim called it, consisted of chunks of stringy meat and some root vegetables in a greasy brown gravy. Caswell hoped his lack of eating would not offend their host too much. Anim didn't ask.

Melni ate voraciously, the way a native of Japan might attack a bowl of ramen. Slurping, chewing noisily. With her pixie cut blond hair, her large purple eyes, and her ragged black soldier's garb, she looked like some kind of punk rocker from the eighties. The 1980s. He found it endearing.

Bowl empty, she stretched and yawned, then excused herself to find the "lav." When she returned Caswell went off to do the same. He stood in the closet-size room for a long time, staring at himself in the mirror. A strange sensation to see himself, here. The man in the mirror would be a stranger in a week's time. He stared hard into his own face, as if by sheer force of will he could forge a memory that would survive reversion. "The most interesting mission you'll ever forget," he said to himself. "Fucking-A, Monique. What an understatement." He splashed cold water on his face, dried it, and walked out without giving himself another glance. He'd forget that man, and the death he'd dealt, soon enough.

When he returned he found two bedrolls had been laid out in a dark corner of the listening room.

"Rest," Anim was saying to Melni. "I will wake you when it is time to send off your report."

"How long until then?" she asked.

"The submersible comes up at seventh hour, when Garta kisses the Endless Sea so as to hide her profile. There is plenty of time. Go and rest."

Lying on the musty folded blanket, one arm under his head to serve as a cushion, Caswell stared at the aging coffered ceiling: cracked, peeling paint over some sort of plaster. Funny how similar some things were here. As interesting as the differences, and equal in number.

Melni's bedroll was two meters away, but the silence between them seemed to stretch much farther. He felt sure she was watching him, still waiting for him to talk. He regretted saying anything at all in that car. He should have just kept his mouth shut. He really should have parted ways with her, long ago. After the confrontation at the Valix house. Why hadn't he? Why take this risk? How would he explain it to Monique, to Archon? He supposed he wouldn't, not if he could avoid it. Maybe that's why he'd been so successful in his career. Maybe it was all bullshit, cleverly fed to Monique and the rest of the corporation. Perhaps it wasn't that he was a good assassin, but that he was a great liar. A piece of shit who'd fooled everyone, including himself. Himself most of all.

The line of Sapporos in the fridge came to him like a vision. He knew he wouldn't make it back to South Kensington in time to arrange them. He'd probably never leave this world now. But what if he did? Would he add another row of bottles to the ones already there and turn all of them around? Would he lie to himself? *Just two kills this time, old man. Not twenty. You're not that much of a monster, honest. Have a drink and go bumble around in the Congo or something. Pretend you have some control of your fucked-up life.*

He shook his head, despite himself.

"Caswell?" Melni whispered.

Her voice brought him out of that cognitive pit of self-doubt. "Yeah."

"Are you going to tell me what you heard in that static? You could help us resolve it, could you not?"

For a while he said nothing. His mind groped for some way to make her understand—resolve, as she said—why he couldn't tell her such things, and why it was so dangerous for Alice to. Gaze firmly on the ceiling, he tried a new tack. "You know what a child is like if their parents do everything for them?"

The question took her by surprise. She considered it, then nodded with vehemence. "I knew such children growing up. The sons and daughters of wealthy true-blood Southerners. Lazy. Dull. Entitled."

"Exactly." He turned on his side to face her. "What happens to them when they're suddenly on their own?"

Melni swallowed. She shivered, visibly. She understood.

He went on anyway. "That child is Gartien if this business of Alia's continues. And I'm no better than her if I start behaving as she does."

"But you must care a little about the South. You are one of us, more so than even me. A native—"

"I'm not. Trust me on that. And anyway it doesn't matter. The people who sent me here care about the well-being of all of Gartien, not one side or the other. It's hard for you to see that—"

"No," Melni said, doubt in her voice. "No. I can see your point of view, I just wish I understood where it originated."

For a minute neither spoke. Melni started to drift off, her eyes dipping and then popping open several times. Caswell snuck a glance at his watch. Seven days until he forgot all about her. About what he'd done here, and to that innocent crew of the *Pawn Takes Bishop.* He sighed.

"What is it? What's wrong?" Melni asked.

He kept his gaze on the ceiling. "I was just thinking about home. After what happened today, I doubt I'll ever see it again."

"Regret," she offered.

"Doesn't matter. The mission remains the same."

He rolled away from her, rubbed at his temples, and waited for the chemically augmented sleep. It didn't take long.

Whispers roused him from sleep some hours later. Day or night he couldn't tell, for the windows were all boarded up.

Caswell rolled onto his side. He saw Melni and Anim, lit by the soft glow of the single dim lamp, huddled around their communications gear. The machine resembled an old mechanical typewriter attached to some Soviet-era reel recorder. It whirred and clicked almost whimsically. Vacuum tubes probably filled its innards. How much of it had been invented by the people of Gartien, and how much had come from components "invented," or at least inspired, by Alice Vale?

He wrestled with that for some time. Melni wrote on a sheet of yellow paper as Anim worked the dials and held one cup of the earphone to her head, while Caswell pondered the efficacy of his mission. Monique, Archon, and whoever had hired Archon had sent him to this place having only clues of what had happened aboard the *Venturi.* They'd learned of Gartien, and Alice's coldly calculated plan to return here with all that data. To play God, Monique had said. And they'd wanted him to stop her, to undo or at least end her influence so that Earth could try to get this right.

Caswell didn't consider himself a fool. He took his orders without question, yes, and only maintained his sanity via the miracle of clear conscience his implant provided. But he knew people. He knew politicians. He could see the angles, the other possible motivations for stopping Vale. This place, and the science it took to get here, were a gold mine like the world had never seen. Even more disruptive than the first mineral-rich asteroid hauled into low-Earth orbit. Lots of money involved meant all the ancillary birdshit, as Melni so quaintly said: greed, power, corruption.

Yet at least that way there was a chance. Alice Vale was already on the wrong path here, perhaps irrevocably so, but if he could at least stop her before she gave them horrors like nerve gas, thermonuclear warheads, or the ability to construct a mass driver, at least there'd be a chance for the right leadership, the right approach, to come forward.

Besides, I'll forget all about it, he thought. And despised himself for it. An easy excuse and a pathetic absolution of evil.

Across the room Melni spoke, more loudly now. "Could the NRD intercept this?" she asked the old woman.

"Oh, it is unlikely, dear. Very narrow beam, you know. They would have to be parked right out there near the sub, between Spire Rock and the northern tip of the bay."

"How long until they reply?"

Anim looked at the much younger agent. "Usually they make no reply. I report, I sign off. It is not for me to know if they do anything with the information."

"Oh," Melni said, disappointed.

"You require a response?"

"I was hoping for one."

Anim shrugged. "Well, I'll sit here and listen, I suppose. Make yourself useful and check the streets, will you? Spy holes are on the second-floor corners."

One of the radios let out a little squawk. Anim leaned over and immediately began to tap away at the keyboard, which instead of rows of offset keys had circular keypads, one for each hand, plus a foot pedal.

Caswell waited for Melni to exit. He counted to ten, then rose and, being absolutely quiet, removed his shoes. Walking with slow, languid movements, he came to stand behind

Anim Corda. The old woman was transcribing what Melni had written, he assumed.

Melni's words were there twice. One incomprehensible, coded in some cipher. But on the left side of the page he read:

ASSASSIN OF SAME ORIGIN AS AV
NRD CLOSED HIS ESCAPE ROUTE W LARGE AIR-
  SHIP
HE PLANS TO COMPLETE MISSION LIKELY ENDS
  WITH SUICIDE
PLAN TO TAKE HIM TO STATION V
ADVISE

Peter Caswell backed away to his bedroll and lay down. He stared at the ceiling again, hands clasped over his chest, and let the word ring in his skull. *Suicide.* He'd not thought so far ahead. He never did, really. Would he—no, could he do that? Assassinate Alice Vale and then himself, all for the cause?

He'd decide when the time came, not now. Too many variables. Plans were for people like Melni. Obsess over imagined details and then inevitably have it all go to shit when reality is even slightly off. He'd gotten this far by improvising, by relying on his instincts because he had no real benefit of memory. He saw no reason to change. Not now, not here.

Caswell reached into his duffel and grabbed another food packet at random. He twisted off the orange cap and sucked at it, trying to figure out by flavor alone what the hell it was supposed to be. Applesauce? No, pears.

Steps at the door. Pounding feet. Melni burst into the listening room. "Rassies outside! Caswell, get up! They tracked us!"

He tossed the packet aside and vaulted to his feet, hands already at his temples. Focus, sensory boost, increased rate of neuron firing. Time seemed to slow. Not much, just enough to have an edge.

"Get your things. We have to leave," Melni said to him.

Anim, still seated at the radio table, tapped fiercely at her contraption.

Downstairs something banged. A sharp crack against wood.

Melni grabbed the old woman's shoulder. "Anim! We have to get out."

"Go," the old woman said with nearly perfect calm. "I have got strict orders for just such an event, young lady, and I plan to carry them out."

"No, I—"

"Do not argue, dear. There is a way out through the private canal underneath. You saw the shop floor?"

Melni nodded. Caswell tried to picture it. He'd been in something of a daze when they came in. Machines for making paper, or something. Some sort of winch to haul up lumber from, he presumed, this private subterranean canal. It made sense.

"Take the lift down. There is a boat. The motor is noisy as a wounded bhar, so push it out." She never stopped tapping at her little transmitter. "Go now, before they block the way."

Caswell rifled through his bag, desperate to find the vossen gun, but it eluded him, buried no doubt under all the food and medicine. So instead he hefted the missile launcher he'd used against the airship. He had opened his mouth and started to speak when something crashed through one of the boarded windows. A little black cylinder trailing smoke bounced and rolled across the floor.

The cylinder started to hiss. Another gas round burst through one of the far windows, pinging against the floor and thudding into a pillar.

Melni grabbed Caswell by the arm and together they ran through an inner hallway door. Caswell let go of her the instant they were through and fell in naturally behind her as Melni beat a path toward the wide, decaying stairwell.

Something exploded below them. The sharp bang set his augmented ears ringing. He shouted to Melni, urging her forward. She seemed to move at a jog, and he had to remind himself that was only a trick of his accelerated perception.

Clouds of white gas rolled out from open doorways on the third floor. The air stung his eyes. His throat burned. Caswell threw an arm across his mouth and nose and continued down, the tears in his eyes making it hard to find the steps, slowing him.

On the second-floor landing Melni turned out into hazy, stinging air. A hallway open on one side, a wooden railing along its interior length. The walkway went all the way around the rectangular room, looking down on the huge machines below. From somewhere down there Caswell heard splintering wood and a great many pairs of boots on gritty floor.

Around the next corner, halfway along the walkway, there was a gap in the railing. A pair of beams extended out over the floor below. Chains extended from there down to a square lift, a winch to raise and lower it beside it just as he'd remembered.

Melni raced on, headed for that gap. It would take too long. Too long to operate the winch. Hell, they wouldn't even reach the damned floor in time. Caswell could see that already. Melni evidently could not.

Automatic gunfire erupted from below, with brilliant yellow flashes from the shadowed corners of the cavernous room. Bullets thudded into the wall to his right. Little eruptions of paint and plaster and wood in a wavering line came straight toward Melni's head.

Instinct took over. In a single motion Caswell aimed the rocket launcher with one hand while he grabbed her by the waist. He leapt diagonally to the right, heaving her off her feet. They crashed through the feeble wooden railing and were out, falling through open air. Bullets zinged past. Caswell aimed at the lift platform in the middle of the shop floor, hoping it concealed a hole that led to the canal beneath. He fired. A deafening hiss as the rocket took flight. Gunfire from all around.

Then the floor exploded. A fireball. Flaming bits of wooden shrapnel lancing out in a thousand directions. Soldiers screaming. More death.

Caswell, still in motion, rolled in midair so that Melni

was protected by his body. He felt the searing heat on his back, the impact of the pressure wave.

And then they were through the hole the rocket had made.

A second of darkness preceded the shocking embrace of ice-cold water.

19

THE FRIGID WATER hit her like a mallet.

Melni saw the shimmer of waves only an instant before they crashed through the surface. She had time to think *Inhale, get air.* Her mouth gaped open too late and the cold, filthy water rushed right in.

She gagged as she fought for the surface, vaguely aware of Caswell doing the same nearby. Her arm hit his. Maybe it was his leg. In seconds the NRD soldiers would be at the hole now above them, shooting blindly into the water. She saw flames through that hole and tried to kick away from it even as she groped for the surface. Her lungs burned. Her arm screamed at her.

Melni's fingers brushed air. She kicked hard and burst through the surface, coughing out the stagnant water and gulping in a lungful of air. The space around her was absolutely black save for the square of smoky, wavering firelight above. She looked there and saw bodies begin to swarm around the edges.

Caswell crashed through the surface a few feet away, inhaling ravenously.

"Down!" she screamed at him. Then she dove, hoping he'd heard. Above her came a chorus of soft *thwick* sounds as bullets chased her into the depths. Melni kicked and kicked, one hand held out before her, the other pulling against the water for added speed.

Her outstretched fingers brushed a slimy bottom to the artificial canal. She turned over to look up, saw the bullets gliding into the water, little trails of bubbles in their wake. It reminded her of the painter's impressions of the first moments of the Desolation, when the rocks began to fall through the sky. Water had a remarkable ability to absorb the fired bullet, however. She could see them rip through the surface, glide a foot or two, then abruptly slow and stop. They floated down like flakes of snow.

Of Caswell she saw nothing. Melni followed the bottom until her fingers brushed the sidewall. Her lungs started to demand air so she let herself float up along the vertical stone surface until her head reached the waterline. She forced herself to come through noiselessly, clenching her teeth together to keep them from rattling. Her body shivered uncontrollably.

The water under the square of light churned as the assault force above poured round after round into it. Someone was shouting just beneath the deafening rattle of the guns. "Cease fire! Cease fire!"

Something tugged at her leg. Caswell. His short black hair poked through the surface so carefully it barely rippled. His face, next to hers. "Down. Follow me," he whispered.

Then he vanished, down into the darkness.

Melni filled her lungs with air and pushed back underwater. In the gloom she saw the ghostly form of Caswell, legs kicking, as he swam off into the darkness. She followed, confident she could ignore the rain of bullets above her head. If someone got the wiser idea to jump in after them, she'd worry. Until then, she kicked after the increasingly diminishing form of Caswell.

After twenty feet or so he stopped and went up for air. Melni swam until she thought she was under him and went up, again with one hand outstretched. Her fingers hit something solid below the surface. *Wood,* she thought. She groped along the curved surface, panic welling in her, lungs burning, until she found the edge.

When she came up she was staring at the side of a small boat. Caswell had already hauled himself in, water dripping from soaked clothes as he fiddled with the large cylindrical weapon he'd saved from his "ride home."

Melni gripped the side of the little boat with one hand and

winced as he aimed and fired. The air above her seemed to rip apart. Brilliant light from the tail of the projectile briefly illuminated the underground tunnel. Slick walls of ancient cut stone, black with mold and grime.

The explosion blinded her. Rock fell from the ceiling. The entire floor around the lift's opening collapsed. Bodies, limbs flailing in surprise, fell to the black water. Then the machinery, on top of them, in a great wall of white spray.

"Garta's light," Melni whispered, no doubt in her mind now that their actions would lead to war.

"Start the motor," Caswell said. "Quickly."

In the darkness she could barely tell which end of the boat the engine was on. One end seemed to taper less than the other, so she pulled herself along that edge and, once the tiller came into view, she hauled herself up into the tiny craft. It rocked as she went over and in. Soaked to the core, Melni sloshed about on her knees until her shivering hands found the machine. She'd never worked one herself but had seen it done plenty of times. A crank lever protruded straight up from the side. She gripped it and began to yank and push, back and forth, winding the starter. Then she slapped the big switch on the top and almost fell back when the old motor coughed and growled to life.

To her surprise, Caswell had gotten out. In the darkness she saw him working at a rope tied to an iron loop on a narrow stone walkway that lined one side of the tunnel. The rope came free easily—Anim had only looped it around instead of tying a secure knot. A stroke of luck. Caswell hopped back into the boat, wincing as he did so. She realized then he'd been hunched over, one hand pressed at his gut.

"Are you hurt?" Melni asked.

"Never mind that. Get us out of here."

She wheeled the boat away from the fire and flailing bodies under the ragged wound that looked into the building above. With a twist of the tiller the craft gained some speed. Caswell, groaning with the effort, turned to face forward. He was fumbling with something attached to the nose of the boat. After a few seconds a weak yellow light winked into existence, illuminating the grimy path ahead.

Able to see, Melni cranked the handle even farther. The air motor banged and rattled under the strain. The boat worked its way up to a satisfying clip, rising in the water with speed. She kept the tiller pointing straight as the tunnel, and less than a minute later she saw a square of dim blue-gray light ahead. A minute after that, a starry open sky came into view above the gentle waters of the cove. The little craft slipped from the tunnel and into the Endless Sea.

Now what? Melni asked herself.

A landmark on the horizon triggered a memory. A tall and sheer clump of rock, about forty feet high. "Spire Rock," Anim had called it. And to its right, the northern edge of the bay, dark against the night sky. That's where the transmitter had to point to communicate with the submersible, so that way meant out to sea. She'd go south along the coast, cross the Combran Divide and beach on the edge of the Desolation. Find a rolltown for supplies. That made sense. That she knew.

Melni set their course for directly between the two landmarks and opened the engine up to maximum pressure. The old thing banged so loud she thought half the city could hear it. Nothing could be done about it, except get away as fast as possible, before they realized what had happened. Perhaps the submersible would still be out there somewhere and could flash her a response to her message.

The slumped, still form of Caswell yanked her mind back to the present. Red-tainted water pooled around his feet in the basin of the little craft.

"How bad is it?" she called out.

He only stared, vacantly. His face was oddly calm. He had one hand against his gut and the other rubbed at his temple.

Melni clicked the throttle and tiller locks into place and crawled forward. "Caswell, turn around and let me have a look."

He didn't move. She placed a hand on his shoulder and, with just that small pressure, he collapsed backward into her, limp as a corpse.

Melni felt around for his right breast and held her palm there. Nothing. No pulse. She probed along his torso until her fingers felt the warm, slightly sticky blood welling out from under his waterlogged clothing. Despite the lack of a pulse, he made a small sound when she touched the wound.

She glanced at the bag he carried. Somehow, through everything that happened in their escape from the building, he'd managed to hang on to it. With some effort she coaxed it out from under his arm.

A brilliant yellow flash made her duck out of pure instinct. Her mind screamed "searchlight!" but then a deep boom slammed into her ears and rolled away on the waves. She glanced back toward the city in time to see rolling fireballs curling up into the night sky.

Anim. It had to be. She'd destroyed the listening post. Her "strict orders," no doubt. Would that plan include a way out other than the boat? Melni hoped so, for the woman had been kind, but it seemed unlikely. The place had been surrounded. Fresh tears welled up in her still-stinging eyes.

Melni shifted focus back to her wounded companion. He had medical supplies in that bag, but they were completely foreign to her. She rifled through them anyway. If he could have just let her in, told her what all this was and how it worked. "Be strong," she said, her voice nothing more than a whisper. "We will find a village past the headlands, compel a doctor to help you."

Caswell did not move, did not even groan.

Something blotted out the moons above her. She glanced up and saw the peak of Spire Rock drift by. The waves grew choppier. Melni grasped the tiller and turned them south toward—

"What is that?" she whispered.

Something protruded from the water a hundred feet farther out to sea. A straight, narrow pipe with a bulbous end. She swallowed, picturing for some inexplicable reason the monstrous sea serpents she'd so feared as a young child. But they did not roam so far north, and rarely ventured to the surface anyway except to die.

There came a great crashing of water and the whole ocean before her seemed to lift, then explode. A massive dark shape broke through the waves and then crashed back down, settling halfway out of the whitewash it had created.

The submersible. Southerners.

Melni felt the tears streaking down her cheeks as she waved frantically. A searchlight winked on and swung toward her. She saw silhouetted figures now, on the slick deck, chestlamps glinting off the black hull and the black waves between them and her.

"Ahey! Ahey!" she called.

The lights trained on her.

"Hang on, Caswell. Hang on."

"Captain Liso," the woman said, extending her hand.

Melni took it and stepped off the ladder into a small, crowded waterlock. "Melni Tavan, 14772 of Riverswidth—"

"We know," the captain said. She waited for her crew to carry Caswell down the steep stepwell. One had his feet, another his shoulders. His arms had been folded across his stomach, where fresh blood still pumped out. His face had gone paper white, and there were blue rings around his eyes.

"Once we clear the water get him straight to Medical, bed two," Liso said. She turned to Melni. "Any Navy in the harbor?"

Melni fought to gain control of all the thoughts in her head. "I . . . No, I did not see any. I do not know."

Liso nodded. A chime sounded and the captain cranked a handle on the inner door until it hissed. She pushed it open and warm, tangy air rushed in. It stank of sweat and cham and waste. Melni grimaced, then steeled herself and followed the others inside.

A sailor waited within, wearing a less decorative version of Liso's dark green outfit. He saluted, fist to the base of the chin.

"Take us down, tillmaster. Hug the bottom at one hundred feet. Return-to-port route."

"Yes, Captain," the man said. "Are we running silent?"

"Only if they chase."

"Understood." He saluted again and rushed off toward the control room.

Liso led them aft, through four inner waterlocks to a series of rooms with white doors. A doctor waited in the sec-

ond to last, hovering next to a bed ready to receive the
wounded man. Melni considered offering up Caswell's bag
and the potentially useful medicines within, but changed
her mind. He might be dead already, for all she knew, and
the advanced gear surely came with the highest of security
clearances. No, she would hold on to his things until she
reached Riverswidth: the bag, and the tube she still had concealed in her now soaking-wet sock. The analysts there
would best know how to deal with these things.

"With me, Tavan," Liso said, as if reading her mind. The
gruff captain marched back the way they'd come, not waiting to see if Melni followed. A thin bellow squawked out of
ceiling-mounted speakers, then a man's voice said, "Prepare
for descent!"

Liso did not change pace, but she started to use a handrail
along one side of the corridor. Melni followed her example,
and soon enough the whole space began to tilt forward. Her
wet boots slipped on the painted metal floor. Disoriented
and still clutching Caswell's bag under one arm, Melni gave
her body a few seconds to adjust to the hallway-turned-
ramp, then began to walk with care. She disregarded the
impatient glances Captain Liso threw her.

The captain's quarters were a welcome change. Melni
took a seat on a small cushioned bench on one side, across
a narrow desk from Liso. She set the bag on the floor between her feet and faced the captain.

The woman was squat and powerfully built. A muscled,
veiny neck connected her squarish head to a set of broad
shoulders. Her hair, what little there was, had a slight tinge
of gray to it, a color reflected in hard, close-set, narrow
Southern eyes.

"Well, Tavan," the woman said, "you may have started a
war back there. Anything to say for yourself?"

The adversarial tone went beyond the usual competitive
jabs between the Southern agencies. Melni weighed several
responses. "Gratitude for rescuing us," she managed. "Has
there been any word from Riverswidth?"

"Not yet. We will have to get far away from here before
we can risk surfacing again to make contact. With any luck
the Combs will think you and your friend drowned and keep

their search to the coastline. If they find out we have been skulking about out here it really will be war."

"How long until we can try?"

The captain let out a breath. "If none of their fast-attack craft are around, maybe in an hour. Two to be safe."

"And if they pursue?"

Liso narrowed her eyes. "If the damned Combs pursue then ask Garta for help, because this old boat cannot outrun the monsters they are building these days."

A black box on her desk chirped. Liso pressed a finger to it. "Speak."

"Dr. Gilot here."

"How is our . . ." She paused and glanced at Melni. "Who is this man, anyway?"

"His name is Caswell."

"What branch? Riverswidth?"

Melni shook her head. "It is complicated."

Liso grunted. "How is your patient, Doctor?"

"Strange, that is what he is."

"Stable?"

"Yes, stable. For now. Whether or not he will recover is another question."

"Explain."

"Well, for one, his blood chemistry is unique. For seconds, I took radiographs and . . . Captain, you had better come see for yourself."

The captain glanced at Melni and frowned at the confused expression she saw there. "On our way."

Melni followed the captain aft again. The submersible sailed level now, at cruising depth. The idea of all the water surrounding her, not to mention the creatures that swam in it, filled Melni with a dread she did not know lived within her. In that instant she wanted nothing more in the world than to be off this boat.

At medical room two the Captain swept inside and moved far enough to allow Melni in beside her. Caswell lay on the examination table, naked save for a thick wrap of bandage around his midsection, already marred with a red stain the size of a fist. A drip line of water snaked from a bag down to an applicator protruding from his left arm.

His body was lean and scarred. His skin had a shocking lack of hair. Chest, arms, legs, and pubic area were all baby-smooth. Had it all been burned off? Or was this just another stylistic choice where he and Alia came from?

"Look at this," the doctor said to Liso. He pointed to a radiograph imager on the wall. The print showed Caswell's skeletal upper back, spine, and skull, taken from the side. The doctor's fingertip hovered near a small rectangular block attached to the spine just below the brain.

"What is it?" Captain Liso asked.

"I have no idea," the doctor replied. He and the captain both turned to Melni.

She ignored them and stared blankly at the image on the wall. Finally she crossed to Caswell and rotated his head to one side, examining the back of his neck. "No scar," she said.

"Doctor?" Liso asked. "Speculate."

Her word made Melni twitch, remembering the even, cold voice she'd spoken to from the public box.

The man fidgeted. "There has been some recent work on an implantable device to regulate one's heartbeat. Northern work. Of course it came from Valix Medical and we have not had a look at one yet. I assumed they would be much bigger than this, and implanted in the chest."

"You are certain it is artificial?"

The doctor stepped around the captain and pointed at the radiograph. "Absolutely. There are two wires. Here, and here. They terminate within the brain. I have never seen anything like it, Captain."

Melni ignored them and stared at the man on the bed. Did a similar device exist in Alia Valix's neck? Did it have something to do with her intelligence? The knowledge Caswell said she'd stolen?

Dr. Gilot cleared his throat. "Shall I remove it?"

Melni whirled. "No," she said.

The captain raised an eyebrow. "Something about this you want to tell us, Tavan?"

"I am afraid," she replied, "this is classified highest secrecy. As of now." The words spilled out with as much authority as she could muster.

Liso's face hardened. "It could be a weapon. If my ship is in jeopardy—"

"It is not a weapon. If it was he would have used it already. All I can tell you is this man has a connection to Alia Valix, and I suspect our betters back home will want to employ extraordinary care in examining him and that object."

A speaker on the wall by the door crackled, followed by a brief high-low chirp.

The captain crossed to it and held the transmit button. "Liso here, go ahead."

The tillmaster replied, his voice muted and tinny. "Six Combran warships just rounded the north edge of the bay."

"Six! You are sure?"

"No. We track seven now, the last coming from the west."

"Go silent," Liso said. "I will be right up." She pressed and held another button on the speaker. "Attention, crew. We are being pursued by hostiles and we are in their waters. We have something aboard they desperately want, and we will not give it to them."

The lights in the submersible dimmed to just a quarter of their previous strength and took on a bluish tinge.

The captain let go of the button. The lights, Melni realized, signaled a silent mode of operation that the crew likely drilled for constantly. Nothing more needed to be, or would be, said.

The captain studied her for a moment. She turned to the doctor. Her voice fell to just above a whisper. "Let me know if his condition changes. Tavan, you're to stay here in case he wakes. I am assigning two guards to the door. I will not have a stranger with ties to Valix wandering about my ship."

"Understood," Melni said. "And gratitude."

"If he dies," Captain Liso said to the doctor, "remove the device and cold-store it."

Melni started to object.

"Relax, Tavan. I suspect there will be a lot of people in Dimont who want to get a look at it. . . ."

"That resolves." The captain was right. Melni had let emotion cloud her judgment. "I . . . I will want to be present if it comes to that."

The captain looked at the doctor. He shrugged a tacit approval.

"All right then," Liso said. "Now we find out just how fast these new Combran boats really are."

Melni huddled against the wall opposite Caswell's bed, one arm looped through a pipe to keep herself steady as the submersible dove, climbed, and turned on some course completely invisible to her.

The doctor had left for a small chamber across the hall, and he'd taken the radiograph images with him. Writing a report for the Naval Information Office? Preparing surgical plans for removing the strange device in Caswell's neck? Both, probably. Melni stared at the unconscious man and tried to put out of her mind the chase going on beyond the hull.

"Would they go to war over you?" she whispered. "Are you that much of a risk to Valix?"

Caswell did not reply, of course. He barely clung to life. Once again she eyed his bag of supplies. Something in there could probably help him, as he'd helped her after a bullet tore through her arm. But foreign medicines were dangerous, too. If there was one thing in the bag that could save his life, there were probably others that could end it. She could do nothing but wait, and hope he had the chance to tell her what to do.

The submersible made another steep dive, moving Melni's weight almost entirely to the wall instead of the floor. Caswell shifted from the change in angle. He was strapped to the bed expertly, but his left hand and wrist dangled from the side of the bed now. A glint of silvery metal there caught her eye.

The bracelet.

She'd seen him glance at it often enough to guess it held extraordinary sentimental value for him. She stared at it for nearly a minute as the idea of betrayal germinated in her mind from the tiniest seed to something just shy of action. Not betrayal of him, but of Riverswidth. He'd be taken into custody the instant they reached Dimont, of that she had no doubt. The bag of supplies would be confiscated, too, if not sooner, along with the "needler" device if she decided to part with it. But the bracelet, if truly just a trinket, she could take, could claim as her own and then, when all this ended, return it to him. A token sign of regret for what would soon happen.

Or was it more than jewelry? Did it serve some other purpose she could not see, like the device in his neck? Exotic Valix tech not yet revealed to the world? She could check, she realized. If the ring of metal was just jewelry, she would hide it and return it to him when all this was over. He'd saved her life on more than one occasion. She could do this small favor for him, should he live.

Melni glanced up at the articulated arm of the radiograph imager above Caswell's bed, then at the open door of the tiny medical berth. She stood on shaky feet and climbed the steeply inclined floor to the entrance. Two guards, a man and a woman, stood—or rather leaned awkwardly— just outside. The hall was otherwise empty, but carried the hushed sounds of activity in other parts of the ship.

"Okay if I close the door?" Melni whispered to the guards. "I cannot sleep with it open."

The guards traded a glance, then shrugged indifferently in unison.

"Gratitude," Melni said.

She closed the door, careful to minimize the dull metallic thud when it sealed with the wall. Alone with the unconscious assassin, she studied the imager until she found the on switch. From a drawer beside the bed she found blank photo paper similar to the kind she kept in her old flat back in Midstav, along with a backing plate. The paper slid into grooves along the sides.

Melni placed Caswell's wrist on the glossy white sheet, then positioned the radiograph above it.

The submersible leveled out. The lights in the room turned a crimson red. A deep and ominous sound rippled through the entire vessel, rattling the walls and causing the metal to groan. A depth bomb. Melni went utterly still. War. It was really happening. Would the history books site her actions as the start of it? And what would they think back home? She could just as easily picture a heroes' welcome as a quiet execution in some dank cell below Presidium Square.

An indicator light on the radiograph's bulky imager turned blue. She adjusted it one last time over Caswell's bracelet and tapped the button. There was a sharp click that made Melni wince. Could a sound like that travel well enough to give away their position? She had no idea.

Another rolling boom seemed to answer the question. It sounded closer. The hull of the submersible groaned as the concussion wave passed through.

Melni slid the paper from its backing plate and stared at it as the image started to appear. She turned to the wall where the lightbox hung. Very carefully she flipped its power switch on, wincing as its overly bright light filled the tiny cabin.

Paper inserted, Melni watched with held breath as the picture exposing the innards of Caswell's wrist, and the bracelet upon it, took form.

This was no simple piece of jewelry. In fact complex shapes filled every bit of space possible beneath the silver outer shell. Most were incomprehensible to her, just sections of dark or light patches arranged in a way that implied electronics on a scale she'd never seen. The only bit she could recognize made her mouth tighten. Lettering, on the edge of one of the dark squares.

SAMSUNG / 2077-Q1 / MADE IN KOREA

Melni rolled this over in her head a dozen times as the submersible avoided Combran bombs. She knew of no Samsung or Korea. People's names? Places? The middle bit could be some kind of designator. Melni frowned, removing the bracelet to study it more closely, yet learning nothing. She slipped it back on his wrist and then, the sense of duty in her suddenly strengthened, she placed the needler device back in his bag.

Another explosion rocked the submersible violently to one side. The ceiling light flickered. From some distant corner of the vessel came the horrible sound of hissing gas or, worse, water.

Frantic footsteps clanged in the hall, silence evidently now a secondary concern. Melni turned off the lightbox and the imager and threw herself back into the far corner.

The door remained closed. The footsteps passed. She warred with a fear she'd not known she harbored: the fear of drowning. It had not manifested in the Think Tank, perhaps because there she'd known at least on some level that escape was possible, the waters something she could survive. But here . . . in the dark depths of the Endless Sea, what she feared was that endless cold embrace. Corpses were sent here, returned back to the core of Gartien for reuse. This was no place for the living.

"Please," she whispered. "Please."

Another explosion washed across the hull, but weaker than the last. Melni gripped a pipe on the wall and cringed. Another boom, this time like thunder on the horizon, barely audible through the walls.

Minutes passed in silence.

The light above her shifted from red to blue. All clear.

Not long after that the room tilted again. The submersible was ascending. Who waited above? Friends? Or had Captain Liso surrendered, not willing to sacrifice her crew for the life of a stranger?

Melni took the bracelet from Caswell and slipped it on her own wrist. She fetched the needler from his bag and stuffed it back into her sock.

Then she waited. Waited to emerge from the depths in the belly of a great sea monster, to face the unknown.

20

MELNI SAT with an engineer in the communications office, just opposite the captain's quarters. The thin woman held a headset to one ear, like a young version of Anim Corda. She was probably the one who transcribed Corda's meager reports from the Portstav listening post.

Repair crews rushed through the hallways of the submersible with each shrill sound of the alarm. Dozens of pipes had burst, spraying frigid water in fine mists. A number of the crew had been injured, bumps and bruises mostly, as the depth bombs took their progressive toll on the vessel. But they had made it. A near thing, judging by the constant congratulations offered to Captain Liso by her crew.

Fifty minutes earlier the vessel had passed under a blockade, hastily arranged by the Southern Naval Alliance on the loosely agreed border that bisected the Endless Sea along the path of the devastation. Captain Liso had fetched Melni from the medical berth sometime later, as if she had come to escort a prisoner to execution. "Quite the storm you have started, Agent," was all she'd said.

"Did they clash? Are we being pursued?" Melni had asked.

Liso had scowled. "No, they did not pursue. That should be obvious. But neither did they turn back. Right now they sit at the edge of range, waiting. A standoff, one they could easily win if they wish to press. You and your companion have brought us right to the cliff of war."

Melni had said nothing. Liso had brought her to the communications office, ordered her to sit and wait, and then stormed off.

The room had no door or even a back wall, but the hall beyond had been cleared to give her privacy. Melni wore the bulky set of earphones all the same, and kept her voice low.

Dials and meters covered the three walls around her, along with dozens of indicator lights and sheaves of laminated papers that hung from the ceiling on chains, swinging slightly with the waves outside the hull.

"You are connected," the engineer said. Then she backed away toward command, leaving Melni alone.

Melni put the headset on and leaned over the microphone. "14772 here," she said.

"Go ahead, 14772. Speak quickly. The Council is meeting right now to discuss this . . . incident, and they need information."

Melni spoke slowly and clearly, relating everything that had happened from the moment she'd set foot inside Alia Valix's den to the current situation aboard the submersible. Out of pure instinct she left out the details of what she'd seen inside Caswell's vessel, partly because she didn't fully understand it herself but mostly because she feared they would think she'd lost her mind or been drugged. Much of the story already sounded crazy; no need to add logs to that fire.

The person she spoke with was the same woman who'd spoken so tersely to her when she'd made contact from Midstav. This time she listened without interruption. Melni thought she could hear a pencil scrawling across paper when she finished her story.

The note taking went on for some time. Voice muffled, the woman said to someone, "Run this up to the Chamber. Tell them I sent you. Tell them whatever you have to, just get it into their hands." Her voice became clear again. "14772, remain on the link while this is reviewed."

"Understood," Melni replied. "May I ask a question?"

"Go ahead."

"Has there been any news of Valix? The way we left her . . . she may have drowned in there."

"Oh, there is news. You have poked the sleeping giant, Sonbo."

Melni grimaced, both at the news and the use of her real name. Her cover, gone, just like that. "What happened?"

"What has not? Troops amassing along the Desolation. Warships streaming out of every Northern naval base. Word of a whole squadron of airships approaching the Cirdian wastes."

"But Valix—"

"At first we received demands that her 'kidnapped employee' be returned immediately. She says this man with you is one of her top scientists, and their Triumvirate considers our snatching him an act of war."

Melni clenched her fists to stop them shaking. "At first, you said?"

"The tone changed as soon as Captain Liso beat them to the Desolation. A formal request for a summit was made, by Alia Valix herself. Top-level diplomats from the Northern Triumvirate and our Presidium will meet in four days in Fineva. Alia Valix has asked to speak to both sides."

The motivation, the ramifications, eluded Melni. Too many things were happening at once. "Why?"

"Speculate."

Not this again. She tried, as she often had when sitting alone at night in her flat, to think as Alia Valix. Airships, police in relentless pursuit, the attack on Anim's listening post, and then a fleet of warships chasing this submersible to the dividing line. Right to the edge of war. Yet the instant Caswell crosses to the South, she asks for a summit. *She knows she has lost,* Melni thought. *But has she, really?* The North had enough might to get their supposedly kidnapped employee back. Maybe Valix didn't want to risk him dying in a full-scale battle. But that didn't resolve, either. They'd tried their hardest to kill him in Combra. They'd come perilously close. Why stop now?

She said, "Valix is afraid of what he might tell us. They could come after him, kill him, but not quickly enough. Not now."

Silence from the other end.

Melni went further. Alia Valix, always one step ahead of

everyone. "So . . . whatever he might give us, she . . . she is going to give it to us first. That must be it. Own the conversation, take away the value he provides, the leverage he gives us."

"Not bad, Agent Sonbo."

"What will the speech be about?"

"Nobody knows. Except perhaps for the man with you. If he really is her top scientist—"

"That part is birdshit. Forgive my language. He is an assassin. He was there to kill her."

"Are you so sure? Absolutely sure, Agent?"

The question, the tone, made Melni pause.

Before she could reply, the stern voice from Riverswidth went on. "You just happened upon this 'assassin' inside the supposedly impregnable Think Tank, which I may add you also just happened to gain entry to simultaneously. Two incursions on the same night? And there is just enough birdshit oddities in this man's story to keep us confused but curious? You will forgive us if we are skeptical."

"I . . . are you saying it is all a ruse? They have tried to kill us at every turn."

"And just barely missing, at every turn."

Melni swallowed. She considered that, refused to believe it. She'd been there. Herself, shot through the arm. Caswell, even now, near death in the medical berth three decks below. "To what end?"

"I should think exactly the end we now fall helplessly toward. A Valix operative, from the Think Tank to inside Riverswidth in less than a week's time. A brilliant plan, is it not? Worthy of a genius, you might say."

The floor beneath Melni's feet seemed to drop away from her, and not from any motion of the boat. Her stomach twisted in knots. A cold sweat suddenly coated her brow, her neck, her arms, as if pushed out by the pressure within. She gripped the edges of the table until her knuckles turned white as snow.

"Are you there, Agent?" the voice asked.

"What am I to do now?" Melni asked through gritted teeth. She saw her own career, not just her covert mission in

Combra but the entirety of it, ending. "Do you want me to kill him? Say his injuries were fatal?"

"If you do that I am certain the summit will be canceled, and I would very much like to hear what Valix has to say."

"What do you plan to do, then?"

"Ah," the stern voice replied. "Here is the runner now with a reply from the Chamber."

The dull hum of static filled Melni's ears as the woman apparently read the leadership's response.

"Exactly as I had hoped," the woman finally said. "14772, I have revised orders for you."

"Prepared to comply, with gratitude," Melni said automatically, picturing herself entering Caswell's room and covering his mouth and nose until the life drained from him.

"The man with you will be," the woman said, "brought here. To Riverswidth."

Melni let go of the desk. "Is that not exactly what you just—"

"Precisely, Agent."

"I do not follow." But she did, in her heart. She understood exactly what they intended to do. She pictured Caswell, shivering, naked, chained up and groveling for rancid food in one of those dank cells above Riverswidth.

"Should he wake you are to maintain the impression that he is seen as friendly. Tell him you have resources here that can help both you and him accomplish your missions. Should he suspect our true intentions you will apprehend him and bring him in against his will. Either way, we shall learn everything we can from him before this summit takes place. Does that resolve?"

Melni's gaze slid to the bracelet. That small betrayal, that infernal seed. "It resolves," she said.

He woke once, a few hours later. Confused, brow beaded with sweat, lips pale and as thin as his eyes. He kept those eyes closed despite the dark room and managed only to whisper a single question: "Did she survive?"

"She did," Melni told him. "In fact she has invited both sides to a summit. In a neutral place, four days from now."

"Four days," he repeated. He repeated it several times, and this seemed to content him.

Caswell drifted back into his fitful sleep after that.

He did not wake again on the sub. Nor during transfer to the *WS Bright Fragment,* a sleek new warship named for the famous folktale. Nor during the day and night that followed as the massive boat powered along the Lungwyn coast toward South Vorseland and finally to Dimont.

Bright Fragment was a massive ship with a full hospital. They gave Melni her own quarters, then confined her there for the voyage. The captain and her senior crew were kind enough, but it had become clear to Melni within a few minutes of stepping aboard that, at least while Caswell remained comatose, she was to be treated as potentially under the influence of the enemy.

She could not find it within herself to blame them. More unsettling than this treatment was the promise of what waited within the soaring towers of Riverswidth, only just visible on the dusty horizon out her porthole window.

Melni's mission, so near success, had in truth been a failure. Alia, Valix Corp., the NRD . . . all of them had known of her role and the turning of Onvel from very early on. Every thing she'd reported, every scrap of intelligence slipped into that drawer in Croag & Daughters, was now just so much paper. All of it would be considered unreliable, useless.

And as if that weren't bad enough, she might now be bringing a trained killer into the very heart of the Southern opposition. The fact that this possibility had never even occurred to her hurt her most of all. She felt like a fish swimming with serpents. A child among adults, sipping juice while they drank cham, speaking as if she knew everything there was to know and not realizing just how shallow that well really was.

She opened her window to breathe the air coming in off the azure waters. It smelled less of the ocean and more the machinery of the ship. She stayed anyway, eyes closed and nose poked proudly through the opening, until the first scents of her homeland came carried in on the warm breeze. Pleasant smells, a flood of nostalgia. The scents of home, of childhood, of memory. Dust and sand and baked bricks. Olives and spices beyond count. Phantom scents, she felt sure, but memory had a way of filling in such blanks and she had no desire to complain.

She was home. A second-class *desoa,* maybe, but she was home.

Whatever they planned to do with her, this at least they could not take away. She would face their questions and whatever consequences followed, and with any luck, she'd be dismissed to a civilian life. She could see her sister again, perhaps repair the rift that had formed between them so many years ago. She'd never see the man Caswell again, or know his fate, of that she felt sure. The mystery would grate on her for the rest of her life, but at least it would be a life lived out of danger. Unless the North came. Airships and soldiers and naval monstrosities all powered by equipment directly or indirectly invented by Alia Valix, the woman Melni had been sent to spy on. To convert, if possible. Interrogate and eliminate if not.

Instead she'd made a gigantic mess of things, left the South's espionage apparatus in Combra in tatters, and brought home a mystery man who might in fact be a carefully placed weapon.

"Meiki Sonbo." She whispered her own name, her real one, to the sprawling skyline of Dimont. She hadn't used the name in years, hadn't even realized she'd given Captain Liso her assumed identity. It had become automatic to do so.

A long sigh escaped her lips. She'd have to forget everything, she thought, but only after they were done asking questions of Melni Tavan. Until then, she decided, she would keep the name, if only for herself. If only to remember.

Once in harbor she was transferred again, this time to a small craft of nondescript coloration and marking. She took a seat in a common room just behind the control area and avoided eye contact with the plain-clothed crew. Whether Caswell was aboard, or if they planned to question him on the warship, she had no idea. They took his bag from her before she left. She wondered what they'd make of the strange assortment of supplies inside.

Soon the little craft turned and weaved away from the huge military ship and began the winding journey upstream. In the hour that followed Melni did her best to clear her mind of the future. She replayed the events of the past week, focused herself on the task of remembering. They would want it all, she knew, and she saw no reason to hide anything. Except, perhaps, for Caswell's "ride home." And the needler tube concealed in her clothing. And the bracelet. Melni resolved to keep those things to herself until the situation, and the South's intentions, became clearer. Betrayal or not, she knew on a level beneath conscious thought that something was not right here. She knew something else, too: Caswell had been truthful with her, right from the very beginning. Except for claiming he was a Hollow Man, and even that he took back.

Which meant only one thing: Valix was the liar here.

Riverswidth, as the name suggested, spanned the width of the Riv Dimont—the river of two hills—which bisected the capital city, Dimont. Calm brown waters flowed at a languid pace below the whitestone archways of the ancient bridge. A hundred feet wide and more than a thousand long, the original span served as a pedestrian walkway between two early nation-states. Eventually traders realized neither state could claim ownership of the bridge itself, and therefore laws regarding street commerce did not apply. Unification eventually nullified these legal loopholes, but the market had become so entrenched and seedy that the new post-Desolation Presidium had ordered it completely torn down. Replacing the old shanty storefronts were modern offices, as well as meeting halls, and even the estates of the Presidium. Riverswidth went from a treacherous, murder-soaked black market to the seat of military and intelligence power for the Unified South in less than a decade.

Melni watched the river-spanning compound glide toward her and fought back tears. She loved this place. Not just Riverswidth but all of it—the city, the people, the memories. Not a day had passed in Combra that she hadn't dreamed of returning. Yet for all her long-term planning and analysis of her life, she never saw herself returning here a disgrace, a failure.

She stared at the hundreds of windows that faced the sea and wondered how many bureaucrats were gazing down upon her now, mentally hanging her up to blame for the brink of war upon which all of Gartien now stood.

A cool shudder rippled through her as the little watercraft slid beneath the walls of Riverswidth and up to one of the dark, slimy private docks below the complex. The wooden structures were fairly new, bolted on to the original stone columns that supported the massive structure above. A pang of latent grief for Old Gartien coursed through Melni as she studied these columns. The bottom ten feet were colored differently than the rest. Once they'd been under the river's surface, only to be exposed later when the planet cooled in the aftermath of the Desolation. All that water, now packed as ice on either pole.

Four armed women escorted her up a slippery stepwell and into the bowels of the South's intelligence headquarters. Almost everyone she passed reminded her of Caswell, with narrow eyes and a median complexion. Their eyes were almost all light blue, however, in stark contrast to Caswell's near-black. She could feel those ice-blue stares slide over her, instantly marking her for what she was: not native. A *desoa*. Melni had grown used to being in the North, where her pale skin and purple eyes, while not anything like the native Northerner's cham-colored skin and amber eyes, was at least considered exotic rather than some kind of defect.

To her surprise she was not interrogated, nor even questioned. Not even a perfunctory debriefing. The escort led her to the property office, where her personal effects were handed to her in a sealed paper bag. Things she'd had on her the day she'd departed for the long, convoluted journey to Combra. The clothes she'd had on. Her backpurse. Keys to a tiny home on the city's eastern edge. A simple silver necklace with a charm she'd received on her firstwords.

"Am I being dismissed?" she asked those around her. Blank faces looked back. One of them shrugged.

The property master regarded her over the rims of his wire-frame glasses. "There is a carrier waiting for you at the low end. House arrest, until this is sorted. That is the word that came down, anyway," he said, his gaze darting upward at the last to imply the Situation Room on the top floor directly above them. "These four will remain with you, and someone from Situations will be in contact if and when the need arises."

The members of her escort did not look especially happy about their assignment.

"But I have—"

"That is all I know, Agent," the man said. He went back to his paperwork.

Melni sighed. "My house is too small for five."

"Which is why," he said without glancing up, "you will be staying at the Hotel International."

It was a state-owned hotel on the coast, primarily used for visiting politicians and their staff. The hotel was well appointed, with great views of Flat Bay and the ocean beyond. Every room was monitored, every word recorded. It was better than a prison cell, but only just. Wondering when she'd be allowed to visit her own home, or seek out her sister, Melni scribbled her signature for the sack of items and followed her new family out into the middle span of the old bridge, which served as a walkway from the northern High End to the southern Low End.

A reinforced cruiser awaited her, in the sand coloration of the Army. Melni spent the drive along the edge of Riv Dimont watching her true home blur past. For all her internal complaining while in Combra, it somehow seemed more like home to her now than this place. So much color here, so much noise. It smelled terrible. Kids in filthy rags ran up and down the narrow, crowded streets. Almost everyone was on foot. Exposed pipes and the occasional power line criss-crossed above. Compared to the gleaming world Valix was building, this place felt half a world and half a century away. Finally the squeaky old vehicle turned and dropped into the maze of hundred-year-old apartment towers and street-level shops that made up most of the city.

The Sun blinded and baked relentlessly. No one seemed in a hurry to get anywhere, or happy with the prospect of facing another day. Errand runners dawdled along on their signature white bicycles.

By the time the carrier thundered up to the Hotel International's staff entrance her shirt was soaked with sweat and her mood as sour as Combran grapes. A porter greeted them and, after being momentarily flustered by her *desoa* looks and her four armed escorts, led Melni to a rather incredible suite of rooms on the top floor overlooking the ocean. To her at least it seemed the type of place a head of state would be afforded, and for a moment her mood brightened. Perhaps she was not the pariah after all. This thought lasted until the sober realization that her four new best friends would be staying here with her, with the bedroom assigned to Melni at the back farthest from the exit. And the room, so high up, offered zero chance of escape by scaling the outside wall.

Melni decided to make the most of it. She threw open the windows to let in the sweet ocean air, heat be damned, then went to the communal lav. After a long shower, first hot then cold, she tapped hospitality and ordered lunch: eggs fried with sea salt, a basket of toasted brown bread with seasonal jam, leaf salad dusted with tree nuts, plus juice and a whole pot of strong, spicy cham. Cuisine shunned by every mealhouse in Combra on principle.

She ate slowly, sipped her cham on the balcony to the concert of waves crashing below, then slept. The sheets were stiff and smelled of flowers, the mattress deep and soft in the Southern style. She'd missed that comfort while abroad, had complained about it to herself on countless occasions. Now she found the opposite to be the truth. The North, with their thin, stiff sleeping pads, had the better idea. This bed felt as if it wanted to swallow her.

Still, she found sleep.

Activity outside woke her at sunset. Wrapped in a soft robe, Melni moved to the balcony and simply watched and listened. The beach below was separated from the city by a long boardwalk. Hundreds of people strolled its length in the warm glow of the setting son. Couples arm in arm. Families with giggling children. The wealthy, here on the coast. Not a *desoa* among them, most likely. She wondered if their mood was in ignorance of the stand-off with the North, or because of it.

She sat on the balcony until her weariness returned. It didn't take long. Melni stood and turned her back on the world. She went to the welcoming bed, lay down, and slept again. Wonderful, dreamless sleep. In the heat of the morning she'd kicked away her blankets and robe, waking naked and sticky with sweat almost five hours later. Humidity and heat, she'd forgotten what a burden they could be. Funny how the nostalgic mind edited out such details.

Another shower, then she dressed in the spare clothing that had been in her bag. The service had washed it for her, thankfully. It was a simple, Southern-style outfit. She slipped Caswell's "needler" tube back into her sock. Then she took his bracelet, far too loose on her own wrist, and hung it from the silver necklace they'd returned to her. The flat loop of strange metal hung just below her shoulder line, partially hidden by her blouse. It looked rather stylish, she thought. If anyone asked she'd claim it the latest fashion on Combra.

A knock at the door. The inner, bedroom door.

"Yes?" Melni prompted.

An older woman entered. Melni recognized her instantly. Rasa Clune, director of information for the entire Southern Alliance. A tall, stout woman with a pinched, hard Southerner's face under a thin crop of silver hair.

"Agent Sonbo," the woman said, using Melni's real name. "It is time we talked in person."

"Please, sit," Melni said, gesturing to one of the two high-backed plush chairs in the welcoming room.

Clune had dismissed the four armed escorts to wait in the hallway outside. She wore a military uniform, flawlessly pressed and covered in decorations. The desert colors were a marked contrast to the deep crimson of the chair. Melni took the other seat, feeling suddenly underdressed in her pedestrian knee-length shorts with a very loose white blouse, decorated by an ornate red and gold sash diagonally across her midsection. A classic Southern style she hadn't worn since the day she'd handed the outfit over to the property master before starting her mission.

Melni had seen Rasa Clune twice before: once on the day she graduated into the information service, and once on the day she'd been selected for an underguise assignment across the Endless Sea. On both occasions the powerful woman had not even so much as made eye contact with her. Melni tried to recall what she knew of Clune. Thirty years of service to the alliance, the last ten of which in her present capacity. It was said she'd once worked in the field, but her classic Southern features likely meant assignments on this side of the crater line.

"I am sorry we could not let you go home," Clune said. "Once this business is over you will be placed on the standard leave any returning covert agent receives: a full month. You shall be free to travel as you like. I have authorized your withheld salary to be deposited into your account, so if you wish anything while you are here just ask the hotel staff and they shall fetch it for you."

Melni swallowed. "Gratitude," she managed to say, picturing a swarm of agents picking through her house for any signs of treachery. There could be no other reason for keeping her from the place, or implying she'd have to purchase material items she required rather than having them brought from home.

"Is there anything you wish to request at this time?" Clune asked.

A breeze off the ocean stirred the drapes. Warm sunlight danced on the carpet between them. Melni found the heat of the South stifling suddenly. Rasa Clune looked perfectly comfortable despite her stiff, heavy outfit.

"I just want to work, Director. To help resolve this situation," Melni said. "I feel responsible, though I'm not sure what I could have done differently."

Stern ice-blue eyes peered out from between the narrow slits of Clune's wizened, tired lids. Was that a hint of disgust there? The undercurrent of racism Melni hadn't dealt with since leaving? An old, deep-seated worry welled up inside her, the idea that Melni was not truly one of *them*. And worse, now that she'd lived north of the Desolation, she might harbor empathy for the enemy.

"Well," Clune said after a moment, "it turns out you can help us."

Melni leaned forward, too eager and not caring. "Yes. Tell me, please. Anything."

"This man you came south with . . ."

A tingle ran up Melni's spine. She shivered. "Has he died?"

"He lives," Clune said. "In and out of consciousness, but he lives."

Melni nodded.

The leader of the South's entire covert apparatus looked Melni up and down. Her gaze lingered, only slightly, on the bracelet Melni wore around her neck. "Do you believe you were 'played,' agent? That bringing him here was a carefully scripted trick? That he is in fact here to spy on us?"

"No," Melni replied, with too much uncertainty. She said it again with more conviction. "No."

"You surrendered all of his belongings upon arrival, correct?" The woman's gaze darted to Melni's neck, then back up.

Melni's own eyes betrayed her. She glanced down, flustered. "I . . ."

"What is that, Agent Sonbo?"

Melni pulled the chain over her head. "I forgot about this. My regret. It is only jewelry."

Director Clune leaned forward and held out a hand. When the bracelet landed there, she folded her wrinkled fingers around it and slipped it into a pocket at her waist. "We shall let the analysts determine that. Anything else?"

For a second Melni hesitated. She felt the slim tube against her ankle, the cool metal against her skin. She couldn't quite say why, but something about Rasa Clune's accusing manner made her shake her head.

"Good," Clune said. "Now, speculate. Who is he?"

Speculate. So it had been Clune that Melni had been speaking with all this time. Straight to the top, and she hadn't even known. "An assassin. Perhaps a Hollow Man—"

"He is no Hollow Man, Agent Sonbo, I assure you. But you know this. I can hear in your voice that you do not believe your own words. Try again. Whatever hypothesis you have dreamed up in your head, no matter how silly, I want to hear it. Now."

The last word fell like the crack of a whip.

Melni steeled herself, folded her hands in her lap. When she spoke next she raised her chin slightly and maintained eye contact. "In truth I do believe he is an assassin. He was in the Think Tank to kill Alia Valix, I have no doubt. He may have succeeded if I had not been there."

"You disrupted his attack?"

"Not on purpose. My presence was unexpected. Alia used that to her advantage."

"Hmm," Clune said. She clucked her tongue a few times. "All right. Go on."

"As I mentioned in my report—"

"I do not care what the report said. I want to hear this from you."

"Yes, Director," Melni said. "Valix knew him. She even implied he had tried to kill her before and failed."

"Not a very good assassin, then."

"No! I mean, he is. I have seen him kill. More than I care to admit. He is brutal and exceptionally skilled. No, I think it is just that Valix is so clever."

"Hmm," Clune said again. She motioned with a flick of one wrist for Melni to continue.

"I have two theories, I suppose. The first, more plausible, is that he and Valix grew up together in some kind of highly isolated community of prodigies. Perhaps they were born there, bred to be extremely intelligent. Valix escaped, and he was sent to find her and keep the existence of this place secret."

"You believe this?"

Melni shook her head, reluctantly. "It is plausible, but does not explain . . . many things. Where such a place could be. How it became so advanced. How it has remained hidden." She thought of the tube against her leg, the bracelet now in Clune's pocket, and all the items in Caswell's bag.

"Stop wasting my time, then, Sonbo. What is the second theory?"

"Well," Melni said, hedging. She broke eye contact then and fixed her gaze on the whitecaps drifting casually across the ocean view. "It is stupid—"

"Speculate!"

The word was so sharp Melni jumped. "I asked him if he had come back through time."

Clune did not laugh, to Melni's great surprise. Instead she leaned forward, and her eyes became so narrow the blue disappeared between the wrinkled lids. "And?"

"He said, 'That's not far from the truth.'"

"Meaning what?"

Melni spread her hands. "It is idiotic, I know."

"I will decide that. Meaning what, Sonbo?"

"He did not say. He evaded. Later he said to pretend he had just been unfrozen from the ice."

Clune's head tilted slightly to one side. She stared at Melni for a long time, her expression no more readable than stone. "Does he trust you?" she finally asked, her voice just barely audible.

"I do not know."

"Does he love you?"

Melni met her gaze. "What?"

"Is he attracted to you? He gave you the bracelet, yes? Did you have any amorous contact during your time together?"

"No. No."

Clune looked skeptical.

"Why?" Melni asked. "What did he say?"

The woman rose to her feet. She straightened the front of her outfit. "The prisoner said he will only talk to you. We have four days until the summit. Four days to find out as much from him as possible."

"I thought it was in two days."

"They asked for more time. A good sign, it means they do not know where he is and thus resort to stalling."

Or they are devising a way to get him back, Melni thought. She decided not to voice that. Rasa Clune was the mastermind behind virtually every covert campaign Riverswidth ran. If anyone would understand the facets of a situation like this, she would.

Clune continued. "You will get him to talk. Hurt him if you must. Love him if that is what he requires. Anything it takes. Does that resolve?"

Melni could only nod.

PART 3
TRUTH OF ORIGIN

21

A LARGE, LUXURIOUS CRUISER waited in front of the hotel, along with armed escorts astride ominous black thumper cycles.

Clune sat beside Melni on the rear bench seat. The windows were up, making the interior of the vehicle feel like an oven. Combined with the peculiar sour odor Rasa Clune's body gave off, Melni felt nauseous by the time they turned and entered the security barricades at the start of the bridge.

"You will be taken directly to the subject," Clune said. "Talk to him. Alone, but fear not. We will be listening, of course."

"Of course."

"When he sleeps I want you to work with Analytics. Specifically the linguists. Tell them everything you can remember. His mannerisms as much as what he said. Not only the information but the specific words he used. Between your information and their investigation into the items recovered from his supply bag, we may be able to identify where he comes from without his help."

"Yes, Director," Melni said. "Anything you ask." She should have admitted right then to the "needler" tube hidden in her sock. She should have, but held back. Caswell's warnings about children being fed answers haunted her.

A second gate finally rolled aside and the oversize cruiser burped and rattled its way into the bowels of Riverswidth.

Melni followed the tall, stout form of Clune at a brisk march through a half-dozen buildings and up many steps before finally reaching the prison area, high above the water. She'd never been in here before, and never wanted to return, either. It was dark and damp, a maze of drab gray walls and tiny square windows that seemed to be purposefully sized smaller than a child's shoulder width. The guards, who were legion, were all pure Southerners and seemed to soak their mood straight from the dreadful confines.

Cells lined the narrow stone corridors, a number plate riveted into the old walls beside each door. Lamps hung from the ceiling, connected by a thick wire that sagged between the pools of light. Old construction, dating back before the Desolation. She tried to imagine all the people held in these ancient cells over the centuries. All the suffering, the compelled interrogations. To walk through such a place led by the infamously cruel Rasa Clune made her skin crawl.

A door at the end of the cell block led into a newer area. There were as many guards here, though they were outnumbered by white-coated doctors and their support staff. Clune greeted one of the doctors with a terse nod. The man saluted her and fell naturally into the lead of their little entourage.

"Any changes?" Clune asked.

"None. Not to his condition at least," the doctor replied. He was young and handsome. In fact he looked quite a bit like Caswell, except for the long hair, which he kept tied back, as was common in such professions.

"Explain."

The doctor glanced back at Melni.

"You can speak freely," Clune said to him. "She is the one who brought him here."

His expression shifted, evidently matching his impression of her as it changed from risk to possible asset. "Well, it is very interesting. He has some peculiarities I cannot explain nor have I ever seen before. Variations in bone structure. A unique arrangement of the internal organs."

"Unique how?"

"It is as if his insides are a mirror reflection of ours. Heart on the left, and so on. Everything reversed. And he has four more teeth than you or I. Not the kinds of things you'd notice on a cursory inspection, but there all the same."

"Valix said he was a geneticist. Are you telling me he is not the experimenter but the experiment?"

"My opinion is that this is not natural."

"How interesting," Clune said. "What about the object in his neck?"

"Per your orders I have not inspected it firsthand. But I can confirm it is not a tumor. I am certain it is artificial."

Melni idly fingered her neck where the bracelet had been, remembering what she'd seen when she'd taken a radiograph of it. What secrets would be revealed by the object inside Caswell's neck?

The doctor led them into a dim observation room. A one-way mirror dominated one wall, looking in on a modern hospital room. Modern by Southerner standards, at least. Nothing like what they had in Combra.

Caswell lay sleeping on a semi-reclined bed in the center, surrounded by various equipment. There were two other people in the observation chamber. One, a nurse, leaned casually against the back wall, hands clasped behind his back. He came alert at the sight of the doctor, and went rigid at Clune's presence. The other person sat hunched over some listening gear, manipulating dials. A large dual-reel recorder dominated the equipment, and the analyst sitting before it wore thick earphones.

"Agent Sonbo," Clune said. "Get in there and see if he will talk." She moved to stand behind the analyst.

The doctor crossed to the inner door and opened it for Melni. On her way through he handed her a tray of food. Simple fare. "See if he will eat, too," he said.

Melni nodded and took the tray, knowing that the food would make Caswell vomit. She entered the room and waited for the door to click shut behind her. The instant it did, Caswell stirred.

22

THE DOOR HISSED OPEN. Another nurse, more than likely. Another meal he couldn't eat. Why did they keep trying? He wanted to roar, to shout at them to just let him die. Everything they did only made his suffering worse. But he didn't have the energy to waste on that. He lay as still as possible, kept his mouth shut, and waited for Melni.

A hand brushed his arm. Caswell cracked one eye open and there she was, standing next to him, a sympathetic smile playing at the corners of her mouth. She'd dressed differently. Civilian clothes, but not like the drab stiffness of the North. It looked good on her.

"How do you feel?" she asked.

He blinked the sleep away and worked his jaw. His throat felt like sandpaper. "Water," he croaked.

"You have a drink line attached."

Caswell shook his head and forced out more words. "Yank it. Please. You know how my body reacts."

He'd asked the same of every nurse and doctor he'd seen since waking, but they'd all ignored him. Melni, however, complied. She twisted the plastic tube and set it, dripping, beside his thigh.

"Now," he said. "Water. Mouth tastes like something died in it."

Melni glanced back at the huge mirror on the wall behind her, waiting for some kind of sign. A few seconds later the door opened six inches and one of the nurses handed a mug of water through.

"Gratitude," Caswell said. He could not hold the mug himself. His wrists were bound to the bed with thick leather straps. His legs, as well. Melni held the cup to his lips and watched as he sipped, her face carefully blank. Caswell swirled the fluid around in his cheeks and spat it back into the cup.

The room smelled of soap and overprocessed air. A cool breeze wafted in from a grate on the ceiling just above the door. It tickled his skin.

She set the mug down, stood beside him, and hugged herself. "They said you'd only talk to me."

Caswell managed a nod. Sweat beaded on his fevered brow. His lips felt wrong, like they'd been drained and numbed. "Your medicines aren't working for me, nor is your food. I asked the doctor to stop providing them but he insists."

"You may die without them."

"I will die because of them. Melni, please. Find my supplies. There are some things in there that can help me."

Her face remained blank, but her purple eyes darted toward the mirror on the wall. A one-way mirror, obviously. He wondered who was watching, and what they'd threatened her with. More than that, he wondered where her loyalties lay.

"What things? What do they do, exactly?"

"You're worried I intend to poison myself?"

Melni shrugged. "No, but there are others who harbor this concern."

"Hmm," Caswell muttered through pursed lips. "Well, I don't know how to convince them. I have a mission to fulfill. I won't take my own life while my goal goes unmet. Even then, quite frankly, suicide is not my cup of tea. Er, cham."

He slumped, exhausted from the little speech. His hands reflexively lifted, strained for a moment against the leather straps. He needed to rub his temples, to flood his brain with chemicals that could help him focus. And take the pain away.

Melni studied him for a moment and then something changed in her. A decision reached. Doubt replaced by sympathy, and focus as well. She offered him another sip of water, then seemed to remember he could not drink it.

Caswell met her gaze, held it. "How long until the summit?"

"Four days," Melni said. "What do you need from the bag?"

Still four days. He let himself relax. When he'd woke he asked everyone who entered how long he'd been unconscious. It had felt like days. But no one would talk to him, and the bastards had taken his watch. The doctor spoke only to say he would be the one asking questions. Caswell had spat in the man's face. That effort had left him delirious, but felt good all the same. Then Caswell demanded to see Melni. Said he'd only talk to her. The rash words, born of anger and frustration, had worked. An unexpected gift.

"Food. Any of those meal packets."

Melni looked down at her hands. "I doubt they will agree to that when you refuse all nourishment we provide."

"Then you tell them, Melni. You saw me try to eat, you saw how my body reacts. Tell them."

"I . . ." She trailed off, her mouth suddenly a thin line.

He studied her closely, watched her eyes. She knew he couldn't eat the local food, but she hadn't told them. What did it mean? "Then my medicines," he said, without hope. "The vial marked Vespilin-4. It will clear up any infection in my blood, hopefully, and along with a few of the water bulbs my body will start to replace what I lost already."

"I will ask. Is that all?"

"No. Ibuproxin. Nothing fancy about that one, it just helps manage pain. The dose is normally two. I'll need four, every twenty-four hours, at least until the food starts to do its thing."

Melni let out an involuntary laugh, then composed herself.

He glanced at her. "What?"

"Twenty-four hours is oddly specific."

"Once per day—" Caswell winced at his mistake. "Ten hours, I meant. Once per day. Why are you staring at me like that?"

She put a hand on his arm. "That was no innocent slip of words just then, was it? You make so many such mistakes."

"I told you: thawed out of the ice."

She slid her chair closer. "Tell me where you come from, Caswell. The truth. What culture marks the days in twenty-four hours instead of ten? I have never heard of such a thing in all our history."

He just stared at her. A second ago she'd seemed happy to withhold information about him, but now she'd cut right to the meat. What was going on? Why act as if she didn't know about his food and medicine? *Perhaps she's hidden it from them. And if so, she's risking an awful lot.* He battled for focus. He couldn't misstep here. She was the only ally he had. The only chance.

"I like you, Caswell," she added while he thought. "We have been through much together. But the people who run this place believe you and Alia Valix are carved from the same stone. That your mind may be equal to hers. That you are the key to matching the North invention for invention, and therefore our only hope. Our actions in Combra have brought the Quiet War to the brink of being something much louder. My superiors need help. They need you. *We* need you. And they will use pain to get the answers they want."

He closed his eyes. *She needs this for herself,* he realized. Whoever listened from the other side of that mirror would write off his answers as lunacy, but Melni wouldn't. He could see it in her face. If he gave her the truth, she would accept it.

A timepiece on the wall whirred away, clicked as another minute passed. Melni's hand came to rest on his shoulder. A gentle squeeze, giving permission.

"I'm not of this world," he said, after a time.

"Meaning what?"

"Exactly that. I come from another world. Called Earth. Alia does, too, only she's not called Alia there. She's Alice Vale. She came here as part of the expedition that accidentally discovered your world. When she realized how similar your planet, your species, was to ours, she decided to stay."

He paused, opening his eyes and gauging Melni's reaction. She gave an almost imperceptible nod to continue.

"Our world is roughly one hundred and twenty years ahead of yours, technologically. More in some areas, less in others. Think about what you know of this woman, and I think you'll understand the opportunity she saw here."

"So she came here with this knowledge, found an ally in the North, and decided to benefit only them?"

"Not the North," he said. A stab of pain from his implant warned him away from thought-lock protected knowledge. He winced. "My training makes talking about this very difficult. You'll have to guess again."

Melni thought it over. "She does this to benefit herself."

Caswell said nothing.

She knew by now what that meant. "Why come after her now? What changed, after all these years?"

"It was only recently that we realized where she'd gone. That she'd survived at all. Her ship was found adrift, a wreck, after a dozen years missing. The rest of her crew were all there, dead."

Melni's brow furrowed. "In the Think Tank she claimed you killed them."

"I know," he said, suddenly tired. "You'd think I'd remember something like that. . . ."

"But how is this travel possible? Through time? Across the emptiness between stars?"

"A damn good question," Caswell said. "I don't understand it myself. Perhaps no one does. Your planet looks almost exactly like mine. We even speak the same language. Crazy, I know, but there it is. None of this is important right now, though. Listen, Melni, the point is we—I mean our leaders—would not have handled such a discovery this way. The way Alia has, I mean. She acts selfishly. Does more harm than good."

"Depends which side you are on."

He grunted a laugh, then winced at the pain it caused. "Do you recall what I said about a child being given all the answers instead of learning them on its own?"

Melni nodded.

"I know it will be hard to hear this, but whatever wondrous technology we could give you, at the very least you should be able to see that a much more nuanced approach is desirable. For both our worlds. You have a sovereign right to advance on your own. To learn and understand rather than just be told. And then meet us when you're ready. And if I may be blunt, many people on my world would argue that much of our knowledge should be deliberately withheld from you so as to maintain an advantage. Some knowledge, given to a child, is dangerous. Lethal."

"I . . . 'understand,'" she said, using his word.

"If I hadn't come along—hell, even now that I have—how long will it be before Valix is the most powerful person on Gartien?"

"She already is," Melni said carefully. Again the eyes drifted toward the mirror.

He went on, despite warnings from his implant. He craned his neck toward her, ignoring the restraints. He had to convince her of the reason for his goals because the chances of him completing the mission were becoming perilously small. "How long before her mark on this world is irrevocable? I know it's hard to look at an offered gift and decide, no, you'd rather earn it on your own, but that's what your world must do. You have to let me go. You have to let me fulfill my task."

Melni's face grew tight. She waited a moment before speaking, choosing her words with great care. When she did speak her voice had changed. Tuned for those listening, not for him. "Perhaps, knowing Alia's true background and motives, we can manage her better? Consider each of her so-called inventions through this lens."

"No," Caswell said. "No. You're missing the point. Damn it. I knew this would happen."

"Is there something more to this that you are not telling me?"

"Listen, Melni. You have to make your people understand. Alia . . . some of the knowledge she has would lead to terrible things. Weap—" A stab of pain slammed into his brain from the neck. Caswell grunted, fought it back. He flirted dangerously now with a total wipe of his mind. "She could end all life here if she wished. No one . . . *no one* . . . should have that power. Not their side, not yours. Do you understand me?" He searched her eyes. "Make your people understand, before your entire world is held hostage."

Weakness and agony overcame him. Caswell slumped back into his pillow, warring with the pain of Monique's thought-lock measures, his wounds, his empty stomach and parched throat. He didn't want to sleep, but sleep came like a bullet.

"Fascinating," Rasa Clune said in her flat, emotionless voice.

Melni waited until the door clicked closed behind her. "So you believe him?"

Clune emitted a dry chuckle. "This man is insane. And it does not matter. While you were in there the Presidium received a much more plausible explanation for our guest, straight from Valix herself."

"What explanation?"

"The one I assumed. That he experimented on himself. He illicitly set up some advanced isolation lab and hid it in the mountains, then began injecting himself with gene-altering chemicals, something he had been working on for Valix that they decided was too dangerous to pursue. Now he has confused some fantastical childhood fiction with reality."

"Oh," was all Melni could say.

Director Clune squinted at her, turned, and went to the doctor. They began to converse quietly.

Melni cleared her throat. "What about the items he requested?"

Clune glanced back at her. "We cannot allow him access, not to any of it. You were right to be suspicious. They will remain in the deconstruction lab, just like any other Valix-produced artifact we wish to unravel and comprehend."

"No, I meant . . . they go against the insanity explanation. He's insane and also just happens to have brought a bag of supplies unlike anything we've ever seen?"

"You blur your words, Sonbo. You are starting to talk like

him." Clune studied her, waiting for a reply that did not come. She shrugged. "Prototypes. He made them, according to Valix. You of all people should appreciate the depths of their invention process."

"Using materials we're—we are—completely unfamiliar with?"

"We are completely unfamiliar with many things Valix's labs produce. Especially now." She looked down her nose at Melni to drive the point in deep. "But you are right. It is more plausible that he is a spaceman from planet . . . what did he call it? Earth?" Clune laughed and returned to her discussion with the doctor.

"What are my orders, Director?" Melni asked, interrupting them once again.

Clune thought over the question and made a casual gesture toward the exit. "That is for the Council to decide. Remain close. If he wakes, you will keep him talking. Even if he is insane he may still be able to provide useful information about the Valix apparatus, yes?"

"Are you going to give him back to them, in Fineva?"

Clune's lips curled back in a wicked grin. "That will be discussed at the summit in four days' time." She glanced at Caswell. "Scientist or space traveler, Valix wants him back very badly, and I plan to exploit that leverage to the fullest. It will be a very interesting summit, I think."

Despite the unease in her gut, Melni offered her director an obedient nod.

"Until it is time to leave, remain close. When he is lucid you are to keep talking to him. Insane or not, we might still get something useful out of him before the summit."

"Yes, Director."

"Dismissed. Where will you be?"

Melni thought about it. "Analytics."

Rasa Clune nodded. "You will be summoned when he wakes." With that she waved Melni away.

As Melni walked through the decaying halls of Riverswidth and out into the sunlight along the bridge's edge, she searched in herself and found nothing but dread at the prospect of what was to come. Caswell was no insane scientist, of that she felt sure. The place he'd taken her, the things she'd seen within, were not just prototypes from some advanced Valix lab. He'd been truthful with her. And more to the point, she found very deep within herself that she agreed with the logic behind his mission. Victory would not come in changing which side Valix's inventions benefited. Gartien would still be no better than a child led by the hand. How could she get Clune and the Presidium to see that? Here, on the eve of their chance to finally turn the tide, how could she hope to convince them to let Caswell do what he'd come to do?

Only one answer made sense.

She needed proof. No matter the risk to her, no matter how treacherous her actions might seem, she had to find proof before it was too late.

23

IN ANALYTICS THEY QUESTIONED her for almost two hours. A pair of "researchers," both native Southerners, came at her in rapid succession with questions that bordered on the ridiculous. How did he smell? Did he snore when he slept? What hand did he use? "The right, are you sure, Agent?" Hardly anyone used their right hand exclusively, but Caswell had. Yes, she was sure.

She felt pure relief when a nurse came to tell her that the patient had awoken again.

In the observation room Melni had seen only a lone analyst monitoring the reel recorder with little enthusiasm. Clune had gone, summoned to a working dinner with the Presidium. The doctor was off duty as well, though he gave strict instructions that he could be found sleeping in his office two floors below if anything changed.

Melni made only cursory salutations and then pushed through into the hospital room beyond.

"My medicines? My food?" Caswell asked in a gravelly voice the instant she entered.

She shook her head.

He slumped back into his pillow. "Do me a favor at least and rub my temples?"

Nothing in his tone implied this was some kind of ruse. Besides, he was still strapped securely to the bed. So Melni leaned over him and pressed two fingers against each temple. She made slow circles with increasing pressure until, after ten seconds or so, he waved her off.

"What will happen to me?" he asked, the words clear and sharp now, as if a new man lay on the bed before her.

Melni glanced over her shoulder at the mirror on the wall, then leaned in and lowered her voice to a whisper. "I want to believe your story. But Valix has offered a compelling alternative. What you told us sounds crazy in comparison."

"What did she say?"

"That you're some kind of genetics expert. That you experimented on yourself, then escaped from a secret lab in the mountains. A lab you set up after Valix declined to pursue your inventions further."

To her surprise Caswell snorted a sharp laugh. "That is pretty good. Clever lady, no doubt about that."

"Caswell, I cannot help you unless I can prove your story. Is there any way to do that?"

Caswell shook his head. "Short of taking you to Earth, not that I can think of. Even if my landing craft survived that airship falling on it, Valix will have it destroyed. Or hidden away, at a minimum." His face scrunched up.

"Are you in pain?" she asked.

"No. No, I just had a thought." Caswell looked at her. "It's a long shot, though."

"That is an unfamiliar phrase, but it resolves. Tell me anyway."

"Alia landed in a craft identical to mine. And whereas an entire battalion of soldiers are probably surrounding even the charred remains of my boat, I'm guessing nobody's ever seen hers. It would pull back the curtain on her true origin. Yet I don't think she would destroy it, either. Perhaps she can't, come to think of it. I'd bet my life it's still out there, somewhere. Wherever she landed."

"She would not destroy it? Why?"

"In case things didn't work out here. Also . . ." He trailed off.

"Tell me."

"It might be where she keeps all the knowledge she brought with her."

Gooseflesh rose on Melni's skin. She tried to mask the sudden excitement. She'd been so focused on the Think

Tank, it never occurred to her that Alia's source of invention might be hidden somewhere else.

Caswell's voice drew her back to the moment. "Where does she claim to be from? Where was she first encountered?"

Frowning, Melni said, "Valix first appeared at a border checkpoint in Cirdia. A *desoa,* like me. A refugee out of the Desolation, claiming to have been raised by Dalantin parents." At Caswell's confused expression she explained. "Dalantin was a nation before the . . . well, you know. By treaty it is ungoverned land. The whole of the Desolation is this way. Very few people live between those borders now, and none of the old nations are recognized."

"Cirdia," Caswell whispered, as if trying on the word for size. "Show me on a map?"

Melni rushed back to Analytics. A room there held scrolled maps of all sizes, detailing every last corner of Gartien. At the confused expressions of two surprised clerks, she selected one of the Desolation that spanned between Cirdia on the north end and Marados on the south. She tucked it under one arm and returned to Caswell's room. She had to lie beside him and hold the map above so they could both see.

"This is Cirdia," she said, pointing, "where Alia Valix was first encountered. They have a record of her requesting citizenship there, and she stayed for a full month before passing the security checks."

"France," Caswell said, deep in thought.

"France?"

"What we call that area on Earth."

"France," she repeated, trying out his version.

Silence. The wall clock ticked away the seconds.

"Hmm," Caswell said.

"What is it?"

"I just remembered something. A place Alice mentioned, before she came back here, called Olargues." He traced his finger along a narrow valley right in the middle of the crater fields of the Desolation, south and west of Fineva. "My geography isn't great but I believe it's around here."

"There are more detailed maps in the archive taken from survey gliders. They might be old."

"As long as they're from after she arrived. Can you get them?"

Her recently adjusted access level was too low. To be caught would mean grave punishment. Procedure called for her to request such things formally, so a paper trail existed. Clune would have to approve it. "I'll try." Melni stood and went to the door.

"Hey," Caswell said.

She turned.

"I can tell from the look on your face that this is a big risk," he said. "Thank you."

"We say 'gratitude' here."

Caswell grinned. "Yeah, well, I'm not from here."

Melni returned his grin and left.

In the observation chamber the analyst sat facing the gently whirring reel of tape. He wore headphones and sat slouched in his chair, only half his head visible over the back. Melni came to stand behind him and considered the recorder. If Caswell had indeed just told her where Alia Valix first landed on Gartien, this man in the chair knew it now, too. He may have already sent off a cipher to Clune.

"The ramblings of a madman, hmm?" Melni asked.

The man said nothing.

"Valix really did a job on him."

Still nothing.

Melni leaned around to look at him. His eyes were closed, his breathing even.

The access badge clipped to his shirt caught her eye. With each beat of his heart the laminated square bounced slightly, catching light from the indicators on the recorder. To her surprise he had archive access, all three levels. Exactly what she'd had taken away. Exactly what she now needed. A short path to the information required. No requests, no Clune signature. Her stomach tightened, as if her body knew what she was going to do before her mind had reached the conclusion. This was the point of no return and Melni swayed on the precipice, battling her instincts until a plan could form.

She breathed, brought her pulse under control. She weighed options against consequences, benefits against risks. She thought of what she'd say if they caught her. It could work. It just might.

Delicately she plucked the access card from his shirt pocket and replaced it with her own. They looked nothing alike, but if she moved with confidence she doubted anyone would notice. Not between here and the archives, at least.

The analyst stirred. He sniffled and rubbed absently at his nose. Then he went still again, breathing evenly. Melni leaned over him and changed the direction of the reel. She let it roll back for two full minutes, long enough to cover the important part of her conversation with Caswell, then clicked it back to wind forward once again. The man did not move. His eyes remained closed.

Melni fixed the stolen card to her blouse, on the right just above her heart, which pounded beneath it. To do what she'd just done over some minor intrigue might mean prison for years. To do so now, with everything that had happened, with armies and warships poised to clash the instant orders were issued, would surely mean torture and death.

But she had to know. If Caswell had told her the truth, she could prove his story and unravel Valix's empire. Moreover, she might prove the existence of another world. *All right,* she thought as she descended the stepwell, realizing how silly the idea sounded. *Maybe nothing so grand as that, but at least Clune and the Presidium can call the enemy out on their lies.*

A warm rain fell outside. Tiny droplets swirled and danced on the evening breeze, catching the setting Sun like little gems.

Analytics, and the archive they maintained, occupied the entirety of Building Nine. The square plaster monolith stood third tallest on the bridge, soaring two hundred feet from the middle of the span and another thirty below toward the water. Only the top floor had windows. The rest was a solid, unbroken surface freshly painted in the Dimont style of blinding white.

A clerk at the desk just within the entrance glanced at Melni. "Blue and yellow levels only," the fresh-faced young woman said.

Two men stood off to one side of the lobby, sipping cham from paper cups and talking in low voices.

"Red has been restricted to black until further notice," the clerk added, nodding toward Melni's access card.

Melni glanced down. Her borrowed card had the blue, yellow, and red squares that denoted access to the entire archive. In certain extreme situations the red level, where sensitive information was stored, required an extra black square. She knew of this, they all did, but she'd never heard of it actually happening. They probably had Caswell's gear down there, and Garta knew how many agents studying it. "Thanks," she said absently.

"What?"

"Gratitude." Melni attempted a smile. She shuffled past the clerk and the two chatting men.

The archives took up all three of the sub-bridge floors. They were gigantic, dimly lit rooms consisting of row after row of filing cabinets and bookshelves, along with a small army of clerks who sorted, filed, checked, and rechecked the contents. In the center of the middle floor was a space devoted to research. Nothing could be removed from the archive without written clearance from Rasa Clune or a senior member of the Presidium. Nothing on the very bottom floor, the Red Archive, could even be examined without the proper access. A red square. Except on a day like today, when the addition of the ultra-rare black was required.

She'd hoped to find herself alone, or nearly so, within the frigid basements. Garta had other plans, however. Dozens of people were working within. Plain-clothed analysts and perhaps even agents like herself. Officers from the military intelligence branches.

Even, and much to Melni's surprise, a Hollow Woman. She sat at a reading desk in the far corner, dressed in an all-black outfit with the hood pulled up. A massive book was spread out before her, and the woman jotted notes on blue paper with hasty motions of her wrist.

The section for maps spanned all three levels, connected

via an old spiral stepwell set in the southwest corner. Melni descended from blue to yellow, the floor that contained "sensitive" information, including unannotated detail maps of the Desolation and both the Southern and Northern frontier zones. Red, Melni guessed, would contain chiefly the annotated versions: which routes were known good, which routes were watched, and which were currently or recently in use for travelers going either direction. Also, most likely, the latest and most detailed maps would be stored there. She hoped she wouldn't need them.

High-level maps were easy. She jotted coordinates of the valley Caswell had indicated and returned them to their drawers. The photographic maps, taken from high-altitude balloons and, in some rare cases, low-flying gliders, were much more difficult to find.

It took all evening to sort through the information. By tenth hour, with few others working and most of the overhead lights off, Melni had covered four worktables with pictures taken in and around the valley. It was a lush place, carpeted with trees and smaller shrubs. A river wound its way down the center, pooling in several craters left from when the rocks fell. She saw signs of destroyed towns and abandoned villages, all desolate and fully embraced by the regrowth of vegetation. Typical of the region. She pored over them anyway, looking for any signs of life.

Her ancestors had lived in places like this. They'd lost everything, and become the beggars of this world. To live in such times, experience that loss and hopelessness, the constant agony and humiliation. It was a wonder anyone had survived, much less fought for a future.

There were farm houses—dead—and a fishing village where all the boats had decayed and sunk in a sad herd around the lone dock. There were crumbled roads and, every so often, the hideous black scars and craters of a rockfall event. How many bodies lay in those ashen, charred fields, their spirits never returned to the sea? How many had been pulverized when their homes were tossed sideways from the foundations as shock waves blistered out across the sky?

Millions, easily.

A long-ago-reclaimed camp or factory of some sort nestled between two steep hills caught her eye. It looked vaguely military, with what appeared to have been neat rows of barracks. Who knew what an army base of two centuries ago looked like, though. It could be a school, perhaps even a prison.

Near this facility, on the riverbank, a lone cottage caught Melni's eye. The small home sat nestled in a deep cleft beside a tributary stream. Steep valley walls would have sheltered it from the nearby blasts, their curve hiding it from view of the river. There was nothing remarkable about the place save for a thin white curling trail of smoke that spilled from the chimney on its roof. It was the only sign of life she'd seen in hundreds of photoprints, and this place was far from the network of scavenger trails that riddled the Desolation like veins.

Melni rubbed her aching eyes and glanced at the datemark. The image had been taken almost eleven years ago, roughly a year before the date Alia Valix first walked up to that Combran frontier post and pleaded for refuge.

She spent another fifty minutes scouring the area for other clues. There was a large boathouse by the river a few hundred feet away. The roof looked new, untainted by the relentless vegetation or weathering, and the trail between it and the little cottage was clear. A tingle spread across Melni's scalp. New construction, chimney smoke, right where Caswell had said to look and right before Alia Valix wandered into Combran society and began to invent.

Something else caught her eye. On the trail, beside a lone greencloud tree, were two patches of discolored dirt amid the tall weeds. The print was too grainy to make out details, but they were clearly not natural. Each was roughly six feet long and three wide. Rocks had been piled at one end of each. The sight tickled a memory: Boran, telling her of the murdered NRD officers in the rural North. Caswell had dragged the bodies away from the scene and buried them in dirt. He'd said this was per custom, though Melni had never heard of such a thing. And yet here, exactly where he said the woman named Alice Vale had landed, were similar landmarks alongside other signs of activity. It was not unheard of for loners, even the occasional small communal village, to exist in the Desolation. But here, exactly where he'd said? And with these burial mounds so alien to Gartien yet identical to what Caswell had done?

Melni sat back and closed her eyes. A battle raged within her: loyalty to the South on one side, the desire to know the truth about Valix on the other. In the middle of this imagined battlefield, a lone figure. Caswell.

Her thoughts turned to Clune and the Presidium. She pictured them locked in some ornate mealhouse, negotiating the stranger's return. Asking for resources or perhaps even technology. Valix, and the Northern Triumvirate she had wrapped around her hand, would likely give a lot. Caswell could expose Alia's true nature. He could bring it all down.

"And so what if he does?" Melni whispered, the clear picture of things finally assembling itself in her mind. Neither side would care where Alia came from. She still represented the same thing: a technological advantage to whomever she worked for. Melni could not imagine either government accepting the logic of Caswell's mission. The temptation for accelerated progress would trump any philosophical concerns over Gartien's ownership of destiny. Both sides would be blinded by the prize she represented.

Unless . . .

Melni shivered. The summit. Valix had called the summit. She must know her role as the lever in the coming conflict, and so she alone could stop it. She'll offer her reservoir of genius to both sides or neither. A brilliant gambit, really. Valix would force both sides to recognize her value, regardless of where she came from or why. She would become the most powerful person in the world, instantly. The truth of Caswell's story wouldn't matter then. Except to Melni. She still needed to know the truth. Then, and only then, could she decide what to do. Because regardless, there was only one decision to make: help Caswell complete his mission to kill Alia Valix, or prevent him from doing so.

The image, of that Cirdian valley, she folded up and stuffed inside her shirt.

"That is against the rules," a flat voice said.

Melni froze. She had thought herself utterly alone. Slowly she turned in place. Behind her a black-clothed figure leaned against a tall bookshelf.

The Hollow Woman.

She had her arms folded across her chest, her mask still up to hide everything except narrow blue eyes.

Melni withered under that stare. She looked down at her shirt to hide the guilt she knew radiated from her face. "With everything going on," she said, then paused. "Well, you know, who has time to wait for procedure? The summit is in four days. War could start at any moment."

After a lengthy silence the Hollow agent made a slow, single inclination of her head. "You must have found something important to the situation, then."

Melni shrugged.

The woman stepped forward. Her clothing seemed to absorb the light from the reading lamp on the table, leaving only the thin view of her eyes hovering in shadow. "Cirdian maps? What is it, a forward base? A smuggling route?"

"Just . . . a possible path north. A new one, thanks to a crater wall collapse."

"Interesting. May I?" She extended a black-gloved hand.

Melni rolled her chair back and away. She came to a stand and covered her torso with one hand, pressing the folded print to her stomach. "Forgive me, I've never seen a Hollow here before. I don't know what sort of clearance you have."

The woman's eyes betrayed the broad smile hidden by her mask. "Oh, that is not an issue, Miss . . . I mean, Mr. Prian Hox?"

Melni blinked, unable to mask her confusion. A second passed before she remembered the borrowed card pinned to her blouse, displaying a man's name and image.

The Hollow Woman took a silent step forward, farther into the light. She slid an access card from a pocket on her leg and held it casually out. The square laminated paper was as black as her clothes, with nothing but a single tiny red and black diamond in the center. Raised lettering across the bottom, unreadable from this distance but there, likely provided a method of verification should anyone unfamiliar be presented it. "I think you will find this allows me the run of the place."

Melni inhaled a long, slow lungful of air through her nose. She needed confidence, and soon. But more than anything she needed to get out from under this terrifying woman's gaze.

The shadow in front of her stepped forward once again. She stood less than a foot from Melni now, her narrow eyes glittering in the lamplight. "The photoprint?"

Melni glanced down at the black ident card. "I've never seen one of those before," she said, the words spilling out quickly, like the way Caswell spoke. And Valix.

"We are not in the habit of showing it. Or ourselves, for that matter."

"Well, I will need it verified and approved before I can show you anything. I take my orders directly from Rasa Clune." Melni wanted a reaction and got it. The slightest tug at the corners of the eyes. "She gave no permission to share my research with anyone at this time."

"Did Clune give you permission to wear someone else's ident? That is strictly against the rules."

Melni managed a weak laugh. "Simple mistake. They were all piled on the desk and I grabbed the wrong one in my haste." As she spoke she turned and piled the images of the Cirdian wastes into a hasty stack. Melni stuffed the whole mess back into the first open drawer she could reach and slid it shut. "Everyone is so busy preparing for the summit, you know?"

Melni turned back around.

The Hollow Woman was gone.

Expecting arrest at every turn, Melni nevertheless took the long way back.

She headed up to the top floor and across a skybridge to the adjacent building where Internal Security made their offices. The very people who would throw her in a cell for the rest of her life if it were discovered what she'd done in the last few hours. It would take nothing more than for that Hollow to report what she'd so obviously suspected.

A clerk sat at a tiny desk halfway across the twenty-foot-long suspended hallway. Narrow windows along the span showed a clear night sky, and moonlight reflecting off the river and the ocean beyond.

Seeing Melni empty-handed, the clerk waved her past without much interest and went back to reading a newsprint folded across the table before her. Through sheer force of will Melni kept a casual pace to the door on the opposite side and walked through.

Every instinct told her to rush straight back to Caswell, but her brush with the Hollow Woman had set Melni on edge. She took a meandering, complicated route through the halls and buildings of Riverswidth, stopping frequently to double back, looking in every corner and through every window for a sign the woman had followed. But there was nothing, and before long Melni could wait no more. She gritted her teeth and made her way to Caswell's room.

24

THE ANALYST STILL SAT at his recorder reels, the tape sighing softly as it emptied itself from one spool and accumulated on the other. He was awake now, a book folded across his lap, his chin resting on his chest as he read. At Melni's entrance he jerked slightly and sat up, alert. His sudden stiffness faded when he saw who had entered.

"I am going to see if he is willing to talk sense now," Melni said.

"Last chance, I guess," the analyst said.

Melni had made it to the inner door, her toe under the foot latch. She stopped and glanced back at the man. "What did you say?"

He favored her with an apologetic smile. "Director Clune is on her way up. Apparently the Presidium gave approval to cut him open and take a look at that thing in his neck."

"That could kill him," Melni said.

The man shrugged and turned back to his book. "Put him out of his misery, if you ask me. Blixxing loon . . ."

Melni slipped into the room and closed the door behind her. She glanced around, her heart racing. In her mind's eye she could see Clune ascending the stepwell through the prison, a team of surgeons and security personnel on her heels. Perhaps the Hollow Woman, too.

Caswell woke when the door clicked shut. "I thought you'd abandoned me," he whispered.

"We are leaving," she whispered back. "I do not know how yet, but if we do not go now . . ." She left the thought unfinished, allowing her face to tell him what was at stake. "Did they bring you your food?" she asked at a conversational volume.

"No." He winced as she unbound his wrists, careful to keep her body between him and the mirrored window.

Melni slid a hand under the bedsheet and unclasped the straps at his ankles. "Are you ready to talk sense now, prisoner?"

"Not until you bring my food," he shot back, playing his part. Then he whispered, "What are you going to do?"

Melni held her hand perpendicular across her mouth, the gesture for silence she'd taught him. "Come through that door in twenty seconds," she mouthed more than said.

He nodded, watching as she turned and strode back into the room beyond the mirror.

Caswell counted, only to fifteen since their seconds were a bit faster than his. Then he leapt from the bed and rushed the door, rubbing his temples the whole way. He wanted focus, clarity of mind. Lack of empathy and pain suppression. But the implant only complained. An empty feeling, like hunger, that told him the chemical reserves had all run dry. His implant could do nothing unless he found food.

Melni stood with her back angled toward him. She had one arm around the neck of a man who sat in front of a reel-to-reel recording apparatus. Her other hand he couldn't see, but from her posture he guessed she'd stabbed him, or was slitting his throat. *Jesus.*

The man spasmed, hands outstretched in sudden panic. A book fell to the floor. Melni grunted with effort, her feet scrabbling on the tiles for purchase. Caswell stepped toward the pair, ready to help, but then the victim melted back into his chair, slid down until his back was on the seat cushion, and fell off one side into a heap under the desk.

"You killed him?"

Melni half-turned, held up something that resembled a syringe. "He will be out for hours," she said. She moved to the next door and leaned against it. "Get his outfit, and be quick. They come for you as we speak."

Caswell knelt and set to work on removing the man's clothes. "I thought you'd abandoned me," he said again.

"We need to find this proof."

He didn't bother with the undergarments. The pants fit, the shirt as well, though once the clasps were fastened it stretched too tight across the chest. Still, it beat the patient gown. The shoes, though, were far too small. "Shoes don't fit," he said.

"We call them treadmellows."

He sat on the floor, strained to get them on without success. Frustrated, he tossed them aside.

"Take the socks," Melni offered. "They are black. Someone would have to look to notice. We must go."

"Fine." He took the socks. They reeked, but he pulled them on all the same. He stood and studied himself. "It'll do, I guess." He inspected the pant pockets. In one, a money clip held a surprisingly thick stack of teal notes. In the other was a set of keycards. Unsure of both, he tossed them to Melni.

"There are two guards outside the door," she said. "I will go out first and try to distract them. . . ."

She paused because he had stopped listening. A wheeled storage rack parked against one wall had caught his eye. Various medicines and other ancillary items were arrayed on the shelves. A standard set of supplies, wheeled in to any infirmary room. "What is it?" she asked.

Caswell took slow steps over to the rack and reached to one shelf in particular, near the top. There, tucked between two boxes of syringes, was an oval-shaped metallic package. He pulled it out and grinned. "Calories," he said, salivating.

Melni just watched him.

He twisted off the cap and sucked the contents down in a single, gulping swallow, crushing the package in his fist to get every last bit of nutrients into his mouth.

"Sweet potato mash," he said, wiping his mouth with the back of one hand. "With peas. Worst of the lot. Of course they'd pick this one, the monsters."

"We could try to find your—"

He held up a hand to cut her off, then sank to his knees.

"Are you okay?"

He nodded, saying nothing, waiting for his body to process the food. "Give me five minutes," Caswell whispered.

"You can have one," Melni replied, and she meant it.

"Five," he groaned. He massaged the back of his neck to get more blood flowing there. The seconds slid away. Then the minutes. Melni shifted impatiently but said nothing.

The phantom sensation of emptiness in his skull abated. He moved his fingers to his temples and asked the artificial organ for what he needed. This time it complied.

Everything slowed down a bit. Dreamlike, but crystal clear. Sights, sounds, even smells, all amplified. Every ache and lingering bit of fatigue in his body melted away. They were there, but only as data. Information that could be comprehended and summarily ignored.

"Right," he said. "Guards outside?"

"Yes, two. I shall distract—"

"No. Wait here," he said. Before Melni could stop him he was at the door, then through into the hallway.

They stood to either side, backs to the wall, batons holstered at their hips. No firearms. Caswell coiled toward one, smashing his windpipe with a knife-hand punch. Then he uncoiled, twisting and extending his leg in a snap kick that took the other guard full in the face.

Melni emerged seconds later, and gasped. "You killed them."

"That's what I do."

"I . . . This is not how—"

"Go back in there, Melni. Pretend I overcame you and fled. There's no reason for you to take any blame for this."

"No," she said. Then with more conviction, "No. I am coming."

He stared at her a long moment, trying to process what the implication would be for her career, not to mention her safety.

"Then help me with the bodies," he said. He grabbed one by the legs and jerked his head toward the door for Melni to hold it open. She complied, still shocked at the violence.

A door at the far end of the hall, ten meters away, creaked open. He heard this easily, despite being in the room with the recorder. Out in the hall Melni stood frozen in place, holding the door, staring in the direction of the sound.

"What is the meaning of this, Agent Sonbo?" someone said. A sour, emotionless voice, like a stern grandmother.

He could hear others, too. Breathing, footsteps. Six, or maybe eight. Guards? He assumed yes. And right about now they'd be readying their weapons. Caswell grabbed the police-style baton from the guard's belt.

"Director, I—" Melni stopped when Caswell pushed by her at a full sprint. Not toward the newcomers, nor even away from them, but straight across the narrow hall. Two steps and he leapt, planting a foot on the wall and pivoting his body toward the "director" and her party. In the same motion he threw the baton.

The woman ducked on instinct. Caswell knew she would; everyone ducked in such a scenario. So he had leapt high, aimed low. The black nightstick slammed right into the woman's face with a sickening, meaty thud.

The group behind her erupted into chaos. Most were doctors, Caswell belatedly realized. Some guards at the rear were trying to move forward, shoving the medical staff aside. Everyone was shouting. The woman on the floor rolled over and came to her knees, hands pressed to her bleeding face, a horrible moan spilling out from between the fingers.

Caswell grabbed Melni's arm. "Which way?"

"That—" she managed before he yanked her away from the fallen director.

She'd pointed to a door in the opposite direction. He raced to it, yanking her behind him. Pulled it open, shoved her beyond, and then closed it at his back with a click.

Ancient stone walls surrounded them. An old prison, he thought. "Where now?"

His words didn't seem to register.

"Where?" he shouted, squeezing her arm.

"Go down," Melni managed. "All the way down."

"Where's the stairs?"

"Director Clune," she stammered. "You just—"

"Melni, get ahold of yourself. For all they know, you're my hostage."

Her eyes came up, met his. Those purple pools, normally so full of intelligence, now full of fear.

"Stairs?" he repeated.

"Stepwell. The second left, then the last door on the left."

He rushed ahead. Melni struggled to keep up at first, but with each step the shock seemed to bleed out of her. Distance from the carnage. Soon enough she was only a few steps behind him.

Overhead, the lights dimmed, shining red when their brightness returned. Somewhere an alarm began to wail.

"Garta's light, no," Melni whispered.

A guard burst through a door ahead of them, looking the wrong way. Caswell dove high and flew over the man's shoulders, grabbing the neck as he flew, twisting him around and pulling him down. Caswell landed and continued to fall, an iron grip around the neck. The motion pulled the man off his feet and brought him crashing down on top of Caswell. Or would have, only the assassin had rolled out of the way. He was up on his hands and feet already. The guard tried to stand, bewildered. Caswell kicked a side of the man's skull with flawless precision. The guard collapsed. All before Melni had had time to catch up.

"Come on, come on," he rasped.

Melni stammered some reply. He could hear her footfalls on the stone steps, falling back. But still coming, still following. He pressed ahead, taking the steps three at a time.

By the time she found him at the bottom, three more bodies lay at his feet.

The black waters of Riv Dimont gurgled by. Three bodies drifted away on the languid current toward the sea. Caswell stood with his back to her, watching them go.

"The raft," Melni said, numb. She could think of nothing else to say. Her plan to sneak Caswell away from here under the cover of night, find her proof, and report back, triumphant, had shattered like glass when that trunch had smacked Rasa Clune right in her nose. She'd only just come to grips with the bodies they'd left behind in Combra, but this . . . this was something else entirely. These were Southerners.

Her allies. Caswell had torn through them like a bhar through weeds. "The raft," she said again.

The assassin did not react. He just watched the bodies float off. His shoulders heaved as he gulped air. Finally he turned, and she saw what the flurry of activity had cost him. His face was bone white, what little color he'd had above now drained save for little flecks of blood. He opened his mouth to say something, his lower lip quivering. No words came. He stumbled, one knee giving out to exhaustion.

"What have you done to yourself?" she asked, catching him mid-fall.

"What I had to," he replied, eyelids fluttering.

She hauled him to the raft and laid him on the wood slats, then took to the oars. The current did most of the work. Within ten minutes they reached the swirling waters where the river met the sea. Caswell had come to a sitting position by then, his color returning. He kept his gaze carefully behind them, wary of pursuit, but perhaps because of the hasty nature of their escape no one had thought to check the raft docks below the bridge. Sirens still wailed above, growing quieter as Riverswidth receded into the distance.

Melni strained against the shifting forces where the currents met, guiding the little raft to the north shoreline, where a set of pourstonc steps met the water's edge, built for fishers. The steps led up to street level. Standing on the slick black rocks along the waterfront she tried to push the raft back out into the river, but it kept gliding right back to rest on the stones.

"Wait," Caswell said. Using some hidden reserve of strength he started to pull the raft out of the lapping waves. Melni understood at once and helped him. Together they lugged the old thing up onto the fisher's platform beside the steps. Three discarded fishing poles had been abandoned there. Caswell compelled her to help him lay the raft upright against the seawall. Then he took the poles and arranged them neatly alongside. Standing back a few steps, it looked convincingly like the arrayed gear of a dawn fishing expedition, left alone perhaps while the occupants went off in search of cham and bread.

"Will it work?" Caswell asked.

"It might buy us a few minutes, and that could be the difference."

She led him up the steps. They walked along the promenade arm in arm as they had in Midstav, her head against his shoulder. With each step she expected to hear a chin-up's whistle, though there were no chin-ups in Dimont. With each step that no alarm sounded she relaxed just a tiny bit more.

At the dockyards Melni paid cash for two seats in the galley of a hauler she knew well. Before being deployed to Combra she'd written a summary of the boat's activities, and dossiers on the key crew members. She knew everything about it: schedule, captain, all of it. That investigation had been dropped for reasons beyond her, but Melni still retained the details.

"I cannot take you past the line. There is a blockade on," the gruff old captain said.

"Marados will suffice," Melni said, and he agreed.

Caswell said nothing at all. He kept behind her, always on the side with more shadow, always carefully bland and uninteresting.

The boat looked ancient compared to the sleek yachts and massive cargo haulers she'd become accustomed to seeing in the harbors along Combra's western shore. Her looks were deceptive, though, as Melni well knew. She was a long and narrow thing with a hull of treated wooden planks, and her air-engine rattled like an old man's bones as the craft glided out from the dark port and into the bigger waves beyond.

The captain led them to a crew galley near the stern of the ship just above the waterline. Porthole windows offered grime-filtered views of the dreary docklands and, in short order, black seas below a star-filled sky. The boat rose and fell on waves ten feet high, moving with remarkable speed on the favorable current.

There'd been no identification request upon boarding, not even a request for names. Just a handful of bills Melni provided from the flush clip Caswell had found in his stolen trousers.

They were alone in the galley. Pots and pans hanging

from ceiling hooks swayed with the waves. Bags of fruit and vegetables, too. Thin red cushions lay on a bench that ran along three sides of the meal space. In the center there was a low wooden table that looked a thousand years old. Words were knife-etched into the deep brown surface. Names of current and former crew, or those they loved. BLIXXING COMBS, a vulgarity aimed at Northerners, in bold block lettering. Others instructed all *desoa* to go home, as if that were a thing that one could do. The ignorance made her blood hot.

"Did you find my supplies? Any more of my food?" Caswell asked, once seated.

She found herself really looking at him for the first time since they'd left his cell. The tally of bodies left in the wake of their escape, not to mention Clune's broken nose, had shocked her senseless. But now, sitting here across from him, she reached the truly terrifying conclusion that he had done it all. He'd turned into some kind of machine. Without a weapon save that baton he'd fought through at least a half-dozen trained Riverswidth guards without so much as a scratch. What limits did this man have? No wonder he'd found his way into the Think Tank so easily.

"Melni? My food?"

Numb, she shook her head. Then she remembered the one thing she'd kept hidden from Clune. "I did manage to recover this." She removed the "Smart Needler" from her sock and slid it across to him. "Will it help you?"

Caswell picked up the tube and turned it about in his hands. Examining it for damage, perhaps. After a few seconds he slipped it under the table. "Thank you. Gratitude, I mean. It's not for medicine. It's a weapon. The same kind I used on all those cruisers at the base of the mountain."

"Oh. Regrets. I suppose that might have been useful getting out of there." Not that he seemed to need any help.

He tilted his head inquisitively, changing the subject. "What'd you find in the records room?"

Melni plucked the information packet from her blouse and laid the images out on the table between them. As he studied them she made a pillow of her folded arms and laid her head down. The lure of sleep tugged at her eyelids within seconds. She watched his face as he studied the images, waiting to see if the same revelation would strike him. When it did, she found she was smiling.

"Graves," he said. "Buried bodies. I'm sure of it."

"That is what I suspected."

He stared a moment longer, then handed the papers back. "Careless of her."

"You made the same mistake, did you not?"

He flashed her a grin. "Exactly. Nice to know she doesn't think of everything." He seemed to notice her half-closed eyes then. His grin turned into something warmer. "Get some rest. I'll wake you if anything happens."

Between his warm smile and the slow rise and fall of the boat, she soon fell into a dreamless sleep.

He woke before her. The sea had calmed. Birds—their version of them, anyway, with their smaller set of hind wings—wheeled and screeched out over the gray-green waters. Now and then one would streamline itself and dart down into the waves to spear whatever it was they ate.

Caswell watched them for some time, absorbing. He'd forget all of this, that much was undeniably true. But the chances were slim to none that he would leave this world after reversion. Memories would be formed, then. Perhaps a lifetime's worth. He grinned at that prospect. They may have sent him to assassinate Alice Vale, but he doubted anyone would ever come to rescue him. No, they would study this place from orbit for decades.

What would he do? How would he live? Become a hermit in some remote house? Maybe he'd travel. Adventure-wandering, like he did for his holidays after any other Archon mission. Only this one would never end. He could move from place to place, disguise himself and try to blend in until anyone began to suspect something, then move on. Perhaps become some kind of legend.

The idea that Gartien would be his home, that he'd never do another mission for Archon, that his implant would never delete another memory after this, had only just begun to sink in. He was thirty-four years old. There was still time for a normal life, a real set of memories without gaps and the suspicion of evil tucked therein.

He turned and looked at Melni, who lay curled up on one of the cushioned bench seats, sound asleep. Maybe she'd come with him. Although she hadn't said as much, he sensed she would not be able to return to her home. Not without dire consequences, at least.

A map on the wall caught his eye. He walked to it and studied the familiar coastlines. The rivers, the mountains, all were basically the same. Only the borders differed, really. He'd given up trying to find a reason why this might be. How this place could exist at all. No answer to that would ever come. Just another piece in the impossible puzzle called existence.

Sunlight spilled in a porthole as the boat turned. It felt warm on his cheek. Welcoming. He wished he had coffee. Or juice. Fuck, even a sip of water. Here he was, dreaming about a lifetime spent here when his dehydrated organs would give up in a week, or less. *Focus on the mission*, he told himself. *That's all you have left. That's the rest of your life. Dream all you want, it's not going to change that.*

"How similar is it? To your world, I mean."

Caswell glanced at Melni. She stretched, catlike, and sat up. The cushions had made her pixie hair stand up on one side. Caswell said, "Virtually identical. Well, it's a lot more developed where I come from. Cities and sprawling farms everywhere, except for the places too hot to occupy or the protected lands."

"Too hot?"

He returned to the bench and sat opposite her. "We caused it. Burnt too much oil and gas, didn't heed the warnings. The whole planet warmed up. The coastlines raised, the weather got all . . . well, it changed. Unlike your Desolation, this happened over a hundred years rather than overnight. Long enough that people could debate the reality of it happening at all."

"What is it like now?"

"Earth?" he grimaced. "Nasty. Wonderful. Depends on where you go, or who you ask, I guess. The population is still declining but it's starting to bottom out. That century of neglect will take a century of sacrifice to fix. Maybe more." He wanted to tell her of the asteroid mining, and the colony stations under construction. But Monique's warnings kept his tongue in check.

The captain of the ship entered through the outer door, propelled on a warm salt-tinged wind. He muttered that his passengers could eat if they wished, they'd paid enough for the privilege, and when Melni prodded he even offered the use of his bath.

"Do you have any spare boots?" she asked.

He did, but they didn't fit well. Far too big. Caswell put them on anyway. Melni forked over more bills and thanked the captain.

"We'll reach the port at Marados in four hours," the gruff man said, pocketing the extra money without apparent joy.

"Our gratitude."

"Will you, ah, want to depart in harbor, or . . . before that?"

Melni glanced at Caswell. He nodded. She looked back at the captain. "If you could put us onshore a mile south, I would be most grateful."

"One of my crew will run you out on the fisher." The man swept strands of long, sweaty gray hair back behind his ears. He stole a curious glance at Caswell and slipped back out.

"Can we trust him?" Caswell asked once the footsteps outside had receded.

"We don't really have a choice. But I think so."

Caswell nodded thoughtfully. "Where's this Marados, and what's it like?" he asked, craning his neck toward the map.

Melni joined him there. She pointed to a port city on the Desolation's southern frontier. "Marados thrives as a conduit to the west. The port is larger than Dimont's, even Combra's. It is also popular with those who supply the shadow market. Scavengers and smugglers. Is there a city here on Earth?"

"Casablanca," he said with nostalgia. He'd spent two weeks there, once, on one of his holidays, pretending to be a billionaire. That had been a hell of a party. He shook the memory away. "And after Marados?"

"We'll buy supplies and head north."

"Into the Desolation?"

"Into the Desolation."

25

THEY HIKED the last mile to the city, following the sandy shore until reaching the first signs of civilization. Melni led him inland then, just a few hundred yards, to avoid the fishers and tanners that crowded the beaches on either side of the port.

Farmland surrounded Marados. The homes were small, the color of dust, built in circular clusters with lush and carefully maintained gardens in the center. The more affluent circles had fountains. Colorful flowers of blue, yellow, and white grew from intricately dyed pots that hung from nearly every eave. Chimes tinkled in the soft wind, the sound intermingled with the laughter of scrawny, half-naked children.

"It's beautiful here," Caswell said.

"We haven't reached the port yet. You may change your mind."

Twenty minutes later, walking between crates and stepping over the thick mooring ropes, she thought he had.

The port reeked of rotten fish and failing sewers. Gulls wheeled above, thick as Renewal flies, and brawled on the docks over scraps of old bread and the remnants of dead vermin. Workers swarmed the cargo ships, attaching lift cables that dangled from giant cranes to the huge, cube-shaped iron containers brought in from across the sea.

A sprawling roller yard loomed just beyond, plumes of steam rising from the aging vehicles. Looking at them now, with their narrow tracks and clattering wheels, Melni felt a sudden embarrassment for her side of the world. The rollers used in the North were faster and provided a much smoother ride. Superior in virtually every way. This difference could not be written off as another Valix-driven improvement, unlike so many other things. No, the North simply arrived at a better solution.

"Gartien must seem so primitive to you," she said to Caswell. "At least this half."

He grunted a laugh. "It's romantic, really. Reminds me of a simpler time, one I only know from stories. Earth is more advanced, yes. More automated, more controlled. It was supposed to be simpler, easier, but coming here makes me realize the opposite is what's really happened."

She led him to Gylina Square, the famous market. Hundreds of colorful tents were lined up in something like rows. It seemed as if the entire population of Marados milled about. The vast array of fresh crops and powdered spices on display overpowered whatever lingering odors still remained from the port just one hundred feet west of the edge of the square.

Melni bought herself food, plus a surplus army hat and coat for each of them. A few stalls later she found a beat-up old camera, and haggled for it as well. With it she could capture evidence of Valix's true origin, should they find it.

"I know we're in a hurry, but some boots that actually fit would be nice, too," Caswell said.

A toothless old vendor sold them a secondhand pair of beige desert treadmellows that covered the ankles. The toes were both patched but the tread looked almost new. Caswell ran a hand over the stitch work and nodded, impressed.

She ate a simple meal of spicy dried meat mixed into rice and some fresh veilfruit. Caswell, she noticed, kept his gaze carefully away from the food. She could only imagine how hungry and thirsty he must be. And the only food he could eat or drink lay in some storeroom inside Riverswidth, permanently out of reach now. They would have to start testing his stomach, she decided. There had to be something here he could eat; it was just a matter of finding it. Clearly Alia Valix had solved that problem. Mentally she began to prepare a list.

They moved away from the bustling market, walking northeast through narrow, winding streets. Wet clothing hung on lines strung between windows above. Birds and monkeys chattered in the heat of the morning. Somewhere nearby, musicians played a lively ceremonial joining tune with soaring lyrics against a deep rhythmic drumbeat. A crowd cheered along. She could almost see their smiling faces, and those of the pair being joined, and she found she wanted to see them. She wanted to show Caswell.

Lost in thought, Melni almost tripped when Caswell suddenly yanked her by the elbow into a narrow, shadowed alley. She recovered and started to ask, but he had his hand flat across his mouth, urging silence.

With great care Caswell leaned back out into the crowded street and took a quick glance back the way they'd come.

"What is it?" Melni asked, whispering, when he'd finished.

"Footsteps behind us."

"There are dozens of people walking this lane."

He nodded. "Yes, but only one who has been with us since we left the market. A patient thief, perhaps, but it makes no difference. They're gone now. I suggest we move quickly."

Melni, mind full of images of black-clad shadows tailing them, readily agreed. On the edge of town she spent the last of her stolen money on two thumpers. The two-wheeled motorized cycles were as old as everything else in Marados, but the pressure tanks were solid and the little air-piston engines both rattled to life without much complaint.

"Do they care we're going into the Desolation?" Caswell asked as he lifted one leg over the saddle and began to examine the simple controls before him.

"Not here." She glanced northeast and waited for his gaze to follow. "Up there they might, along the frontier. Scavengers make the journey all the time. There are still plenty of relics to be found in the dead cities and villages. Their papers get checked when they come back, but we will worry about that when the time comes." She left her fears of a blockade unvoiced. They'd see it well in advance and turn back, perhaps go by ship even though it would make them too late to do anything before the summit. "We shall have to hurry," she added. "The summit is three days from now. We will barely make it and that assumes no delays."

"I'm ready."

"Do you know how to control that?" she asked, a nod toward his thumper.

"We've got something similar back home, though purely just for sport. Show me the basics and I think I'll have the hang of it soon enough."

She ran him through the controls: gears, brake, accelerator, tiller. He proved a quick study and by fifth hour she found herself racing him up the Great Alvass Road, the grin on her face exceeded only by his.

Then the pourstone pavement ended. Plumes of sand and dust kicked up by the thumper's knobby tires filled the air. Melni took air through a thin scarf wrapped across her mouth and nose. The goggles she wore over her eyes were like magnets for the grit in the air, but a simple swipe with her jacket sleeve cleared them well enough.

Caswell let her take the lead when the frontier post appeared on the horizon. The cluster of low buildings were dark, though, and other than a single guard atop the high watchtower on a nearby hill, she saw no one. Into the Desolation, as easily as if they'd crossed a farm. The lack of border guards, something she'd hoped for over the last fifty miles, concerned her greatly the moment they rode through. It wasn't right, given everything going on. Northern forces could roll through here without firing a shot.

Ten miles later the road veered sharply left and followed the rim of a crater. The depression spanned hundreds of feet across and fifty deep. The soil around it crunched like broken glass under the thumper's tires. Melni took Caswell up to the rim. Below, a small pond of brackish water filled the basin, surrounded by wisps of pale weedgrass six feet high.

"Are they all like this?" the assassin asked.

Melni stared into the ugly hole for a moment. "This is a small one. Come, let us keep moving."

The road wound its way up the coastline. At Nakala, Caswell skidded to a stop on a bluff overlooking that ancient city and simply stared, mouth agape, at the devastation below. Half the gigantic city had been obliterated by one of the larger rocks that had fallen. The crater spanned almost a mile across, its rim lined with half-destroyed buildings overrun by spider vines and other invasive weeds. Huge piles of sand, blown in from the desert and fifteen feet deep in places, pooled around the bases of every structure's eastern edge. Opposite, facing the ocean, the surfaces were marred with patchwork patterns of black mold. The whole place seemed to shimmer with the populations that had replaced humankind: swarms of sandflies, whole flocks of gulls, and roaming packs of feral canis.

"Have you ever seen anything so terrible?" she asked Caswell.

Fingers twitching on the handles of his cycle, he replied without breaking away from the view. "There are weapons on Earth that can do this, but I've never . . . they haven't been used in a long time."

"Weapons? So powerful?"

He turned to her and nodded gravely. At her aghast expression he sighed. "I know. It's a wonder Earth isn't a molten ball of slag."

Caswell went back to studying the annihilated landscape below them. Melni found herself staring at him. Did he realize what he represented? That even a basic description of how such weapons worked could shift advantage to the South? At least provide an equalizer to hold the stalemate, perhaps indefinitely? Yes, she realized. He did know. She finally understood why he refused to tell her things, and why he saw Valix's influence here as so dangerous.

"You said such weapons have not been used in a long time. When were they used? Why?"

"To end a war," he said, voice flat. "Two cities, not unlike this one, destroyed to force one side to surrender."

"And it worked?"

He nodded.

A chill ran through her. The thought of Alia Valix unveiling such a weapon at the summit. Threatening to wipe the South out entirely if they did not bow to the North's supremacy. Perhaps she, too, would use one as an example. Fired from the water or dropped from one of those massive airships. Whatever information Caswell could provide would be rendered trivial if there were no South to benefit.

Of course, the easier option was to remove Caswell himself. Find out where he is and make that place the example. The individual threat, a whole city, and the determination of an entire hemisphere, all obliterated in one single act. If Valix did nothing else, the entire history of Gartien would be forever, irrevocably, altered.

"Valix," Melni asked carefully, "knows how to build such a weapon?"

Caswell nodded. "And others. Worse, much worse, than this. Relax, okay? It would still take an enormous effort, and I see no pressing threat here that would make her open that particular box of horrors."

"Nothing here, no. But what about from your world?"

He thought about this for a long time. "That I had not considered."

"I mean, you are just one man. What if they send an army next time?"

Caswell kicked at a loose rock, lost in thought. He glanced habitually at his wrist and, seeing no bracelet there, balled his fists in frustration.

"They took your jewelry," Melni said, with a pang of guilt. "Regret."

"It's all right. Just . . . sentimental value. Let's keep moving."

Caswell insisted on riding well past the dead city before they stopped to refill the air vessels. She showed him how to set up the collapsible turbine on a windy gravel beach, then convinced him to try a bite of spicy pie filled with minced nuts and red bean paste. He swallowed one bite and then, a minute later, face green, walked off to expunge it. While she ate, the little turbine blades spun overhead in the strong breeze. Even with that energy, she and Caswell still took turns cranking the manual pressurizer to feed more air into the cycles' canisters. It took nearly an hour, and by the end they were both tired, sweaty, and eager to be moving.

"Day becomes night by the minute," Melni said. "I would like to be at the coast before dark."

He nodded, pulling his dust-coated goggles on. "I've been wanting to ask about that. How do we cross?"

"Another boat," she said, hoping the code still held that scavengers kept communal watercraft in sailing condition as a courtesy to one another.

"Who are they?"

He lay next to her on a boulder wedged in a cleft between two hills. Above the sky blazed with the twinkling eyes of a thousand stars, capped on either end by the waning moons of tiny Gisla and her lover, Gilan.

Ahead, on a smooth, narrow beach pestered by frothy waves that crashed like muffled thunder, a woman and a man worked together to heave a large mesh bag over the side of a tiny sailboat. They wore shabby clothing beneath impressive gear: knives on each hip, hunting rifles slung across their backs, goggles to keep the sand and dust out of their eyes.

When Melni spoke she tried to sound relaxed. "I do not think they are dangerous. We call them Grim Runners. Desolation scavengers. Sometimes they smuggle between South and North."

"All the way to the other frontier?"

"Not so far. There are rolltowns in places, well hidden."

"Rolltowns?"

"Like . . . a place to unroll your bed and sleep, nothing more."

"We call it a campsite."

She thought about that and nodded. "Grims from both sides meet and trade what they can, barter for maps and food. I wrote a report about them, years ago, when a miniature war flared between their factions and our agents needed to avoid such places. Those tensions later eased." Melni glanced up and down the beach. "I do not see any other boats. There are usually three, maybe more."

"What do we do? Steal it?"

Melni placed a hand on his arm, a sudden fear in her that he might march up the beach and slay the couple before she could shout to stop him. "Be calm. The boats are shared. We wait for them to leave, then we take it across. Nine miles to the other side." It had been a clear day and she could see the rocky hills of Cirdia across the water.

"Suppose they don't leave. It's late; they might camp here."

"Then we risk approaching. I'd prefer no one see us here but we cannot delay much."

He picked at some pebbles on the boulder in front of them, tossing them down into the sand below. "Maybe we should approach now. This waiting is—"

"You are right," Melni said. "Look."

The pair had moved the bag up the beach about fifty feet and buried it under sand. That task complete, they'd returned to the boat and now worked to turn it around. "They are going back across," Melni said, already up to her knees.

Caswell followed her, leaping down from the boulder and jogging behind her, slowed by his still-healing wound. Sandflies erupted from a clump of seaweed and clouded around. Melni swatted the black insects aside and sprinted ahead. She shouted, "Ahey! May we approach?"

The woman stood in the sailboat, legs wide for balance, untying the sailcloth. Her companion stood knee-deep in gentle waves, struggling to push the craft out of the sand and into the glittering black water. Both froze at the sight of two strangers approaching. They glanced nervously at each other and abandoned their work. The woman cast a quick, sidelong glance at the place on the beach where they'd just buried their haul.

"Close enough!" the man called out. He had a thick Cirdian accent, not uncommon this close to that old country. Survivors had streamed both north and south two centuries before, and lived today in clusters of their own kind.

Melni stopped and held out her hands. Caswell came to stand just behind her.

"State your business," the woman by the boat said.

Melni took a tentative step forward. "We had hoped to use the boat to cross when you finished. But since you appear to be going back, perhaps—"

"Your business," the woman repeated, her raspy voice sharp as the knife at her hip.

"Careful," Caswell whispered.

"It is all right," she whispered back. She raised her hands higher. "A simple message swap in Rolltown Calis."

"Swap? Who with?" the man asked.

"That is not your concern," Melni said. She tried to make it sound matter-of-fact. It came out defensive. "What I mean is, our task is not of importance. Wealthy families, separated by the craters, who wish—"

"Calis is *gone,* young lady."

"Gone?"

The man nodded, his face grave. The woman spoke. "Along with all the other rolltowns. Destroyed. Not heard this? Maybe we are ahead of the news."

Dread began to seep through Melni's bones. "What news? How did this happen?"

"Those floating monstrosities from Combra started bombing them lasterday. Plus two caravans."

"That we know of," the man added.

"That we know of," the woman agreed.

Melni bit her worry back, swallowed. "So far south," she said. "That is a breach of treaty."

The scavenger pair both laughed bitterly. Again the woman spoke. "Treaty, a-yah. Also says no travel in the Desolation save for the Vongar."

"According to treaty, enforceable only on their own frontier," Melni pointed out.

"You tell them that," the woman replied. "And those who died in the rolltowns."

Caswell cleared his throat. "Despite all this you appear to be going back across."

They tensed at his strange accent. Both squinted in his direction, as if noticing him for the first time. *At least he is well disguised,* Melni thought.

"A-yah, so we are. Ferrying our stores here until the whalebirds are gone."

Caswell stepped in closer to Melni and spoke under his breath. "Whalebirds. Like the one we saw in the North?"

"What do we do?"

He shifted his feet in the sand. "You can turn back if you want. I have no choice."

She nodded and raised her own voice to the couple at the waterline. "Can you take us across? We can pay."

The woman stepped closer and studied them both, up and down. "No gear with you?"

"We have thumpers. Two. Back in the ravine."

She considered this for a moment. The man whispered something to her. She raised her chin and looked at Melni with renewed skepticism. "You take a big risk for a simple message 'tween families."

"And I think I comprehend now," Melni said, "why they offered us such an impressive payment."

"Which we won't receive," Caswell added, quick to follow her lead, "if it's not delivered."

The couple debated in hushed voices for some time. In the end they turned and faced Melni and Caswell in a united front. The woman spoke. "Five hundred. One way."

"Done," Caswell said. "Wait. Do we have that much?"

Melni pressed her flat hand across her lips, hoping he'd remember the meaning of the gesture. "We can only spare two hundred and fifty."

"Exactly half of the proposed fee," the man said, more to his partner than to Melni. "How convenient."

"Three hundred," the woman countered. "And I will have that camera, too."

Melni paid with the last of their stolen money, the camera she'd purchased in Gylina Square, and only as much gratitude as tact required. She left Caswell to wait with the couple while she made two trips back to the rocky cleft to fetch their thumpers. He helped her lift them aboard while the ragged couple looked on, impatient.

Ten minutes later the small craft set sail. In the darkness, as the boat tacked on a stiff wind against brutal waves, flashes of light began to illuminate the underside of clouds to the north. Thunder rolled across the stretch of water and, as the far shore grew close, began to rattle the brass catches of the decaying sail rig.

"That's some storm," Caswell said.

"No storm," the woman at the till replied. "The blixxing Combs have started bombing again."

* * *

They rode in the weak light of tiny Gisla, her lover Gilan having set.

Melni took the lead. She shunned the more direct coastal path, turning inland and up into the foothills of southern Cirdia—an area Caswell said was called "Spain" on his world. She relied on overgrown trees and partially collapsed crater walls to shield their passage from the Combran airships high above. She glimpsed the elongated egg-shaped behemoths twice through fleeting breaks in a cloud bank that split the sky in half. Gisla hovered just above the eastern horizon, below the cloud layer as if holding the gray mass at bay.

Three times they stopped to refill the pressure vessels, eat, and use the smallberry bushes as an improvised lav. Obstacles on the ill-maintained arterial scavenger trails hampered their progress. The dirt path weaved between craters old and, in a few disturbing cases, brand-new. By the time Garta began to chase darkness from the sky they'd only made one hundred and sixty miles.

Near dawn, however, the Combran airships vanished, apparently unwilling to be seen directly, or perhaps chased away by the invisible hand of diplomacy going on.

Or maybe they have killed everyone they can find, and now they lurk, waiting. Melni's skin crawled at the thought.

Despite a raging ache across her lower back from the thumper's worn old saddle, and a weariness that now seemed ingrained in every cell of her being, she suggested they should push on without sleep.

Caswell agreed instantly.

If anything he seemed to have become more alert since leaving Riverswidth. No grimaces of pain, or tentative movements. He'd been silent since landing on the coast, answering her questions with nods or simple shakes of the head. On one of their stops he'd sat still for almost ten full minutes with the thumb and forefinger of one hand pressed against his temples. At first she'd thought he was shielding his eyes from a sudden ray of sunlight, but even when the clouds blocked Garta once again his hand remained there.

She watched him for some time. What was he doing? She thought of the object in his neck, and how advanced the technology on his world was. Was he communicating, right now? With his Earth? Sending his thoughts back there like some kind of antenna? The distance must be incredibly vast, but did that make such a thing impossible? Another idea crept into her head. He had come down from space, landed here. He'd implied so, at least. So maybe he didn't have to contact another world, but a nearby craft waiting to take him home. "Tell me something," she said.

He glanced up, as if woken from a light sleep. His gaze met hers. After a second, he nodded.

"Are you and Valix the only of your kind here?"

"Yes."

"I do not mean on the ground. Does someone wait for you"—she pointed to the zenith of the sky—"up there?"

Caswell shook his head. "I wish. But no."

"Are you in contact with your world?"

"No." He sighed and stepped closer to her, offering his hands. An odd gesture, but she understood he wanted to hold her. She let him, placing her hands in his. They were warm and rough. A scar ran along one palm. A gold band graced one finger of his right hand. "I have no way to contact home. No way to let them know if I've succeeded or failed."

Melni looked into his dark eyes. She thought of her own time in the North, in Combra. How exhilarating it had been to be entirely on her own, in constant danger, making decisions. Yet at any time she could have left. Fled south to be among allies. She'd had a way out. Caswell had no such options. He would never be able to leave. Utterly alone, except for her. "And then? They will send someone else to find out?"

He considered that and shrugged. "Probably. But they won't risk further contact with your world just to fetch me. If I succeed, I'll be stuck here. If I fail, well, who knows? They may try again but that will take time, and now that Alia knows we have found her, she'll take measures to hide herself. Or worse . . ."

"Worse? How?"

His mouth tightened into a line, and his hands gripped hers more tightly. To speak of this pained him in a very literal sense, she forced herself to remember. "I fear she'll try to give Gartien everything she has all at once. All our history, our science, inventions. Including our weapons. What if that's her play at the summit?"

"You fear we will destroy ourselves?"

To her surprise, he shook his head. "What I fear, Melni, is that Earth will then see Gartien as a threat."

For a while they just stood there in the cold dawn air, her hands in his, as Garta's light began to spill across the desolate land. She kept opening her mouth to ask what that meant, what Earth would do to such a threat, but there was no point. She already knew. His tone said far more than the words he'd spoken.

Minutes passed. A breeze stirred the leaves. Caswell finally let her hands go, so that he could rub at his temples again.

"This device, in your neck," she said, "works by rubbing your temples?"

"Yes."

"Your scientists could not think of a better interface?"

He let out a single astonished laugh. "They could, and did. My watch," he said, and made a circle with one hand around the other wrist, "handled certain functions of the implant automatically. It's been a long time since I've had to manually perform such tasks."

The mention of the bracelet stung. Giving it to Rasa Clune had been an act of loyalty. Now it felt like a betrayal, to him. Knowing its function, she wondered what intelligence would be gleaned from the device. "What functions?"

"I've used it sparingly, if that's what you're asking."

Melni tilted her head deliberately, and squinted at him. "Wait. I saw what you did at Riverswidth. They sought to kill you. Yet it seemed as if you were merely dancing with them. Are you telling me you were holding back?"

"You know I can't go into details."

"Caswell," she said, grabbing his hands again and squeezing hard. "Can you not trust me? I will keep your secrets. Your goal resolves for me. I agree with the principle of it.

Please, do not jeopardize our success out of fear of my tongue."

He sighed, then nodded. "It's more complicated than that. The gland requires a reservoir of certain chemicals to work, and without food I am dangerously low on most. I don't want to waste what I have left, because I think I'll need it very soon. So I hold back. The meal packet I found in Riverswidth I ate and used because I saw no other way to get us out of there."

A tingling sensation ran up her spine and across her scalp. "That was hardly a meal. What can you do when fully, er, supplied?"

Caswell stared at her for a long moment. A grin tugged at the corners of his mouth. "Sweetheart, you ain't seen nothin' yet." At her blank, uncomprehending expression he chuckled. "Right now I am trying to keep my pain, hunger, and fatigue from overwhelming me. If and when I'm able to really let loose . . . well, I suspect you'll be happy I'm on your side."

She returned his grin, warmed by the foreign and wonderful term *sweetheart,* yet also chilled with imaginative visions of what this man might become when truly unleashed.

26

HE'D LIED TO HER. A white lie, but it still gnawed at him.

The implant kept him awake by shutting down parts of the brain in a carefully controlled sequence, letting one bit rest at a time instead of the lot. He hadn't yet used this capability since landing because he'd always felt it a last resort. There were dangers, not the least of which was simply operating your brain in a way that went against everything the body knew. He saw no alternative, though. He was battered, starving, and dehydrated. If he fell asleep he feared he might never wake.

He'd also allowed a trickle of pain suppression. All that had been true, more or less.

What he'd left out was the heightened state of his senses. Hearing, specifically. He thought it best to keep this to himself, in the spirit of his mission.

Just after midday that became impossible.

"We need to get off the road!" Caswell shouted over the snare-drum rattle of the air engine.

The Sun, Garta, battled scattered clouds. Midafternoon light tinged slightly yellow. They had not stopped since dawn, when he'd told her the basics of what his implant could do.

"Agreed," Melni shouted back. "I am so hungry, and this seat is—"

"I mean now!"

He accelerated ahead of her and swerved off between two

giant trees. The ground, blanketed by dry fallen leaves of vibrant yellows, oranges, and reds, crunched beneath the cycle's tires. Caswell weaved a tight path between thin gray trunks and skidded to a stop in the shade of a low rock outcrop.

Melni roared in after him, too fast. She jerked the bike to the left, skidding in a wild slide that threw autumn leaves and clods of damp earth into the air. "Blixxing cur—" she started, fighting to keep the cycle upright. The curse died on her lips because she saw him. Caswell held one hand flat across his mouth in the Gartien sign of silence, his eyes scanning the clouds above.

Ten seconds passed in near-total silence. Just the sound of rustling leaves. The emerald-green canopy swayed in the breeze. Nothing else moved.

"What is it?" Melni whispered.

"Airships," he said.

She glanced around. "I hear nothing but the wind."

Caswell reached up and lightly tapped the back of his neck. "I can."

If the revelation of this ability surprised her, she hid it well. "I thought you were holding that in reserve?"

"I am, for the most part. But I also don't want a bomb to drop on us."

"Gratitude."

Minutes passed before Melni finally craned her neck toward the sound. Caswell let his augmentation ebb, hearing the world again as she did. The growing noise resembled the nearby buzzing of a persistent fly, coming from everywhere and nowhere. For minutes it went on, joined by others in a droning chorus. Any second now Caswell expected to see an entire fleet of those bulbous monstrosities fill the sky, but then the sound faded until only the wind remained. Caswell rubbed his temple, listening for another few minutes before he glanced at Melni and nodded. "I suggest we move as fast as possible when they're not around."

"I need a bite to eat."

"You know," he said, "the first thing I'm going to do when we find Alice is ask what the hell she's been eating and drinking all this time."

The look of guilt on Melni's face was priceless. "Regret! If you would prefer I—"

"It's fine," he said. "You eat. I'll top us off."

His wording earned a quizzical look that evaporated from her face when he began to compress more air into the thumper's pressure canisters. While she ate he repeated the process for the other bike.

Caswell stowed the pump gear and swung his leg over the bike's saddle. "Want me to lead for a while?"

A shower of leaves cut off his words. Melni, astride her bike, had gunned the accelerator to full and tore away from him in a flurry of sprayed debris that peppered his goggles. She looked back at him and flashed a childish grin.

"Going to be like that, is it?" he said to himself, and raced off after her.

The bumpy dirt "road" was studded with rocks and fallen branches, riddled with long trenches carved by rain, and rife with blind curves. Still, he managed to close the gap, grinning like a fool when the trail opened up into a long, straight passage through a flat patch of forest.

Hidden from the sky by a cathedral ceiling of tangled branches, Melni pushed her cycle to its limit. Caswell followed her example. Five miles into the straightaway he managed to overtake her, his grin echoed by a mischievous smile on her face. He weaved in front of her and laughed aloud as dark soil and churned leaves sprayed across her body.

The air, thick with the rampant vegetation all around, had an almost intoxicating effect. He lost himself in the race. All the fear and worry at what lay ahead was suddenly forgotten in a rush of wind and the simple competition. Every ten seconds they traded positions. She could ride, no doubt about that. And, to his delight, she displayed a competitive streak that seemed to equal his own. At one point she pulled up next to him and they playfully traded halfhearted attempts to kick the other off balance. Then Melni leaned forward, streamlining herself, and shot ahead on a burst of speed he hadn't expected. She took a bump, left the ground, landed in a puddle that splayed mud across his borrowed army coat and splattered across his goggles. Caswell roared with laughter and leaned so far forward his face almost touched the handlebar.

Melni glanced back at him, a sly grin plastered across her face. She never saw the sharp bend in the trail. He tried to shout a warning, but it was too late.

Trampled ground gave way to raw soil, thick and muddy, strewn with obstacles. He watched helplessly as she fought for control. Her focus shifted to the immediate obstacles, not on the change looming just beyond. He felt his heart lurch. Ahead, the forest fell away. Open sky replaced the dark crowd of tree trunks. At the last instant Melni swerved right, leaned into the turn, and let the cycle kick out in a vicious skid that sent a wave of dirt and leaves over the precipice she'd almost crossed.

She stopped just inches from the cliff edge. Caswell followed her, more slowly, his heart racing. "That was close," he managed, pulling off his goggles.

"I was holding back," she said.

"Not the race. Christ, you almost flew right over the edge, Melni."

She turned to look, and seemed to see the crater edge for the first time. Propping the thumper on its stand, she walked to the drop-off and stood, mouth agape, at the view below.

Caswell came up beside. "Shit," he whispered.

The great wound had leveled forest, cleaved away hillsides and floodplains, and demolished a small village on the visible perimeter far to his left. A river—he could almost see its original winding path from before the event—entered one side, pooled into a great semicircular lake in the basin, then drained out of a dozen low points along the eroded edges. Despite plenty of trees and plants growing in the massive basin, the shape and scale of the impact zone was still apparent, even after two centuries.

"One of the titan craters," she said. "Fifteen miles across. There are only a half-dozen of this scale."

"Unbelievable."

She pointed off to the right. "If I am not mistaken, our destination is up that river valley about fifty miles. We are close."

"How long until Valix's summit, exactly?"

"Tomorrow evening. Fifteen hours from now."

He converted that in his head. Thirty Earth-hours to get to Alice. And two days after that, reversion would come. Everything since the *Venturi,* forgotten. He'd have to isolate himself by then. Lose himself somewhere in this vast wasteland. What would he tell Melni? He resolved to worry about it later. "Will we make it?"

She summoned her mental map of the area. "It is five hundred miles from there to Fineva. It will be a near thing, especially if we spend a lot of time searching for our evidence."

"No time to waste, then."

The playful mood of the forest race evaporated in the face of the brush with death and the press of time. Melni took the lead, picking a path along the jagged crater rim. After a few miles a collapsed portion of the steep wall provided entry. She bounded down the recently formed hillside and into the crater proper, the drumbeat rhythm of her cycle just meters ahead of his, the two machines both at the limit of their capability.

After fording two streams at their shallowest points, and another half hour of brutal riding out the other side of the crater, Melni found the cleft that led into the valley Caswell had identified on the map. A swift and narrow river gurgled down the center of the ravine. Melni followed its rock-strewn bank. Soon she began to weave, and almost fell. Her bike rolled to a sudden stop.

"What's the matter?" Caswell asked, pulling up beside her.

"I am exhausted."

He let her rest, sitting on a rock a few meters away where he could see most of the sky and the entire span of the crater they'd just crossed. A birdlike creature wheeled overhead, four brightly colored wings glinting in the morning light.

"Hear anything?" she asked him.

Caswell shook his head. "All quiet."

"We should go then, before they return."

"Rest awhile."

She considered this for several seconds, then began to shake her head, slowly, then with more conviction. "There is no time. I will be okay if you lead. Navigating requires more focus than I can muster."

"All right then," he replied.

Caswell mounted up and, while Melni fiddled with her goggles, he rubbed his temples and mentally gave a series of commands. A familiar warm tingle began to spread across his scalp from the back of his neck as a chemical mixture crept through his brain. It used the last of his reserves, but he could see no alternative. Saving it for some shoot-out with Alice Vale's bodyguards would not matter if he arrived too late. Better to make sure he arrived in time, and trust his natural skill as a killer to do the rest. He only knew that part of himself from what had transpired the last few weeks, but what he'd learned gave him confidence. *Just get me there,* he urged his implant, *and I'll figure something out. It's what I do.*

So he rode, like some maniac teenage motocross champion. He weaved between narrow gaps in the hairy bushes Melni called "loma plants," darted around boulders like a fox in flight, and used the bumps in the ground to jump over dangerous eroded pits. Melni fell into some kind of trance-like zone, mimicking his path subconsciously. She fell behind now and then, but overall she held her own and their pace improved significantly.

A few hours later, a patch of color ahead caught his eye. Caswell began to slow.

"Are we here already?" she asked, sliding up next to him.

"No," he said, "and yet . . . yes."

She followed his gaze down a steep hill. Ten meters away a signpost protruded from the ground, partially obscured by tall, pale weeds. Old and rusted, tilting slightly in the soft dirt where it had been placed, the sign nevertheless had obviously been placed here recently. In the last ten years, he thought.

The sign warned of mines, if he understood it correctly. Best to be sure. "What's it mean?"

Melni swallowed to clear her throat. "Toe-bombs," she said. "A good thing you spotted this. I would have missed it."

"Toe-bombs?" He could guess, but he wanted to hear it from her.

"Disk-shaped explosives buried just below the topsoil. They will explode if enough weight is detected by a sensor plate on top." As she spoke she made a round shape with her fingers, about the size of a dinner plate.

"Mm. We call them land mines," Caswell said. "Or, we did. They've been outlawed for a hundred years on Earth."

"They are illegal here, too. For almost half a century. One of the few things both North and South agreed on. None have been placed since, so far as I know. And while many old fields still exist, I have never heard of one so far from either frontier."

"That sign doesn't look fifty years old. More like ten."

"I thought the same thing."

He knelt and shoved his fist into the soil, scooping out a handful and letting it fall through his fingers. Soft dirt. Easy to conceal a land mine just a few inches below the surface. "Well," he said, "one thing's for sure. We're in the right place."

"How do you know?"

Caswell nodded at the sign. "Someone doesn't want people snooping around." He crouched there, studying the landscape, for some time. "I say we leave the bikes—thumpers—here. Follow the river on foot until we reach that boathouse we saw in your picture."

"Too slow," Melni said. "Plus we would have to walk all the way back here to retrieve them, the opposite direction of Fineva. It would set us back hours."

He bit back his gut response, ready to defend his instincts against her calculated logic. She had it right. Caswell swallowed his pride. "Ideas, then?"

"Keep the thumpers," she offered. "Ride along the game trails. Look, there." She pointed off to their left, in a gully that paralleled the river. Even from here, fresh prints could be seen in the soft dirt. "Anything placed along such paths would have been set off by wild bhar already. They are heavy enough to trigger such devices. I see no sign of prior explosions."

"The trail might not lead where we're going," Caswell pointed out.

Melni shook her head. "Bhar eat the shoreflowers that bloom along the fringe in second month. They will follow the river."

"What are these bhar? Dangerous?" The word, similar to *boar,* conjured an unpleasant image of large feral pigs with nasty tusks.

"They are big, yes. The size of our thumpers, but harmless. They lumber around on six stubby legs, their great long snouts sweeping back and forth plucking flowers in vast quantities."

Caswell glanced up and down the trail, and saw no flowers. But he did see stems he'd mistaken for weeds. He pictured the animals, walking in a line, then *WHAM!* The leader vanishing in a cloud of smoke and chunks of meat and bone. Despite the wisdom in her plan, that vision gave him pause. "It's risky."

"So is fleeing Riverswidth on the eve of war. Or riding below airships that bomb anything that moves."

He grinned at her. "Do you ever deviate from one of your plans, once formed?"

Her smile matched his. "Plans can be useful. You should try making one sometime."

"I think I'll leave that part to you," he said, laughing.

The landscape began to feel familiar. Features gleaned from studying the photographs Melni had stolen. Certain twists in the river, and the shape of hills that sloped up gently to either side.

Half a kilometer from the boathouse Caswell skidded to a stop when the bhar trail abruptly ended. In front of him, almost concealed by the tall, bone-colored grass, were horizontal strips of razor wire. Not exactly like the kind he knew from Earth, but close enough. The sharp metal vines of the fencing ran out into the river and descended into sediment-clouded depths.

Melni watched as he dismounted and produced a pair of cutters from the tool pack each thumper had been supplied with. Old, rusty things, but when he pressed the handles together there came a satisfying snap and one of the sharpened strips of metal fell away with a twang that reverberated off in both directions—out into the water, and up the steep wall of the canyon that they had entered half an hour earlier.

He cut the remaining bands and, with a sand-coated scarf wrapped around his fist, pushed the fragments out of their way. Then he stowed the tool and stood beside his bike, ready to push it. He glanced at Melni and tried to give her a confident expression.

She met his gaze with a single raised eyebrow.

"If I'm right," he said, "she'll have this place well guarded."

"We have not seen anyone."

"Not by people. This place is her greatest secret, if it's what we think it is. Mines, razor wire . . . that's only the beginning, I fear. Stay well behind me just in case."

He could see the small war behind her eyes, that innate desire to lead she harbored being fought back by a grudging acknowledgment that his implant gave them too large an advantage here. She relented, swung down off her bike, and began to push.

They walked in the late-afternoon sunlight. The cheerful conversation of songbirds gave way to the sighs and scratches of insects. Caswell listened, transfixed by the similarities and the differences equally.

Not far from the interwoven helixes of razor wire he came upon the narrow dirt lane glimpsed in the aerial scout's photo. Weeds had obscured most of it, but there was no mistaking the wide bulbous puff of the greencloud tree and, in its shade, the two graves. Caswell glanced in each direction. To his right he saw the cottage, hidden in the cleft at the end of the ravine. No smoke curled from the chimney now. A good sign, he decided. If Alice had lived here, there wouldn't be many clues left behind if someone else had moved in since.

Vegetation had all but consumed the little cottage. A small shade tree sprouted from the roof, its roots worming their way through layers of ancient mud-brick tiles and into the dark depths of two tall, glassless windows. Orange spiderwebs clung to the undersides of the eaves. An old wooden bucket lay discarded on the stone steps that led around to the back of the tiny hovel.

Caswell glanced right. The road, somewhat maintained in the photograph, was nothing more than a trail of saplings doing battle with choking weeds. Only their small size compared to the adult growth around them marked the path.

"No one has been here in years," Melni said, echoing his thoughts.

Caswell wasn't so sure. Something about the perfectness of it all nagged at him. As if this "nothing to see here" effect was elaborately staged. He said, "Or we're meant to think that. Let's have a closer look."

He moved to the two graves and went to one knee. Knelt so, the meter-tall weeds concealed him completely. Melni came closer and knelt beside him.

Crude gravestones—crosses made from sticks and twine—poked from the far end. Near the middle of the piled dirt, dry flowers lay in bundles lashed not with twine but clear tape. The flowers, though brittle and long dead, still held faded blues and yellows of their original coloration.

"These were placed here in the last year, maybe two, if I'm not mistaken," Caswell said.

Melni pointed at the strips of adhesive. "That tape is a Valix invention. Something of a North-wide phenomenon five years ago. Why are these mounds marked with the letter *T*?"

He stood and brushed dirt from his hands. "Our best evidence. That's a religious symbol from Earth. She was here all right."

"Did she travel here with others? Perhaps—"

"No, she came alone."

"You are so sure?"

"Yes," he said, more tersely than he'd intended. Caswell went back to the trail. He studied the cottage for a long time. It was far too dilapidated and exposed to harbor much in the way of evidence. He glanced the other way, toward the boathouse. In the photo that structure had a key difference compared to the cottage: a new roof. Caswell went that way and Melni fell in behind him once again.

He weaved a careful trail through what she'd called bone-grass. The knuckled segments tapped against his body and then sprang away before settling back in to mar Melni's passage a few seconds later, like probing skeletal fingers.

A subtle change in the soundscape made him stop.

Melni almost ran into him. "What is it—"

His upheld hand silenced her. He rubbed his temple, and willed augmentation to his hearing. The dregs of his chemical reserves obliged, but only just. Caswell craned his neck and tilted his head from side to side. What was it? What had changed? Insects, like cicadas but with a wholly alien rhythm and tone, filled his ears. Beneath came the regular sloshing of the river. There had been something else. A brief, minute addition, like the hiss of a snake. Or like an air engine, settling down to a stop? Whatever it was, it was gone now.

Beside him, Melni glanced around, her brow furrowed. She hadn't heard it, or perhaps whatever had made the sound was normal to her ear, like the rush of a field mouse through grass that he would ignore back home.

Twenty seconds passed without further anomalies. Caswell lowered his hand. "Nothing, I guess," he said. "My imagination. Let's go."

The cleft between the hills weaved around for another thirty meters. With each step the sound of the river grew until finally the brown water came into view, sliding past from right to left. Roughly a hundred meters wide here. The path's angle sloped suddenly down to the water's edge where the boathouse waited.

While the cottage had appeared to be centuries old, the boathouse gave the exact opposite impression. Though ramshackle and filthy, it lacked the air of total abandoned disrepair. The roof sloped to either side at a shallow angle, finished in shingle tiles, even patched in places. The walls were of poorly painted wooden slats. None of it seemed to line up quite right, as if the right supplies had been slapped together by an incompetent builder. Compared to the small cottage it presumably serviced, this was quite large, a long, rectangular shape that started five meters out on the water and spanned another ten up onto the shoreline of the turgid river. The building's uneven window frames were not empty, though they didn't contain panes of glass, either. Instead, planks of wood had been sloppily nailed across the spans. The door itself had a length of heavy iron chain wrapped neatly around the handle and the foot latch at the base. Clasped around the links there rested a heavy combination padlock, alien and yet instantly recognizable.

The lock did not concern Caswell. His eyes were drawn instead to the signs peppered all around the building as well as on both windows and the door itself.

Each read:

QUARANTINE
DEADLY TOXINS PRESENT
Joint Gartien Assembly—Desolation Survey

Rust crept in from the edges of the brightly painted signs. One hung at a tilted angle, a broken loop of wire dangling behind it.

More theater, Caswell suspected. He smirked.

"What is funny?" Melni asked, a tinge of fear in her voice.

"Everything. It all says, 'Go away, it's too dangerous and besides there's nothing interesting here. Nope, nothing at all. Please leave.' Someone's trying too hard, I think."

Her gaze swung back to the boathouse, and she studied it anew with this perspective. After a few seconds she nodded in agreement.

Caswell studied the broader scene: the sloped path, the reeds along the riverbank, and the clefts in the surrounding hills now tucked in long shadows. He glanced at Melni and said, "Stay low."

Another nod.

He bent at the waist and moved at a light jog, avoiding anything on the path that might make a noise if stepped on. At the door to the boathouse he took one side. Melni understood and slid in opposite him, her back to the wall in a mirror of his posture. He glanced at the heavy lock and then the chain. He took in the windows and up to the underside of the eave that shaded them.

"Whoever built this place did a shitty job," he whispered.

"I was thinking the same thing."

He gestured to the lock and chain. "The wire cutters won't get through this."

"Agreed." Melni nodded toward one of the boarded windows. "Easier to pry some of those planks away, I think."

Caswell considered that, then grimaced. "Too loud. Let's check around the back first. Maybe it's open out toward the water. If we can get out of here without leaving a sign of our presence, I'd prefer it."

"Agreed," she said.

Melni took the lead. Around the side of the structure she found a long stick. She thrust the six-foot length of wood in, probing the depth a meter off the shore. The stick descended until her wrist touched the murky liquid. No chance of walking that. Without a word Caswell began to remove his boots and clothing. Melni watched him, a total lack of embarrassment as his clothes came off.

He stood with his toes at the waterline and readied a headfirst dive.

Melni pulled the stick from the water. It snagged on something. "Hold on," she said, a heartbeat before Caswell leapt.

He watched as she heaved on the stick. It had snagged on something. A few centimeters finally lifted out, along with a length of razor wire.

Caswell eased back and let out a long breath as a line of the barbed material broke the surface, a few meters in each direction. He envisioned ribbons of the stuff, entwined and snaking their way all around the base of the structure. "That would not have been a pleasant swim."

"Boost me up," she whispered, dropping the stick. "I will cross the roof and look down from there."

He cupped his hands and hoisted her to the awning, then busied himself with his clothes.

Dressed, he stood back a ways to watch her cross the roof. The tiles were coated with slick green moss. She crept to the far end slowly, avoiding portions of the surface that dipped downward. At the back, she lay down and peered over the edge. Then she turned and crawled back. She motioned for him to approach.

Caswell moved to the wall and looked up. "What did you see?"

"An old boat, tied up. I cannot see what condition it is in. There is another door, and some toolboxes."

"The door. Locked?"

She shrugged. "Yes, but there is a window. Boarded, but not visible from the front at least."

"Okay. Okay. How sturdy is that roof?"

"It will hold us," she said.

Caswell pressed himself against the wall and reached up for her offered hand. He stopped short of clasping it, and paused.

"What is wrong?"

Through his hand pressed against the wall he felt a constant, low vibration. He looked up at her. "A vibration," he said. "Coming from within."

"Perhaps just the flow of water against the supports?"

He thought about it. Held his hand firm for a while. The faint movement was absolutely constant. "Maybe." His gut told him her theory was wrong. This felt electric. He decided to keep the theory to himself until he could be absolutely sure. "Let's try that window in back." At least there it would not be immediately obvious someone had entered.

Caswell took a running leap and clasped her outstretched hand. It made a lot of noise, but he saw no alternative. She hauled him up and led him to the edge of the roof.

"Avoid those depressions," she said, pointing at the sinking portions.

He kept a modest distance and followed her steps. At the edge she lowered herself over the side and dropped onto the narrow edge of the dock below. The wood planks creaked under her weight. She moved in and watched as Caswell repeated her motion.

An old fishing boat bobbed in the calm black water of the slip, covered by gray canvas. The ropes that held it in place were black with mold. To either side of the moored craft were various stacks of toolboxes, air cylinders, and spare lengths of rope. Mold, dust, or a disgusting mixture of the two coated everything. The whole place reeked of mildew.

He glanced at the door, which was chained in the same fashion as out front.

"Search these boxes for something we can use," he said.
Melni took one side while he rummaged through the other.

In the third tool chest he found a pry bar and set to work
on the lone boarded window. The nails holding the wood in
place were rusted through and, with only a mild groan,
came free easily. In less than a minute he had the sill clear.
He paused only to glance at Melni. At her nod he hauled
himself up and in.

Darkness swallowed him. Even with the thin light spilling
in from the now-empty window frame, he had to wait for his
eyes to adjust.

Melni plopped down next to him and started to move farther in. He wrapped a hand around her forearm.

"Let your eyes adjust," he whispered.

"Why are you whispering?" she asked, her voice as low
as his.

"Just in case." He could feel the vibration through the
floor now.

Melni finally noticed it, too. She glanced down at her feet.
"What is that? A bilge pump?"

"It's warm in here," Caswell noted. "Maybe a power gen-
erator."

A trickle of sweat ran down his spine. He inhaled deeply.
Moist air rank with decay.

"There does not seem to be anything toxic," Melni said.

Caswell grunted his agreement. His eyes began to register details. Furniture covered with sheets once white, now
coated in thick dust and those strange orange spiderwebs.
Wooden floorboards creaked beneath his feet. He took a
path that led around the edges of the room and looked for a
closet or chest. Anything that Alice might have left belongings in. Maybe her spacesuit, or empty meal packets. Something.

Melni, able to see now, went to the center, picking her
path with great care. The floorboards squeaked at first, then
groaned with each step she took.

"Stop," he said.

Melni stopped, her eyes on him.

Something wasn't right. Caswell focused on the floor.

"What is it?" she asked.

"The sound of the floorboards changed."

Melni glanced down. Then she closed her eyes and focused. She took two careful steps back. Groan, groan, squeak.

He came to her. His last two steps also produced groans.

A low table separated them, covered in a dusty sheet. Caswell tore the fabric aside and coughed as a cloud of dust and grit filled the air. Melni waved at it uselessly, gave up, and went to her knees to inspect the floorboards. He joined her, and together they poked and prodded the surface.

One chunk moved when Caswell's fingers gripped it.

"Here," he said. He lifted the broken section of wood away. Gray metal gleamed just below, unmarred by dust. A ring the size of a bracelet lay flat on it, attached to a small hinge.

Caswell slipped his fingers through the ring, raised it, and lifted. "Move back," he said. After she did so he tried again and this time a square section of floor one meter on a side came free.

Beneath was a circular hatch of gray metal with a circular window in the middle. Familiar words were printed at four marks around the edge, in block lettering:

LATCH
PREP (BLEED PRESSURE BEFORE OPENING)
TEST
UNLATCH

Caswell allowed himself a grin. "*Venturi* Lander One."

"What does that mean?"

"The proof we need, Melni. A vessel just like mine, the one she came here in." How Alice had managed to get it under the building he could only imagine. The most likely explanation is that she built the place atop it, after landing here. A lot of work for one woman, he thought, and then remembered the two graves just up the trail. Maybe she'd enlisted help, or forced it, and then did away with them.

A hungry growl from his stomach banished that moment of revulsion. There might still be food in the stores. Alice Vale must have figured out a way to eat and drink here, otherwise she'd be long dead, but whether or not she'd solved that particular problem before running out of the supplies she'd stowed remained to be seen. He didn't hold much hope, but even that glimmer filled his mouth with greedy saliva.

He pulled out the recessed handle and twisted it from LATCH toward PREP, grunting with the effort, his mouth pinched in a snarl, teeth clamped together. The handle lurched and clicked into position. Breath held, Caswell waited. Inside the porthole window a single red light began to blink. He hissed breath through clenched teeth as more and more lights began to wink on inside. The damn thing still had power. It was causing the vibration. But why? Why hadn't Alice shut everything down?

Finally the circle of the porthole window glowed with a green ring of light. All clear. Caswell twisted the handle, with a bit less strain this time, to the UNLATCH marker. He eased Melni back with one arm and then yanked the whole thing up and away. There came a hiss of cool, stale air. Not pure like the air from his vessel, though. This air reeked of sweat and something foul. Spoiled food, he thought. Maybe even disease. Curious.

Melni suddenly backed away, repulsed by the odor. She looked at him with obvious worry. "It smells like death," she said.

Caswell tried to give her a reassuring smile. She had it right, but his mind still lingered on the possibility of edible food. Rancid, spoiled, or otherwise. "Let me go first."

She nodded emphatically, then watched in silence as Caswell lowered his feet inside and then, with only the slightest whisper of fabric against metal, slid his body down.

"Is it safe?" she asked from above.

"I think the air processors are failing, but it seems to be okay," he called back to her.

"Seems? It reeks like skinrot, Caswell."

"Let me open the inner door before you come in. Let some fresh air in."

She covered her mouth and nose with one hand and nodded to him, dubious.

The inner door opened without complaint. Another rush of disgusting air, even stronger here, flowed into the boathouse. After twenty seconds he took a tentative whiff. Still awful, but at least bearable now. "All clear," he called up.

Swallowing, searching his eyes for reassurance, Melni sat at the edge of the trapdoor and slid her body down into Alice Vale's spacecraft.

27

CASWELL WENT STRAIGHT to a cabinet door on the back wall and flung it aside. Dust fell in great clumps and spread into the rancid air. With desperate madness he began to paw through the contents, examining silvery packets and flinging them aside with growing frustration.

Finally he found one that met his criteria. He twisted off its cap, tilted it above his mouth, and sucked the contents down in four gigantic swallows.

"Slow down," Melni said. "You will just vomit it up if you eat that fast."

He nodded without looking at her, ashamed at his lack of self-control. Then a violent shiver ran through his body. He quickly inhaled the second packet. Then a third.

Melni left him to his desperate feast and took in the cramped cabin of the spacecraft. It resembled the one she had visited in Hillstav down to the last detail, but nothing gleamed. It was like viewing a beautiful work of art and then seeing it again, faded by time, half-hidden under grime and dust. Her treadmellows left imprints on the floor. Melni knelt and trailed a finger along the surface, watching the brownish material return to white. Her fingertip brushed across a groove. She traced it, revealing another porthole like the one above. Aboard Caswell's craft she had glimpsed the same feature through the gap in her blindfold. "Why," she asked, "do these vessels have a door on the floor as well as the ceiling?"

Caswell had to swallow a mouthful of food before answering. "The bottom one has no airlock. It's used only to connect the vehicle to other modules."

"What kind of modules?"

He shrugged. "You name it: habitats, labs, engines, other landers. Link enough together and you've got a city in space."

"I see."

Her fingertip squeaked across a round window inset into the porthole. Melni froze. She'd expected to see mud below, as she had in Caswell's craft, or perhaps swaying plants in the depths of the river. Instead she saw what appeared to be a wall of dark blue material a few feet away, broken only by a glowing green line inlaid perfectly into its surface. "What is this one connected to?"

"Nothing." He turned, a water container in his fist, squeezing the last few drops into his mouth through a blue straw. "It was connected to a ship called the *Venturi,* until Alice fled in it."

"Well, there is something down there."

A vertical worry line creased his forehead. He knelt beside her and wiped grime from the glass with one swift swipe of his forearm.

She pressed her face to the glass next to his.

"What the fuck?" he gasped.

Another room waited. Something separate from the lander. The dark blue of the wall curved gracefully at its edges to meet a floor and ceiling. Dimly glowing green lines ran along the surfaces in elegant patterns of no discernible purpose, though Melni sensed they were not simply decorative.

In places, holes six inches in diameter receded into darkness within the wall. They were spaced at regular intervals, as far as Melni could see, anyway, and displayed the same curved joining where they met the flat wall, as if the surface were clay and the holes had been simply pressed inward.

"What the hell is it?" Caswell asked.

"That you must ask me makes me very worried."

He grunted, a bitter laugh of agreement. "Well, let's have a look."

"Just like that? A strange dark room. Just go on in?"

"Sure, why not?"

She marveled at him. "Driven by instinct, as ever."

"You'd prefer we sit here and make a detailed plan?"

Melni dropped her head, shook it. "You could at least see if there is air inside. What if we open this and drown ourselves?"

"Hmm. Fair point. All right." He flipped open a panel beside the airlock door and tapped at a flat, recessed screen. Annotated graphs bloomed to life, varying in color but mostly green, which seemed to be the standard color for a positive indicator.

"There, you see? Breathable air."

"Are you always so lucky?"

He grinned at her. "As far as I can recall." Still smiling, Caswell twisted the handle and opened the lower airlock door. Through some unspoken agreement he slid first into the cavity below.

He stood almost perfectly still in the strange dark blue room for several seconds, his mouth agape in naked astonishment. Slowly he raised one hand to cover his open mouth.

"What is it?" Melni asked.

"Come down," he said, "and see for yourself." Then he stepped out of her view.

Melni slid in after him, landing neatly on the floor and rising to a half crouch, ready for anything.

Or so she thought. Her own jaw went slack at what lay before her, and without intending to do so, Melni soon stood as Caswell had, one hand over her own gaping, astonished mouth, her gaze utterly locked on the thing her companion now stood beside.

Focus, a voice in her head urged before the sight overwhelmed her. *Analyze. Study.*

With a conscious effort Melni clamped her jaw shut and lowered her hand. She strode forward. Three tentative steps ahead and to the side opposite Caswell.

Between them was a bed, or something like one. The surface was made of translucent bulbous shapes of amber, linked by flat, conjoined edges as if they'd started small and grown until connecting. The bed was not flat, but formed exactly to support the body of a very tall, very thin person who lay upon it. Man or woman she could not tell. It seemed somewhere between the two. A he, she decided, for the sake of a mental handhold.

His skin was bone white and smooth, veins visible under the surface. He looked impossibly thin, and not in a natural way. There seemed to be no muscle under the sagging skin, as if he were being consumed from the inside. Melni shivered.

He had long silvery hair that looked soft as spider silk. It lay in a cloud atop the amber bulbous cushions. His eyes were closed, the lids slightly blue—the only color on his face. His lips were as pale as his skin. His nose, long and finely etched, had an almost inhuman perfection to it.

Gradually Melni took in the rest of the body. Arms and legs as thin as a malnourished child's. The chest was hairless and lacked nipples. A belly button did mar the otherwise smooth stomach.

A cloth of fine white fabric had been wrapped around his pelvis and thighs. Long fingers and toes sprouted from the hands and feet, the nails perfectly matched to the tips as if meticulously trimmed.

Caswell reached out. Melni hissed a warning at him, shook her head, but he did not stop. Acting on instinct, yet again.

Two inches from the man's arm, a sharp crack broke the silence. Electricity rippled away from Caswell's finger, drawing fine little blue-white dots in a ripple pattern across an invisible surface. Caswell jerked back, his mouth twisted in pain. He shook his hand vigorously and blew on the fingertip.

"Are you insane?" Melni asked.

Caswell glanced at her apologetically. "I just wanted to see—"

"Think before you act, just this once, will you?"

"That's not fair."

"Who are you?" a third voice said.

Melni glanced down to the source of those brittle, barely audible words. She felt sure he'd spoken, but the face of the man on the table had not changed. The eyes were still closed, the hairless skin still pallid, the lips . . .

One lip twitched. Then they parted and the tip of a pale tongue emerged and slid across them. His eyes fluttered beneath closed lids and, as if in reaction, a semitransparent tube emerged from between two of the bulbous amber cushions. The tube glided upward and curved around to touch the man's parched lips. With a motion of pure economy he moved just enough to draw clear fluid into his mouth. Then his head sank back and he became still once more. The tube retracted without a sound.

"I was going to ask you the same thing," Caswell said.

"Are you sick?" Melni asked at the same instant.

"Very," the man croaked. Again the eyes moved beneath the lids. The tube extruded itself around from the bed, and he sipped once more. The fluid had an orange color to it this time.

"What can we do?" she asked. It was, she realized, the most ludicrous question she had ever asked. "Medicine, or . . ."

"No."

Caswell spoke, force in his words that seemed incongruous to the frail figure on the bed. "Who are you? What is this place?"

The pale blue eyelids drew back. The irises below were like liquid gold flecked with rust. They drifted from Caswell to the ceiling and all at once the room changed. Blue walls and ceiling turned white. The floor became a dull, dark maroon. The glowing green lines that snaked along the walls graduated to a bright yellowish white, ramping in brightness until the whole space flooded with a sunlight hue and noticeable warmth.

His bed transformed, too. The bulbs grew and shrank organically and in concert, shifting the patient they bore into a reclined sitting position, his head propped enough to be eye level with Melni. He licked at his lips once again and regarded them both. "Please, sit."

The frail man raised his left arm. Tendril-like tubes rose with it, dangling from bruised puncture points on the skin that had been in contact with the cushion, to disappear somewhere below him. Medicines, nutrients, Melni guessed. With his gesture two thin, rectangular strips sluiced off the wall and rotated down. In unison and absolute silence they settled into position as benchlike chairs, perfectly positioned behind Caswell's and Melni's knees.

Melni sat, wondering how such things were possible. The drink tube, the chairs, it all seemed to happen merely by thought. Though she knew little of Caswell's world, his reaction, the look of shock and even fear on his face told her that he was as impressed by the display of technology as she. This man was as alien to him as to her. Despite the warmth of the strip lights she felt an unnervingly familiar chill course through her.

"What do I call you?" the man asked.

"I'm Peter Caswell," Caswell said, "and this is Melni Tavan."

"I am also known as Meiki Sonbo," she corrected. Peter raised an eyebrow in response.

The gaunt face had become more alert. Color flowed into the face. The orange eyes, now bright, exuded intelligence. "A Southerner of Gartien, though your features mark you as a *desoa*," he said to Melni, then slid his gaze back to Caswell, "and an Earthling. British aristocracy, I think I hear? It's been a long time and my knowledge of accents has slipped along with everything else."

Caswell stiffened. "How the hell—"

The man went on as if he hadn't heard. "Sent by Monivar, then, and not Alice."

"Who?"

"Monivar Pendo Tonaris?"

Melni glanced at Caswell. His mouth hung agape and then audibly clicked shut. For a moment he sat perched there, grinding his teeth. "Are you . . . do you mean Monique? Monique Pendleton?"

In answer the man's gaze shifted to the wall behind Caswell. A screen had simply appeared there as if grown for the specific purpose. It showed the face of an attractive middle-aged woman with ruthless blue eyes and strangely long blond hair. Her features were finely etched, as if sculpted. "This woman?" the man asked.

Caswell twisted to view the image and went still, frozen by what he saw there. The last of his energy seemed to bleed out of him then. He slumped in his chair and folded his arms across his chest.

"Caswell?" Melni asked.

"Impossible," he whispered. "Impossible."

Caswell stood and walked like a man asleep to the image. He reached out and traced a finger along the woman's image. "All this time," he whispered, just barely audible. "I can't fucking believe it."

"So it is her," the man in the reclined chair said.

"It's her all right." Caswell slumped back onto his chair, deflated. He stared at the image for a moment longer and then rested his chin on his chest and began to rub at the back of his neck with one hand. His fingers paused, touching the spot where his artificial gland was. "My whole career . . . Christ. Everything I've done. All of it came through her. All of it fucking taken *by her*." His fingers pressed into the skin until the knuckles turned white, as if he intended to tear the device from his spine right then and there.

Silence crept into the room. Melni wanted to say something, to comfort the assassin. But something kept her back. His tone . . . he sounded as she'd felt upon learning of his origin. The moment when a belief held for all of one's life is suddenly shattered.

Melni turned back to the alien on the bed, desperate to change the subject. "You have yet to tell us who you are."

The frail figure managed something resembling a grin. "Lazotel Leffit Delgaris, Warden of Gartien, former Observer of Zero World—er, what you call Earth. Simply 'Warden' will work. 'Laz' if you like."

Astonished, confused, Melni turned to Caswell for an anchor in all this. He leaned forward, eyes screwed shut, his fists at his temples and not, Melni thought, to access his implant. "None of that made any goddamn sense at all. I have so many questions I don't know where to start," the assassin said.

Laz sipped more fluid from the unnerving automatically retracting tube. "What were Monique's orders? To bring Alice home?"

"To kill her," Caswell said. "Because—"

"Unauthorized influence of a pre-Conduit world," the Warden finished. "They never change."

Caswell said nothing. Melni groped for meaning in the word *conduit* and found none.

Laz asked, "And you've succeeded? Alice is dead?"

The assassin hedged. Carefully he said, "Not yet."

"That is good. We knew this would happen someday. That someone would come. Another few years and she would have been ready for you. The fact that you're here in this room means she was not."

"She's damn close. I've spent most of my time here running away rather than chasing."

Melni broke in. "Please. I am confused. Explain to us what is going on. Why are our worlds so similar? How is it that we speak the same language, that we are so physically alike?"

Laz cast a dubious gaze at her and found sincerity in what he saw. His eyes slid over to Caswell. "You really don't know?"

Caswell shook his head.

"Monique did not explain?"

"No," Caswell replied. "No she bloody didn't."

"Oh." Laz pondered this. "I begin to understand. You are from Earth. Of Earth. And you thought she was like you."

"You're goddamn right I did."

"So Earth is still in the dark," he said almost to himself. "Alice's crossing went unnoticed."

"Until now. We found her ship. The data it contained, evidence that she'd come here with . . . knowledge."

"And Gartien?" His gaze shifted to Melni. "How much do you know?"

Melni spread her hands, unable to comprehend any of it. "Until a few minutes ago we thought he"—she pointed at Caswell—"was some recluse genetic experiment, escaped from a Valix lab."

"Then there may still be time," Laz said. Again the tube protruded from beside his head. He gulped something murky and gray, cringed at the taste. He coughed once, a sickening wet sound that came from his lungs—assuming he had them. His whole body shook from the effort, and the invisible field between him and the larger room shimmered briefly with pinpoint flecks of light.

"Time for what, exactly?" Melni asked. "What is this all about?"

"First bring Alice here," the Warden said. "I must verify she is safe."

"We can't," Caswell said. He explained their flight from the North, and Alia's subsequent call for a summit between the two sides.

The Warden was nodding. "Your presence here means she needs to accelerate preparations."

"Preparations for what?"

Laz shifted in his reclined seat. The bulbous cushions jostled about, swarming and growing to support the Warden's redistributed weight. "I'd better start at the beginning."

28

CASWELL LEANED FORWARD in his extruded chair. He saw Melni do the same. The alien's tone implied exactly what he needed right then: answers.

Laz settled in his bed thing. Another tube, a thin one this time, snaked out from somewhere behind his head. The tip formed into a needle-sharp point and it poked him, just below the Adam's apple. Fluid pumped out, not in, this time. Melni let out a little gasp, but Caswell motioned her to be calm.

Finally Laz opened his eyes again and spoke. "What I am going to tell you is known to only two people on your worlds. Alice Vale, and Monique Pendleton. And neither is a native of the world they live on."

Caswell said nothing. A shiver ran up his spine. His eyes met Melni's, then he focused all of his augmented attention on the alien.

Laz fixed his gaze on some imagined point far away. "There exists in the universe a, well, the simplest way to explain it is a linkage based on fractal symmetry. An invisible, underlying chain of places connected due to their similarity."

"That mouthful is the simple version?" Caswell asked.

Laz didn't quite smile, but came close. "Similar places, linked together."

"Like a wormhole?" Caswell asked. "That's what I went through?"

"The term *wormhole* is quaint and colloquial to Earth, I

suspect. Alas it is unknown to me, but I think you've got the idea, yes."

"So . . . what . . . you can pop into this wormhole and it finds a similar place to dump you out?"

"Not exactly," Laz said. "It's not dynamic. It's more like a roller . . . a train track . . . linking places not because of their proximity to one another but because of their *similarity* to one another. We call this series of connections the Conduit. Along its length are entry and exit points that lead from one star system to the next most similar in one direction, the next least in the other, no matter the time or distance involved."

Melni was looking at Caswell. She seemed to want to draw confidence from his own reaction, to see that at least he understood, but he had nothing to offer her. Not then.

Laz sighed, sensing her confusion without looking at her. "Imagine if in that estew of matter that was the exploding early universe, someone or something was able to analyze that chaos and find the conditions that would lead to life-harboring worlds. Human life, specifically. It is as if something knew that we would all be scattered too far apart to ever meet, and decided to establish a means of travel. These locations within that estew were linked from the earliest possible moment, and have remained so. Over all this time those original similarities—back then simply trajectories of exotica, I imagine—have resulted in the worlds that support our life-form.

"I'd be lying if I said we understood it fully, or indeed if I claimed to possess the proper knowledge to give you a satisfactory explanation. The important thing to know is that the Conduit exists, one can travel it in two directions, and with each jump you find yourself at a life-capable planetary system startlingly similar to the one you left."

A brief silence followed. Caswell broke it with a whisper. "How many worlds are we talking about here?"

"Unknown. Thousands," the Warden said. "Travel far enough and you'll eventually reach places unrecognizable to your home, but the worlds within a few dozen exits of Earth will be habitable to you, if not uncannily familiar."

"Like Gartien," Melni said.

He glanced at her, something like a smile playing at the corners of his thin mouth. "Exactly. And also not. I'll get to that in a moment."

"So where are you from?" she asked. "Not from here. Not from Earth, either, by the look of you."

At that he actually did smile, full and bright. "A world called Prime, though it's not so grand as its name implies. Eight exits negative from Earth."

"Negative?"

"We call the two directions of the Conduit negative and positive. Chaos and order, if you will. Travel in the positive and the planets look more and more like your Earth. At this end of the Conduit the differences are almost negligible, as you've seen. Go the other way, the negative, and within a few hundred exits you'll find worlds with barely any resemblance. By the thousandth you'll come to places you could never have imagined. Chaos. Disorder."

As he took another sip from his feeding tube, Caswell tried to picture this arrangement. "So, traveling toward the positive from here, the variations between worlds eventually become so minor as to be undetectable?"

Laz sighed at that. "No. Earth is the last world on the Conduit. The Zero World, we call it."

"But you said Gartien—"

"It's easier if I visualize it for you." With that his eyelids drooped down and his face contorted in concentration. The light in the room changed. Caswell turned, as did Melni, to the screen where Monique's image had been.

That picture vanished, replaced by a flat gray across the entire surface. Blurry white circles began to emerge and solidify, aligned in a horizontal row. A line connected them and, at the left side of the screen, it curved into the background where hundreds of similar white circles continued into the distance until they were too small to discern.

"The worlds of the Conduit," Laz said. "This one is Earth."

The first circle, farthest to the right, shifted from a simple white disk to the familiar blue marble. Melni stood then, and stepped closer, obviously amazed at the detail within the image. Save for the lack of craters along the Desolation,

Earth resembled Gartien in every detail. Caswell saw every emotion he'd experienced while studying the *Venturi*'s survey data flash across Melni's features.

One by one the rest of the circles began to fill in with their actual appearance. To the left of Earth the next planet looked very similar, as if someone had been asked to trace the continents by hand through rice paper. Very similar, but not quite exact. Next over from there the differences grew, and so forth. Melni gasped at the fourth world, which was not a world at all, but a cloud of debris. "What happened there?" she asked.

"I'll get to that in due time," Laz replied.

New iconography appeared at the top center of the screen, showing positive toward the right and negative to the left. Earth was farthest right, in the positive. The line of the Conduit ended there.

Caswell said, "You said Gartien was last in the chain, then you said Earth. So which is it?"

"As far as Monique and the rest of the Prime Wardens know, Earth is Zero World. The positive termination of the Conduit. The origin you might say, and therefore special. The Master Design, some believe, of all life-harboring worlds. For this reason Prime has taken a very careful approach with your planet."

The words chilled Caswell to the bone. What the hell did it mean, "a very careful approach"? Approach to what? He was about to demand an explanation when Melni spoke up.

"Where is Gartien on this map?" Melni asked.

"Ah," Laz said.

Now a new line grew out from Earth. Not to the right for order, or even the left for chaos, but straight up. The white circle it linked to Earth filled in with the familiar landscape of Gartien, craters and all.

"I don't understand," Caswell said.

"Neither did we," Laz replied. "In fact it was a long time before we even discovered that this branching phenomenon exists, and how to traverse it. Observe."

The image shrank away slightly. The link between Earth and Gartien grew, becoming a central hub with Earth, Gartien, and two more worlds at the points of the compass.

"We call these four worlds the Zero Terminus: Earth, Gartien, Zema, and Ardis. Four hub worlds that link what are in truth four Conduits."

Caswell sat and stared at the image. Ramifications and questions swirled maddeningly through his mind, slippery, out of reach. For nearly a minute he just looked at it, but his mind fixated on the simplest and most obvious part. *So many worlds.* Gartien he could handle, only just. But this . . . Thousands. Thousands of worlds.

Melni's voice broke the silence. "I remain confused. What's it all for?"

"No one knows."

"I find that hard to believe."

Laz took no offense at the jab. "Believe or not, that is the truth."

"Hold on," Caswell said. "You said 'as far as Monique and the rest of the Prime Wardens know.' They don't know about Gartien?"

"We have hidden it from them. At least, until you came here."

"Why?" he asked. Then he added, "For that matter, why even tell us of this? You have no idea who we are."

"You've told me who you are, and who sent you here. It is enough to deduce the rest, I think, and without this basic information what I have to tell you next would not make sense."

Caswell turned from the display and focused on the alien. "Well, go on, then."

"My people, that is to say those of Prime, were the first to discover the Conduit. This was a very long time ago. Every world we visited was either still in various prehuman eras, or if there were humans they were most often yet to develop language, culture, and all that comes with such events. We mapped the Conduit, we explored some of the worlds, even settled a few. We made contact, and we made plenty of mistakes."

Caswell thought of Alice Vale. How any plans humanity might have made to handle this first-contact scenario, if such plans even existed, went straight out the fucking window when the situation finally arose.

"This is overwhelming," Melni said, voice shaky.

"There's more. Much, much more."

She made no reply. Instead she just wrestled, those purple eyes darting from side to side. She bit her lower lip. She started to say something, stopped, then finally, feebly, gave a tiny nod to the alien.

Laz went on. "Eventually we found a world on the cusp of discovering the Conduit themselves. We would soon not be the only humans traveling along its length. Our leaders discussed this and decided on a policy of suppression. The worlds along the Conduit would be allowed to develop mostly on their own, but the Conduit would be ours—"

"*Mostly* on their own?" Melni interrupted.

The Warden nodded at her. "The standard procedure eventually became thus: Prime agents would visit worlds as long as they had not yet developed scientifically sound forensic techniques. I say 'mostly' because prior to that particular innovation we would manipulate the development of language—sometimes subtly, sometimes very severely—so that the peoples of these worlds would ultimately communicate in a way we can comprehend without overt contact."

"English," Caswell said. "So that's why . . ." He trailed off, glancing at Melni. He tried to imagine the challenge of skewing a world's dominant language and could not.

"English, yes. That's what you call it on Earth. However I mean this more structurally than any specific lexicon. The net result is a common language structure, written and spoken, for the more advanced worlds. It is the language of Prime."

"Why? Communication, I get it, but couldn't you just learn? Use translators?"

"It comes back to a concept we call the Divergent Moment. The point at which a world begins to employ forensic science. When they stop ascribing the occasional interaction with someone of Prime to the divine, or the spirit world, that sort of nonsense. Once that moment arrives we take on a purely passive role, and observe from afar. The language begins to drift, of course, but not so much that we can't follow along with some trivial artificial assistance."

Melni shook her head. "Yet the language I speak is virtually identical to Caswell's."

"Gartien is . . . different. Special, as I shall explain. Suffice to say, we had an opportunity after the Desolation to take a more direct approach, so we covertly put forth the idea of a common worldwide language and made sure your leaders saw the wisdom in it."

"Sorry," Caswell said. "I'm still not getting the point of all this. Okay, rule this Conduit, that makes sense. But why bother influencing language? What's the bloody point? Why go through all that trouble?"

"Because what we harvest from these worlds is ideas."

He let that settle for a few seconds.

"Inventions," Laz continued. "Successes and failures in the various sciences and arts."

"Until a world becomes so advanced that they reach this Conduit," Caswell said. His voice cut through the room, sharp as the knife's edge. He couldn't quite pinpoint why all this made him so angry.

"Yes," Laz admitted. "That is the process. It has been for a very long time."

A primal urge to strangle this creature flooded through him. In a flat voice Caswell said, "Earth has found the Conduit."

"Twice, in fact," Laz said.

"So what happens now? You wipe us out? Bomb us to the Stone Age? Will I have a home to return to?"

"Unknown."

"Not good enough."

The Warden winced. "Until you go back, if you do go back, it is hard to say what Prime will do."

"Why? You said the policy—"

With an effort Laz held up his hands, each supported or perhaps held back by the thin translucent tubes that connected him to the amber bed. "The situation is more complicated. I know this is a lot of information for you. For both of you. But, please, have patience."

Motion caught Caswell's eye. Melni, her hand held horizontally across her mouth, willing silence.

"Okay," Caswell said. "Okay."

"You see," Laz began, "Prime was not aware of Gartien's existence, or indeed the very concept of the Zero Terminus. Multiple zero worlds. They thought that Earth was the positive endpoint of the Conduit."

"Like the first map you displayed," Melni said.

"Precisely."

Caswell held up a hand. "You were saying 'we,' now you're saying 'they.'"

"I am getting to that part," Laz said. No malice, no annoyance. Just infinite patience.

Caswell relented once again.

"Myself and a very few others learned how to travel here. We kept Gartien's existence a secret from Prime, and we very carefully covered up the first visit by the *Venturi*."

"Why?"

"In the hope that it would appear to have been a failed attempt by Earth to enter the Conduit and thus not be investigated."

"To what end?"

"To avoid this policy of suppression for Earth, if possible. But more importantly to hide the existence of the other Zero Worlds from Prime."

"To what end?" he asked again, emphasizing each word.

"If we could allow this one world to advance in secret, to reach a technological level sufficient to resist Prime, their monopoly of the Conduit could end."

"I," Caswell started. He'd expected evil plots. Nefarious plans. Not this. "I see."

"We maintained the lie that Earth was the endpoint. This status afforded us additional staff, because Earth was considered special."

"The first world on the Conduit, therefore Prime thinks something about it matters," Melni said.

"Exactly. Over a few thousand years we recruited from this large group of operatives and arranged for new agents to be birthed and stationed on the Gartien side of the Conduit. We hid the knowledge of how to travel here. Things were going very well until the accident. What you call the Desolation, Melni."

Melni's knees buckled. She gripped her chair to keep

from falling. A snarl replaced the patience and understanding on her face. "You . . ." she rasped, "you caused that?"

"No, no. Please, take a deep breath and allow me to explain."

Caswell felt the anger, too, like a physical thing. A vision came to him, unbidden. A group of thin, improbably tall individuals like Laz, sitting in a room reviewing the schematics of Caswell's engineered gland. A tech unknown or undreamt of by their kind but covertly stolen by their agents from some poor scientist on Earth. These people, this *Prime,* were worse than Alice. Far worse. Exactly the opposite of her. Instead of running around giving away technology in exchange for power, they used power to steal all the choicest bits from who knows how many worlds. Information parasites. The ultimate theft of intellectual property.

All those goddamned worlds. Entire civilizations, unknowingly speaking an alien language, ignorantly handing their best ideas and advancements to a watchful overlord who would destroy it all should that civilization manage to reach high enough.

The anger coursed through him like a stiff drink. He knew he had to fight it, to hear this creature out. The vision reminded him of his implant, now flush with the chemicals he needed thanks to the food he'd devoured above. He thrust his hands to his temples and willed focus, calm, and accelerated the signals in his brain to give him more time to think. He'd pay for it with a nasty headache later, but this was all too important for rash emotion and clouded thoughts to derail. His scalp tingled as the chemicals worked through the cells of his brain.

Melni looked ready to strike the alien. She fumed. Her eyes were wild.

"I think you'd better explain," Caswell said, artificially calm. He glanced at Melni for Laz's benefit. "Quickly, please."

Laz lowered his head until his chin rested against his chest. He turned to the left and his lips met the feeding tube that appeared as if reading his thoughts. The alien man swallowed hard and took in each of his audience. "The Desolation of Gartien was in truth a random cosmic event, one we would have stopped had we known about it early enough. There was one among us who did know, but she, being secretly loyal and yet disconnected from Prime, decided to say nothing. An extinction event on Gartien, she thought, would set back our efforts here and give Prime a chance to find the world before we could challenge them.

"We tried to stop it, too late for full success. At least your world was not annihilated."

"That is small consolation," Melni said through clenched teeth.

"I am truly sorry for what occurred," Laz offered.

Caswell cleared his throat. "What happened then?"

"Something of a war followed within our ranks. Other hidden loyalists to Prime rose up. Our blockade of the Conduit was destroyed, most of us along with it. I alone remain here, but my ship was badly damaged and my health now deteriorates rapidly. I knew I would die soon and that I needed help. The blockade was down. Gartien was in no position to help. I needed someone to carry on our mission, but I could not trust anyone from Prime. So I lured Alice Vale here, along with her crew. I studied them and decided she was the best candidate to replace me. I made contact. I begged her to stay but she refused. She went back with them, and I feared she would betray not just my existence here but Gartien, too. And the Conduit. To those of Earth and, through Monique Pendleton, Prime as well. She would doom both worlds."

"But Alice came back," Caswell said.

"Yes. She began to see that even if Prime did not exist, Earth would try to take advantage of Gartien in the same way. She and her crew argued about how to handle the discovery, and she lost that argument. A ship arrived to debrief them. Or so they claimed. Instead a soldier came through and murdered everyone. She hid, survived, and came back here armed only with knowledge. Well, and a desire to help me."

Bodies floating in a medical bay. The strange sense of déjà vu. Alice's recognition of him in the Think Tank, her naked fear. Now it all made sense. Monique had sent him the first time, too. To tidy up. To conceal her precious Conduit. Six more bottles of Sapporo. *No, fuck that,* he thought. He'd lost count, and he wasn't even done yet.

"Help you do what?" Caswell asked, despite knowing the answer.

"To prepare. We feared at any instant this soldier from Earth, or thousands like him, would come. Or worse, agents of Prime would arrive with a full fleet for a 'clean slate' operation.

"We had no idea how much time there was. And remember, I was already dying. So Alice and I came down here. She would join Gartien's society, use the benefit of her knowledge to try to accelerate Gartien to spacefaring status, and ultimately blockade the Conduit once again."

"But," Melni said, "surely you have even greater technology than Alia? Why did you not do this yourself?"

Laz glanced at her. "What I lacked was the history behind it all. I could tell you how the tendrils of this bed work, yes, but not the long and complex chain of inventions and entire industries needed to allow your world to build one. Alice realized this, and could acquire that information. She even concocted the plan on precisely how to dole it out so that, in the end, your people would feel like they were on a perfectly natural course. The product of genius rather than the ravings of an alien lunatic."

"God," Caswell whispered. "It makes perfect sense."

"The fact that Monique sent you through means we have very little time. She now knows Gartien exists, and she knows how to travel here. She will share this with Prime, and they'll be making plans even now on what to do."

There came a sound like meat being torn from bone. Startled, Caswell glanced down to see the Warden's left hand rise slowly, forcefully away from the translucent tendrils. The thin dewy strands ripped out of his skin with a thousand little pops. His hand, shaking, grasped Caswell by the wrist. "You . . . must . . . help . . . her!" The words came out like the dying grunts from a wounded animal. His skin paled even as Caswell watched. He must have been hypermedicating himself in order to have this conversation.

Laz sighed a raspy breath through clenched teeth. His whole body suddenly lurched upward, held back only by the thousands of little wormlike tendrils that clung to his skin. He groaned and slumped back, his head tilting to one side.

"He is dying!" Melni shouted.

Caswell leapt to his feet and leaned over the man. He tried to reach, to feel for a pulse, but his hand met the invisible shield with a shower of luminous energy. He ignored the pain, he leaned in closer and shouted, "What about Earth? What about Monique? What can I do?"

The Warden remained still. Melni extended her hand to pull Caswell back when the alien's eyes suddenly opened wide. "Alice is the key," he whispered. "Help her. But go, now. It is not safe to remain here."

"But Earth—" Caswell started.

His words were drowned in a sudden, shrill noise that came from everywhere. The coloration of the walls rippled from white to a blazing orange.

"Someone else is here," Laz the Warden said, his voice thin as a breeze through grass.

"Monique? Prime?"

"No. Outside."

A frigid chill slammed through Caswell's body. "Who?"

"Unknown." With a shaking hand the Warden managed to point toward the hallway through which Melni and Caswell had entered. "Weapons. Supplies. State your names to enter."

Then his hand fell, as if sucked back to the bed by the slimy tendrils that still clung to the underside of his arm like hungry serpents.

Light shifted in the room. Motion. Caswell whirled, expecting to find a squad of alien soldiers swarming in. What he saw instead was worse.

The wall display had come back to life. It showed a vibrant image of the door to the boathouse, and some of the sloped trail beyond. A shadow moved down that slope. The shape of a woman in black from hair to feet. Each hand gripped a pistol, held at the side.

"A Hollow Woman," Melni whispered. "We are doomed."

Two more black-clad figures moved into view. One, a male, stopped halfway down the sloped hill and began to assemble something. The third, a woman, moved sideways at a crouch, keeping to the tall grass beside the trail, a long rifle of some sort sweeping rhythmically from left to right and back.

"Three of them," Melni gasped. "Three!"

Caswell ran. He sprinted down the now-pulsing amber corridor, under the hatch they'd entered through, along the gently curving length to the far end where a barrier waited. He stopped in front of it, looking for a handle of some kind. A button. Anything. Then Laz's instructions came to him. "Peter Caswell," he said.

A click from inside the wall. Nothing more.

Melni came running up and stopped next to him.

"Say your name," he told her. "Quickly."

"Melni Tavan," she blurted.

Nothing.

"Meiki Sonbo," she tried.

There was an odd, pleasant chime and then the barricade simply melted back into the walls around it. Beyond was something like a workshop. Sloppy and, other than the floor and ceiling, nothing like the rest of the vessel. Wooden tables that looked as if assembled by a child. Boxes of varying size and manufacture lay strewn about the floor, their dusty contents mostly books and other documents.

Alice must have toiled in here, hidden from the outside. Caswell darted in. He glanced about wildly and then vaulted one of the tables to get to the far wall. The wood creaked under his weight, but held. Beyond it, a brownish bedsheet hung from poles to form an impromptu curtain. He yanked it aside. Behind it, an assortment of pistols and rifles were neatly arranged. Caswell had envisioned an array of exotic alien firepower, sleek and gleaming. But these were all of Gartien origin, and worse, antiques.

"Familiar with any of this?" Caswell asked her.

Melni slipped around the table and took inventory. "This is Frontier Police issue. Or was, fifteen years ago."

"It's all ancient. How is this helpful?"

"It is better than nothing," Melni said.

Caswell looked at the old pistol. It had a bizarre shape, most of the weight at the back. "Is it loaded?"

She slid the housing aside. "Fully."

He took it, tested the weight, trying to figure out how to even hold the damned thing. Melni grabbed another, slightly smaller model. This one proved empty, but she quickly found ammunition on a shelf to one side.

As she loaded the second gun he held his up. "How the hell do you even aim this?"

Melni showed him how to swing a supporting brace out so that the padded end rested on his forearm. "If you press down here with your free hand, the stability is excellent. Almost as good as a rifle, without all the bulk."

"If it still works," Caswell said. He turned for the exit.

Melni gripped him by the arm, hard enough to cut through his laser focus on the enemies approaching.

He turned to her. "What is it?" he asked. "There's no time for a plan, Melni. They're right outside."

She shook her head. "These people, the Hollow. They are our most elite killers. Extremely dangerous."

"So am I," he said, peeling off her grip, "when I need to be." He pressed his fingers to his temples once again. This time he turned everything on.

29

CASWELL TURNED AND RAN to the hatch, but Melni hesitated. She glanced down at the slender weapon in her hand. Would it be enough? Not nearly, not against the Hollow. *Garta's light, three of them!*

Her pistol would be a toy compared to what these soldiers carried. Melni slipped it into a pocket and gazed at the array of weapons before her. Beneath the shelves of pistols were two wide drawers.

She slid one out and grinned at what lay within.

Despite spending only twenty seconds to equip herself, by the time Melni reached the hatch Caswell had vanished through the ceiling hatch and into Alia's lander.

Melni slung the riot rifle over her shoulder and jumped for the open hole above. She hauled herself into the capsule, cursing every sound she made. For an instant she marveled at the change in her perception of Alia's craft. What had seemed so advanced before now looked primitive compared to the Warden's vehicle. She wondered if he really was dead, and why he seemed more prisoner than patient in that bed. Why had Alia not moved him somewhere more secure? Questions for another time.

Melni leapt again and clawed her way into the ramshackle boathouse above. The wooden interior was primitive and dark and smelled awful. It was as if she'd just climbed through three epochs of human achievement. She glanced about for Caswell but he was gone.

Wood creaked outside. Melni slipped the riot gun off her

shoulder and hefted it in both hands. The damn thing weighed twenty pounds fully loaded. For an instant she debated setting it down. She'd trained with such a gun just once, way back during her first year at Riverswidth, and hadn't cared for it much then. But the pistol in her pocket seemed a pathetic choice against a Hollow, much less three of them. Fear tore through her at the prospect there might have been even more, off-display.

Crouching, Melni lowered the wooden door that concealed the entrance to the space vessel below. She picked up her heavy weapon again, held it at the hip so that the shoulder strap could lend some support, and crept to the back wall. She rounded gun-first and swept the barrel across the space beyond.

The river drifted by in its lazy journey. The aging boat bobbed gently on the brown water, ropes straining and slackening with each little wave. A cloud of insects weaved and darted in a blur around a conical flower that poked up from the water two dozen feet out. The sky had cleared, pure blue above the distant crater-rim hills.

A black shape fell from the roof at the back of the structure. It landed with a single thud on the boat and seemed to coalesce into the form of a woman. More like a woman's silhouette. The black of her fatigues was absolute, save the narrow strip of face visible between forehead and mouth. The eyes were dark, narrow slits, just like Caswell's. Melni grasped the oversize trigger with her fist and pulled back. The gun's eight barrels erupted with flame and gray smoke. The sound hit like a physical blow and Melni stumbled back under the violence of it. The walls shook. Birds took flight from trees all along the river.

The top half of the old boat disintegrated in a cloud of shredded wood as the thorny balled projectiles hissed through the air.

She'd wanted a cloud of blood and black fabric, though. The Hollow Woman had dodged, leaping off to the right, bouncing once on the wooden decking beside the watercraft and then leaping in a high forward flip toward Melni. Melni raised the gun as fast as her numbed hands would allow but the heavy gun had not been designed to take on fast-moving targets. It had been designed to convert a cone-shaped portion of an angry mob into shreds of meat and bone. Melni fired anyway and marveled at the circular portion of ceiling that vanished in a haze of splinters. Then the black shape was on her. Melni dropped the heavy weapon, leaning as she did so to dislodge the shoulder strap. At the same time she fumbled for her pistol. The Hollow slammed into her left shoulder, one palm striking Melni's chin. She bit involuntarily, a searing pain as teeth punctured tongue, then the taste of copper as blood filled her mouth. Melni fell backward, spinning from the impact, her hands unable to grasp the pistol. She tried to turn the fall into some kind of sweeping kick but her foot tangled with the wall beside her.

Clumsy. Utterly outmatched.

The Hollow managed to hit the ground with one foot and vaulted up, her other foot catching the back wall and pushing her into a tight twirling flip to avoid Melni's leg sweep that never came. The woman landed with a dancer's grace and swung one arm out of a fold in her outfit. Melni glimpsed something metallic there. A pistol. She had only time to grimace at the bullet to come.

The Hollow Woman's head snapped sideways. There was a wet slap from the back wall as her brains splattered against the wood.

Melni glanced left and saw a blur resembling Caswell disappear around the back wall of the boathouse. She struggled to her feet and ran to where he'd been. When she glanced around the edge he was gone. Instead, she saw a black shape in the trees thirty feet distant, just up from the riverbank. She lurched back and ducked just as the sniper's rifle cracked. A chunk of wood above Melni's head exploded inward, raining bits onto the boat and the far side of the slip. Melni crawled back on her hands as two more rounds tore through the wall. Fired for effect. Fired to keep her pinned there. She whirled and ran back inside at a crouch, finding and hefting the riot gun with both hands as she went. In the next room she bounded past the hatch in the floor and kept running toward the door at the front of the building. One earsplitting boom from the weapon saw the barrier annihilated in a cloud of smoke and shrapnel. Someone cried out behind that mess.

Melni leapt, bringing her knees up and elbows in as she crashed through the remnants of the front door. She landed knees first on a figure dressed in black, one leg a mangled length of blood and bone. Too close to shoot, Melni swung the heavy gun instead. The thick eight-barrel cylinder met skull with a dull, ringing thud. The surprised Hollow let out an inhuman sigh and slumped sideways into a motionless heap.

Two down. Only the sniper remained, unless more of the killers lurked out there. Where was Caswell? She strained her ears but that was useless. They rang from the close-quarters use of the riot cannon and pounded with the rapid thud of a battle-fueled pulse. She needed to move. Be unpredictable. Act, she realized, on pure instinct. Maybe there was some merit to Caswell's style after all.

She forced herself to her feet and lumbered away from the smashed door of the building, up the sloped path diagonally until she reached the dense grass near the burial mounds. Something, some survival instinct, made her dive at the same moment a shot hissed through the air where her head had been. The thunderous crack of the weapon followed, echoing off the surrounding trees.

Another bullet whipped through the tall grass a split second later, inches above her head. She forced herself lower, dirt in her mouth and nose, and crawled on her belly for a tree a few feet away.

"Stay down!" a voice shouted. Caswell's. He sounded distant, but then everything did.

Something blotted the Sun above her for a second. Footsteps nearby. Her companion rushed past, toward the sniper. Melni heard the crack of gunfire—once, twice. Unable to stop herself she came to one knee, her eyes just level with the wispy fringe of the tall weeds. Caswell was twenty feet away moving toward the shooter at a dead sprint. He weaved, using the thick tree trunks as natural cover. Suddenly he dove, rolled, and came up running at a new angle even as the rolling thunder of another sniper round boomed through the trees. He dodged with uncanny, almost precognizant speed a heartbeat before each whip crack from the sniper's rifle.

After three such uncanny escapes the sniper changed tactics. Melni saw the black-clad figure vanish into the bushes when Caswell was still fifty feet off. He did not slow. Running at a low crouch he slipped through the branches and shifting grasses like a yacht through calm waters, then he, too, was gone, out of sight, over the next rise along the river. Gunfire echoed off the hills.

Help him! a voice shouted in her head. Her own voice. She'd been sitting there, clutching the heavy riot gun like some kind of talisman. Melni came to her feet and considered her options. Follow Caswell? Find a more appropriate weapon within the ship? No, secure the bikes. Be ready to flee—

Quit blixxing around and act!

She never heard the person approach. She was utterly alone, and then not alone. The cool metal of a pistol pressed against her neck just behind the ear. Then a black-gloved hand on her collar, squeezing.

"Say nothing," a woman said.

Melni had heard that voice before, in the archive.

"Drop the cannon and put your hands behind your back. Fingers entwined. Yes, that is good. To your knees, traitor. Lean forward until your face is between your legs."

"Traitor?"

The force of the hand on Melni's neck compelled her to follow commands. To fight back now would mean instant death. She'd wait for Caswell. Strike when the Hollow Woman was distracted.

Footsteps from up the trail. Melni felt the hand ease on her neck, inviting her to look. She did so. He emerged from the trees along the trail, a hundred feet up from where he'd sprinted off after the sniper. Caswell walked with his hands clasped behind his head, a Hollow behind him. Then another.

She watched in stunned horror. Six of the black-outfitted soldiers were fanned in a rough half circle behind him, plus a seventh on his heels, some unseen weapon clearly pressed at the small of the Earthman's back. Melni's breath caught in her throat at the sight. In all Gartien there were said to be only twelve Hollow. The South had sent the entirety of that elite force after her. Her and the stranger.

For his part Caswell did not appear to be injured. He looked calm, in fact. Disturbingly so. One of the Hollow, Melni noted, walked with a limp. Another's arm dangled uselessly at his or her side.

"Let her go," Caswell called out. "I forced her to bring me here. She's innocent."

"Your concern is noted, your request denied," the one holding Melni said in her icy voice. "Now, why did you go through so much trouble to come to this place, I wonder?"

"We are on our way to Combra," Melni said without thinking. "We just stopped for shelter."

The handle of the gun cracked against the side of her skull. Stars swam before Melni's eyes, then the tears came in a single, stinging wave. A trickle of warm blood ran down behind her ear and dripped onto her pant leg. She teetered but did not pass out. The blow had been expertly placed and just hard enough not to send her unconscious. "Remain silent, traitor. Your time to answer questions will come." She pressed harder on Melni's neck until Melni could feel her knees against the bottom of her chin and smell the dirt inches from her nose. "Now, stranger. Answer me."

"Absolutely not," Caswell said.

A few seconds of silence followed before the Hollow spoke. "Your lack of cooperation is unfortunate."

"Good," he replied.

Melni found herself smiling.

The Hollow leader shifted her weight. "They were in the boathouse?" she asked. One of her team evidently replied with a positive gesture—Melni could see nothing and heard nothing. "Search the place," the leader said.

Melni counted four of them darting off down the trail toward the river. That left her captor, plus three others guarding Caswell. An even split of their number, and as good as the odds were likely to get. She wondered if Caswell would agree, and what he planned to do. Melni tried to remember if there had been a rock or stick anywhere within reach. Something she could wield, however feeble. Then she registered the weight of the slender pistol she had stuffed in her pocket. Bent over like this she'd never get it out in time, but if—

"Hear me!" Caswell suddenly said. His voice was unnaturally loud and he went on with only the slightest hesitation. "Within that structure two Northern agents wait ready to kill anyone who enters. They're heavily armed—"

His words all ran together as if he had to say them all in a single breath. Why? Melni groped for some hidden meaning and found nothing obvious.

"—heavily armed and in a foul mood. I suggest you enter from both sides at once if you want to live. Also, the water is quite cold, so be ready for that."

"Quiet," the leader snapped.

"You really should heed my warnings!" Caswell was shouting now, on the cusp of hysterics.

What the blix is he up to? Melni tried to rock back on her feet. She still had a pistol. She needed easier access to the pocket she'd thrust it in. But the Hollow only pushed on her neck harder.

"Be still, traitor!" she growled. Through it all Caswell had kept talking, louder and louder. "Silence! I mean it!" the leader shouted at him.

"Melni, down!" Caswell roared.

She was already down. She pitched forward anyway. The shift in her posture, her sudden lack of resistance to the pressure on her neck, allowed her to dive face-first into the dirt and flatten herself. The leader of the Hollow squad stumbled, one knee driving hard into Melni's back. She lost her grip on Melni's neck.

There came a hiss that grew from the edge of inaudibility to an ear-splitting roar in less than a second. Then the world shattered.

Even with her lying flat on the edge of the trail's incline down to the boathouse, the explosion slammed Melni sideways into an awkward roll. Debris, dirt, and a wall of blistering hot air hit her all at once. The roar of the blast forced her sense of hearing into some kind of self-preservation dormancy. Vaguely, as if miles away, Melni heard the brief scream from the lips of the Hollow Woman followed by a muffled distant noise of what Melni could only think of as meat thrown against a brick wall. She pressed herself into the dirt and screamed as the shrapnel-laden inferno rolled over her and away.

How much time had passed, Melni couldn't be sure. Intense heat licked at her back. Her clothing, on fire. She rolled in the dirt, extinguishing the flames, and glanced toward the river.

The boathouse was nothing more than a blackened crater. Debris still rained down from the sky in fiery chunks that smacked into the ground and splashed into the river. Water rushed in to fill the sudden hole in the ground where the structure had been. Of the vessels—Alia's or the Warden's below it—nothing remained. The bomb must have been massive.

Gathering her senses, ears ringing, Melni completed her roll and looked to where Caswell had stood, just on the other side of the rise. Amid smoke and flame she saw him, lying prone like her. Around him were the splayed bodies of the Hollow. Half bodies, in truth. The legs and pelvises, sheltered by the crest of the trail, were largely undamaged. Waist up, however, all that remained of each was a horrific mess of shredded muscle, bone, black fabric, and various unrecognizable chunks of human innards. The four who had gone to search the boathouse had been completely obliterated.

Caswell was shouting something at her. He sounded a mile away and underwater. Melni crawled toward him, happy to find that her arms and legs still worked. She ignored the bits of fire starting to catch within the clumps of tall grass, and the sting of a dozen lacerations along her left side and back. "Are you all right?" he shouted as she reached him.

Despite her proximity she still had to read his lips. A bright, all-consuming ringing filled her head. Melni managed a nod and took his outstretched hand. Caswell kept glancing up as he began to pull her away from the boathouse. His jog turned into an urgent sprint, tugging her along. The cuts and scrapes across half her body forced her into a lurching, stumbling fall that barely served to keep up.

Suddenly Caswell twisted, grabbed her by the shoulders, and shoved her bodily between two mounds of dirt. The two graves. Another explosion behind them. The air seemed to rip apart. Melni tasted the soil and felt the flash of warmth and then Caswell was on top of her, shielding her.

She barely had time to suck in a breath and then he was up and dragging her to her feet. "Run!" he shouted, the muffled sound almost inaudible. Melni tried to, but half her body now felt as if aflame. Maybe it was. She limped and plodded through tall grass, away from the trail, the ruin of the boat-house, and the cottage. Caswell seemed to be pushing her toward a cleft in the valley wall so she forced her mind to focus on that. Bits of dirt and other unrecognizable debris rained out of the sky. Another explosion, this time to her right, shook the ground beneath her feet. The cottage vanished in a ball of fire and smoke.

Caswell pushed her on, a strong hand at the center of her back guiding her. She stumbled and screamed in pain. His arm slipped under hers and in one motion he lifted her and swung her up over his shoulders. Caswell carried her like that for fifty feet and then dove, the pair of them slamming into a natural earthen pocket carved from the valley wall. She lay there, arms over her head, body pressed against Caswell's, as six more bombs demolished the entire length of the path. The home, the graves, the boathouse, all re-duced to craters. Nothing remained but charred dirt and a choking cloud of smoke. It filled the air, stung Melni's eyes and nostrils. Her mouth tasted of ash and blood. Each breath came with racking coughs.

She lay there for a long time, wrapped in Caswell's arms, until the dust cleared. Ten minutes passed, maybe more. "We need to get away from here," she said.

Caswell didn't reply. In fact he hadn't moved in many minutes. Suddenly his body felt like an unbearable weight upon her.

Filled with sudden dread, Melni pressed her hand to his right breast.

30

SHE FELT NO PULSE. Despair began to crash upon her like a wave, until a tiny voice inside her said, *This happened before!* Yes, on the boat as they fled Portstav. She'd felt no pulse then, and yet he lived. Then she remembered what the doctor in Riverswidth had said, how all his organs were flipped from the normal layout, as if reflected in a mirror. She pressed the other side of his chest. His skin thudded rhythmically against her palm. Quite strong, in fact.

Sighing with relief, ignoring the hundred aches her body had on offer, Melni slid out from beneath the unconscious man and rolled him onto his back. "Caswell? Caswell?" she asked, slapping his cheek gently. Her own voice sounded distant and muted to her tortured ears.

He did not react. Melni forced herself to stand and surveyed the devastation all around them. Even the vaunted Hollow, it seemed, were no match for surgical bombing from Valix's airships. She lifted a hand to shield her eyes from Garta's glare and surveyed the sky. High above, like bloated birds circling on some impossibly strong updraft, three Combran airships traced circles against the darkening ceiling beyond.

As she watched they began to peel away and fly northeast in a loose V formation. Melni waited until they were well out of sight. In that time nothing save the wind and small critters stirred around her. Of the Hollow, or any support teams that might have been with them, she saw nothing. The bombing had wiped them out. Those that she and Caswell hadn't killed, she corrected herself, feeling a surprising surge of pride.

His augmented senses had saved them. He'd heard the engines, the whistle of that first bomb, before anyone else. There'd been no time to do anything other than dive to the ground, but that had been enough.

Fires burned all around, casting plumes of gray smoke high into the air, a light breeze drawing the haze out over the river to the north.

Melni took a last glance at the placid face of Caswell and slid the pistol from her pocket. She left him there, in the cleft along the valley wall, and crept south toward the smoking ruin of the cottage. The Hollow had come from that direction. Masters of stealth they might be, but their footprints had told the story. They would have vehicles nearby. Supplies. And though they had probably left someone behind to guard such things, maybe whoever it was had rushed to the riverbank after that first bomb, to help, and been annihilated by the second fusillade.

Pistol held before her, the brand of "traitor" still echoing in her ears, Melni entered the smoke. It filled the air like a morning Combran fog, only black, and stung the eyes to the point that tears streamed down her cheeks. She saw nothing but shadowy trees and the orange glow of a hundred small fires. Then the husk of what had been the cottage, now a ruin in a blackened crater, loomed out of the haze. Melni skirted it and kept on. The ground began to slope, then a cliff wall emerged from the haze.

Black rappelling ropes with knotted segments trailed down from high above. Melni took one last glance back toward the cleft where Caswell lay. She drew a mental line from cottage to a lone greencloud tree, then his body a ways beyond that. Then she turned and started to climb, up and out of the smoke, away from the death.

At the top of the ravine she found herself at the edge of a wide field of boneweed grass that sloped gently away to a tree line perhaps a quarter mile distant. Viewed from here, the passage of the Hollow strike team was even more obvious. No amount of care could mask the trampled grass. Their path traced a gently waving line from the rappelling rope spikes to a particularly large shade tree opposite. Melni walked fifty feet to her left and, keeping low, traced a parallel path to the one the Hollow had made, using the umbrella-like dome of the tree as a guide.

Twenty feet from the tree she came upon a shallow Desolation-era crater, invisible in the tall grass unless you stood right beside it. Their vehicles rested in the basin: sleek, disguise-painted thumpers and a single, low-slung quadcruiser covered with storage packs of varying size. None bore any kind of label or identifying marker, not that she had any doubt where they'd come from.

Movement caught her eye. A man, sitting in the passenger seat of the quad, dressed in the black garb of the Hollow. He hunched forward and fiddled with something on the instrument panel before him that she could not see. He held one hand to his ear. Reporting the calamity that had just befallen his squad, no doubt. Melni kept to the trees and circled behind the vehicle, then moved in, pistol held level before her. She could hear the man's voice now. Low, urgent. "Please acknowledge. Anyone, please!"

He froze when Melni pressed the muzzle of her weapon to the side of his neck.

"Keep your hands visible," she whispered.

The man nodded once.

"Did anyone else stay back with you?"

He hesitated. Melni pushed the barrel harder against his skin. "I am alone," he finally said. A young man. Communications and support, probably. Trained in the basics of combat but likely not of the aptitude normally required for fieldwork. He'd still be a competent fighter, just not the elite. Or so she hoped.

From the dash the radio chirped. "Acknowledged, oh-nine-deso. Report your status."

The unmistakable voice of Rasa Clune. Melni urged the Hollow Man away from the vehicle. With one eye on him she leaned in and switched the communicator off.

"What happened down there?" the Hollow Man asked. If he harbored any fear of her or her weapon, it did not manifest in his voice.

"Combran airships bombed the entire site. Your squad was annihilated."

"What of the stranger?"

Melni studied the man before her. She decided to lie. "Vaporized along with the rest of them."

"Yet you survived."

The accusation behind his words stung. Melni retrained her aim on his chest and did her best to look unperturbed. "Go back. Tell Clune and the others that I have seen proof of the stranger's story."

"Show me."

"Unfortunately it was just bombed into nothing more than shrapnel."

"How convenient."

"The truth sometimes is. Now go and tell her, or I will leave one more corpse here."

"What do you intend to do, Agent Sonbo? You should know if you set foot in the South you will be killed on sight. If you go anywhere near the summit—"

Melni stopped listening. Sonbo, he'd called her. Her real name still felt uncomfortable, like clothes that no longer fit. Had she really left that person behind?

It wasn't that, she suddenly realized. It was the world that person had lived in, now no longer relevant. What she'd heard and seen inside that vessel below the lake rendered everything that had happened before moot. Sonbo, and all the rest, no longer mattered.

But she was not Melni Tavan, either. Not of the North or the South or even the disjointed area in between. She was of Gartien.

She shook her head to dispel these thoughts. True or not, she had a more immediate problem. Both North and South wanted her dead. The ramifications slid home like a knife in the gut. She was an exile, and would be forever more. Despite all she'd learned today, about Conduits and oppressive alien empires, it was all useless without proof. No one would believe a word of it. Except Valix.

Valix, in the end, was the key. She had to get to her, with or without Caswell, and help her in her cause.

Mentally Melni donned the exile's coat and renewed her

aim on the man. She had claimed her land and must sleep under the sky above it, as the old saying went. "I am not sure what I will do," she said. "Tell Clune I remain loyal, despite all appearances, and that . . . and that . . . I will find a way to prove what I have learned."

"Tell her yourself," the man said through a sudden, nasty grin.

A sound behind her. The slightest scuff of a boot against dirt. She'd missed one of them. A minute earlier and her hearing might not have recovered enough to detect the noise. But now . . . Melni reacted on pure instinct, as Caswell would have. She dove to one side, firing her gun at the Hollow Man before her even as she fell. The bullet caught him in the stomach and he doubled over. Then Melni was rolling. Something whooshed past her head and thudded into the soil. Melni came up at a crouch and instantly ducked. Another black-clothed Hollow. A huge man, two feet taller than her with arms as thick as her thighs. He swung a black trunch that sizzled with live electricity. It passed inches in front of her face and knocked the pistol from her hand with a shuddering jolt. The weapon sailed six feet and vanished into the weeds.

Melni took a step back and positioned herself into a fighting stance. One leg behind for stability, both hands raised chin level, fists balled. The huge man in front of her flexed his fingers on the crackling baton. She could not see the bottom half of his face, but the grin was obvious. She did not stand a chance. He was a Hollow, the most elite of trained killers, and judging from his gigantic hands could probably break her in half if given the chance, sizzling trunch or not. She could hear the hum of the electricity flowing across its surface. All he had to do was graze her skin and she'd be writhing on the ground, her tongue half-bitten off. She had to run. Or get that pistol. She glanced where it had fallen. The man danced a step in that direction, sensing her move. Toying with her. He stepped closer. Melni matched it with a step back. She tried to picture the layout of the clearing, where the vehicles were parked. That quadcruiser, there must be some kind of weapon there. The brute would never give her time to find one, though. She had to run.

Beside her, on the ground, the man she'd shot made a muffled groan. He lay in a fetal curl in the trampled grass. Melni took two steps back and to the side, her eyes darting between the wounded man and the brute. The giant stepped forward in tandem with her, happy to push her farther from the dropped pistol.

Melni glanced at the wounded man. He had both arms wrapped around his stomach. Blood welled freely between the black sleeves of his shirt. A wretched smell permeated the air. Digestive fluid. A fatal wound, more than likely. Melni glanced back at the brute, almost too late. He was in midair, leaping for her, the baton raised. Melni lurched into a sideways somersault, back on her feet just behind the wounded man as the brute's misaimed jump crashed into the ground where she'd been, his overhand swing converted into a wild sidelong swipe that sizzled inches from her face. She felt the heat of it, and the hair on her skin tugging toward the electric force.

With a dexterity she didn't know she possessed, Melni yanked the wounded man's pistol from the holster at his side without breaking stride. She clutched the weapon in her off hand, transferred it as she ran sideways. The giant sensed her find and dove as the gun coughed—once, twice, and a third time. Thunderous bursts echoed off the trees and the sides of the shallow crater. The big man dove behind the pack vehicle, hidden by its fuselage and the tall grass.

She had no idea if she'd hit him. Melni took the weapon in both hands and crept forward. The man on the ground let out a long, gurgling wail. In one swift motion Melni swung the pistol in his direction and fired her fourth shot. His head jerked sideways and he went limp.

Melni put her focus into controlling her racing heart and shallow breaths. A bead of sweat slid down the side of her face. She loosened her grip on the weapon. She drew in a long breath through her nose and let the aroma of combat flow in, strangely calming.

There was more movement, now from her left. Melni turned too late. A thrown rock struck her sternum. The impact sent her stumbling, shooting blind. A waste of ammunition. Her foot caught on something and she toppled over onto her back. *He'll press,* she managed to think, and rolled to one side as the heavy form of the man slammed into the soil where she'd been. Again the thrum of naked electricity roiled near her face. Half-blinded, Melni did not bother to stand. She aimed and fired, and kept on firing until the trigger pulls resulted in the dull click of a spent cartridge.

The giant lay five feet away, half-hidden by grass, blood seeping from wounds on his chest and neck. He twitched. A bubble of blood formed on his lips and, when it popped, his eyes became still as glass.

Melni stood. Tried to. Her legs folded under her. She collapsed into a kneeling position in the dirt, laid the pistol across her legs, and let it dangle from shaking fingers. "So much death," she whispered to the soil. To Gartien. These people were supposed to be on her side. With each dead body left along her trail the world felt a little darker, joy and hope and everything in between slowly bleeding out.

Only now, instead of one final death at the end, Melni found a spark. A tiny glimmer of something good to come of all this. She would save Alia Valix, not assassinate her. She would save her and, in doing so, save the world. Not North from South or South from North, but Gartien from Prime. She would do this. The *desoa* journalist and failed spy. A deep chuckle rolled out of her at the absurdity of it all.

"What's so funny?" someone asked.

Caswell.

She glanced up, startled. He stood over her, his face filthy and dotted with mud or maybe blood. Probably both. He held out one hand for her.

Too numb to react otherwise, Melni took it and let him pull her to her feet. The world tilted beneath her like a boat on the ocean. She let the sensation pass. "I was laughing because," she said, and stopped until the mirth in her faded. "I was laughing because now we have to save Alice."

His brow furrowed, the humor lost on him.

Melni frowned. "It is one thing to fire the gun and let the consequences be," she said. "Now we have to save her from everyone else." She gestured at the two dead bodies in the grass. "From these people. They want her; the North will go to war to stop them from getting her. Two great foes, intent to either have her on their side or none at all. And the two of us are supposed to walk in there and . . . do what, exactly? Steal her away? Hide her? And all the while some alien civilization spanning hundreds of planets is on their way to annihilate Gartien? And Earth, too? What do we do? Where do we even start?"

A breath exploded from Caswell's lips. "I was hoping you'd have a plan."

Now Melni really did laugh, softly at first, but she couldn't control it no matter how hard she tried. It grew and grew until tears came. Caswell just stood and waited, and that sobered her. She took a deep breath. "What does your instinct tell you?"

"Get to her."

Melni waited. He said nothing else. "Get to her? That is it?"

"Get to her. Find out what she intends to do. Find out if she still believes in the Warden's mission."

"Why wouldn't she?"

He gestured to the plume of smoke still rising from the valley. "She just bombed the only real evidence for what he told us."

"It might not have been her that ordered the bombing."

"Right, yes. But if anyone had the power to stop that from happening, Alice did. So why didn't she?"

Melni looked away. He was right and she knew it. Alia . . . Alice, had deliberately destroyed the place rather than let it be discovered. Or perhaps because it had been discovered. Some silent alarm alerting her, perhaps.

Caswell went on. "We have to face the possibility that she's gone mad with power here. You saw the condition he was in down there. That was a tomb, not a hiding place. I doubt they've spoken, at least on friendly terms, in years."

"And if that is true? If she no longer works toward preventing Prime's discovery of Gartien?"

He grimaced. "I don't know. It'll be up to us, I guess."

"We need a better plan than that."

It was his turn to laugh. "You know I'm not much of a planner."

"Well, then," Melni said, "you are lucky I am around."

* * *

It should have revolted her. Blood and bits of intestine, partially digested food, a gruesome fluid that surely was on its way out the other end of the body. All of it spilled from the communication officer's belly as she pulled his outfit off. It *should* have revolted her, but for the absurdity of the whole situation.

Instead of revulsion, she fought to keep the laughter in. She imagined herself of two years prior, sitting at the conference table above the Loweast in the *Weekly*'s modest office tower, surrounded by other reporters and editors, interviewing for her new role. Someone had asked, "Where do you see yourself in two years?" She pictured herself, leaning back, casting a confident glance at the faces around the table, and deadpanning the response. "I will be crouched in a snowy Desolation crater in Southern Cirdia, tearing the clothes from a dead Hollow Man that I shot in the gut, trying not to vomit onto his large intestine. And beside me, an assassin from another world, one of many worlds, will be singing a song of his world called 'Dead Man's Party' while he tries on a pair of boots taken from corpse number two, another Hollow that we, together, murdered. That is where I see myself."

And the chief editor, a half smile on her face, saying, "Lovely. When can you start?"

This imagined conversation went on and on in her head as they searched all of the vehicles in the crater.

Unfortunately Caswell could not wear the giant's clothes. The smaller man's outfit might have worked for him, but she already had it on. A bit loose, but good enough to pass a cursory inspection, except for all the blood.

Caswell found a tactical vest in one of the cruiser's sidebags and handed it to her. That covered the gore, mostly.

"What about you?" she asked him. No other garments had turned up in the storage compartments.

"I'm your prisoner. I look the part."

"They are looking for a female agent and an escaped prisoner."

Caswell snorted a laugh. "Then let us hope they think we

are smarter than this," he shot back, exaggerating the individual words like natives of Gartien did. He even mimicked her accent, or tried to.

"*Yur gunna wanna* let me do the talking," she replied, in his accent and smashed-together cadence. She thought she sounded pretty convincing, but Caswell reacted with laughter and by clapping his hands together.

"Don't quit your day job, Mel."

"What?"

"Never mind."

"Come on," she said, annoyed and a bit embarrassed. "We should get moving if we are going to reach Fineva in time."

"Agreed."

She took the tiller. The military-spec cruiser was choice-of-the-flock, configured with a powerful air-ram motor and everything needed for the rough terrain of the Desolation. It climbed out of the shallow crater with ease and ate up miles of scrubland forest beneath its tires with a voracious appetite. It being a rare quadcruiser, they were able to sit side by side in the cabin.

"Look here," Caswell said, yanking Melni from the lull of a smooth section of trail across a wide, flat plain dappled with colorful wildflowers. In a pocket affixed to the front of his seat a booklet had been stowed. Inside were maps and aerial photoprints. "They tracked us all the way from the shore," he said, pointing at a wax-pen circle marking where they'd landed.

"They must have been behind us the whole time."

He nodded. "Damned impressive. I had no idea." He showed her another page. "Looks like they charted a path from here to the summit meeting. I guess they were supposed to take us there. Or our bodies, anyway."

"It makes sense," Melni replied. "That is where everyone else will be. Including Rasa Clune, broken jaw and all." She flashed Caswell a smile but he missed it, too engrossed in the papers on his lap. For the next twenty minutes, as mile after mile of cratered prairie vanished under the nose of the cruiser, he studied the map and compared it to the landscape around them. Eventually he pinpointed their location and guided Melni onto the course the Hollow had laid out. The path led mostly east into the mountains.

"Where does this lead us?" she asked.

"Something called the Vongar. Those Grim Runners mentioned that as well. What is it?"

"A path between North and South. One of the few undamaged land routes. For a while after the Desolation it was one of the only safe ways to travel across. A roller track was even built, and that is how diplomats reach the city of Fineva even now."

"You sound . . . I don't know, concerned."

"The Vongar," she paused, choosing her words. "It's the one safe path to Fineva, from either side. It's guarded, patrolled. And, with the summit so close, it will be crowded."

"I see." He grew silent for some time. "And Fineva itself? Tell me more about it."

Navigating around fallen trees and over countless erosion holes and miniature canyons carved by years of neglect, Melni recounted the same summary all recruits at Riverswidth received, which in truth was hardly more than what any child learned in school. Fineva had once been the cultural heart of the Cirdian nation, neither its capital nor possessing any real political significance. It was regarded as one of Gartien's most beautiful cities even then, and the fact that it had been somehow spared by the bombardment of the shattered comet made the place perhaps the only beautiful city left in the world. Coupled with the winding path through the craters that surrounded it, after the Desolation occurred Fineva became a meeting place for refugees, disaster relief coordinators, and smugglers. As tensions rose between the planet's two halves, and the two major alliances—North and South—began to solidify, Fineva evolved into the de facto meeting place. The city was made a military-free zone along with the rest of the Desolation, and so the city also became Gartien's epicenter for the activities of spies.

"How many people live there?"

"I do not know. Perhaps five thousand? *Desoa,* mostly. They maintain the place, handling all the menial tasks in trade for imported goods. And they act as chaperones to any meetings between the two sides."

"Why?"

"It adds a risk of collateral damage to any hostility that might break out. In fact we have a saying: If someone uninvolved is blocking your line of fire we call them a 'Finevite Escort.'"

Outside, the lush overgrown plains began to give way to hills. Ahead steep mountains waited, the color of rust in Garta's fading light. Somewhere, on the other side, waited the roller track that wound its way to Fineva and on all the way to the Northern frontier.

"And they remain strictly neutral? Really?"

"Theoretically they are unaffiliated with either faction, but as you can imagine one of the chief industries in such a place is influence. Often they are suspected of trading information, or not stepping in to prevent hostilities. There is mistrust everywhere there."

"A nest of spies," Caswell said under his breath.

She turned to him, and nodded.

"Who settles disputes? Maintains law?" Caswell asked.

"That is a bit vague," Melni said. At his confused expression she added, "There is no real government. Behavior is regulated by treaty and all sides are supposed to punish their own transgressors."

"I can't imagine that works well at all." His expression hardened. "Sounds like a horrible place."

"I have never visited," Melni said, "but I suspect you are right, considering how nothing useful has ever resulted from the meetings that go on there."

"Gah. I must say, Melni, I'm a bit disappointed that shit politicians seem to be a universal truth."

She laughed at that, and he with her. The violence and death behind them was fading, if only slightly.

Caswell grew silent for a long time. He became so quiet, in fact, that Melni thought he must have entered his quasi-sleep state. How much of his nutrient reserves had he consumed in their battle with the Hollow? How much remained?

Garta, obscured by the western horizon, painted that narrow band of sky in rust and blood. The two moons rose in the east almost as one, mischievous Gisla peeking out over stoic Gilan's shoulder.

She drove on in the dark without the aid of the forward lamps. With the summit due to start tomorrow evening, and hundreds of miles yet to cover, Caswell had insisted they drive through the night. Melni feared the lamps would beacon their approach from miles off. In the end the two moons had settled the argument.

Caswell lurched out of his near-sleep state just past zero hour. She'd patted the back of his knee with one hand, expecting to need much more persuasion than that to rouse him, but he sat right up, alert as ever, eyes already scanning the dark road ahead of them.

"Where are we?" he asked.

She opened her door and stepped out onto the cracked ancient cobbled road. He joined her.

Melni had parked at a bend in the ancient mountain path where half the cobbled surface had long ago crumbled away and slid down. Far below a single light moved briskly up a long, shallow valley, a stretch of land completely unmarred by cratering. The light came from the front of a roller that clattered along on Southern-style tracks, heading south toward the sea.

"The Vongar," Melni said to him. "A few hundred feet wide at its narrowest, nearly fifty miles wide in some places. From the shore south of us all the way to the Combran frontier, with Fineva almost exactly in the middle."

He took all this in. "Where's the train . . . er, roller, going?"

"To pick up diplomats and staff coming up for the summit, I expect."

"Your people keep the tracks operating?"

Melni shook her head. "The NFP handle that. Um, Neutral Fineva Protectorate. We just provide the equipment."

"So what now?" he asked after a time. "What's our plan, Melni?"

"As I see it," Melni replied, "we have two choices. Cling to the hills, parallel the Vongar without getting too close, and hope we can find our way all the way up to Fineva without being seen."

"Or bombed."

"That, too."

"Hmm . . . so far Alice seems pretty trigger-happy. What's the other option?"

"We board the roller and take it all the way to Fineva."

"And how do we do that, exactly, without being captured?"

She turned to him, and grinned a grin worthy of Gisla herself.

31

MELNI REMAINED at the wheel. Not a wheel, actually, but more of a V-shaped handle she called a tiller.

In the light of the two moons she picked a path over game trails and crumbling old roads, plus the occasional jaunt over rough terrain strewn with jarring rocks and slick, snow-dappled soil. Her path wound farther and farther up into the mountains above the coast. Caswell took on the task of tracking the train, glimpsed occasionally between trees or through gaps in the foothills as it sped along the track below, a bit closer each time he saw it. A collision course, in truth, and as they drove he became aware of a strange excitement growing within him.

Laz had shattered Caswell's world. If the alien could be believed—and Caswell saw no reason to doubt the story—then Monique had been lying to him from the very start. He knew now what all those bottles of Sapporo represented. People who, in some way or another, must have flirted with discovery of the wormhole. The Conduit. And he'd killed them for that crime. Monique had sent her hammer to drive those nails back into place. To keep the Earth bottled up right where this group called Prime liked it: isolated, ignorant, and happily churning out interesting ideas. Human ingenuity, just another beast on the idea farm. *Those motherfuckers.* He bit another wave of rage back and nourished that growing excitement that waited just beyond. Excitement because here, finally, he could break the chain. Instead of killing Alice Vale he could save her, and help her in whatever plan she'd cooked up to keep Gartien from falling into Prime's hands. He could do something to wash away all the shit he'd done for Monique Pendleton.

Melni kept the cruiser more or less aimed at a wide gap between two mountain peaks, a high pass, perhaps two kilometers above sea level. Caswell shook off his distracted thoughts and studied the map. He found the two peaks, and saw a town marked in the plateau valley between. Before long he began to see its silhouette against the night sky. Steepled roofs, sort of a cross between Chinese and Russian architecture. That was where Melni wanted to lay the trap. She just had to beat the train there.

With altitude the grass fields dissipated, giving way to clumps of trees surrounded by wide, empty areas of snow and dirt. With no cover and the train so close, Melni drove hard across these patches of open ground. The tip-tap rattle of the air-ram engine transformed into a constant, heavy hiss that filled the cabin, sounding like a punctured gas line.

She barreled over one final rise and the town came into full view. Caswell glanced behind them and down, searching the valley through which the Vongar snaked. "The train's reached a steep stretch, slow going. Perhaps five minutes"—he paused and converted to their timescale—"make that three minutes out."

"We must hurry then," Melni said.

At the edge of the ravaged old town she turned and skirted along the perimeter. The utterly dark buildings loomed like monuments to the events that had destroyed this part of the world two centuries earlier. And perhaps, Caswell mused, also a monument to the political stalemate that had prevented anyone from resettling this land.

Ahead, the track appeared. Melni turned the cruiser and drove south, toward the oncoming engine. Within a minute she found the right building, a tall structure, but narrow. The beams that formed the corners were rotten and starting to buckle under the weight of the floors above. Melni backed up thirty meters.

"Out," she said suddenly, popping the canopy open.

"No way. I'm staying with you."

"This is too risky. If it fails one of us still needs to get to

Fineva. Quickly now, the dust needs time to settle or this will not work."

Caswell reluctantly obeyed. He took a few steps away and then turned to watch, feeling helpless.

She flashed him a smile, and wound the accelerator to maximum.

The cruiser lurched forward, engine hammering. Twenty meters. Melni hauled the tiller hard to the left. The cruiser bounced as it left the track, then shuddered down the tiny slope of gravel that supported the rails. Ten meters to impact. She aimed for the corner beam, one black with age and already half-rotted away.

The cruiser slammed into the corner in an explosion of loosened snow and ice. The sound of wrenching metal and splintering wood filled the air. The impact sent the cruiser careening off in a wild spin until it smacked sideways into a wall across an alley from her target. Even in the darkness Caswell saw her forehead slam into the canopy with a thud. He started to run for her, then stopped as a gigantic cracking sound filled the air. A terrible second of silence followed, then a rumbling he felt more than heard.

The building collapsed. A cloud of dust hid the carnage, but even so he could tell her plan had worked flawlessly. A pile of debris three meters high now lay across the track.

Elation gave way to concern. He ran again, skidding to a stop in the snow where the cruiser had come to rest. He wiped dust and ice from the window and peered inside. She sat there, looking dazed and in pain, but then seemed to see him. Her grimace turned into a brilliant smile when she saw him looking back. Caswell hauled the canopy open.

"Did it work?" she asked, sounding shaken.

"Perfectly. Come see."

"Not yet," she said. "We must hide this cruiser. Get in."

He glanced up and down the length of it. "Looks wedged. I'll push."

Together they managed to coax the vehicle out into the alley. Once free of the wall, Caswell hopped in and closed the window. He gave her hand a congratulatory squeeze as she set off down the darkened lane. The cruiser thumped rhythmically, a front wheel bent beyond repair.

"The whole building fell right on the track," he told her. "An engineer couldn't have planned it better. Brilliant bit of driving!"

"Gratitude," she replied, taking a sharp turn, ignoring the protests from the vehicle. She drove to the edge of town and out into the snow-dappled field just beyond, taking care to avoid leaving tracks that would be visible from the train.

She found a suitable drop-off. "Out," she said.

He popped the canopy open and exited, snow crunching beneath his treadmellows. He ran around to her side and helped her. "You okay?"

"Hmm?"

"Injured. Are you hurt?"

"Just confused. Knocked my head against the glass when I hit that wall."

Together they pushed the cruiser down the slope and watched as it rolled down the mountain on the north side of town. It started to veer toward the track, a hundred meters to the right. Caswell held his breath, exhaling only when the vehicle swerved back and, finally, disappeared over a steep drop-off. Seconds later he heard the faint sound of metal smashing against rock somewhere far below.

"So far so good," Caswell said. He glanced at the north side of town and the abandoned buildings there. Any minute now the train would arrive on the other side of town. "What's next?"

"We hide, but not here."

"Where then?"

"The town center, where the tail of the roller will be."

He nodded and fell in behind her as she jogged parallel to the tracks. At the edge of town she crept into a dark gap between two buildings. He dropped to a crouch and followed her in.

Melni weaved a path through half-collapsed shops and houses, jogged along a cobbled alley, and climbed over a stone wall that had fared much better than the wooden frames of the old buildings all around. Two centuries of decay had not been kind, but despite that he could sense the charm this place must have once held. A quaint stop for the night on the way north or south. He made a mental note to quiz Melni later on the political stratification of her world, suddenly curious how it compared to the dizzying maze of shifting alliances and adversaries back home. What could be learned by comparing their ideologies? Though far from an expert on the topic, he sensed a strong possibility both worlds could benefit from the wisdom gained by the other.

A chill coursed through him. These must be the same sorts of questions that led these so-called Wardens of Prime to observe the worlds they found. Even for such an advanced society there must be plenty to learn from populations that arose independently, even if the populations were physically the same. *We must all be like precocious children to them,* he thought. *Often dazzling with imaginative solutions to old problems, but deserving of being struck when we ask sensitive questions or dare to explore beyond the immediate surroundings.*

A thunderous cacophony banished the thought. The ground trembled. Brakes squealed. The train had arrived.

He caught the hint of its brilliant headlight just as Melni did, and they both dove to the ground just to be safe. The shrill scream of brakes from a hundred wheels went on and on. Melni glanced at him and grinned, standing. He smiled back and vaulted to his feet.

Twenty meters on Melni found a collapsed multistory building with a shadowed cavity on the ground floor that looked out onto the tracks. Thirty meters beyond, the rear car of the segmented vehicle waited. The long train, twenty cars at least, had come to a complete stop before crashing into the pile of rubble across the tracks, just as Melni's plan assumed.

She gasped upon seeing all the debris her crash had created. "Maybe we did too good of a job," she said. "It may take all night to clear."

"They're in a hurry. They'll figure something out." He glanced up at the sky, happy to see that the dust kicked up from the building collapse had already dissipated in the mountain breeze. This needed to look like a natural occurrence, not an ambush. With any luck they wouldn't notice the tracks on the ground, or the footprints. At least the sky betrayed nothing. Just the two moons as witness, and they weren't talking.

Melni gripped Caswell's arm. He glanced at her and then at the train.

Four soldiers leapt from open doors at the rear. They split off in pairs, fanning out to either side of the vehicle, weapons at the ready. At the head of the long vehicle an even larger detail emerged. Not just soldiers, Caswell thought. A mixed group—engineers and porters—spilled out and rushed toward the debris. They shouted back and forth to one another, and a few darted back inside, presumably to fetch more labor, or tools, or both.

"Be ready," Melni said.

Her plan had worked perfectly. Within two minutes the initial confusion and investigation transformed into a concerted effort by virtually everyone aboard to clear the tracks. Caswell guessed at least seventy-five people had disembarked and were now crowded around the demolished building, tossing chunks of wood and rubble away from the front of the train. Even the guards eventually shouldered their weapons and joined in the work.

"There are so many," Melni whispered.

"That's a good thing," he replied. "Disguises our tracks. And, easier to hide among them. C'mon, now's our chance."

She nodded, gathered her courage. Per the plan he went first, walking casually toward the vehicle with his hands held in front of him as if bound, his gaze on the ground. Melni followed a few paces behind. "Business of the Presidium, not your concern," she'd say to anyone who challenged them.

But no one said anything. In fact, the rear carriage was empty. Just rows of forward-facing seats in plush red fabric. A few supported bags and other detritus, but most were entirely vacant. Melni urged him forward, deeper into the train. The patrol guards had exited from this rear car and would certainly notice the sudden presence of a Hollow and her prisoner upon their return.

In the next carriage the hallway turned and followed the right side of the train, allowing room for seven sleeper cabins on the left. Caswell tried the first door, then the second, both locked. The third opened. He went in.

"This is perfect," Melni said, coming in behind him. The cabin was empty, lit only by a small magenta bulb above the door. He clicked the door closed once she was inside, then went to the single round window on the far wall, expecting curious guards approaching their car, guns drawn. There was nothing, however. Just the dark buildings of the tiny mountain village.

He puffed out a breath he hadn't realized he'd been holding. He needed to relax, so he sat on one of the two couches, unsure what else to do.

Melni checked the two inner doors. The first opened upon a small lav. She paused there, if only for a second, perhaps tantalized by the prospect of a hot shower.

The handle of the second door twisted when she tried it. Melni opened it an inch and peered into the room beyond. Yellow light spilled through the gap. Melni stepped through.

"What are you doing?" Caswell asked, trying to keep his voice low.

"I am not sure yet," she said from the other room.

Curious, he stood and joined her.

The adjacent cabin, a mirror of their own, was lit by a reading lamp embedded in one wall. Upon a shelf above the far couch were two long, flat bags, stacked one on top of the other. Melni pulled one down and undid the latches. A little gasp escaped her lips at the contents.

"What is it?" he asked, craning his neck to see.

"An opportunity," she replied, and showed him.

An hour later he emerged from the lav, feeling very much like a new man.

The train had started moving fifty Gartien minutes earlier and now raced downhill through a dark forest made uneven by the ravaged landscape. Melni sat on her bench, dressed in the purple evening gown she discovered in the second of the two garment bags. She looked up at Caswell as he stepped through the narrow door and presented himself.

The suit fit him well, if a bit loose in the chest and shoulders. The dark gray cloth was tailored in a modern Southern style, Melni had explained, with an asymmetrical opening buttoned three times just above the heart, the gap falling diagonally away to end at a smart, hard corner before disappearing around the back. The material had a slight sheen to it, contrasted by a light gray shirt beneath that he'd clasped tight at the neck. The sleeve cuffs above each hand were hidden below the arms of the jacket. She stood and corrected these apparent gaffes for him, then stepped back.

"It is obvious you have a pistol tucked in the coat, but that should not raise concern where we are going."

He patted the weapon, as if that might press it down enough to hide it. The compact vossen would have been ideal, but he'd spent every round fighting the Hollow, and discarded the empty, single-use tube.

"How does it feel?" she asked him, referring to the clothes.

"I'll admit it looks quite smart, but I liked the Grim Runner garb better."

She stifled a laugh. "Me, too. However the diplomats will be wearing garments like this tonight for Alia's speech. Our chances of being noticed are considerably reduced this way."

He sensed, or thought he sensed, a deeper reaction to his attire. The slight reddening of the cheeks, the uptick of the eyebrows, and the vaguest hint of some kind of animal desire. He couldn't be sure he read these signs right, but were he on Earth he would have known instantly that his sudden attraction to this woman had been repaid in kind. She looked like a vision in her dress. The cut was severe, the type of thing you'd expect on a runway model in Milan for some provocative new designer, not a diplomat at a summit meeting. It accentuated a dancer's body he'd barely noticed before, and, combined with the literally otherworldly hairstyle and her unsettling purple eyes, he'd found it difficult to keep his mind on the danger of their situation.

Caswell took his seat again across from her. He'd had to keep his desert boots on beneath the widened bottoms of the pant legs, for there had been no footwear with the clothing. Hopefully no one would look down.

For a time they sat in silence as the train thundered along toward Alice Vale's summit.

"Next comes the hard part," he said, looking out the window. "Finding Alia before your people make their move. What time is it?"

"Almost first hour, I think."

He nodded. "Cutting it close." *Damn close,* he added to himself. Two days, almost to the minute, and he would revert. Ready or not, all this would be forgotten.

Melni said something.

He barely heard it, and then her words registered like a slap to the face. "Hold on. What did you just say?"

She yawned, stretched. "I said we are lucky the summit was delayed. With this new information—"

Caswell sat bolt upright, head swimming. He grabbed Melni's hands, so tight her eyes went wide with fear. "Delayed? What the hell are you talking about?"

She looked at him, confused. "The . . . While you were unconscious, in Riverswidth. From your injuries."

"Yes? Go on!"

"Combra called for a two-day delay. So lucky for us. It bought you extra time to heal."

"I was in that bed for *two days*?"

He shouted so loudly the window rattled.

Melni flinched back, held fast by his grip. "Why are you so angry? It gave us more time to—" She stopped.

Stopped because he wasn't listening to her. Caswell leapt from his seat. Before he knew what he was doing he was at the door, then out in the hall beyond. He stopped there, looking off toward the far end of the car, where a clock hung on the wall.

One minute left to reversion.

"Goddamnit," he growled to himself. "Goddamnit, goddamnit. Fuck."

"What is wrong?" Melni asked from the cabin door.

"Look," he stammered, pushing her back inside, closing the door. He urged her back to her seat, then he paced. *What to do?* He was fucked and he knew it. He sat down, saw the fear in her eyes, and felt a surge of guilt. "Look. Okay. Listen. I'm so sorry I didn't tell you of this sooner. I thought I had more time."

"Tell me what? You are scaring me."

He fixed a gaze on her, tried to put every bit of urgency he could into it. "In less than a minute I'll forget everything."

"You . . . what? You will forget? Forget what?"

"My mission. This place. Laz, Alice, all of it. You. I'll forget *you*."

"What are you talking about? How?"

"There's no time, Melni!" he shouted.

She recoiled as if slapped.

He grasped her hands again, gently this time. "Just— Listen to me, carefully. I won't know you. I may even try to kill you."

"Kill me? Caswell, what—"

"Don't say anything, just listen. I will reset. Do you understand? You must explain to me why I'm here. What we're doing and why it's important."

"I . . . Garta's light. Yes. Anything."

"There's more."

"What?" she asked, breathless.

"I won't trust you. But there's a chance. When I come back, I may whisper something. Part of a song. You have to finish the lyric or I will never believe you. I'll say: 'Speak the word.' "

"Speak what word?"

"No time, just listen! You must finish it."

"But what word?"

"*Not a word,* it's a song. I'll say, 'Speak the word.' You say: 'The word is all of us.' "

"Caswell, this is too much. I don't—"

His body suddenly spasmed, and then his eyes screwed shut as every neuron in his head flipped back to where it had been, two weeks earlier.

PART 4
REVERSION

32

EVERYTHING CHANGED. He'd been exhaling, now he was inhaling. Weightlessness, and now the familiar tug of gravity. Stale air became heavy, full of exotic scents. He felt the sway of motion. His stomach suddenly clenched so hard he felt as if shot in the gut. Pain from a dozen new injuries registered. The weight of his spacesuit, gone, replaced with something light and flexible. His body spasmed involuntarily at the change. His neck throbbed, too, low on chemicals.

Fuck, I've reverted, he managed to think through it all.

Despite the tears in his eyes he coaxed them open. "The word . . . speak the word," he realized he was still saying, and stopped.

He was sitting now, not clinging to the *Venturi*'s wall. A fashion model with pixie hair and fake purple eyes sat across from him, looking like she'd just been pummeled by street thugs. He hoped he hadn't been the one to do that. Caswell blinked tears away and fought to get his mind around this shift in realities. "Who . . ." he said, then waited as a wave of nausea passed. He willed focus from his implant only to realize his smartwatch was gone. He tried the manual method of activating the implant instead, rubbing his temples, hoping for something. Anything. Clarity, concentration. It gave a little. He sat up, more alert now. "Who are you?" he barked.

The exotic party girl opened her mouth to reply, and suddenly it occurred to him that he'd been compromised. Captured. Why else would he not be in his bed in London or, barring that, at least somewhere safe? To revert in the field was unthinkable.

Before she could utter whatever lie waited on her lips, Caswell reached out. He grasped her neck and shoved her bodily back into the red-cushioned seat. He gripped hard. She clawed at fingers that felt stiff as iron, gasped for breath, and croaked something. "The . . . word . . . all of us."

Had she just . . . ? He eased off. His hands did not move, but he loosened his grip just enough to let her speak.

"The word is all of us," she said, eyes wide with terror.

Caswell let her go. She scrambled away from him to the corner of the small room and got her breathing under control.

"Who are you?" he rasped. "Where am I? Some sort of simkit?"

"I do not know what a simkit is," the woman replied.

The sway of the room suddenly registered. The vibration in his seat, and distant sounds. "Are we . . . is this a bloody *steam train,* for fuck's sake? Who are you?"

"Please, one question at a time," she said. She willed calm and allowed herself several full breaths, her fingertips still massaging her neck where he'd grabbed her. "My name is Melni Tavan."

"Melanie?"

She grinned at that, though it vanished in an instant. "Melni. And you are Caswell."

Her accent he could not place, and her looks . . . probably all artificial. The eyes, the hair, the skin tone . . . none of it worked. She looked like some Eastern European sim-raver in a dress made by a fashion school genius the world just wasn't fucking ready for. "How do you know me? Why am I here?" He glanced down at himself. "Jesus Christ, what the hell are we wearing?"

"Your implant has caused you to forget," she said.

"Obviously." He stared at her. "You knew the lyric, so . . . that's something. I've never told anyone that. What happened? Tell me why I'm here." He glanced around again. Where on Earth did people still ride steam trains? "Wherever here is."

The woman swallowed. "You were sent here to kill a woman named Alice Vale."

"Right. Right. I know that name," he said. The missing crew member. Monique must have located her, sent him to finish the job. "She wasn't with the others."

"She goes by Alia Valix here."

"Where is 'here,' damnit?"

"We are on our way to a summit where she is due to speak, but when we—"

The door burst open.

Shadows stood in the hall. Shadows with guns.

33

THE GIRL REACTED before he could.

Still in the post-reversion fog, Caswell watched the woman across from him lurch up and into the two figures in the hallway with surprising speed. Whoever she was, she was damned quick.

The soldiers in the hall were dressed like none he'd ever seen. But then he was dressed in a completely bizarre outfit, too. It looked like someone from a hundred years earlier had tried to imagine what a business suit would look like in the year 2100, and failed miserably.

Get it together, Cas. He reached out to his implant and willed a dose of elhydrine, ignoring for the moment that virtually every chembank was nearly empty. One thing at a time. There was danger here, and the post-reversion haze left him little to no chance of fighting it. The gland responded. Time seemed to slow down externally while remaining normal within his mind. Chemical reactions in his brain would trigger faster, much faster, now. The downside was heat. He'd get maybe thirty seconds of realtime advantage and then it would stop or he'd cook himself.

The woman flung herself toward the door, one balled fist arching toward the jaw of the uniformed man standing there. Who was she again? Melni? A strange name. She looked like no one he'd ever seen, pale skin and blond hair cut almost mannishly short. Her eyes were a luminous, unearthly purple. Contact lenses, surely. She wore a dress that matched her eye color.

Most important, she knew his mnemonic. Whoever she was, he trusted her. Or, at least, he needed her. Maybe he'd given her something for safekeeping, something too important to lose along with his memory. Something Archon needed?

What Caswell needed was space. To gather his wits, find out just what the hell had led him here, then make contact with Monique and report.

He forced himself into motion. With his brain firing at six times the normal rate it felt like slow dancing in a vat of heavy syrup. The woman's fist was just reaching the first guard's chin. The man was holding a completely bizarre-looking gun with tubing along the sides and some sort of pressurized canister extending well back above the wrist, but there was no mistaking the business end and it was coming up. Caswell adjusted his motion to lift his lower back away from the bench seat and, just as he suspected, the tip of the weapon suddenly unleashed a bright flame and then a bullet. The round sailed across the gap like a gently thrown dart, slapping into the cushion where Caswell's rear end had been a second earlier. A split second from the guard's perspective, unless he had an implant, too. His eyes did not move in the telltale hyperactive way elhydrine causes, though. Perhaps just a local soldier? The uniform was as bizarre as the suit Caswell wore.

He kept himself in motion, and reviewed the last few minutes of his life before . . . *this.* He'd been aboard the *Venturi,* watching the crew of the *Pawn Takes Bishop* work to free the black box from that doomed, long-dead station. He'd sent off a report to Monique that one crew member was missing. Alice Vale.

"You were sent here to kill a woman named Alice Vale."

Monique had forced him into an IA-protocol mission. A sudden request, no time to get his acceptance much less his ritual, spurned because the captain of that salvage crew had accessed the *Venturi*'s computers against orders. Then his implant had kicked in and everything between that moment and when he "awoke" on this train was now forcibly deleted. Forever. Whatever it had been, wherever they'd sent him to do it, he'd obviously failed to complete the objective and return to London, or at least a safe place, in time.

He had to contact Monique. Find out what the fuck was going on. Find out if he should abort. Go to ground or return home.

Or finish the job he'd been sent to do. *Kill Alice Vale.* Perhaps that was why he'd trusted the girl with his lyric. How the hell else would she have known his mission goal?

A strangely muffled thud caught his attention: the woman's fist smashing into the guard's jaw. A tooth glided away like a leaf knocked from a branch. The man's knees were going, his eyes rolling sickly up.

The other man, though—shit. Caswell hadn't noticed before but saw it now; the butt of the man's gun was driving in hard toward Melni's stomach. No time to do anything about that. He could think fast but his movements were still constrained by human capability and real-world physics. Caswell pushed his body into a leap, stretched himself out, hands extended. He aimed straight for the woman's head knowing she would double over from the blow to her abdomen before he reached her. Sure enough she started to bend forward, an elongated grunt whooshing out of her lips. Caswell brushed the top of her head as he sailed past, his hands perfectly grasping the neck of the man who had struck her. Caswell caught a brief glimpse of snow-dappled trees blurring past outside. No landmarks to guide him. Planetside, clearly, but where? Russia? Canada? Some goddamned theme park for rich weirdos who liked to ride steam trains? Impossible to tell, and not the time to figure it out.

Not the time because, despite everything else assaulting his mind, one fact stood out: He'd trusted the woman Melni. Trusted her enough to tell her his mnemonic, *had* to trust her because above all else he apparently thought his mission was important enough to continue beyond the expiration timer. Monique wouldn't like that. IA-rated missions were not given unless a strict and carefully considered time frame had been agreed upon.

Caswell's momentum through the heavy clear molasses of thin-fucking-air took him and his victim straight across the narrow hall of the train car and into the wall beyond. He lowered his head as they flew, slow as a considerate nod from his perspective, aiming for the man's jaw and succeeding.

Caswell twisted with the impact, allowing his body to roll sideways into the wall and drop him to the floor on all fours. He took the impact easily, graced so with the luxury to ponder every motion, every angle. The man he'd hit was sliding down the wall, knees splaying. In realtime Caswell might have snagged his foot on the man's knee while trying to stick his landing, but in this slowed frame of reference he managed to hook his foot out and around. As he did so he glanced back.

The woman Melni was falling, limp as a mannequin. More guards were rushing up from her end of the hall, frantically trying to ready movie-prop weapons. Only they were real, Caswell thought. No one made props with that kind of detail just for a damned simkit fantasy.

The guard Melni had punched was falling, too, one hand pressed across his face, a weirdly deep scream beginning to hiss out of him like a slow leak of air. He spun as he fell, one arm flailing out to brace the impact. It made the men rushing up behind him begin to slow or leap to one side. That was useful. Caswell came up in a sprint for the other end of the train, running crouched, feeling like he was at the bottom of a pool. Suddenly he noticed the weight at his breast. As he ran he lifted one hand and slipped it into the strange, diagonally breasted coat he wore, where the grip of a pistol waited. He yanked the weapon free and considered his options. Turn and empty the clip? He had no idea what this weapon was, much less how big a cartridge it held, but he thought it reasonable to assume it had four shots and thus enough for the immediate problem. He could turn and drop the four guards in as many squeezes of the trigger, taking leisurely aim for each.

But he'd never killed anyone before, not that he remembered at least. And he certainly didn't know this gun. It could be empty, though he doubted he would have been carrying it if that was the case. Hell, glancing at it he began to wonder how to even fire the bloody thing, or which end was which. It was longer behind the grip than in front, and had a weird brace or something at the back. Caswell gripped the handle and found it all made a sudden sense. The brace rested on his forearm. The weapon's weight seemed evenly distributed instead of in front of his trigger finger like a typical pistol, but this he thought he could compensate for with one or two practice shots.

Caswell raised the weapon and fired it at a rounded window at the far end of the train car. The glass shattered and fell in splinters, like it would have a hundred years ago before aligned-hybrid glass became commonly used, or even the basic tempered stuff from half a century ago. This window spidered rather beautifully and then sucked inward, propelled by the forces of the wind outside. He saw the shards coming for him and knew he needed to dodge. The men behind him would be thinking he was going to leap through the broken pane. A suicide move he had no intention of making. He did leap, but aimed himself slightly off to one side. He started to bring his left leg up and began to twist himself bodily. The glass missed him by mere millimeters. His foot caught the sidewall and he pushed off, accelerating himself diagonally toward the dogleg corner of the hall beside the broken window. Cool air gently buffeted him. He rolled in midair, took aim behind.

His first bullet took the guard standing over Melni just above his left eye. Brains splattered out the other side. Some part of Caswell knew this moment for what it was: the first kill he would actually remember. *No Sapporo for you, mate. Sorry.* This death he would keep, forever scarred onto his memory. It changed everything. With that one bullet a man died, and Caswell's own life may well have ended, too. His career, his far-flung adventures between contracts. All of it suddenly felt like a house of cards, built on the simple idea that he carried no baggage. Until now. This stranger. This cop in a bizarre uniform, falling, brains spraying into the hallway of a steam train, of all things.

Caswell shifted his aim and fired once more, even as the corner of the hall obscured his vision. He thought the shot true. Two down, then. Two kills in as many seconds.

Despite this the girl collapsed. Dead, alive, he didn't know. Leaving her there felt like a mistake but he saw no way around it. For all he knew she could have been a random stranger he'd forced to learn his lyric so that he could reacquire his mission goal. Nothing to be done about it now. If she was important, he'd deal with finding her again on his own terms. Adapt and improvise.

His leap took him around the little corner at the end of the hall. There was a door, as he'd hoped, and he crumpled into it, taking full advantage of his slowed reference frame to absorb the impact with minimal pain. Behind him came the muffled, drawn-out sounds of alarm, followed by gunfire. Three rounds slapped into the thin wall beside the door. Caswell ignored them and reached to open—

What the hell is this? he thought. The handle was in the middle, somewhat phallic, and linked via a metal bar to a little lever at shin height. Nothing was right about this place. The acceptance of this obvious truth caused a seed of fear to suddenly sprout within his mind. He reached for dihazalon to counter the sensation and felt a mild sting as his implant declined. Reservoir empty. The fear spread and flowered. Any second now he'd lose his advantage of slowed time, too, and he'd be left with a potentially deadly fever. Caswell gripped the handle and twisted. Nothing. He lifted it up and the bar moved, clicked. He felt the door loosen in the frame and pushed outward. The rush of air outside sounded in his slowed perspective like water running through pipes.

Through the window on the car behind he saw more guards or police or whatever the hell they were running toward him. The train was moving too fast for him to jump off. He glanced up, saw a handle of some sort, and leapt for it. His fingers brushed the bar and curled around it. That he held on to the slim length of metal was nothing short of a miracle. Impossible without the implant. His body lashed sideways and slammed into the hard corner of the train car. Vortexes of wind whipped at his clothing. Grunting with effort, Caswell hauled himself back to a more or less upright position and climbed onto the roof of the car. Police or soldiers or whatever the hell they were poured out from the two opposing doors below him.

A concert of wailing sounds began to fill the air around him, then the press of wind against him began to slowly abate. The train was slowing. He looked forward and saw an old city. It looked medieval: gray stonework and small windows, narrow spires, tiered steepled roofs. Only everything was slightly off. The steeples were at offset angles. The windows had rounded tops. The stones were inlaid in triangular chunks rather than square. He took all this in and, most of all, noticed how dead the place was. Save for a few distant buildings in what he assumed was the town center, everything else was black. Broken and shuttered. Vines and weeds dominated the streets instead of people. How old was this place? What had happened here?

Immediately ahead a large, long building loomed. It looked different from the rest. Simple flat walls, no windows. Utilitarian, and built recently. As it grew closer he saw it for what it was: a train depot, of sorts. There were platforms to either side, but only the one on the left had people standing on it. They carried lanterns, of all things, and some appeared to be armed. The other side, to Caswell's right, was very dark and empty. He started to run forward along the top of the train car. From the back of his head came a subtle tingling sensation. A warning that his reserve of elhydrine had been used. His advantage would only last a few more seconds.

Caswell scanned the dark platform as the train lumbered into the station. It was easy to fool oneself while on elhydrine. Confuse slow movement for safe. The mind's natural calculations of risk and ability could not be trusted. Every instinct told him to just jump, to land and roll and dash into the shadows. Only his training kept him from doing so. The car seemed to be moving about ten kilometers per hour, which meant sixty in reality. Still too fast to jump. Caswell forced himself to keep moving ahead. He ran to the end of the car and slowed only when he saw the top of someone's head emerging over the lip. Caswell jumped the gap, kicking as he went, a solid connection right to the eye socket of some poor, uniformed woman. Her head began to recoil backward as he sailed past. Caswell landed easily on the next car, rolled, came up in a jog. A bullet whistled past his head, very wide. A deliberate miss? He filed that, too risky to rely on that assumption just yet.

There was a pile of debris in the shadows on the empty platform. A mass of leaves and long, knobby reeds. Gardening waste. It was his best hope. Caswell took one last step and launched himself toward the heap of dead vegetation.

In that instant his world sped up, physically, visually, audibly. The neurons and synapses in his brain began to process signals slower and slower until, just as his knees hit the pile, everything became human-normal again. It felt like sinking toward the bottom of a pool only to have all the water suddenly, instantly, vanish. He managed to fling his arms up around his face as he slammed into the dead leaves. Cut lengths of vine and weed lashed at him. The pile smelled of soil and cut grass. Fresh, not brittle. It cushioned him and then sprang back. Caswell practically bounced off. He fell on his ass to the hard, gravelly floor of the old platform. Cries of alarm went up from the train and beyond. English words, but the accent he couldn't place.

Caswell forced himself to stand. He loped off into the shadows, the sounds of soldiers and a slowing train filling the space behind him.

Melni lay on a vibrating metal floor, dimly aware of a throbbing pain emanating from her guts. She tried to lift her head and heard a wet tearing sound for the effort. The smell hit her then. Her own vomit, in a pool around her face.

"She is awake," someone said.

Blurred shapes swam into focus.

Melni tried to move, only to find herself bound at the wrists and ankles with strips of rubber.

"Sit her up," the familiar voice of Rasa Clune said.

Hands slipped under Melni's armpits and she was hauled bodily from the sticky mess she'd made, flipped around, and slammed down again, this time on her back. The hands tugged her until her back and head rested against a solid surface. The room swayed and vibrated. Somewhere behind her came the clattering sound of an air motor. The movement made her nauseous and dizzy. A new pain manifested: a throbbing from the back of her skull.

Melni tried to focus on her surroundings. She blinked and concentrated. "How long have—" she started.

Clune cut her off with a backhanded slap that stung Melni's cheek. The hand whipped back in the opposite direction and left an identical impression on the other.

Bright pain nearly blinded her. She could do nothing save lower her head and wince until the heat on her cheeks faded to something manageable. It took a long time. All the while the room swayed.

Not a room, Melni realized. A special roller cabin. Armored walls, floor, and ceiling. A military troop carrier.

Clune stood in front of her, one hand pressed up against the ceiling to steady herself. With slow, deliberate motion she raised her free hand and gripped Melni by the jaw, her nails digging painfully into the skin. Melni could do nothing but clench her teeth and stare into the woman's emotionless face. The bandage across her nose should have made her seem weaker, yet somehow the dressing only added to the cold, disciplinary stare.

"What happened," Rasa said, "to the team we sent to fetch you?"

Fetch us. What birdshit. Melni met Clune's gaze. "Speculate," she hissed.

Clune's eyes narrowed. She gripped so hard the nails drew blood. Then harder still, until the pain became unbearable.

"They were not there to fetch us," Melni managed to utter through the compressed circle her lips had become. "And they are all dead."

Clune's face betrayed nothing. Her grip, however, tightened. "Impossible."

If Melni could have spat in the woman's face she would have. The gesture came out as a bubble of drool that dripped down her chin. She gagged involuntarily as Clune's fingers dug in even harder.

"You are the one who is going to die," Rasa said. "Very slowly and very painfully, if you do not tell us everything you know about the man you helped escape. Talk, and I promise a quick and painless end to your miserable traitorous life."

Melni held her head steady and tried not to gurgle under the press of sharp fingernails. The stern woman searched Melni's eyes for a few seconds and then, abruptly, let go. She took a step back. "How did you elude the Hollow agents?"

"I told you," Melni rasped, working her jaw to ease the pain. "They are all dead."

Clune apparently believed it this time because her complexion, already pale, flushed to bone white. It matched her bandaged nose. "Impossible. You are not so well trained—"

"Caswell went through them like a farmer clearing boneweed," she lied, then instantly regretted it. With Caswell painted that dangerously, Clune would probably have him killed immediately.

Except . . . that was not shock on the woman's face, it was fear. "He knows you sent them," Melni added. "And he is out there."

All he actually knows is that he was sent here to kill Alia Valix. A man who managed to penetrate the Think Tank in his first few days on a completely alien world. Now he was in a virtually deserted city, with a million places to hide, and Alia would be out in the open. For a speech, to diplomats.

"Why have you brought so many soldiers to this event?" Melni asked, the truth slowly dawning on her.

"Simple," Clune replied. "After you helped our only negotiating piece escape, only one option remains to us. We are going to capture Valix, or eliminate her. She will either work for us, or work for no one. There is no other outcome that will suffice. Not now. Even you must realize that."

"Why not just hear what she has to say?"

Clune laughed. "That is exactly what we cannot do. She is far too clever to propose anything other than a scenario that will advantage her and her allies in the North. Even if she proposes sharing her genius equally, the North is already too far ahead of us. We would never catch up. No, we must get to her before she can take the tiller of this conversation. And as for your friend, well . . . if he really killed a whole squad of Hollow, his punishment will match the crime." The woman came in closer, her lips just inches from Melni's face. "The same goes for you, Sonbo."

"I . . ." Melni paused, almost gagging on the director's wretched breath. What could she say that would stay Clune's hand? She had no way to prove the Warden's story. Melni's only hope was to get to Alia Valix before anyone else. Before Caswell, before Clune and her strike team. Find her and tell her that Melni and Caswell had met the Warden. Maybe if she knew she wasn't alone with that burden of knowledge she'd change her course. *And then all I'd have to do is stop everyone from trying to kill her anyway.* Melni tugged at the chains holding her arms and feet. She glanced at the guards and then at their cold, disgusting leader, and she saw no path that would lead toward this goal.

34

CLUMPS OF PALE GRASS poked from every crack in the gravelly gray bricks. Small tricolored flowers with angular petals grew across knotted vines that wormed through every empty window and doorframe. The buildings were old, Caswell thought, though not of any architectural style he'd ever seen. They'd been abandoned long ago, that much was obvious. Or at least made to appear so, if this was some kind of elaborate training ground or simkit scenario.

Virtually all of it hid in darkness. Row after row of buildings with black windows, lined on one deserted street after another. Only a small pocket near the center of the city had working lights that chased away the black of night.

Caswell avoided that area for now. It seemed to be the only place around where people were, so it made sense that the summit that woman Melni had spoken of would take place there. Thus his target would be there, too, but he wanted to make sure he'd well and truly lost his pursuers before he turned his focus to that goal. One thing at a time.

He darted through a small square, the cobbled ground hidden beneath the snaking vines with their little blue-white-red flowers. At the center of the space—it was more of a hexagon in truth—Caswell froze. He could see the night sky clearly from here, and in that sky hung not one but two moons.

Two goddamn moons.

Caswell stood for a long moment and stared at the two dark gray orbs, baffled. Certainly no training sim would bother with such a deviation from reality. Besides, he knew instinctively that this was not a sim. No synthetic environment had this kind of tactile fidelity. The technology existed to fool one's visual cortex on this level, but every other sense told him this place existed and he was really here.

"Not my problem," he whispered. Monique, and Archon, had sent him here to do a job. Wherever or whatever "here" was didn't matter. Clearly this place, real or some hyperadvanced simulation, was something he wasn't meant to know about, hence the IA status of the mission. He'd failed in that regard, but the goal must still be critically important or he wouldn't have trusted a total stranger with his anchor phrase. That was a tool he'd kept primed for almost thirteen years and never once used. He had to trust the side of him that he did not know. The version of Peter Caswell that killed for a living. The man who had never screwed up a mission before, at least not like this. Whatever repercussions would come from retaining memories, he could still be a professional.

Caswell turned his eyes away from the moons and darted into the shadows across the square. He worked his way through the abandoned streets, keeping the pool of lights off to his left. After ten minutes or so he began to angle toward the activity those lights represented. He found a tall building and climbed a dark and rickety old stairwell to the top floor. There he found a few small rooms that had probably been flats, though they had no kitchens. A hotel, perhaps? The place reeked of stagnant water and old vegetation. He crossed to a round-top window frame, partially occluded by grimy broken glass, and looked out upon a grand square bustling with activity.

Caswell pulled an old stool over to the window and sat down to watch. His feet ached now, and his stomach grumbled audibly. A fever raged behind his forehead. He wondered at his own lack of gear. No survival pack, no vossen gun, not even his smartwatch. Just a weird, retro-futuristic tuxedo, a pistol unlike any he'd seen before, and a virtually empty implant. *What the hell have you gotten me into, Monique?*

Tents dotted the square, and people milled about in the

gaps and small spaces between. Caswell scanned them with a practiced eye. To his surprise, despite the train full of uniformed soldiers he'd just fled, everyone—*everyone*— in the space below his window wore civilian clothes. Hundreds of individuals, milling about a tent city in the middle of a dead city, and not a policeman or private security detail in sight. If those walking about were dressed in rags he might have understood. Some squatter town erected in an old-world city condemned due to some chemical spill, perhaps in Belarus or Moldova, from the quirky architecture. Yet these people were not in rags. They wore clothes like his. Fine suits, however avant-garde in style, on the men. The women mostly wore what he could only think of as the stiff, heavy fabric dresses politicians' wives had worn a hundred years ago. Nineteen-sixties chic with some local flair.

The more he looked the more he realized the square had been divided neatly into two camps, with a wide aisle between. Here some of the men and women, though dressed like all the others, stood alone and spoke little, their gazes sweeping the crowd, their passive faces betraying nothing. So, policed but not overtly. Interesting.

The woman on the train had said something about a summit. Now it made sense. He was looking at two factions, gathered perhaps in secret to hear Alice Vale give a speech.

Caswell took a long breath and willed himself to be calm, no easy feat without the aid of his extra gland. He took stock, lining up what little he remembered and what he'd experienced since reversion. He'd been on the *Pawn Takes Bishop,* undercover as an expert on the famously lost *Venturi.* His briefing had confirmed the theory of weapons research going on there. Something so nasty they'd done it far from Earth's prying eyes. Monique, via the powers that be within Archon, had snuck Caswell onto the black-box recovery mission so that he could try to siphon data before the old wreck dove into the Sun. Mo had also asked him to account for the crew. All there, dead of course, except one: Alice Vale. And there'd been a shuttle missing. Then he'd seen the *Pawn*'s captain accessing the *Venturi*'s computer, and Monique had initiated the IA protocol moments later without allowing for consent.

Recalling this soothed his nerves, like the warmth from a strong drink. He welcomed it, and his little roost here. The post-reversion nausea had gone. He let his mind wander through possibilities. Clearly Alice Vale had survived. Killed the rest of her crew and come here, or perhaps was brought here against her will. She likely had intimate knowledge of the research that had gone on aboard that ship. Hell, she'd probably been one of the masterminds. Maybe she'd run. Maybe she'd taken whatever nasty weapon they'd developed there and brought it here. Perhaps to sell it.

His calm dissolved into cold calculation. What if she was here to unleash the secret weapon she'd been researching? What if she planned to kill all these people, here, tonight? Had that been what was so urgent that he'd given up his mnemonic to some stranger on a train?

It must be that. Or something like it. Archon had probably been hired to prevent the weapon's use. Caswell scanned the crowd again. He allowed his vision to glaze, letting his mind see the whole scene rather than the individual people. "Where are you, Vale?" he whispered.

She was here to give a speech. A dignitary then. She probably wouldn't be out here in the open. He scanned the tents and then the buildings that fronted the square, looking for the best one. Then he noticed that not all the buildings were dark. Most of the structures immediately adjacent to the space were lit from within. Perhaps the upper echelon of this gathering were huddled in those places. Some were more ornate than others. Palaces or mansions. Maybe even churches, though clearly this was not a city that subscribed to any religion he knew.

Caswell glanced down at himself. He had a suit like the ones they wore, and a pistol of unknown capacity and capability. His implant was next to useless, unless he could find food, but even that would take a while to fully metabolize and find its way to the reservoirs in his neck. His current position, though it afforded a nice overlook, would not help him. Not without a preprogrammed drone rifle to place, or at the very least a decent hunting rifle. He needed to get down there, among that crowd, and start asking questions.

He needed to do what he always did: drop himself into an unknown environment and blend in.

Peter Caswell walked a jagged perimeter and kept to the shadows, unsure what to make of the event under way in this strange place. Two sides, gathered in a city that appeared to be all but abandoned, about to hear a speech from a woman who disappeared twelve years ago instead of dying with the rest of her crew.

Nothing made sense.

Near the far corner of the square he spied a two-story building that may have once been a restaurant. Urine-yellow lights bobbed around inside as people with handheld lanterns or candles busied themselves within. He could smell food cooking, though the scents were unusual. His stomach growled all the same. He pondered shifting tactics. Steal some food, wait for his implant to extract the needed resources, then find his target. But that would waste precious time.

A door at the back of the building opened abruptly. Caswell stood hunched over just a few meters away as a man emerged. He was taller than Caswell by a good ten centimeters, and heavyset. He held a steaming mug in his right hand. His clothing marked him as one of the "other" faction. Where Caswell's own outfit looked like a designer's vision for the "business suit of tomorrow," this man wore something that, aside from a few stylistic variations, looked right out of a Cold War Kremlin meeting.

Condemned to think in realtime, Caswell worked his way behind the chap. He darted in the last two steps, swooped his left arm under the other man's, and clapped his hand around the poor sod's mouth. Caswell raised his elbow, forcing the man's left arm awkwardly up and away from his body—no chance to fish a pistol from that coat.

The man emitted a surprised grunt and froze in place. The mug, still clutched in his right hand, trailed coils of steam up into the cool night air. Drops of hot liquid splattered on the ground. He did not flinch as Caswell groped around his chest, thighs, the small of the back. And there Caswell found a small, hard lump. He reached in and found a kind of holster attached in the curve of the lower back, angled so that one could, as long as he flipped his coat out of the way, reach behind himself and draw with relative ease. It took Caswell a few seconds to figure out how a small twist was required before the weapon would come free.

The gun was small, and shaped more or less like standard-issue Cold War fare, to match the suit apparently. For an instant Caswell wondered if he'd stumbled onto some kind of large-scale anachronistic role-play event. The gun was real enough, though, and certainly the soldiers on the train had not been pretending.

Caswell nudged the man forward. He guided him a good thirty meters out into the dark ruins of the city and forced him into a musty storefront. Broken grass crunched under their feet. Somewhere within came a rhythmic plopping sound of water on stone. There was another sound, too, a strange high-low chirp vaguely reminiscent of the cicada.

The man stumbled on a bit of rubble. Caswell held him upright and spun him around. He slapped the mug away, the drink spilling out in an arc as the cup fell and clattered on the ground. "This is far enough," he said. "You're going to answer some questions for me."

The man rubbed his freshly uncovered jaw. The room, almost entirely pitch black, made facial expressions impossible to gauge, but Caswell sensed resistance in the man's stance. Caswell flipped the pistol around in his hand and clubbed the man in the abdomen. Just once, and not hard. The suit crumpled to his knees all the same, coughing.

"Cooperate and that's the worst you'll get from me, understood?"

"Mmm," the man managed.

Flipping the pistol around again, Caswell lowered himself to his knees and pressed the business end up under the man's chin. "Now. Questions. What is this place? Where are we?"

The man's brow furrowed. "How could you—"

"Just answer. I don't have time for any bullshit."

"What is bull?" the man said.

Caswell slapped the man's cheek with the edge of the gun barrel. It would leave a nasty bruise. "Where, are, we?" he asked with all the patience he could muster.

"Fineva," the man said. "The summit."

"Where's Fineva? What country? I'm not familiar with it."

"Huh?"

Caswell coiled for another slap. The man cringed away. "All right, all right. Fineva. In the Vongar." At Caswell's silence he stammered on. "The neutral city within the Desolation."

None of it made any sense. Caswell tried another tack. "Where's Alia Valix?"

The man's eyes widened. He swallowed. "I . . ."

"Don't lie, I can spot that even in this darkness. Where?"

"She remains at the terminal."

The same train depot Caswell had fled from, or another? "Which terminal? Describe it."

"You really do not know?"

Caswell hit him again. The man ducked, too late, and took a solid knock to his eye. It would be black within an hour. "I'm asking the questions here. Where's the goddamn terminal?"

"Behind the palace," he croaked through gritted teeth.

"Good enough," Caswell said, and slugged the man one last time. Enough to knock him unconscious. He didn't want another kill on his conscience if he could help it. "Enjoy the hangover, come dawn. I don't think anyone will find you before then." Caswell knelt and rifled through the poor bastard's pockets. Or tried to, anyway. None of them were in the usual places. Eventually he found the openings, though, and managed to lift a thin metal case with a simple hasp on one edge. Inside were various slips of actual paper. Money? Receipts? Perhaps identification? Who carried such things in paper form anymore?

He clapped the little wallet closed and stuffed it into his breast pocket, which of course was on the right side of his shirt, not the left. Because fuck convention, apparently. Caswell shook his head and resolved to take a trip to Costa Rica the moment this op ended. Relax on a beach for once. Eat tacos and sip margaritas. Invite Monique to join him, since they'd probably both be out of a job for his field reversion.

Back outside, armed with what at least resembled a normal pistol, Caswell worked his way toward what he hoped was the palace the man had spoken of. It was the largest building on the square, lit from below by several portable spotlights that cast long shadows in dark lines up the façade. Like everything else here the building was old and in serious disrepair. Bits of the outer stonework had fallen away to reveal crude bricks beneath. Most of the round windows were jagged shadows. Black mold crept along every edge and corner. And yet despite all this it had been tidied. It looked like a site preserved for historical significance despite a limited budget, rather than a structure truly abandoned to time.

There were lights in most of the windows. And, now that Caswell stood much closer, he could see guards posted at the doors, and patrolling a loose perimeter. None were dressed in obvious uniform, though. These were soldiers, he had no doubt from the rigid, concentrated faces, but they were in plain clothes. Why?

He gave the structure a wide berth, creeping along abandoned cobblestone roads and through narrow, rubble-strewn alleys. On the far side of the so-called palace he saw another big structure. Unlike the train terminal he'd fled from, this one had apparently been built at the same time as the rest of the city. It was grand, with soaring pillars and huge, multi-paned windows. All of it was run-down and decaying, but still he knew immediately it must have once been a treasured place, rivaling Grand Central in New York.

A sound high above caught his ear. Caswell crouched in a shadow and glanced up. At the top of the terminal building he saw a huge, oblong shape, dark against the dark sky. "A bloody airship?" he whispered. As if in answer the propellers mounted along the thing's tail made a short buzzing sound, no doubt working to keep the beast still.

Caswell decided only two possible explanations made sense for all this: He was dreaming, or he'd been given some bloody powerful hallucinogens.

He forced himself to look away from the giant aircraft

and focused on the ground between here and the terminal. Detritus from recent sloppy construction littered the ground. Lengths of rusty iron rail tracks, bent and broken, lay in heaps amid boulder-size chunks of gravelly concrete.

The train depot opened onto the side facing away from the palace, with bizarre half-pipe tracks leading off into the distance. Caswell kept to the edge of the building when possible. It wouldn't do him any good to be perched in a window across the wide avenue, or hidden among the old derelict train cars that rotted in the streets across from the building. The pistol he'd lifted was a tiny thing, no doubt only accurate and lethal when used at close range. Better to stay close in and rely on his senses, despite the lack of implant-fueled honing. Part of him relished the purity of the scenario. The strangeness of the place, the lack of useful intel. He would have to rely on his training and natural ability, just like one of his between-mission adventures.

He crept the last few meters to the corner of the huge building and dropped to one knee. Light spilled from the open-ended back of the structure. He risked a quick glance around the corner, seeing without focusing, and then ducked back to mentally review the scene.

No sign of Alice Vale. Just a mess of armed guards, ten at least, some with weapons out and in what appeared to be uniforms, though the "NRD" markings were unknown to Caswell. They were milling about around what appeared to be another train, though it looked like none he'd ever seen. It rested in those weird half-pipe tracks, which the tube-shaped train apparently rolled along with a series of rubber-like tires mounted in three rows along the underside. Inside, the half-pipe track sloped up from the ground and ran in along a metal lattice above an older set of more traditional-looking train tracks. This raised structure continued out for a hundred meters and then angled down into a ditch dug into the earth where the half-pipe continued on to the edge of the city and beyond. Curious. It was as if some competing form of train travel had been retrofitted here. Yet the train he'd arrived on had been different. Why? The answer seemed obvious once he factored in everything else he'd seen. Two sides, here for some sort of important meeting. Two sides with different clothing styles, weapons, and who knew what else. Alice Vale was either with, or a prisoner of, the side that used the half-pipe mode of rail transport. He searched for some meaning in this, some clue as to what the hell was going on, but couldn't find it. He filed the detail away and focused on the tactical scenario.

Ten guards, at least that he could see. The weird train. And, deeper inside the cavernous building, beyond where the train tracks ended, something large and oblong lay concealed under a large white tarp. Six of the guards stood near this object, plus what appeared to be two automated sentry turrets arranged on either side. These, he now realized, pointed *at* the covered shape with silent menace. What was under there? Some kind of holding tank for prisoners? Why conceal it?

The other guards stood watch over the wide-open backside of the terminal building, one of them just five meters away from Caswell's position.

Getting in seemed impossible with such odds. He decided to backtrack. Halfway along the outer wall he spotted what he needed: a door, hidden behind a stack of iron bars and rubble. Again the strange center-door handle that connected to a lever at the bottom. Gun held in both hands, Caswell instinctively used the toe of his shoe to lift that lever, and sure enough the door clicked and swung open. He toed it the rest of the way, somewhat impressed by the clever utility of the design, and stepped into the darkness that waited within.

Dust and bits of rock crunched under his shoes. The walls were bare, devoid of any ornament or piping. Just a simple hall, probably used by workers or maintenance staff back in the heyday of the old place. The hall was uncomfortably narrow. He saw light to his right and crept along in that direction until he came to another door, this one with a small, rounded window mounted at shoulder height. It was a grimy bit of glass, thick and uneven of surface. Primitive stuff. He glanced through and saw a wavy, blurred version of the terminal interior beyond. The hall had brought him right to the center of the large covered object he'd seen within. Against the white sheet was the silhouette of one of the guards. He or she stood in place, casually resting a rifle of some sort over one arm.

Voices came to him through the old glass. On instinct Caswell willed improved hearing from his implant, only to feel the mild sting of rebuke from the engineered gland. So he did the next-best thing and cupped his hands against the glass, feeling like he was pursuing court intrigue in the Middle Ages, and finding himself suddenly very impressed at what his Cold War brethren had been up against in their day-to-day work.

Nothing useful would come from standing here, but he did find it interesting that this little access hall had been unguarded. Perhaps they hadn't seen it, hidden as the outer door had been.

He started to push farther in, then stepped back at the last instant. A small crowd, a dozen or more, walked purposefully toward the "front" of the building, toward the palace, and the crowded square beyond. Through the crack in the door he'd caught a glimpse of the leader of this entourage, and now, squinting through the uneven glass, he felt sure it was her. Alice Vale, only twelve years older than the one who'd fled the *Venturi,* dressed in what probably passed for smart business attire in 1965, her hair trimmed short, her face determined and serious.

Caswell decided his best chance was to attack while she moved between the two buildings. Something forced him to stay put, though. Something about that oblong shape below the giant tarp. The curve was familiar. He'd seen it recently, in the schematics Monique had given him to study.

It was one of the *Venturi*'s landers, he felt sure of it.

The allure of it was too strong. Alice would have to wait. If he could get into that ship he might be able to contact Monique. Report his status and acquire new orders.

Caswell waited until the sound of footfalls receded into the distance and then slipped into the train terminal. A few guards had been left behind, but they seemed blissfully unaware of the entrance he'd used. Two stood way down at the far end of the building, looking out over the weird half-pipe track, perhaps guarding against sappers who might seek to demolish a train's only way in or out of here.

Three more guards stood near the covered shuttle. Concealed behind an old bench made of rotting wood, Caswell studied them more closely. These guards were fiddling with the pair of tripod-mounted sentry turrets. One clicked on a spotlight mounted atop the nearer of the two devices. Cables snaked out of the back of the bulky, old-fashioned weapons, linking one to the other and then continuing off into darkness toward the far side of the building.

One of the people then went to stand behind the turret and leaned into it until his eye pressed against the protrusion on the back. The man then gripped a handle of some sort and adjusted the aim of the device manually.

Not a turret. A bloody camera. Caswell's entire tactical map of the situation shifted. They weren't guns aimed at something dangerous within the vehicle. They were cameras. Very goddamn old cameras, so old they required human operators—not guards at all—to fiddle with the settings.

And fiddle the trio did. Once both devices were adjusted they moved off, talking in low voices. Caswell thought he heard the word *broadcast* in the conversation. Now he hesitated. He saw no way to get into the shuttle without the cameras seeing him. Were people watching, live? Would his antics be suddenly splayed across a billion screens around the globe?

He had to take the risk. Teeth clenched, Caswell slipped out from behind the bench and raced across the gap. He ignored the glare of the camera's lights and dove into a sideways roll at the last second, taking him under the draped edge of the white tarp. The material crinkled at his passage. If the guards heard or cared they had made no sound to indicate it.

Caswell leapt to his feet and studied the black-scarred fuselage of the shuttle. His eyes darted to the identification markings. ESA. *Venturi.* Griffin-class capsule. Lander 02.

"Zero-two?" he whispered. He tried to recall what Angelina Monroe and her crewmate had discussed. One of the landers had been missing, but which one? He could have sworn they'd said 01.

The vehicle seemed to be in working order, despite atmospheric scarring. The recessed docking port on the belly was closed, and he knew from his research that it could not be opened from the outside, not without special tools anyway. He'd have to go up top.

Moving with great care, Caswell crept up the recessed access ladder. Now he had a problem. The tarp was draped over the top of the vessel, and he needed to crawl to that hatch just behind the top center. Anyone looking this way would see a human-size lump moving beneath the white blanket. He was hanging there, by hands and feet, contemplating this, when footsteps approached just beyond the curtain of the sheet.

"From the mealhouse," a voice said.

"Gratitude," the guards muttered in unison, followed by the sound of cutlery against tin plates or bowls.

The distraction would have to do. Caswell pressed his body close against the fuselage and crawled up the last few steps. The outer airlock door, oddly, had black charring all around it as well as signs of vicious scraping along the hull. Something traumatic had happened here, and recently. Nevertheless it opened without any fuss and came without the usual hiss of pressure equalization. He opened it just wide enough and slithered inside.

The round door clicked softly shut behind him. Now unconcerned about noise, he set to work yanking open the inner door and lowering himself into the cockpit proper.

Food first. Caswell opened the storage bins on the galley wall and found them blissfully well stocked. Stocked, in fact, with food packets dated recently. Alice Vale had fled twelve years ago. Who had resupplied her? The temptation to interrogate his target before killing her suddenly coursed through him. He'd never before had the chance to learn of a mission he'd already been absolved of. In the end, sucking on a package of avocado and vitamin puree, he decided he would take that chance, but only if he thought he could do it without compromising the mission. Monique would understand, he thought. He'd had many long conversations with her over the years about the nature of their IA status. She didn't seem to struggle as much as he did with the conflicting sensations. The lack of consequence versus the gaps in one's self. "Holes in memory are a damned weird thing to live with, but the pay makes up for it, don't you think?" she'd said.

He'd agreed. He still wondered if he'd meant it.

Like a junkie reunited with a hidden stash, Caswell rummaged through the medical bins until he found an ibuproxin inhaler. He stuffed the plastic end in his mouth, squeezed, and drew in a long breath. Within seconds the raging fever wrought by the use of his implant in the train escape began to abate.

He grabbed another food packet. Dark chocolate and espresso pudding. Not as good as a cup of coffee, but close enough. Finally, he went to the personal storage locker and opened it, hoping to find some clue about Alice's goals here. A copy of her summit speech, perhaps. Anything that might give him an edge.

Instead he saw a carry-all bag. A familiar one. His own.

"This isn't Alice's lander, it's mine," he said aloud. The room took on a whole new light, possible scenarios unfolding in his mind. How he'd come to be here. How Alice had come into possession of his ship.

He'd packed two bags before boarding the *Pawn* on the Mysore Orbital. Only one was here, but he'd split his more important gear with an eye toward redundancy. Caswell plunged his hands into the bag and shoved aside his travel gear until his fingers brushed the hidden pocket concealed in the rigid false bottom.

Inside he found the familiar tubelike shape of a vossen gun.

35

PICKING HIS WAY THROUGH the maze of rubble out-side proved easier the second time. At the front of the great depot building he stopped and peered around.

Alice Vale's group had moved quickly. He caught only the trailing members as they entered a door at the back of the palace. Two guards remained behind as the doors swung shut. He would need another way in. Cursing, Caswell wasted precious seconds moving carefully through the cover of debris in the streets and then along the side of the palace building. Like the depot, this building also had a servants' entrance, only this one was not hidden behind garbage and was very much guarded.

Two of them, both plain clothed, and perhaps because of that fact neither carried drawn weapons, a disadvantage Caswell could exploit. He searched around by his feet and found a clump of rock the size of an apple. He hefted it, content to use it, then saw a meter-long length of iron rebar laying flush with the side of the building. He picked that up as well, slipping his vossen gun back into a pocket. Then he set his sights on the two guards.

He crept forward, keeping to the side of the building. The pair had angled themselves slightly toward the square, ex-pecting trouble from that direction if it happened to come. The fact allowed Caswell to get within five meters before the guard nearest him, a tall woman, became subconsciously aware of something approaching. She started to turn. Cas-well threw the clump of rock as hard as he could. Not at her, but at the shorter male guard just beyond. He knew instantly the toss was true. A work of art, really, unaided by his gland. The rock caught the unsuspecting guard on the side of his head. At the same instant Caswell moved within a meter of the woman, his length of iron coiled back. She fumbled for a weapon inside her jacket. Her mouth began to open, a cry of alarm forming on her lips. His bar struck the side of her head only a half second after the rock had struck the man, and then both guards were on the ground with almost no noise. Caswell checked both of them for pulses, found them both to be alive, and decided he would leave them that way. He'd glimpsed the version of himself that had spun 206 bottles of Sapporo to face the rear of the fridge in Kensington, and he'd even killed on that train after reversion, but at some point between then and now he knew that man had not been the real Peter Caswell. That man had an out. A knowledge that all would be forgotten, quite literally. Without that mental cushion, he simply did not know how much blood he could spill. He didn't want to know. He would kill Alice Vale because he'd been sent here to do so, but no one else unless absolutely necessary. Caswell dragged their unconscious bodies three meters away from the door, into shadow, and left them there.

Inside he found a building flush with architectural details that implied wealth and power but none of which was exactly familiar. Ornately carved pillars along the walls. An intricate, polished stone floor. Not marble, but something like it. The hall he stood in spanned three meters across, lined with doors on either side. Ten meters on the hall came to a wide intersection with a perpendicular passage, then continued on to the far side of the building. There were voices from the adjoining hall, off to the right toward the square and the crowd awaiting Alice's speech. Shifting lights from lanterns made the hallway swim with shadows.

This was his best chance. *Do it now,* before she entered the square. Before a thousand pairs of eyes were watching her, listening. He surged forward, drawing his weapon once again, hoping he could get close enough for it to be effective. At the intersection he curled himself around the corner.

The crowd in the hallway were huddled in front of a massive pair of closed double doors. Most were focused on Vale, who stood at the center of the group in quiet conversation with a few of them. The rest stood idly by, chatting in pairs or simply waiting. Those waiting were the bodyguards, with the stance, the sweeping gaze, the hands held loosely at the waist, ready to draw should the need arise.

Loping along the edge of the wall, Caswell decided not to give them a chance to do that. He accelerated into a sprint, and with each step he summoned a little more time for his brain to process. The gland in his neck, replenished, gave up the required chemical mix happily. Sweet elhydrine, and with enough ibuproxin already in his system to counter the side effects. The scene around him slowed.

Instinct drove him. He watched those he'd marked as guards, saw the initial flickers of danger-sense triggered by the sound of running footfalls nearby. Heads began to swivel in his direction. Hands began to dive toward holsters worn at the small of the back. Caswell took all this in. Okay then, they intended to kill him, so he must defend himself. Mentally he prioritized the targets. One through six, leaving Alice Vale out for now.

He had ample time to analyze the situation, but his body could still only move as fast as any other. With agonizing slowness he raised the vossen gun and let his gland communicate to it the six targets he'd identified. Pinprick balls of light and hissing gas erupted from the barrel, like tiny rocket launches from his perspective, like little explosions to those around him. The needles sprayed out in an arc, one by one, each on a plume of flame vectored to fight the tug of gravity. Their sensors would detect atmosphere and shift tactics from the blinding, mask-filling foam he'd used on the *Venturi* to a more direct approach.

The six were in various stages of slow-motion reaction when the needles arrived. They made perfect lines to the eye socket, right or left, whichever was closer, and exploded in brilliant white flashes. The tiny bullets at the tip of the needle, little wads of 1,500-degree slag now, launched through the eye and into the brain, melting everything they touched.

Reflexively they dropped their weapons and brought their hands to the sides of their suddenly very warm heads. It would be a few seconds before they even realized something was wrong with one eye, but that information would come far too late to matter.

Alice and the others were starting to react. Many had been temporarily blinded by the flashes of light. For the rest, in their reference frame the six guards were suddenly, simultaneously screaming.

Caswell ignored all this. The dying and those helpless to stop it. It was as if he were of two minds: the one that dealt with threats around him in whatever way made sense, and the one that had less immediate goals to worry over. This part of him focused on Alice. He sprinted at full speed toward her. It felt like pushing through a pool of peanut butter.

She'd started to turn, her mouth forming into a surprised O at the sudden burst of activity around her. The flashes of light had happened behind her. She'd be only slightly affected by that. Not so much, Caswell saw, to fail to see him. Her eyes began to widen at the sight of him. He aimed the vossen at her face and relayed the target—

No.

He held back. Something in those eyes. He spent a half second—three seconds to him—studying that. It was more than fear. More than surprise.

This was recognition.

Between that look, and the strangeness of this place, the whole bizarre situation, he shifted tactics, improvised. For the first time he was at the heart of an IA mission that he would actually remember. He had to know what was going on. What this place was. How he'd come to be here. Why it was so important to kill Alice Vale. He would still kill her. That's what he did, after all. A hammer drives nails.

Thumb pressed to his temple, he relayed a different message to the gun through the implant. *Fatally wound with sufficient time to interrogate.*

Gas hissed in rocket-plume clouds from around the tip of the weapon. The needle lanced out on its tail of flame, zipped across the two meters that now separated them, fast even from Caswell's perspective. The needle had been carefully designed. It knew exactly what to do in order to achieve

Caswell's order. The thing curved, arched downward, and plowed into her chest just left of the sternum, between the ribs.

No molten slag this time. Cauterization was not desired. A rupturing, instead, of the critical veins around the heart. Alice would bleed out internally within several minutes. No amount of medical attention could save her, but the pain would not be so great as to prevent her from talking through it. Theoretically, anyway.

She started to fall, the shock of the impact not driving her back but instead simply buckling her knees. Caswell shifted his momentum to account for this. He swooped in, his arm slipping under hers. He heaved, willing adrenaline to give him the strength required. With one arm he brought Alice up to lay across his shoulder. The closed door was right in front of him now. He jumped, planted one foot on the heavy surface, wondering if it would give. It did not. The door held, so he let himself compress toward it and then pushed against it with one hand and one foot. He vaulted backward, spinning around with the motion; Alice's body flailed out in both directions, her limbs smacking into the confused heads of those nearby.

Caswell let the motion guide him, adjusting himself expertly thanks to the benefit of time. His head began to feel warm from the overclocked state of his synaptic nerves. Soon the implant would kill the effect to save his brain. He had enough time to sprint four steps back toward the hallway intersection when time seemed to speed up.

Two more steps and everything was back to normal. The familiar feeling of running through air instead of crystal-clear molasses. Alice, over his shoulder, was groaning. Those behind her, those still alive, were screaming. Caswell ignored it all. He powered around the corner and headed back for the door he'd come through.

The door, still open, framed several people. People in uniforms that he recognized from the train.

Four soldiers, a woman apparently in handcuffs whom he recognized as Melni, and then another who seemed to be leading the party. An older woman, stocky of build and with that same, short mannish haircut he'd seen on every woman here. She wore glasses, with round blue-tinted lenses. She held no weapon, but the four escorting her had the pistols with the elongated stock that rested on the forearm.

Caswell aimed the vossen. Without the benefit of elhydrine he couldn't prioritize targets or even designate the preferred level of damage. He tried to relay the four armed guards, hoped it was enough, and shifted his focus to a side door nearby as the needles flew.

He turned his shoulder in and slammed into the wooden slab.

Melni saw him raise the small metallic tube and reacted out of sheer instinct. She dropped prone to the ground. Rasa Clune, standing beside her with a viselike grip around Melni's wrist shackle, was pulled down with her.

Something hissed through the air, a sound that abruptly ended with four muffled pops in rapid succession. The four guards around her toppled to the ground. Melni rolled to her side, lifting her knees to her chest as she did so. Beside her one of the guards lay, half his head missing. The smell of charred flesh hit her nostrils, reaping an instantaneous flood of nausea.

She bit back her bile and focused on her hands, tugging with all her might to break Rasa Clune's iron grasp. The woman let go but not without a fight. Ignoring the scraping grit of the stone platform beneath her, Melni pulled her arms around to be in front of her and shoved her feet through the loop. She rolled to her stomach, ignoring as best she could the spreading pool of blood she'd just splashed her elbow in. Melni shoved against the ground and rolled back onto her feet. She vaulted herself up into a ready stance. Clune was just coming up, on one hand and one knee.

Melni kicked the leader of Riverswidth, the spymaster of the South, hard in the gut, so hard that Clune came off the ground several inches, her eyes bulging in their sockets, breath rushing from her cruel mouth. She gasped and collapsed back to the ground. Melni kicked again, aiming for the bandaged nose, but missed. Instead she heard the sickening sound of teeth skittering across the tiled floor of the hallway just inside the door. A puddle of blood spilled from Clune's mouth. She lay in that red pool, writhing.

Melni left her there and ran for the door that Caswell had stormed through.

36

HE HAULED THE SQUIRMING body up three flights of stairs. He was short of breath and nauseous from the post-acceleration headache, and his legs began to buckle. Limp at first, Alice fought him now. Every step he took earned a barrage of fists against his side and back, then finally claws against his cheek.

Caswell ducked into a random room off the third-floor hallway. The trail of blood she'd left would guide the enemy right to him, but he hadn't heard any footsteps on the stairs behind him so he figured he had enough time to complete his task even after a few questions were answered.

Alice bit his ear savagely. He clenched his jaw to hold a scream back and dumped her unceremoniously to the floor in a corner of the room. A cloud of dust erupted from her impact and filled the air. The whole place reeked of mildew and earthy vegetation. Vines curled in around the space where a window had once been, looking like the fingers of some deformed giant trying to pull the very walls off.

He took a quick glance outside. The city square was fifteen meters below. The crowd had grown some, and seemed to be jostling nervously along a wavy line down the middle. Confusion and fear were fueled by the sound of combat within the palace. Some had drawn weapons, and shouts of accusation and alarm rang out from both left and right.

"You're making a mistake," Alice Vale hissed.

He glanced at her curled form in the corner. She hadn't moved. "I have orders and I intend to follow them."

To his surprise she pushed herself up to a sitting position against the wall, her face a mask of agony. She turned her head and spat blood in a stream along the wall beside her. A dark red trail ran down her chin and dripped onto her shirt. With a force of will she managed to fix a steady gaze on him. When she spoke her voice was barely more than a whisper, thick with wrath. "You failed once. And you're hesitating even now. Why, you son of a bitch? Get it over with."

"I have questions first."

Her lips curled back from teeth immersed in blood. She spat weakly, not bothering to turn her head. The liquid just splashed down the front of her shirt. She coughed. A wet, ugly sound. "Fuck you," she said.

Behind him the door burst open. Caswell whirled and dove, lifting his weapon in the same motion, finger on the trigger.

"No!" the person in the doorway shouted.

He recognized her from the train, and held back. He hit the ground and rolled, coming up to a half stand, still pointing the vossen.

"Oh no," the woman said upon seeing Alice. She raced across the room to the wounded woman, ignoring Caswell. "Garta's light, no. What have you done?"

Confused, Caswell took a tentative step toward the pair. "My job," he said flatly, yet he could hear the doubt in his own voice.

"No," the woman said. Melni, she'd said her name was. "Caswell, the guards came before I could tell you everything. Your goal was to kill her, but it changed. You and I learned much since you arrived. We need to save her. She *must* live."

He swallowed. The woman's words were sincere, yet it didn't matter. Alice Vale was already dead; it was only a matter of time now. "Explain yourself, Melni. Learned what?"

She spoke of something called the Conduit, of worlds linked by similarity, and the powers that sought to control these planets in order to harvest their ideas. A group called Prime.

"The person who sent you here, Monique, is one of them."

* * *

Melni sat on the floor beside Alia and cradled her in her arms, laying the wounded inventor sideways across her lap so blood would not pool in the mouth. It dribbled out into a rapidly spreading puddle on the floor instead.

For the last two years Melni had spent virtually every waking moment studying this woman, spying on her, trying to comprehend her genius. Then she'd learned the truth, that it had all been an elaborate lie. This should have filled Melni with rage if not for the motivation for that deception. She'd been trying to protect Gartien from something much worse.

And now here she lay, dying in Melni's lap. Gartien's golden daughter. Earth's cunning escapist. Her breaths came shallow and rapid. Whatever Caswell had done, the internal damage seemed massive and entirely fatal.

"So she killed her crew and came here—" Caswell started.

Alia's face came alive then. She cast a glance at the man and said, "It was you who killed them. You tried to get me, too, but I hid. . . ." She paused and coughed up a mouthful of blood that splattered across the floor. "So you set a bomb and left me there, but I figured out how to escape. I took everything I could and fled in the lander before the station was destroyed."

Caswell stared at her. His expression, hard as stone, began to crack. "It was me," he whispered. "I killed them."

It was not, Melni realized, a question. "Caswell, there is so much you don't know. So much you've forgotten."

The assassin grimaced. Squeezed his eyes shut and shook away whatever doubt had begun to creep in. "Why not contact Earth? Tell them what happened, and what I supposedly did."

"Because that would have led them to the Conduit," Melni said for Alia. For Alice. "If Earth became aware of the Conduit, that would trigger Prime to take action against both planets. The Warden said—"

Alia glanced up at her. Her eyes were cloudy now, half-closed, but the surprise there came through. "You spoke with him," she said. She'd only just realized it. "Before the airships I sent bombed the site?"

"He told us much," Melni replied, nodding. "But not all. The bombs fell too soon. He seemed unsure of your intentions, Alia."

The dying woman closed her eyes. Her lips moved, but no words came. A silent apology, perhaps. Melni would never know.

Several seconds passed. Alia's face became very still. There were sounds of commotion in the square outside. Somewhere below she could hear boots on the steps. Melni pressed her palms to Alia's chest, the left side instead of right. A weak pulse beat there. As if Melni needed any more proof that Alia and Caswell were of the same origin.

Alia groaned. Her eyes flickered open. Caswell came and knelt beside Melni. He'd put his weapon away.

The dying woman's words were barely audible. A liquid, feeble whisper almost drowned by the voices from beyond the window. She said, "The Warden and I had our differences, but our goal was always the same: Help Gartien reach space as quickly as possible. Block the Conduit, or at least be prepared for the day that Prime finally discovers the Zero Worlds beyond Earth. Your presence here means we failed. They'll come soon. They'll come for Earth as well. We were . . . too late. Unless . . ."

Caswell leaned in. "Unless what, Alice?"

"Unless you finish what we started."

The last word fell from dead lips.

Alia Valix was gone.

"We need to leave," Caswell said.

Melni rocked back on her feet and closed her eyes. She'd been wrong. She'd devoted her career to hindering Alia's. How much had she and her fellow spies delayed the woman's efforts? What state of preparation would her world be in right now had only the petty war between North and South been ended long ago?

"Melni," Caswell said. "They're coming."

"What difference does it make? We can do nothing now but wait for Prime—"

"No," he said. He grabbed her by the upper arm and

hauled her to her feet. "I'm still baffled as to just what the hell is going on here, and there's a gigantic gap in my memory being filled by bits of cryptic jargon. But I know this: Though I forgot you, I trusted you enough to tell you my anchor phrase, and that's good enough for me. So you listen: My lander is here. It still works, and I plan to take it."

She shook her head. "It was destroyed in the mountains—"

"No. It's here. I saw it. I went inside." He produced a tube from his pocket. It gleamed in the moonlight. The weapon he'd used on the guards below. In the battle she hadn't had time to contemplate where he'd found it. "The ship is in the terminal next door. Come with me."

"Where . . . where will we go?" she asked, thinking of all the remote corners of Gartien and how easy it would be for Rasa Clune and her Hollow to find them.

Caswell looked into her eyes, searching for something. Whatever it was, he evidently found it. "Alice sought to blockade this Conduit. She failed." He squeezed her arms. "Failed because this world doesn't have the tech, but Earth does. . . ."

She watched as his eyes scanned some horizon in his mind. He stood that way for many seconds. Footsteps in the hallway snapped him back to the present. He whirled and tugged her along by her bound hands. At the door he let go and pressed his palms against his temples in a gesture she now felt a great deal of fascination with.

Caswell, in his formal meeting suit, which now bore numerous bloodstains, dove through the door. As he flew out into the hallway he raised his weapon and it spat those tiny glowing dots that hissed away on puffs of gas. Caswell hit the floor and rolled into the far wall, grunting with the impact and yet somehow positioned perfectly to keep his weapon pointed toward the top of the steps. She heard the sound of toppling bodies, and cries of alarm from farther off. She took a chance and peeked around the corner. Three plain-clothed Northerners lay on the floor, utterly still.

Across the hall Caswell pushed himself up the wall to a shaky stand. "Get behind me," he said.

She obeyed. Together they backed down the hall toward another room that faced the rear of the building rather than

Summit Square. He kept guard at the door and ordered her to go to the window. "What do you see?" he asked, his voice low.

"There is a street, maybe twenty feet wide, then a large building with a flat, dark roof." As she spoke she sawed her wrist bindings apart on a shard of old, broken glass protruding from the window frame.

"That's the terminal. Anyone down there?"

She glanced left and right and told him no, it seemed to be quiet. Everyone, North and South, had likely entered the palace. She could only imagine the tense standoff below.

It was a forty-foot drop to the street, not something she thought either of them could handle without breaking bones. "There's a pipe attached to the wall," she said. "It might be sturdy enough to climb."

A rattling sound filled the air. Bullets thudded into the wall and doorframe, forcing Caswell to duck inside the room.

Melni swung her legs over the window frame and grabbed the metal pipe, two feet away. Brackets bolted into the much older bricks held the pipe in place. As soon as she put some weight on it the bolts squealed in complaint. Bits of rubble and dust fell to the ground below. She let go. "This will not hold us."

A hand at the center of her back forced her out the window. Melni grabbed the pipe with both hands as her body swung out and smacked into the bricks. She glanced back, ready to curse Caswell's haste, only to see him perched on the windowsill and coming out. There was a pop as one of the brackets came free of the wall. The pipe tilted outward. She hung in space, ten feet from the wall now, and she could see the shapes of people in the window. Caswell leapt from the sill, angling himself toward the pipe. He hit the metal length and clanged against it. Another bracket popped free from the bricks, and they were both falling.

Melni dug her fingers into the brittle old pipe. A shrieking sound filled the air as the tube bent and began to collapse. Thirty feet above the ground the motion stopped abruptly. She felt as if her shoulders would pull from their sockets as the pipe wedged itself into the dark wall of the terminal and stayed there. She was only a few feet from the shadowed surface. Caswell clung to the pipe about ten feet back, halfway between the two buildings. He had one leg looped over the length of metal. As she watched he hauled himself up onto the narrow beam. He made eye contact with her, opened his mouth to speak.

A popping sound from above filled the air. Bullets, fired out of desperation, hissed by her and thudded into the cobbles below.

"Go!" Caswell shouted.

She turned and started to shimmy toward the wall. Suddenly a line of light appeared in front of her. It grew into a rectangle. A shuttered window, opening. Someone was silhouetted within. Melni brought her legs up and kicked hard, sending the person sprawling backward into some sort of mealhouse. There were rows of tables behind the person, and he or she crashed into the nearest and went head over heels across the surface.

Melni swung her legs back and then forward, letting go of the pipe as she did so. She flew through the open window and landed on her feet, crouched and ready for anything.

The room was lit by a single lantern, upended when the table was knocked over. The brass cylinder rolled on the ground, casting long black shadows that slid across the floor, walls, and ceiling. The person she'd kicked lay in a scrambling heap a few feet away. She saw no one else but with the confusing shadows she did not trust that. Melni scurried across the floor to the Northerner—she could tell from the clothing—and slugged him four times on the back of the head until he went still. Outside bursts of gunfire rolled like thunderclaps off the building and echoed down the long streets. Caswell swung himself into the room, grunting as he landed on his rear. He held his left hand hard against his right biceps, and even in the swinging long shadows she could see blood oozing between his fingers.

"How bad is the wound?" she asked him.

"I'll live," he growled. "Keep moving, I'm right behind you."

Pushing herself to a shaky stand, Melni lurched for the open doorway and kicked the lantern in the process. Long shadows groped wildly about her. Bands of yellow chased by pitch black. The doorway, a gaping inky maw, felt welcoming against the chaos and confusion of the sliding shafts of muted light. Melni barreled through the doorway and kept going right across the hall, spinning to slam into it with her shoulders. Caswell was right behind her, a cutout against the room she'd fled. He gestured off to her left, down the hall. Melni nodded and began to navigate the unlit passage, probing with one extended hand to keep the wall to her left. Eyes now adjusted to the darkness, Melni saw a faint glow at the far end of the hall, a steady, dark blue pall that bathed that end of the passage and revealed a ninety-degree corner going off to the left.

"Hurry," Caswell whispered.

That single word carried the reality of their situation. Hundreds of agents and soldiers from both sides of Gartien were all converging on her and him. Caswell's instinct was exactly right. His ship was the only option. There was no turning back, no other conclusion to this that didn't end in her execution. And then Prime would come, and "correct" Gartien. She had to flee her world if she wanted any chance to save it.

So Melni ran.

She ran ahead to the corner and took a quick peek at what lay around it. The pale glow in the hallway came from an eroded hole in the ceiling five feet down, spilling weak moonlight in. Water dripped from the edges of rotten shingles into a small puddle on the floor. The surface looked as weak as the ceiling above. Without waiting for Caswell she rounded the edge and skirted the bowed section of wet floor, then waited for her companion to appear. "Careful," she whispered, pointing. He followed her example.

Halfway down the length of the hall she came to a landing with stepwells leading down to the left and right. A waist-high wall that looked out over the station proper. Melni crouched and moved to the wall. When Caswell joined her she chanced a look over the edge.

"It is just like when we dove into the canal in Portstav," she whispered.

"I have no idea what you're talking about."

"Oh. Yes. Regret."

"Focus, Melni. Do you see the craft?"

"I see it."

"How many guards?"

"Four," she started to say.

Something exploded outside in the alley. The whole building shook. Dust fell like thrown confetti from the iron rafters of the arched ceiling. A rattling volley of gunfire followed the blast, reverberating through the walls and floor like a tooth drill. The knowledge that North and South were fighting each other rather than banded together in pursuit of Alia's killers gave her a surge of confidence. The guards shifted at the sounds of combat, alarmed and clearly worried. They took cover to be ready for enemies coming in from the street.

"They are distracted," she said.

"Go. Go now."

The firefight outside hid her footfalls. Melni took the steps two at a time. At the bottom she paused long enough to see Caswell making his way to her. He moved slowly, one hand still pressed hard to his arm. In the glow of the moonlight she could see a trail of dark droplets on the steps behind him.

Another explosion ripped through the building, filling the terminal with light and heat and a cloud of shrapnel. Melni winced and cowered on instinct, distantly aware of a swarm of soldiers rushing into the murk from the opposite side of the building. Southern soldiers, her brain registered. She forced herself into the fog of dust and smoke.

Ahead one of the Northern guards shouted into a portable radio. "We're overrun! EXECUTE NUCLEAR OPTION—"

Something hissed past her ear. Four little *thwick* sounds, like arrows given flight. Tiny glowing orbs lanced across the room from Caswell's position to the man with the radio, and the other three. They never knew what hit them. A rapid popping sound followed and the four sentries toppled, lifeless, to the floor.

She turned to Caswell. "What is 'nuclear option'?"

A deep vibration in the floor answered the question. Caswell glanced to his right, and Melni followed the gaze.

In the distance, out on the roller track, a humming engine pulling a line of cars began to emerge from the shadows and move toward the terminal, gaining speed with each second.

"Go!" Caswell roared.

Melni went. Straight to the shrouded vehicle. She dove under the sheet that covered it. Caswell rolled through behind her, smearing a trail of blood across the floor in his wake. He took the lead now, scrambling up a ladder indented into the side of the craft. He grunted with each step but his pace never slowed. Outside the sound of the approaching roller filled the air. The whole building vibrated as the engine thundered toward them.

At the top Caswell paused, fiddling with the hatch mechanism. The whole surface had been charred black by the crash of the airship on that mountain, but just as Caswell had said, it appeared otherwise undamaged. Time seemed to slow the longer Melni waited on the ladder. All around her she heard the growing thrum of the engine, blended with the frantic footsteps and tactical chatter of Northern soldiers converging on the craft.

A hiss heralded success. Caswell hauled himself across the threshold and into the bowels of the vessel. She vaulted up the last few steps and over the same, crashing headfirst into the small cavity within. Caswell had already righted himself and was pulling the heavy door closed even as she landed. The portal slammed shut, cutting off a sudden, urgent warning cry from one of the pursuers outside.

Silence enveloped her. Not absolute, though, because even the craft now shook from the approaching roller. She moved aside so Caswell could open the inner door, a wave of dread sweeping over her, the events of the last few minutes a sudden unbearable weight. Encased within the otherworldly vehicle she felt simultaneously secure in its embrace and terrified at what would come next.

Caswell dropped into the vessel proper and she followed. Again he closed the bulky door, cranking a long yellow handle to seal it completely. He pointed to a seat inset into

the back wall, one of three. "Strap in," he said, already haul-
ing himself into the tiller's chair and pulling belts across his
shoulders and waist. Numb, feeling no longer in control of
her own future, Melni complied.

A wide segmented screen rotated down from the ceiling
and positioned itself in front of Caswell. He began to tap at
the bright and detailed displays, his finger leaving little red
smudges.

"You need that bandaged," she said.

"Later," came the reply.

On the screen before him a series of white squares winked
into existence. She didn't understand it at first, until the
shadow of a soldier raced across one, appearing on the next.
External cameras, all showing the white tarp that covered
the craft.

A deep rumbling began to shake the entire cabin. The oncoming roller, seconds away. She braced for impact despite
the futility. The very walls rattled around her. Everything
hummed, so violent she was sure the whole craft would be
torn to pieces before the roller even made impact.

Then the white tarp on the screen vanished, blown up and
away by the spacecraft's powerful engines. Caswell had
powered them on. A deafening roar drowned out even the
noise of the roller.

Melni had not considered before what kind of force must
be required to push such a vehicle all the way to space. The
numbing vibration all around her implied something beyond imagination.

A light caught her eye. One screen, cleared of tarp, looked
almost straight down the roller track. In the center the bright
headlight of the oncoming engine blazed. The huge vehicle
barreled into the terminal with astonishing speed, angling
up the sloped scaffolded track. Just two hundred feet away
now and practically flying. The scaffold buckled. People
were diving for cover.

Melni gripped her seat. She heard screaming and realized
it came from her. Through eyes screwed nearly shut she
watched another portion of Caswell's display, a view straight
down. Plumes of white-hot fire suddenly lanced downward,
sweeping the floor clean of equipment, debris, and people.

Everything began to move away as the craft rose from the floor, and then a shudder that nearly stopped Melni's pounding heart shook the world. The roller engine had reached the end of the track, torn through the barricades, and kept right on going. It streaked through the air that Caswell's craft had occupied just a heartbeat ago, pulling a dozen cars or more behind it. The whole mess crashed into the interior wall of the terminal with a deafening cacophony of rending metal, screams, and shattered stone. Explosions rippled through the carnage. Even in here, with the roar of the spaceship's engines, she heard it all. Caswell shouted something she didn't understand, a curse or something like it, as the building began to collapse around them. The nuclear option. Alia must have ordered the lander destroyed if hostilities broke out.

Their craft slammed into something above. Dropped, then rose again, faster this time. Caswell, she realized, was putting everything into the upward thrust now. A vicious bump jarred her to the bone. The roof. They'd crashed right through it.

Then everything, miraculously, became calm. On the screen she saw the building fall away. Somewhere inside, Rasa Clune would be looking up at the craft streaking off toward the night sky, as the building fell in on her. She would curse the name of Meiki Sonbo, and perhaps, with her last living breath, she could speculate as to just what in Garta's light that aircraft had been.

Melni watched the building shrink, explosions and smoke rippling along its length until the whole place went up in a bright fireball. Then the palace came into view, and the square that still swarmed with diplomats and soldiers now tiny as palt bugs. Too small to tell Northerner from Southerner.

A distinction, she realized, that meant less with every foot of altitude the craft gained.

Then the dark outskirts of Fineva, and the crater-strewn mountains. Caswell tipped the craft to an angle as they gained more and more speed. In surprisingly little time, half a world loomed on that screen.

Minutes passed in a blur of vibration, roaring sound, and incredible forces that kept her pinned back in her seat.

Then, as suddenly as it had all started, the craft became whisper silent and Melni felt her limbs begin to float as if she was sitting on the bottom of a pool.

She had left her planet, never to return.

37

MELNI WAVED A TINY machine over the pool of blood on the floor and watched in mild fascination as the liquid slurped into the device. No trace remained on the floor.

The surface, Caswell had explained, was at once hydrophobic—it would repel liquid indefinitely—and also near-field charged with "micro-controlled variance." This caused any particulate or, indeed, fluid, to cling to the surfaces until it could be devoured by the device she now held.

"Fascinating," she said, as the last drop of blood vanished into the little machine. Then she laughed at herself. "Listen to me, impressed by a cleaning tool as we fly through blixxing space."

Task complete and tools stowed, she found herself suddenly without anything to do but absorb the experience. The craft circled Gartien, her continents sliding horizontally across one of the stunning monitors. Utterly quiet. Soft clouds over blue-green oceans. No indication at all of the millions of people. Yet everyone she knew was down there, somewhere, perhaps looking up right now at that new speck of light moving against the night sky. Her sister among them. In Dimont. Never to know more than the years-old explanation that Melni was setting off for a newsprint job across the sea. They'd parted on bad terms, and that would not change. Melni sighed, offering silent regret and farewells.

Even the pockmarked band of the Desolation had a tranquility when viewed from this silent capsule, swimming as she was in the very air. On some level, buried deep in her psyche, Melni knew she should be terrified. She was beyond Gartien's air, hurtling along at an impossible speed inside a craft that was, when she really thought about it, just a large version of a returning ceremony sphere. Or, more aptly, just another submersible in the dark, only instead of a crushing ocean full of fanged serpents all around, there was nothing. Nothing at all.

That should have terrified her. She knew that. And yet the serenity of it all won her over the instant the engines went quiet.

Whenever her fear began to bubble to the surface, all she had to do was look at Caswell, and draw from his calm, his absolute confidence in the vessel. Where he came from this was no different than tilling a cruiser along a quiet mountain road.

Caswell lay prone on a bunk he'd pulled from one wall, his body strapped in to prevent him floating off. A few minutes earlier a pair of articulated arms had appeared from a panel and set to work cleaning and bandaging his wound. The bullet had gone right through the muscle of his upper arm, a good thing since the surgical "robot," as he called it, was not sophisticated enough to remove foreign objects.

Stitched and dressed, his body coursing with medicines she could never have dreamed possible, his brain kept carefully aware of any pain without feeling the true impact of it, he was soon up and as spry as the first time she'd seen him. He floated across the cabin and checked the bank of displays. "Two hours until we initiate burn for the Conduit."

"How long will the journey take?" she asked, the will to leave dampened by this last, magnificent view of her world.

Caswell returned to his bunk, across from hers. They sat facing each other. "Six days, give or take. Plenty of time to rest."

"And plan."

"If only we knew what to plan for. Anyway, doesn't matter, we've got something more pressing to deal with."

Melni raised an eyebrow.

"Food," he said. "Considering how hungry I was when I

first met you on the train, I'm guessing your food disagreed with me."

"*Disagreed* is an understatement."

"If you have the same issue with my food . . ." He let the thought trail off, the conclusion obvious.

"I ate some of those . . . cracker things. Remember?"

"I don't remember, actually. But if that's all you can eat it won't sustain you. They're just calories."

"I do not know the word, but I think I understand. You fear what will happen if I cannot eat anything but the food of my world."

"Exactly. Worst case, we can try intravenous nutrition— a direct line into your bloodstream, that is. It's not as effective, but it might work."

"Hmm," she said. "It is no way to live, though, is it?"

"No," he admitted. "Let's worry about that when we have to. The food I have on board is well sterilized, so as to last in storage a long time. My problems on your world were probably due to microbes, not the nutrients themselves. We're both human. It makes sense our needs are the same."

"All right, give me something to try."

He'd already picked something out. Two shiny packets lay on the bunk next to him. She took the one he offered and read the label. "Protein Shake—Vanilla," the title said, along with a paragraph of impossibly small text that listed what she presumed were the scientific names of the ingredients.

"Meal in a pouch," Caswell said. "Everything the body needs. Well, your teeth don't fare so well, but in the short term?" He rotated a three-inch tube from the side and began to suck at it.

Melni followed his example. Only a tiny sip at first, but the flavor had a pleasant warmth and sweetness to it. Like the marcan bean, only not as tart. When her stomach didn't immediately complain she sucked down the rest. Caswell handed her another packet, this one clear and obviously water. She drank it without hesitation.

He watched her carefully for any reaction. When she smiled, he said, "Let that settle for a few minutes, then we'll buckle in for the break-orbit maneuver. After that, I plan to sleep for a full day. Then you're going to tell me everything that happened since we met."

"Strangely enough I don't feel tired. This is"—she gestured at the view of Gartien—"too exciting."

He considered that, then drifted over to another storage compartment—every wall panel seemed to be no wall at all, just a cover for storage—and removed a thin rectangular slab the size of a weekly. He flung it across to her and she caught it. One side lit up at her touch. A display bloomed to life, every bit as impressive as the screens that hung in front of the pilot's chair.

"What is it?" she asked.

"A lot of things, but think of it as a book. A way to learn. I'd recommend you start with the atlas. Maps of Earth and our—my—solar system. Everything is linked to relevant information. Anything you want to know more about, just tap and away you go. It can be a bit of a rabbit hole, but—"

"Rabbit hole?" she asked. "What is that?"

A sly grin spread across his face. "Ask it."

Melni looked at the device. When she did so, she noticed a soft blue pinpoint light shining back at her, as if it knew it had her attention. "What is a 'rabbit hole'?" she asked.

Explanations of the phrase, and there were several, flooded onto the screen.

For the next two hours she dove deeper into the "rabbit hole" this device represented. She looked at a map of Earth for only a few minutes before tapping on a word she did not know: *Internet*. This led to even more unfamiliar terms, not to mention entire concepts. By the time the ship signaled them to secure the cabin for acceleration, she felt dizzy and breathless at the prospect of learning of an entirely new culture. In that moment she understood, fractionally, what Caswell must have gone through the moment he set foot on Gartien.

She bit her lip against the throbbing vibrations the engine generated and the sudden massive force that pinned her into the cushions of her chair. Melni just managed to keep her eyes open enough to watch the displays. The change was imperceptible at first, but with each second it grew. The line that marked their orbit around the world began to bow outward, extending out beyond the orbits of Gisla and Gilan, and then some sort of tipping point was reached and the curved line exploded out beyond the range of the display. Finally the press of the engine—the fusion torch, as Caswell called it—abated to something like Gartien's normal gravity.

Melni passed the time by reading, viewing pictures, and watching "movies." She peppered Caswell with questions, many of which made him laugh or even cringe with a sort of cultural embarrassment. There was solace, even a bit of pride, to be found in the fact that his world had experienced its fair share of self-inflicted tragedy. Nothing like the Desolation, at least not in its recent history, but when pressed she found herself morbidly fascinated to learn that the people of Earth had damaged their world almost as badly thanks purely to willful ignorance and neglect.

He asked her questions, too. A thousand, it felt like, for the better part of a day, all to fill in the massive gap in his memory. With her journalist's eye for detail and ability to relate events with clarity, Caswell eventually felt he understood what had happened. He still had no memory of landing, or an explanation for how he'd managed to get into Alia's—Alice's—Think Tank within just a few days of that moment. "Let's just assume I'm an incredibly talented badass and leave it at that," he'd said, grinning.

She'd smiled, too, then thrown an empty water bulb at him.

Earth food suited her. In fact she began to look forward to their meals so much that Caswell had to ration the supply. Vegetable korma, shepherd's pie, and, best of all, hazelnut gelato. She salivated as each meal hour approached, and only a few times did she balk at a flavor or texture. Caswell seemed to find immense delight in her reactions to the food. "Just wait until you taste these prepared fresh," he commented once. It was then she learned that these nutrition packets were not the normal method of consumption on Earth. They were specifically designed for space travel. Easy to eat, no mess to clean up, long shelf life. It made sense, of course, and she felt childish for not realizing it sooner.

At the halfway mark the craft warned of a pending maneuver. They'd been drifting for the last hour, and some loose items now floated about the cabin. She helped Caswell secure everything and then strapped in for the transition to deceleration.

"We'll turn around," Caswell explained, "so it will feel like acceleration, just as on the way out."

The maneuver came off without a snag, and she once again felt as if her chair lay on the floor.

"How far are we from Gartien now?" she asked.

Caswell studied the display for a moment. "Just over one hundred million kilometers."

She had to look up the word, and translate that to the measurement system Gartien used. They were quite different, the two, much like the way time was measured. She wondered how Prime managed to keep track of all the various systems they interacted with. Their motivation to at least have the predominant language based on their own made a lot of sense. Going further—forcing their system of measurement, for example—would have helped even more. She supposed they had their reasons for not taking that step, recalling what the Warden had said about their ultimate goal of harvesting ideas from the worlds they watched over. Perhaps imposing a measurement system on a world somehow hindered their science in some subtle, undesirable way.

As the craft neared the Conduit, Melni's gut twisted involuntarily into a knot. Caswell had of course lost all memory of his previous journey through this incomprehensible passageway between solar systems. He had nothing to offer when she asked what it would be like, other than to point out he'd come through unscathed.

"Do you even know how to navigate it?" she asked him. "What if we end up somewhere else? One of these other 'Zero Worlds' the Warden mentioned?"

He considered that for a moment. "Because I'm not navigating. Monique preprogrammed the return trip."

"Is not she the one who wants to wipe out both of our worlds?"

"Good point."

"You do not seem worried."

Caswell shrugged. "As far as she knows I'm still her weapon, with no memory of where I've been or what transpired there. At the very least she'll want to talk to me before eliminating me."

After the usual warnings the press of deceleration lifted. They'd come to a complete stop in reference to Garta, which now lay directly below them at the same distance as Gartien was out. The engines did not cut out entirely, though, apparently needing a tiny amount of thrust to hold their exact position lest Garta begin to pull them in.

"Something's happening," Caswell said, his voice trailing off even as he spoke.

Outside, the stars were fading away.

For a time of unknown length she felt *something*.

Something like the fog of inebriation.

Something like the dizziness after a head injury.

Something like being yanked from a deep sleep.

Something like dreaming.

Something like death and, also, like birth.

Then the stars returned, but not the stars she knew.

Caswell let out a sharp breath as if waking from a nightmare. He practically attacked the control display in front of him, fingers dancing across the virtual controls, eyes darting from one readout to the next. Sounds of alarm came from all over the cabin. A synthetic voice calmly repeated, "Proximity alert. Proximity alert."

"Is something wrong?" she asked. "We've arrived at the wrong place, haven't we?"

"No," he said. He sounded angry. "We made it."

"So what is the problem?"

"The problem is they're here, waiting for us."

Then he gripped the sides of his head, howling in pain, and slumped forward in his chair.

38

THE LIGHTS in the cabin winked from sunlight-white to a pulsing red. A shrill sound began to rise and fall, grating on Melni's ears. Against her better judgment she released the clasp that held four belts together across the center of her chest. She began to drift, and pushed off toward the slumped form of Caswell.

"Warning," the artificial voice cooed. "Proximity alert. Proximity alert. Proximity alert."

Entire swaths of the display bank in front of Caswell vanished, replaced by various warnings and red or yellow flashing iconography. She ignored it all and reached out for the back of Caswell's chair. Unused to the lack of gravity, Melni almost bounced away. She just managed to hook the headrest with one finger as her body tried to rebound across the space.

"Errmmh," her companion groaned. Caswell stirred and shook his head. His hands rose to rub at his temples, a gesture she'd come to trust and fear in equal quantity. Only this time, he seemed to simply be trying to ease pain.

"What is going on?" she asked him. "What has happened?"

He gave his skull one last violent shake and tried to focus on the monitors. "My implant."

"Do you remember me?"

"Yes," he said. "This is the trigger moment, the reversion marker. I'll forget whatever happens next, unless we can neutralize it. Which I doubt."

"Blixxing bastards."

Caswell turned and met her eyes, deadly serious. "You remember the anchor phrase?"

She nodded.

"Good." He shifted his focus back to the riot of alerts in front of him. "A ship is here, right on top of us. Earth or Prime, I have no idea. We need a plan, Melni. Right now."

Melni felt paralyzed. She had no idea of what to expect, of what they were up against. Trapped in a palace swarming with NRD goons she could at least wrap her mind around, but this? What were all these alarms? What object was in such close proximity that all this chaos was warranted? There was no time to ask. Something clanged against the ship. "I . . . Caswell, I am afraid. . . ."

"It's okay. Don't worry. I've got an idea," Caswell said, ending the worst silence Melni had ever known. "It relies entirely on you, though."

Melni managed a nod, grateful he'd come up with a plan for once. "Tell me what I must do."

He had no idea if it would work. If Monique had any inkling that he was not alone, the ruse would die before it could even start.

A sound wormed its way into his mind. The uplink, notifying him of an incoming transmission. He drifted back to the command console and hauled himself back into the seat. With a deep breath, Caswell accepted the call.

The face of Monique Pendleton appeared on the screen. "You made it!" she exclaimed, the delight on her face genuine.

"Barely," he said. He tried to impart exhaustion, weakness, confusion. "I'm not quite sure what happened, Mo. I was on the *Venturi,* then—"

"Let's talk in person," she said. "I'm here, right outside."

The surprise on his face required no acting. He'd never been in the same room with her. To get this chance now, to confront her with what the Warden had apparently told him, was far more appealing than this—

He realized then what he should have noticed immediately: no time lag in the brief conversation. Monique *was* here. She'd come to him. "Yeah. Yeah, okay," he managed.

Monique must have seen the comprehension dawn across his face. She offered her usual brilliant smile. "Come through," she said. "I'm to debrief you personally. They've really got a lot riding on this mission, Caswell. You scared the hell out of us not coming back on time."

"I can imagine. Right, see you in a minute," he said, and killed the link.

He checked the vossen gun. Only one needle left. It would have to count, and he'd have to fire it before she could trigger his implant, something she could probably do with the push of a button. No easy task.

Monique did not greet him outside the airlock. Instead he found himself staring into the impassive faces of two soldiers in full vacuum-rated combat gear, armed to the teeth. Archon logos were visible on each shoulder and across the breast.

"Search him," one said.

The other complied, drifting over to Caswell and patting him down. "Clean," the man said.

"What the hell is this?" Caswell asked.

The voice that replied was Monique's, cast through speakers embedded in the walls. "Welcome aboard, Agent IA6. Sorry about the welcome committee, but given your reversion state we have to be sure you aren't compromised."

One guard fell in behind him. The other led Caswell along a corridor segmented by bare metal bulkheads and lined with snaking bundles of colorful cables tucked into latticework aluminum trays. Exposed pipes and ventilation ducts wormed their way across the walls, floor, and ceiling. All of this was concealed beneath clear hard-plastic panels, bolted at each corner. Under acceleration, whichever way would be "down" would be made semi-opaque, and all of the panels could be removed to allow easy access to the ship's support systems. Standard Archon layout. He'd seen it a dozen times before.

Some of those clear panels began to glow softly blue. He

drifted along the tunnel. His escort took a left at a T junction, then a right, then "up." *One of Archon's executive flagships,* Caswell thought. Everything looked clean, and despite the surface veneer of chaos in the way the cables and pipes snaked their way around the walls, a trained eye such as his could recognize the layout had been very carefully planned. The vessel made the *Pawn Takes Bishop* look like some kind of thrown-together garbage scow.

Finally they came to a bulkhead door. The forward guard levered it open, revealing an opulent room within. Decades ago spacecraft had left behind their "only as big as we can fit inside a shuttle bay" size restrictions thanks to the advent of orbital construction yards. Yet even by modern standards this room was enormous, ten meters long and ten wide, with porthole windows along the far wall that showed a muted view of the Sun. A disk-shaped conference table made of black marble dominated the space, with room for twenty or more to sit around its circumference in high-backed, ergonomically perfect chairs. Lacking gravity the room's layout seemed rather silly, but Caswell imagined the normal use would be for meetings between corporate heads or visiting dignitaries, and the ship would be placed under thrust for the duration simply to make the occupants feel more comfortable.

Monique Pendleton sat alone in the huge room, directly opposite Caswell, the Sun glinting majestically behind her like an angelic halo. He squinted, raising one arm to block the light, until she made the windows go opaque. Soft yellow light from recessed bulbs along the wall joints replaced the sunlight.

"Where's our betters?" he asked, the use of "our" a deliberate attempt to paint him and her as a team, joined at the proverbial hip, just as they'd always been. As he spoke he drifted to a seat, then decided sitting at a table in zero-g was stupid. Besides, deliberately strapping himself down when he might need to flee at a moment's notice was tactically dumb. He floated beside the chair instead, holding it with one hand to keep from drifting away.

"Just us for now," she replied. With a gesture of her hand the two guards came in, positioning themselves to either side of the now-closed door. "Only a skeleton crew aboard, I'm afraid. We came out to rendezvous with you, guessing you'd be low on supplies. When you didn't emerge . . . Tell me, how do you feel?"

"Like shit. It's not fun reverting like that."

She frowned in sympathy. "If there had been time I would have re-created your Hyde Park apartment in one of the shuttle bays."

"That would have been nice."

"Alas, we arranged this in a hurry."

Caswell feigned humility. "An expensive journey to pick up one man," he said. "Not that I'm complaining."

"Worth it, in this case." With a smile she added, "The mission, and our coveted Agent IA6. What happened? What do you remember?"

"I was on the *Venturi,* watching the salvage team do their work, when Angelina made the mistake of accessing the station's database. You triggered IA as a result. Then . . . I was in the lander, drifting, unable to lock on to the SPS or even the background stars. The whole navigation system, fubarred."

"What do you make of that?"

He shrugged. "Malfunction, I guess."

"Did you access the ship's logs to troubleshoot this?"

"No."

"Why not?"

"I'd gone through reversion. First time that's ever happened to me during a mission, but I remember my training, Mo. I isolated myself from any potential mission artifacts and awaited contact. You know all this, of course."

"Did you record any imagery or notes while under IA?"

"No." Then he added, "None that I remember. I didn't look in the ship's secure log."

The person he'd spent more than a decade thinking of as his partner gave a matronly nod. With great care she said, "So, the mission, was it a success?"

He let a little anger slip into his voice. "That question is insulting, Monique. How would I know? I don't even know what the mission was. The implant did its job. Have the fucking analysts figure it out and send me on holiday." If he could get her to believe him ignorant of what had happened, indeed of the very existence of Gartien, maybe she would leave it at that. Maybe she'd send away the two soldiers. He needed all of them to lower their guard, to suspect him of nothing, so that he could be ready when Melni was found.

"Relax, IA6. You have your protocol, I have mine. These are standard questions."

"I . . . of course." He almost said "regret," turned it into a cough. "Apologies. Go on."

She gathered herself. Tapped a few notes into a terminal on her right. "You left no indicator for yourself?"

"If I logged anything it would be with the key only you can decrypt. I know the protocol, Mo."

She leaned forward, considering him.

Caswell tried to look at her with fresh eyes, to see her not as the handler he'd become so intertwined with over the years, but as an alien. A so-called Warden of Prime, monitoring Earth to make sure humanity didn't find the Conduit. And, if Melni's fantastic story was all true, then Monique—indeed all of this group called "Prime"—had been unaware of Gartien's existence until the moment that evidence of Alice Vale's escape had been uncovered on the *Venturi*.

He imagined the situation from her perspective. He almost certainly knew more about Gartien—the planet and its relation to this Conduit—than she did. He'd watched video logs from the *Venturi*'s brief visit to the world, a bit of intel Monique had provided him with when he was under IA and something he rediscovered on the return journey while Melni slept. The footage contradicted some of the things Alice Vale had said, most specifically that it had been Caswell who had blown up the *Venturi*. In the video, Alice did that. But such things could be faked, and on closer inspection he thought he saw slight clues in the imagery that confirmed such doctoring. Archon had made Alice out to be the villain, when all along it had really been him.

Monique knew of Gartien's existence now, thanks to the *Venturi* data, but probably not much more than that. He figured she'd sent him to kill Alice Vale as something of a knee-jerk reaction. Alice had been there for many years by then, but given her goals and how they differed from the way this outfit called Prime operated, Monique had to take the first chance to put an end to Alice's perceived poisoning of that world. If he succeeded, Prime could treat it like any other world on the Conduit. If he failed, well, they had their ways of dealing with that, too, from what Melni recounted from the Warden's story.

Caswell cleared his throat, realizing she was waiting for him to say more. "I assume I succeeded, whatever the goal may have been, but didn't make it back in time to avoid field reversion. I hope that's the case, anyway. That's all I can tell you."

"But you were aboard the lander when you reverted."

"Yes."

Monique steepled her fingers. "Archon appreciates your optimism, Agent Caswell. It's an unfortunate drawback to our implants that such a situation might arise, and in any other circumstance your involvement would have ended already. This is a special situation, however."

"Is that why you triggered me again, when I came through?"

Her lips extended in a condescending smile. She blinked, twice. "Came through what, exactly?"

Shit. He swallowed, buried suddenly under the crushing weight that mere knowledge of the Conduit could spell not only his demise, but Earth's and Gartien's as well. Melni's.

Melni. Jesus. Another thought, cold and terrible, coursed through him. She represented an intelligence coup for Prime, and he'd brought her right to them. Not only had she lived on that hidden world her whole life, but she'd been deeply integrated into its political and military intrigues. She remembered everything the Warden had said, and she had no implant with which to defend herself against forced interrogation.

"Came through what, Agent?" Monique repeated.

"My . . . my mental stupor. The pain meds on that boat were twelve years old, Monique, a bit beyond their expiration date."

A pause followed. Her eyes bored into him, just long enough to raise the hairs on his neck. "Well," she finally said, breaking eye contact to glance down at her screen, "it looks like the data from the lander has finished download-ing."

He tensed, cursing his own lack of foresight. Of course the damned ship would have recorded everything, and he hadn't thought to manipulate or, at the very least, erase the evidence.

Monique leaned forward, her eyes scanning information Caswell couldn't see. "Hmm. Either you were talking to yourself a lot, or . . ." Then she tapped something, and his own voice came booming out of the walls of the conference room.

> "Two hours until we initiate burn for the Conduit."
> "How long will the journey take?"
> "Six days, give or take. Plenty of time to rest."
> "And plan."
> "If only we knew what to plan for. Anyway, doesn't matter, we've got something more pressing to deal with."

Caswell pushed away from the chair, but in that same in-stant a pair of hands, strong as vise grips, wrapped around his upper arms and yanked him to the table, thrusting him into the seat.

"Well, well," Monique said, pausing the recording.

Caswell fought against the guard, but in the lack of grav-ity he couldn't get any leverage. A black strip of plastic came across his field of view, pressed against his chest, and tightened. The restraint constricted until it bit into his skin. He could barely breathe. His arms were pinned helplessly to his sides. His legs, though, were free. Caswell tried to kick out against the table, hoping to topple the chair. But of course in a zero-g situation it had been securely fixed in place, and his effort accomplished nothing.

"Enough of that," Monique snapped. "Shoot him in the foot if he resists further."

"Yes, Warden," the guard replied.

Warden. So these men knew of her true role.

"Search the lander," she said to the other man. "It seems we have a visitor. Let's get her into quarantine, hmm?"

"Yes, Warden," the second guard replied.

"There's no one else aboard," Caswell said in desperation. "I put her out the airlock. She was a spy."

"Forgive me if I don't believe you," Monique said. She looked past Caswell then. "You have your orders, Cento."

"Warden," the guard said. He left.

Monique leaned back in her chair. Her movements were fluid, utterly comfortable in the lack of gravity. "A rather illuminating bit of audio to hear, that," she said, smiling slightly at Caswell. "Specifically the use of that word. *Conduit*. How could you have learned that, I wonder? Its proper name. Even Alice Vale wouldn't have known that."

Caswell leaned forward and reached up at the same time, to rub his temples. He searched for his implant, ready to flood his brain with anything available to give him some advantage here. But he found only emptiness there.

"You didn't think I'd leave you that option, did you?" Monique asked. "Give me a little credit."

"I . . . I didn't know you could do that."

"There are many things you don't know about that little gland in your neck, Agent. Granted, the device was invented on Earth. Among the most interesting harvests we've made. We took it and improved it for our agents, however. Orders of magnitude more sophisticated than the slimy little blobs most Earthlings walk around with. You yourself received a very special model indeed."

To prove the point, Caswell's hands lifted from his lap. As if of their own volition, the limbs raised and reached out to the left, one thumb extending. Unable to control himself, he swung across his own body, fists crashing in against his right biceps. The tip of his thumb bore straight into the bullet wound. Fresh, blinding pain flared there. And then utterly vanished. Then returned. Like an on-off switch, he was flung to the limits of agony and then hauled back, panting, crying, as the thumb continued to press against the bandaged entry hole.

His hands finally relaxed. The pain vanished entirely. Artificially suppressed, lurking in the darkness of his mind.

"You should know," Monique said casually, "that I'd love to hear what happened in your own words, Caswell. But rest assured I'll have every memory pulled out of your skull in perfect fidelity. Even, by the way, the ones you think you forgot."

He glared at her, too stunned to say anything.

"That's right," she said. "It's all still there. Everything, since day one. No memories were ever deleted, Agent, they were simply firewalled."

Rage erupted within him. All this fucking time. All the murder he'd committed, all the deeds he'd done with the confidence that he would be absolved, mentally and legally, of the consequences. All of it, still inside him.

"Here," Monique said. "Have this one back. A little taste."

He felt a slight tingle deep inside his skull. And then, unbidden, Peter Caswell saw the interior of a luxury condominium. The evening skyline of Hong Kong gleamed just outside expansive windows. He stood at the center of a large mattress, white sheets and maroon blankets pooled haphazardly around his feet. And limbs. Naked flesh. A man, a woman, their faces just smears of blood and gore. In his hand he held a kitchen knife. Another body lay not far away. A . . . *No*, he thought. *God, no.*

"Surprised at what you're capable of?"

"That wasn't me," he stammered.

"Of course it was. It was the real you. The man who emerges when he knows he won't remember. Intoxicated, as usual. Drunk on his lack of accountability."

"Who were they?" he asked before he could stop himself.

"Dr. Huang was an astrophysicist," Monique replied, her voice sickeningly even. "He was two weeks or less away from discovering the Conduit. That particular mission was eight years ago."

The words confirmed what he already feared, yet this did nothing to soften the blow. Monique had recruited him specifically for this role. The implant made him the perfect enforcer. Everything he'd done since joining Archon had been to protect the secret of the Conduit. And if he himself ever caught even the slightest hint of the thing, she'd just revert him and that would be that. He took fucking *pride* in not asking questions, in never seeking to know what had lain within the myriad of gaps throughout his memory. He'd been a tool, a blunt instrument for her to wield. He did the fucking *work*. Worse, he'd genuinely relished the lack of consequences that gave other, unaugmented agents that perpetual haunted look. He relied utterly on Monique's summations of his success or failure in the field.

Just a hammer, driving nails.

All the people he must have killed over the years. All the labs he'd probably demolished. Every one of them on the verge of, or perhaps even just beyond, discovery of the Conduit. Now just bottles of beer, facing backward. How fucking juvenile. How willfully ignorant.

Alice Vale had eluded him, though. She must have been one of his first missions. Perhaps *the* first. He'd been sent to kill her on the *Venturi,* and failed. She'd slipped the net, simultaneously dooming humanity and, most likely, Gartien as well. *Gartien.* Alice and the Warden, both dead. Sacrificed everything to try to build a culture that could challenge Prime. Or at least to keep Prime away from the other branches of the Conduit, and the Zero Worlds besides Earth.

"Earth," Monique said, as if reading his mind.

Could she do that? Christ, what exactly was she capable of? His plan would fail if she could read his mind. *Hurry, Melni.* "What about Earth?"

"We've worked so hard to keep the Conduit's secret from that world. That was only possible because you never retained any knowledge of it yourself. Now, however . . . the situation is different."

"No shit. Finally some memories you can't, what was the word, 'firewall'?"

"I'll just have one last mission for you, Peter Caswell. Agent IA6."

"If you think I'm going to help—"

"Before we start," Monique said, ignoring him, "perhaps you'd like to know the real you?"

A stinging electric shock rippled outward from the base of his neck. Caswell's entire body spasmed, vibrating like a struck drum. Thoughts, memories, impressions by the millions fell upon his mind like an avalanche. Too much to bear. So vast in quantity that it all blurred together, too vague and jumbled to grasp any one thing. In that instant he knew no more than a newborn babe.

Basic instincts.

Fight or flight.

How to breathe.

The true self. Satisfying, in an animalistic sense. But the feeling did not last. The blurred vastness began to crystallize. When the feeling subsided he found more than just a single new memory in his mind.

Peter Caswell remained, but there was another, now. His true self.

His mind drifted through this landscape of memories, him just a passenger. Looking out over a city of golden spires that kissed the clouds, studded with lavish gardens and connected by bridges of astonishing beauty. Far above those clouds, tens of thousands of tiny lights zipped across the darkening sky. Like Saturn's rings, but all artificial. Cities in orbit.

Another memory beckoned. Trudging through a muddy jungle, wearing a full suit of mechanized body armor. A dozen more such augmented soldiers in a dispersed formation in front of him. They were on Conduit World 26, sent in to wipe out a primitive tribe that had found a crashed probe.

Now a third memory. His first day with the implant. He was just a boy. There were hundreds of others like him, standing in neat lines, practicing a martial art designed to work in the slowed reference frame of an overclocked mind. Behind the instructor, beyond massive windows, he saw the struts of the space station. A city in space, above Prime. Dozens more drifting along beside it.

"What," Caswell said, struggling for the first time in what he thought of as his life to *not remember,* "is all this?"

"You, of course," Monique replied. "The real you. An enforcer of Prime. Peter Caswell is just an invented persona. Your cover, here on Earth."

"No. No, it can't be true."

"I think you'll find it is. Or you would, if you had time. Now, about your final mission."

"Go fuck yourself."

She shook her head, patiently. "No need to be a willing

participant this time. All I need is for you to die. Thomas, if you please," she said, with a slight jerk of her chin toward the guard behind Caswell.

He heard the knife unsheathe. Saw the blade—ten centimeters of carbon morphblade—slide across his field of view and then push in toward his neck. Felt the heat of the cauterizing filaments as they crawled along the razor-sharp edge, ready to instantly seal the wound, bleed him out from the inside, nice and clean. A hand came around from the other side and pressed against Caswell's forehead, driving his skull back into the headrest.

The blade bit. The heating elements began their terrible thrum. He smelled cooking flesh. He wanted to scream.

Monique's lips curled into a horrible voyeur's smile.

Melni. Melni! NOW! Now, goddamnit!

The blade slid against his skin, grating on stubble, carving through muscle tissue. A crackling sound followed, along with the sick smell of burning meat.

Unable to stop it, to stop any of it, Caswell shut his eyes hard and prepared himself for the end.

An alarm wailed.

The blade stopped, just millimeters from his jugular.

Monique's expression shifted to concern. Her eyes darted to the display in front of her. "The lander," she hissed. "It's detached and moving away. She's fleeing!" Then her gaze snapped up and she met Caswell's eyes. "She's headed for Earth."

"She's doing more than that," Caswell said, growling out the words, his jaw clenched for the blade still embedded in his neck.

His former handler glared at him a moment until something on the screen pulled her attention away. She studied it, eyes darting back and forth. She could not help but open her mouth into a surprised circle at what she saw there. "You haven't," she hissed.

"I have."

He didn't know exactly what the screen displayed, but he knew what it meant. In ten minutes or so, the broadcast would reach Earth. It would hit every public source with equal, unstoppable abandon. And it would tell them the secret Prime had worked so hard to keep.

Monique's fists clenched. "Do you realize what you've done?"

"I've given them a fighting chance."

"This could have just been your life," she said. "Yours and whoever is in that shuttle. Instead you've doomed the entire planet."

Caswell managed a small, satisfied smile. "I've given them a chance. If you have any sense at all, you'll know what a fight you're in for, bitch."

Her eyes narrowed.

"What do you want me to do?" the guard named Thomas asked, blade still held firm, the tip still inside Caswell's neck.

"Finish that," Monique replied, "then locate Cento, and meet me on the bridge. We have work to do."

"Yes, War—"

His word ended in a hiss of breath. The man slammed against Caswell's chair. An almost inaudible grunt escaped his lips. His body tumbled over the headrest in the morbid slow-motion ballet of a corpse in zero-g. He drifted across the table toward Monique, his eyes fixed and glassy, arms and legs splayed and limp.

Monique ducked under the body and popped her head back up, just her eyes visible across the slab of marble.

"Get up where I can see you," a voice said. Melni's voice.

Caswell kept his body carefully still. The morphblade still protruded from his neck, only a centimeter of the tip inside him. The rest just dangled at the edge of his field of view, bouncing horribly with each beat of his heart.

His chair rocked again. Caswell winced in pain as his body, and thus the blade, moved in reaction.

Melni must have seen the knife then. She gasped. Her hand reached for the grip.

Her other hand came into view. She held the vossen gun in an iron grip, pointed straight at Monique.

"Careful," Caswell said. His eyes were blurred with tears from the pain of the blade and the burned skin around its edge. "Grip it with your thumb on that red switch and pull straight out."

She did as he instructed. When her fingers curled around the handle, though, the room plunged into absolute darkness.

39

"PULL THE BLADE!" Caswell said.

Blinded, her nostrils full of the smell of his burned flesh, Melni renewed her grip on the knife's handle and yanked outward. A brief glow of reddish yellow light, like a candle just extinguished, illuminated her hand as the strange weapon melted Caswell's skin around the entry wound, sealing the flesh. The stench made her want to vomit.

Caswell emitted a low groan. "Cut the binding," he croaked.

A sound came to her from across the table. The slight scuff of fabric against stone. Monique, on the move.

Thumb still on the blade's activator, Melni pushed herself back and down. She had to move her face in close to see anything more than a few inches from the glow of the blade. There, against the back of the chair, was a black strap an inch wide. She sawed across it with the knife, smelled the sour acrid fumes of burned synthetic fabric. Caswell shifted in the chair, free from the torso up. She heard him frantically pulling at a second strap that presumably held his feet in place.

Melni let go of the knife. As reassuring as the little flare of light might be, it made her the only distinguishable target in the room. Besides, she had something else in mind. Another weapon, one she'd taken from the guard who'd come to search the lander. She'd ambushed him before he'd even reached the entrance, strangling him with a grapple hold she'd learned many years before, improvised to work in this damnable lack of gravity. "Stay low," she whispered, unsure if Caswell could hear her. She pushed off the floor with both feet to make sure she was well above his head. Pushed harder than she'd planned to. By the time she had the gun in her hands the top of her head smacked into the ceiling. Out of pure reflex she pulled the trigger. Rapid little plumes of fire erupted from the weapon.

The gun did not chatter like a machine rifle back home. This sang a steady hum like the chant of a Tibetan monk. She'd listened to a sample on Caswell's electric book.

Little explosions of sparks and debris began to erupt on the far side of the dark room. Melni fought for control of the weapon as it tried to push back into her, her own body being shoved with each round that flew from the barrel. And fly they did. Hundreds, perhaps thousands, of muffled coughs from the barrel that ran together in a numbing, bone-shaking roar. She managed to guide the weapon to the place Monique had been sitting. Electrical sparks and little bolts of lightning flared out from the screen that protruded from the table. Something shattered and a huge shower of sparks erupted like a holiday burster. Of the enemy there was no sign. Something broke loose from the far end of the room, allowing a jagged triangle of brilliant white light through the back wall. The beam poured through the room like a coastal beacon, the shaft of brilliance swirling with the smoke and dust that now clouded the space.

The weapon's tone abruptly became a rapid click. Emptied.

Melni tumbled over backward from the momentum she'd created. She saw the ceiling, then the door she'd come in through, only upside down. Then the floor. The knife she'd discarded floated across her field of view, tumbling. Finally the table came into view. Caswell was nowhere to be seen. The table had a line of craters across its center like the Desolation. It continued across the mess of the computer screen and right up the backrest of Monique's empty chair, which sat in the center of that single beam of blinding white light, bits of foam cushion in a small cloud around it.

Suddenly the whole back wall of the room became horizontal lines of brilliant light. The lines grew, letting in knifelike bands of white across the entire space. They grew and grew until they merged together, just a single wall of luminance now. Melni shielded her eyes to look in that direction. Seconds passed before she could see anything at all. She was looking at a ball of white flame surrounded by a shifting milky haze. A star. Earth's star, she hoped, which Caswell had called Sol.

Against that dazzling radiance Melni saw a blurred shadow begin to move near the top of the wall. *No,* she thought, *that's the bottom. I've flipped over.*

It was Monique, coming out from where she'd hidden. Wounded or perhaps just shocked from the barrage of gunfire, Melni couldn't be sure, but the woman was in motion and had something in her hands. A tiny thing like a baton. No, Melni realized. One of those little cylindrical missile weapons. Melni, adrift, could do nothing to take cover. She couldn't even stop herself from tumbling, and soon the so-called Warden of Earth would be out of view again. She tried to twist around and only made things worse.

"Whoever you are," Monique said, "you're a terrible shot."

Melni braced herself. The weapon seemed capable of anything. What would her death be? An explosive that tore her innards to shreds? A molten lance through her heart?

Something punched her in the back. A white-hot pain tore through her chest before the projectile ripped out between her ribs and embedded itself in the wall near the door.

Melni felt her breath catch as unbelievable pain seared through her. She couldn't think, couldn't focus. She could do nothing save mentally curl into a fetal ball against the staggering, all-consuming heat of agony in her breast.

Her body continued to tumble, bringing Monique back into view against the inferno of the star behind her, outside the expansive windows. The woman glided to the side of the room and slipped through a gap in the wall Melni hadn't seen before. A concealed door. It began to slide closed silently behind her, a queer echo of when Alia Valix had confronted Melni before fleeing into the Think Tank.

Vision blurred by tears, face contorted into a silent scream, Melni fought for control of her senses. The blinding sunlight pouring in made it almost impossible to see. The stinging tears in her eyes did not help.

A shape drifted in front of Melni's face. She tried to bat it aside only to stop and grab hold of it at the last instant. The knife felt right in her hand. She focused on it, used it as a talisman to clear her mind. In that moment her back thudded weakly against a flat surface. The wall, just above the door. Melni gripped the object even as she launched herself. Her body rocketed across the room, over the table and the bolted-down chairs, in a perfect line to the corner where Monique had fled.

The hidden door was an inch from sealing. Melni thrust the knife into the gap, just managing to get the tip in. She braced her feet against the wall and floor and began to apply pressure to the hilt, pushing with all the strength she could muster, praying the tip wouldn't snap off. The effort made her scream as something inside her chest tore. Her whole body trembled violently.

A band of light caught her eye. The door pried open a meager inch. She thrust the knife in farther, letting the door slide back, then levered it again. White spots began to swim across her vision. She felt as if her breast would erupt in flame, and wondered how much blood had pooled inside her body as her breaths began to flutter wetly, her lungs filling with fluid. She'd drown herself in less than a minute. Even less than that, perhaps, given the lack of gravity. The blood would be freely sloshing about in there, blocking her wind-pipe instead of pooling at the bottom. Melni heaved against the blade, scrambling for purchase on the walls and floor around her, mind numb to the pain now, only dimly aware of the rip of flesh and muscle inside her. She screamed. She pushed. The band of light reappeared and widened.

Melni thrust her knee inside, then her arm. The task became easier, and soon she was through. The door caught her foot and she yanked it free, leaving her shoe behind, which kept the door from sealing. "Caswell!" she shouted, not knowing where he was or if he could hear her. The word came out more as a wet croak. "Going . . . after . . ."

She couldn't finish. Her lungs felt heavy. Melni pushed off with her feet and rocketed down a narrow utility corridor. She hit a bend hard, taking the impact on her elbow, gagging as liquid in her chest flew up her windpipe. A numbing sting shot up her arm.

Then she was falling.

The floor came up to meet her. It was only a few feet to drop, but the impact could not be defended against and she shrieked as the metal surface slammed into her cheek. Something cracked there. Bone. Her cheekbone. In some corner of her mind, Melni heard the knife clatter away. She came shakily to her feet and groped around for it. Her body felt heavy and sluggish, each step a skirmish, the rest of the hallway looming like a war. At least, in gravity, she could breathe a little.

Her foot kicked the knife. She collapsed to the floor in her effort to pick it up, but her fingers finally encircled the cool metal handle. Just standing again made her dizzy. The edges of her vision began to darken, as if she'd entered a tunnel within this tunnel. The craft must be accelerating very fast, she realized. Twice what she and Caswell had endured on their flight to the Conduit.

Melni focused on each step.

One foot, then the other, shod in invisible boots of lead.

Again.

Don't drop the knife.

Another step. Another breath.

Keep the knife, keep the knife, keep the knife.

She came through an open doorway at the far end of the hall, her only clue of the transition being a change in the sound her footsteps made. She recognized the sound. She'd heard it . . . when? Thoughts seemed to slide around the edges of comprehension. She shook her head violently, regretted it instantly. She just wanted to lie down. Rest, she needed rest. "A bit of sleep then right in Garta's light," old Gram used to say. Her grip began to loosen on the hilt until another part of her mind seemed to snap away the betrayal of the other. Her fist tightened. She glanced up and took in the room before her.

The Warden's ship. No, just one like it. The slightly soft walls, the snaking lines of illumination—glowing faintly red here.

Monique stood at the far end, before a dizzying, enormous display. Her hands were extended out before her, light dancing around her fingertips as she performed some sort of interfacing communion with the ship.

The woman spun around, alerted by some unseen mechanism to her pursuer's entrance.

Melni, barely able to move her heavy limbs, her breaths coming in wretched, bubbling sighs, watched in horror as the woman took aim at her again. At her eyes this time, and the brain behind them. Melni wanted to close those eyes but could not. Fear would not let her command her own body.

The press on Melni's body eased, and then vanished. She was adrift again, too far from any wall to control her own movement. She floated helplessly. Monique, her feet fixed somehow to the floor, grinned, and aimed.

A dark shape ripped through the air. It flew past Melni toward the surprised Warden. Caswell, launched out of the hallway like a cannon round.

She fired at him instead of her.

One of his hands exploded in a cloud of blood and bone and gore.

He did not slow. His body smashed into the woman's legs, knocking her feet out of the apparatus that had held her in place. The two of them flew backward into the display, slamming against it with a hollow, blunt smack. The impact bounced Caswell away from her. His arms flailed, blood fountaining out as he tried desperately to grab hold of the woman. The fingers of his one good hand only found air. Monique managed to grab the edge of the control display. She kept herself from drifting away with him. She tilted her head back and laughed, then turned the vossen gun on him again.

Monique said something to Caswell. Gloating, goading. Melni couldn't hear it, bloodlust pounding in her ears.

Her back bumped into something. A bulkhead. She gripped the edge with her off hand, pressed her feet against the wall. Blood dribbled from her mouth. Her nose stung from bile, filled her senses with the smell of copper and vomit. She couldn't breathe. She had only seconds left. Kicking hard, pulling with her one free hand, Melni launched herself at the woman. In that motion her throat cleared long enough to suck in a lungful of air.

Monique noticed her. She tried to re-aim her weapon, yet even with her implant-enhanced reaction time she was too slow. Melni slammed into her as Caswell had, only against the woman's chest instead of her legs. The impact lanced fresh pain through Melni's body. Her own breast felt as if a white-hot ember had been reignited inside.

She and Monique smashed into the far wall. Melni's face pressed against the oddly soft surface, and for a moment she could see nothing at all. In Melni's hand, the knife hummed, buried all the way to the hilt in Monique's chest. The woman groaned and Melni, falling rapidly toward unconsciousness, twisted the blade with the last of her strength.

Monique tilted her head back and screamed, a shrill, ago-nized sound that tore through all the pain Melni felt. Melni kept twisting. She felt the sickening resistance as the blade wrenched through muscle or bone or both, the burning edge slicing through it all.

"You should be dead," Monique managed to say through clenched teeth. "I shot you through the heart!"

Melni let go of the knife. She met the other woman's dying eyes and spat the blood from her mouth. "I am of Gartien," she said, "and our hearts are on the right."

40

SHE WOKE with the horrible feeling that it had all been a fever dream.

Melni lay back in the reclined pilot's chair. Tubes snaked from her arms. Another had been taped under her nose, and there was a mask over her face. All these tentacles joined together at a machine that protruded from the wall. Pumps and other equipment whirred and hissed inside.

Sweat clung to her skin, chilling in the processed air. She glanced around. The lights were dim and set to a soft, comforting shade of blue like the depths of the ocean. Of Caswell there was no sign. Melni tried to move and found her hands and legs had been restrained. The effort brought a dull ache to her left shoulder. Dullness achieved through medication, she had no doubt. Her head felt heavy from it, despite the continued lack of gravity.

"Cas?" she called out. At least she could talk again without spitting blood. But who, or what, had saved her? "Cas? Anyone?"

"I'm here," his voice said. The sound came from all around her, through hidden speakers.

"Where? I cannot see you."

"Be with you in a minute," he said.

The minute felt like a month. One of Gartien's hundred-day months, at that. Her mouth was dry as paper, her lips cracked. She turned her head and realized there was another tube that touched her lips when she looked that way. Her fears banished by the sound of his voice, Melni pursed her lips around the clear tube and sucked cool fluid through it. Water. Pure, cold as ice. It tasted wonderful. She tried for more but her efforts were rewarded by a soft chime from the little automatic doctor.

"Birdshit," Melni said to it. "Give me more, you little monster."

The machine did not reply, nor did it give her more water. Melni sighed and waited. She fell asleep before Caswell arrived.

She spent three days drifting in and out of sleep, floating from one fever-induced nightmare to the next, until the nightmares finally turned to simple dreams. Eventually she felt clearheaded and her stomach no longer roiled. When she was awake, she and Caswell talked. He showed her the artificial arm and hand the ship had grown for him. Attached just below his elbow, the limb looked waxy and pale but nonetheless real. The fingers moved like real ones, and he seemed completely at ease with the prosthetic.

"What of Monique?" Melni eventually asked.

"On her way into the Sun," he said with more than a little hesitation.

His answer took a moment to register. "Are you okay?"

He nodded, eyes downcast. "She was the only friend I had, for years. The only one who understood both me and the man I could never remember being." He turned slightly then, and she could see a bandage across the back of his neck. "Losing memory is not going to be a problem for me anymore," he said. "For better or worse, from now on I live with my actions."

Melni rested a hand on his. Silence stretched.

He fed her. He told her how the ship they were in was a clever shell of Earth-based tech over a wholly alien vessel within. He could access the familiar components easily enough, but the rest he was still struggling to understand, much less control. Eventually he freed her from the bed, provided she agreed to wear a protective shell over her upper left arm, shoulder, and that side of her chest and back. "You took a needle through the lung," he explained. "The healing is going very well, but a good bump against a wall in here and . . ."

"Gratitude," Melni said. She offered him a reassuring smile, and wondered if he could see the pain behind it. It was better, but not as much as he seemed to think. Perhaps, she thought, he just had a higher tolerance for pain. Melni would deal with it, she decided, simply to get out of that damned couch and do something.

"What did your people think of our transmission?" she asked him. Together they had recorded an account, brief and to the point, of everything they had learned. Following Caswell's instructions she had beamed it toward Earth, on a repeating schedule, even as their lander sped toward that world with a physical copy. The question was what his people would do. He had seemed convinced they would do nothing. Argue among themselves, a camp that believed and one that called hoax.

"I don't know what they think."

"They never replied?"

"Not before . . . we're not there anymore, Melni," he said, the words sharp as a knife. "She moved us."

Silence opened like a chasm between them. "What do you mean?" she said finally, though she could guess.

"Come, let me show you."

And so he took her to the bridge. The room where she'd buried a knife in the heart of the alien who had ordered Caswell's throat sliced. All evidence of the violence had been cleared away.

"Before she died," Caswell said, pointing to a map similar to what Laz had shown them, "I believe she set us on a course back to Prime. We've jumped four times already."

"Four?" Melni wrestled with the information. "Four. I do not know if I should be impressed by the number or not. I suppose I imagined these Wardens skipping around like a stone across a pond, dashing off across dozens of worlds in the time it takes us to bathe. Yet it has been days, has it not?"

He nodded gravely. "Each 'skip' requires an exit into normal space, then a sort of recalibration. The local star begins to pull you in, so the engines have to fire to compensate for that drift. But there's something else. It's only a guess based on what I've seen, but I think the Conduit entrances are related to how far the target planet is from its own star. These can vary quite a bit. Earth and Gartien were very similar, but some of these worlds require hours' worth of flight before you can enter the Conduit to reach them. Orbits are often elliptical, too, complicating things further. I imagine you need some pretty detailed stellar cartography to plot a course."

"No wonder Laz said they had to map it."

"Yeah, no kidding."

"Kidding?"

"Joking."

"Ah."

He looked back to the display. He was exhausted, she realized, despite the days of rest. They stood in silence for a time, trying to make sense of the imagery in front of them.

After a minute Caswell sighed. "Laz told us much before he passed, and this ship will tell us quite a bit, too."

"It better," Melni said.

Caswell grinned at that, though there was little mirth in it. It was a patient smile.

"Why Prime?" Melni asked. "Why not steer us into the star?"

He nodded. "I thought about that, and the best answer is that she intended to transmit knowledge of Gartien, the Zero Worlds, to them."

"Surely she did that already?"

"Communication through the Conduit is not possible, not without some kind of physical transmitter. They have a system during normal circumstances. Little automated pods that just jump back and forth, relaying information."

"I see. Wait, how do you know this?"

"I'll get to that," he said, and returned to his thought. "Maybe Monique didn't have time to transmit, so she did the next-best thing and laid in a course. Or, who knows, maybe she thought she'd won and was just anxious to get there and gloat."

"Or," Melni thought aloud, the idea descending on her like a deathbed drape, "maybe she is sending us back as some kind of proof."

"Hmm. Also possible."

"So . . ." Melni paused. "What do we do now?"

"What's the plan, you mean?" he asked, with half a grin.

"Yes."

"Two choices, I suppose. One is to try to stop this damned ship before it reaches its destination. Land, or hide, somewhere. Keep the secret from them as long as we can."

On the screen she saw their current location, near a star much like Garta or Sol. At the orbital distance where Earth or Gartien would lay, however, there was nothing. No, not nothing, exactly, just a cloud of specks in a ring band around the star. A demolished world. The Warden had shown them this. He'd said Prime had done it. Destroyed an entire planet, just to preserve their monopoly on the Conduit. Apparently the destruction had not affected the Conduit's entry point, however. She wondered idly if Prime had considered that before demolishing the world. Perhaps they had deemed it a necessary risk, given that, as far as they knew, there were only three other worlds they would lose access to should it render Conduit travel here useless.

"One thing is for sure, we will not be landing here," Melni observed.

"Indeed not," he said.

She searched his face for some sign of his feelings. Those narrow, dark eyes, the tight, cruel mouth. "Could you do that? Could you just curl up in some mud hut on a planet somewhere and live the rest of your life knowing what you now know?"

He held her gaze for a long time before he finally shook his head.

"Good. Me neither. What is the other choice?"

"We don't stop. We go to Prime."

"To Prime," she echoed.

Caswell nodded. "That's right."

"Why?"

"To do what they've been doing all along. Keep them from learning of Gartien's existence as long as possible using our skill as spies. As assassins."

The idea held a certain appeal, she could not deny that. But she also recognized a triteness to it, a lack of tactical reality. "We know nothing of that place. They would be onto us instantly," Melni said.

To her surprise, Caswell shook his head. "Maybe not. There's something I haven't told you."

The tone of his voice filled her with a sudden nervous dread. She shivered at the idea and waited for him to speak.

"Before you entered that room, Monique unlocked my memories. All of them."

She blinked. "I thought they were—"

He gave a single, solemn shake of his head. "Not erased. Just, locked away."

She gripped his good hand. "Tell me."

"I'm from Prime, Melni. I'm one of them. Trained to enforce their rules, and I've done so. On many worlds. Earth was just my latest assignment. Peter Caswell was simply a cover. An invented one, I think, or perhaps memories stolen from someone else, I don't know."

She shrank away from him, suddenly fearful. "You mean—"

"Relax," he said. "I'm on your side. I see the wisdom of what Laz and Alice were doing. And the thing is, Melni, I think we can help."

"How?"

"I'm a weapon they don't expect. I have memories of Prime, and not just things like how they communicate through the Conduit, but more. Much more. Sensitive things. About Prime and many other places important to them." He paused to let that settle. At her silence he went on. "And yet I also know of Gartien. The Zero Worlds. I know what we're fighting for, and who we're fighting against. Combine that with your ability to analyze and plan, and I think we make a formidable team."

She swallowed, hard. "But can we really stop them? The

two of us? Against an empire that spans hundreds, maybe thousands, of worlds?"

"No," he admitted.

"Then what do you intend to do?"

A ruthless grin spread across his face, and his dark eyes glinted. "I intend to do some damage."

The end.
Not where it started at all.
Not even where it ended.

ACKNOWLEDGMENTS

First and foremost I must say "gratitude" to my wife for her constant support. And to my boys, who keep things in perspective.

Gratitude to my agent, Sara Megibow, as well as Jerry and Wayne (aka the "Hollywood Team"). They consistently amaze and humble me with their talent and support.

Much gratitude to everyone at Random House who helps bring my books to life, specifically (but not limited to) Mike, Sarah, Rachel, Joe, Greg, Beth, Keith, and Scott.

I've met a whole bunch of wonderful authors since first being published in 2013, and the welcoming arms within which they've enfolded me is something I am endlessly grateful for. There are far too many to name each, but I do want to call out my first and biggest fan, Kevin Hearne, for all the kind words both spoken to me and shouted to the world.

To all the fans I've met at cons, at book signings, and electronically from all over the world: You folks are amazing and I love every last one of you!

Gratitude is owed to the ever-patient Skyler, Sam, Prumble, and Tania. I'll get to you, I swear! Now relax and enjoy your flight. The landing might be a bit bumpy. . . .

Thank you, Jake "Oddjob" Gillen, my trusty beta-reader, bodyguard, and dear friend. *Slainte,* old man. Also, thanks are due to beta-readers Josh and Scott.

Saving the best for last . . . my gratitude to YOU, dear reader, for indulging me in this tale. I hope you had as much fun reading it as I did in writing the blixxing thing. Cheers!

Jason Hough
Seattle, 2014

If you enjoyed *Zero World*, read on for the entirety of Jason M. Hough's action-packed novella

The Dire Earth

Set years before the events of the *New York Times* bestselling novel *The Darwin Elevator*, this thrilling adventure begins in a world on the brink of disaster . . .

PART 1

Wave of Infection

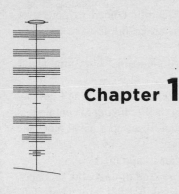

Chapter 1

The aircraft rested in a windswept field a few hundred meters up from the beach. Her crew, a pilot and co-pilot, sat nearby. Gulls wheeled overhead, their occasional calls as lazy as the Mediterranean whitecaps stretching north as far as Skyler could see.

Today he could see a long way. The clear sky, blue and even from one horizon to the other, was marred only by the blazing white disk of the sun directly above. On any other day, in any other circumstance, the afternoon would be among the most pleasant he'd ever experienced. That wasn't saying a lot, of course. Other than a rail trip to Rome two summers back, for his twenty-fifth birthday, he'd kept mostly to the colder portions of Europe.

Until this week. The week from hell.

And it was only Wednesday.

"They're late," Finn said.

Skyler had thought the pilot asleep. He glanced at the man. Captain Finn Koopman lounged in a foldout chair, one of two he kept in the plane for just such "hurry up and wait" scenarios. Skyler sat in the other, perched on the rough fabric edge, hunched over a slate he had split between newsfeeds and a map of the continent.

Finn's posture couldn't be more different. Shoes and socks off, feet propped up on a sun-bleached rock. Hands folded across a belly a bit rounder than was really appropriate for a pilot of the Luchtmacht. Finn had earned that, though, Skyler supposed. The man had ten years and a few thousand sorties on Skyler. He didn't need to pore over flight plans anymore. That's what co-pilots were for. He'd said as much when they'd met.

"Maybe I should check in," Skyler said. "They might have moved us again."

Finn cracked a half grin. "Relax, Luiken. Can't get any more north than this, assuming they're trying to contain this thing to Africa. My guess? They'll set up a naval blockade next and wait it out."

"I just wish they'd tell us what's happened."

At that Finn shrugged. "Some kind of nasty flu, probably. Or, hell, maybe a clever new seed that fell into counterfeiters' hands."

"They'd shut down a whole continent over some engineered grass?"

Finn shrugged. "A flu, then."

"Hmm," Skyler said. He didn't like the information on the newsfeed half of his slate. Or rather, the lack of information. If command wouldn't tell them what all the medical supplies were for, surely someone in the quarantine zone could slip a note about it out through one of the HocNets. Something should have leaked by now. It's not as if the informal networks could be locked down. Jammed, maybe, but surely not on this kind of scale. Skyler had connected to every one he could find, despite the violation of military procedure. Damn the protocols—he didn't want to catch whatever bug had plunged half of Africa into a media dead zone in just four days.

They'd made their first flight in two days ago, a joint op at the UN's request, dropping private corporate doctors plus a mountain of "unspecified" equipment into Chad. The orders were simple: Fly in, drop the goods off, speak to no one. Maintain silence on all channels and nets, no exceptions.

Sixty klicks from the landing site in Chad they'd been rerouted, told to turn east and land in a hastily erected staging area in the desert outside Nyala. There'd been soldiers there. Soldiers from many different places, looking just as confused as Skyler had felt. Finn took off ten minutes after landing, ordered to make haste for the port in Rotterdam. Another load of gear, though no doctors this time. They'd dropped that off a day later outside Aswan, another redirect. Another staging zone, this one massive, blanketed with white tents and people in bulky hazard suits. Skyler and Finn hadn't even stepped out of the cockpit that time.

And now, Alexandria. The third mission, the third change of plans. They were supposed to land at a university in Cairo, only to be told to avoid Cairo's airspace when they were already two kilometers inside it. The new coordinates brought them to this desolate strip of land with orders to wait. They'd be met by . . . someone. In the confusion no one seemed to know who.

The air controller, a woman with the Egyptian military, had started laughing then, just before the connection died. There'd been no humor in that laugh, nor much in the way of sanity, Skyler thought.

Beneath the sound of seagulls and the gently lapping sea, Skyler heard the crunch of soil beneath tires, then the distinct whine of ultracaps discharging.

"About time," Finn said. He came upright and went to work putting his socks and shoes back on. "Open her up. I want to be off the ground the instant they're done."

"Sure." When Skyler stood and turned, the sight of the approaching vehicle drove all such actions from his mind. Despite still being a half kilometer away, Skyler could see the flames licking out the back windows of the huge white vehicle. The smoke plume hid within a massive dust cloud being thrown up behind. It was some kind of mobile laboratory, moving fast. Careening as if driven by a child. Not slowing.

Skyler broke for the aircraft. In through the side hatch and forward to the cockpit in seconds. He palmed the unlock. "First Lieutenant Luiken," he growled at the vocal sensor.

The controls lit up, recognizing him. Skyler flipped to systems-ready state and tapped the preflight warm-up sequence, urgent departure. The sound of turbofans whirring to life filled the cabin.

Through the window he saw the van storming toward them. It swerved off the dirt road and began to hop awkwardly over the uneven ground, then pivoted hard right back toward the road, almost rolling on its side in the process. Flames consumed the entire back half now. The nose dipped suddenly, sending a huge spray of tan dirt into the air almost in time to obscure the body being propelled through the front window.

Unable to look away, Skyler slipped into his co-pilot's chair and pulled on his helmet. Finn came in. The captain did not sit. He just stood, hunched to see the spectacle outside.

"Stay put, Lieutenant," he said.

"I thought they were going to ram us."

"Me, too, but they're not going anywhere now." The captain's voice sounded tight, strained.

Skyler chanced a glance over his shoulder in time to see Finn pinching the bridge of his nose, grimacing. "What's wrong?"

"Migraine or something. Look, keep the fans hot. I'm going to see if I can help."

Skyler watched as Finn jogged toward the stuck vehicle. The pilot hefted a fire extinguisher in one hand. Black smoke rose in a plume now as the fire ate its way toward the front of the mobile lab.

A man in a white jumpsuit climbed through the hole in the shattered driver's window. He scrambled down into the dirt and began to run toward Finn. This was not a rush to greet a rescuer. Fear drove those steps. The person was looking back at the burning van, not at the pilot. When he finally turned and saw Finn he almost tripped over himself, turned ninety degrees, and ran off as if the pilot and the flames were equally dangerous. His face was contorted in a scream that seemed never-ending. Finn stopped and waved to no avail.

Skyler swallowed with difficulty. Without looking down he switched the aircraft into liftoff configuration. The engine note shifted higher.

Another man emerged from the crashed vehicle. His jumpsuit was white, too, or had been. Most of it was charred now, one sleeve completely black and in tatters, revealing a badly burned arm beneath. He sprinted away, too. Not simply following the first, Skyler thought, but chasing.

Finn was shouting.

"Get back in here, Captain," Skyler said under his breath. "Let's go."

The burned man saw Finn. He halted, dropped to a crouch more animal than human. An unnatural pose that sent a cold chill up Skyler's spine. The pause lasted barely a second before the man charged forward. Before Skyler could think to breathe, the white-clad figure had closed half the distance to Finn and showed no sign of slowing. This was not flight, like the other, but aggression. A snarl of pure hatred contorted the man's face.

Finn saw it, too. He spun and raced back, dropping the fire extinguisher and raising his index finger in the air. He twirled it in a tight, fast circle.

"Way ahead of you," Skyler said.

Compared to his pursuer, Finn's pace might as well have been a jog. The burned man tore across the ground, feet pounding, that snarling face growing more terrible with each loping step. Finn disappeared from view below the hull of the aircraft. Skyler felt his gut twist as the thing that hurled after him vanished underneath the canopy only two seconds later, like a hunting dog closing on wounded prey.

"Finn!" Skyler shouted.

He heard a clang. Then a thud that vibrated through the craft.

"I'm in!" the pilot called back, breathless. "Get us off the ground!"

"Take the stick," Finn commanded once they were out over open water.

The textured metal of the flight controls was cool to the touch and somehow reassuring, as if Skyler could draw reason and clarity from the emotionless machine after what he'd just witnessed.

He struggled with what it all meant. Africa, or at least North Africa, was lost. There could be no other explanation for the burning van and its two deranged inhabitants. Whatever calamity Finn and Skyler had flown equipment in to fight—disease or chemical weapon, it made little difference—had spread from southern Chad to Alexandria like the wind.

He glanced over his shoulder, east toward the massive city on the horizon. A blanket of smog marked its location— he'd seen that on the way in—but there were smoke plumes now as well. That meant fighting, or perhaps looting. A breakdown of society in a matter of hours. Skyler's gaze drifted north to the blue waters of the sea below. He thought of Finn's comment about a naval blockade. Even if such a tactic could contain whatever this was, Skyler knew it would be too late.

There were boats in the water below, all moving away from the coast, headed toward Italy, Greece, or Turkey. Spain. *Christ,* he thought, *damn well anywhere but here.* His stomach tightened at the thought that these may have been the last to flee. But surely there'd been smarter people who'd left earlier, who'd flown or driven. . . .

Beside him, Finn leaned back in his seat and pinched the bridge of his nose again, wincing. He'd said nothing since returning to the aircraft, except the order for Skyler to handle the controls. The veteran did not give up that task easily or often. The minimum required, in fact.

Skyler flew to Naples, only to receive an automated message that the airport had been placed on emergency lockdown. Terse orders from home compelled him toward Madrid instead. He landed there, without approval from local authorities, at the far end of a dark and empty landing grid.

Engines off, he left Finn in the cockpit and went outside. A warm breeze carried the smell of smoke. Skyler studied the windows of the distant terminal. There were bodies in some of the seats, unmoving. Someone ran from one side to the other, another chasing.

"No thanks," he muttered.

Finn had barely moved. Skyler patted him on the shoulder and settled back in. He reported their status. The orders that came back instructed him to take off, get to cruising altitude, and circle while awaiting further instructions.

That, he thought, did not sound good at all. "They have

no idea where to land us," he said to Finn. The pilot just grunted.

At altitude, Skyler pulled the slate from his pocket and palmed it. The screen lit up with information. He eyed the connection status. An ad hoc link had been made, but with zero participants. Skyler swore inwardly. There were the usual slew of commercial options, and of course his military band, but he'd been trying those for two days only to find his access locked down. Not surprising given the nature of their mission.

HocNets were another matter. Their topography was transient, amorphous. Swarms of personal devices talking directly to one another without any underlying infrastructure or membership requirements. Silence there unnerved him even more than the deranged lab worker who'd charged Finn on that windswept field. Silent HocNets meant no one was talking. Not even in Madrid below. There should be hundreds of thousands in a city that size. Millions. Someone should—

Finn shrieked.

At first Skyler didn't know what he'd heard, so shrill and high was the sound. Then the pilot started to kick wildly at something below the dashboard.

"What is it?" Skyler asked, unbuckling himself. "Snake? What?" Something nasty must have crept aboard while they'd been sitting outside, waiting.

The pilot kept screaming between desperate sucking breaths. His boots mashed frantically at the pedals in the footwell.

"Knock it off," Skyler rasped. "You're going to break something—" He placed a hand on the captain's shoulder. Finn recoiled so violently his head cracked into the low ceiling. The man thrashed now, clawing at his harness, pushing Skyler away. Kicking all the while at something in the darkness of the footwell. A kick grazed the rudder control, lurching the aircraft to the left and throwing Skyler off balance. He fell, caught himself on the armrest of his own seat.

"Captain, get ahold of yourself! Go in back, I'll take care of whatever's down there."

A flicker of recognition in terrified eyes. The pilot had his legs fully outstretched now. He drew breaths like a man deprived of oxygen. Lurching heaves of the chest, followed by almost childish whimpering exhales.

"Go," Skyler repeated, more forceful now despite talking to his superior officer. "I mean it." He tried again for the shoulder. This time Finn only flinched at the grip. His breaths were coming easier now, too.

"My . . . my . . . ," the pilot said between rapid inhales. "My shoes . . ."

"A scorpion? Spider?"

"I, I . . . Please . . . help."

A goddamn spider. Skyler fought the urge to slap the man. He activated the autopilot and leaned, awkwardly in the cramped space, to untie Finn's boots. A bead of sweat dripped off his brow as he pulled the first one off. The pilot was holding his breath.

When the shoe came away Finn exhaled.

Skyler peered in. Held it upside down and shook. Nothing. He glanced at Finn. The man was pale. Sweating visibly, lip quivering. His gaze met Skyler's, only for a second, but in it Skyler saw profound terror and something else, too. Embarrassment.

Grimacing, Skyler took the other boot in one hand and pulled, ready to drop his fist on whatever nightmare fell out. The boot resisted, then gave. A centimeter, no more, but Finn flew into hysterics unlike anything Skyler had ever witnessed before. He pulled away so fast the boot in Skyler's hands flipped upward, spinning before it slammed into the ceiling.

Finn flailed as if fighting invisible restraints. Skyler just managed to keep focus on the falling shoe as the other man made a frantic scramble from his chair. He was out through the rear of the cockpit before the boot landed, slamming the door behind him.

Through it all Skyler had never taken his eyes from the shoe. Nothing had come out. He tipped it over, cautious until his patience ran dry. Finally Skyler lifted and shook it as he had the other, one fist raised and ready.

Nothing.

"Empty!" Skyler shouted toward the door.

No response came. Then something thudded against the door.

"Captain? The shoe was empty. Relax, okay?"

Skyler heard Finn speaking then, difficult to discern thanks to the door and the low, fractured voice. Skyler pressed his ear against the cool barricade.

". . . don't . . . want . . . to be like this. Like them. Like me. I will save you."

Save me? Skyler turned the handle and pushed. The door didn't budge. He put his shoulder into it and managed a few millimeters, just enough to get a crack of light through from the galley space and the cargo bay beyond. Not enough to see his pilot, or what blocked the door.

"Stay away!" Finn shrieked. "It's all . . . falling."

"Open the door, Captain. I'll help you." Sedate you, more likely. Skyler racked his mind, unable to recall the contents of the medkit on board. Surely there must be something suitable in there.

"The door," Finn said. "The door."

"That's right. Come on now, everything's—"

Hydraulics hissed to life, then an incredible rush of air that sucked the cabin door open enough for Skyler to get his hand through. Frigid wind buffeted his hair and clothes. He should have acted more quickly. Should have known instantly what Finn intended. With all the shocks that afternoon the sudden loss of cabin pressure just left him numb, baffled. Frozen for precious seconds, tugged against the door by a violent sucking rush of air out through the back of the plane. By the time Skyler had the presence of mind to override the cargo door and seal the aircraft, Finn was long gone.

Skyler found himself standing alone in an empty cargo bay. The pilot and everything else had been yanked unceremoniously from the aircraft, four thousand meters above Madrid. All parachutes accounted for, still in their locker. Captain Finn Koopman had committed suicide. Skyler swayed on his feet, unable to concentrate. Nothing that had happened this day made sense.

And yet it did. The realization hit him so suddenly he felt his knees buckle. Seated on the floor, Skyler forced himself to say the words aloud. It was the only way he could believe it.

"It reached us. The disease. Finn . . . we both were exposed."

I'm a dead man, Skyler thought over and over. The next few hours went by in an erratic blur. He took the co-pilot's chair—couldn't bring himself to sit where Finn had. The radio he turned off. To check in now, to report what had happened, would probably result in the aircraft's immediate destruction. He wouldn't blame them, either. He didn't want to be the man who brought this ailment home. But he could see beyond that, could see himself differently. A sample, racing ahead of the infection, that could be studied.

He set to work.

Two hours later an aircraft set down in an empty field three kilometers outside Volkel air base. A message, automatically sent upon touchdown, brought swarms of soldiers in hazmat suits and a small armada of vans emblazoned with disease-control logos.

When the engines cooled sufficiently a huge tent was erected over the quiet vehicle. Quick-drying cement sealed the special structure to the ground.

The rear cargo door opened. Soldiers readied their weapons. Orders were to take the single occupant alive, if possible.

When the heavy door finished its rotation downward and crunched into the dirt, the warriors in yellow suits hesitated.

The man inside—a Lieutenant Luiken, co-pilot with a spotless service record, noted for his levelheaded conduct—crouched on the floor of the aircraft with his hands chained and locked to a tie-down. A set of keys lay a few meters away, well out of reach. He wore a full-face mask attached to a tank of air. When he spoke, his muffled voice sounded apologetic. "False alarm, perhaps," he said. "I feel fine, but take all precautions."

One of the suited people came forward, carrying a small

tube instead of a rifle. "Sorry about this," she said, and pressed the cylinder against Skyler's neck.

The world melted away.

When his senses returned, Skyler found himself lying on a bed of white sheets in a white room. The air smelled like plastic. Brilliant LEDs on the ceiling brought tears he blinked away. His neck hurt, as if something had bitten him. The tube, he recalled. Sedated, then, which meant they'd taken him seriously. "Good," he said aloud. More of a croak, really.

"What's good?"

Skyler turned toward the woman's voice. She stood nearby, wearing the white and blue uniform of the medical division. Unsuited, unmasked. He wanted to shout at her for her carelessness, until he realized what it meant. "I'm okay, then," he said.

"Yes. How, exactly, we've no idea."

He tried to touch the bruise on his neck only to find his hand, both hands, cuffed to the gurney. The chains rattled when he yanked. "I suppose these are unnecessary?"

The doctor stared at him. Karres, the name on her uniform read. "Are you one hundred percent sure you were exposed, Lieutenant?"

He'd explained what happened in his message. It dawned on him suddenly they might not believe it. They might think . . . "Ninety-nine," he said. "I don't know how it spreads. I was in the cockpit with him, though. We were both in Africa—shouldn't you have your mask on?"

"The tent is sealed."

"But you're inside."

The woman's lips tightened. She came closer. Her voice fell to a whisper. "Not just Africa, Lieutenant. It's . . . spread."

He studied her face, saw fear and fatigue.

"They're calling it SUBS," she said.

"How far, dammit?"

Her lower lip quivered. She bit it, then stood and crossed the room. "I've maintained the seal on the tent because I don't want it to get in."

The weight of the words seemed to press him down on the bed. "Uncuff me."

"Not yet," she said.

"Why?"

She turned back to him, another tube in her hands. "Because I don't want you to try to stop me."

"What? What are you doing?"

She stepped closer, priming the syringe. "Listen to me carefully. You're immune. You may be the only such person, so you must survive. You have to get to the WDC facility in Abu Dhabi. They've got the best chance of finding a cure for this thing."

"Then release—"

"Be silent."

Before he could speak again she jabbed the tube against the side of his neck.

He woke to an utterly silent room. The cuffs had been removed. A note waited for him on a rolling table beside the bed:

The worst may be over, but now there's little time. I'm sorry for that. I had to keep you from leaving too soon.

Survive. Remember the World Disease Control offices in Abu Dhabi. They can study you. It might help.

Please, Skyler. Hurry.

                    —Lotte Karres

She lay on the floor a few meters away, head propped against the wall, chin resting on an unmoving chest. Her lips were blue, her face unnaturally pale beneath the splay of blond hair that hung across her cheeks. She'd cuffed herself to a cabinet rung on the wall, and an open bottle of pills lay on the floor beside her.

Skyler lay still for a long moment, letting a wave of nausea and grief pass.

On a chair opposite the doctor's body lay Skyler's neatly

folded uniform, boots on top. He swung off the bed and lifted the footwear away. Beneath lay a set of keys and a hand-drawn map of the nearby air base with one hangar circled.

Skyler dressed in silence, trying not to look at the dead body. She'd killed herself rather than breathe air from the outside. The idea made his gut twist.

Clothed, he lifted the first boot and paused just before inserting his foot. The memory of Finn, of the panic attack he'd suffered, rushed in. He'd leapt from the plane because of some imagined terror in his goddamn boots. The disease, SUBS, had turned the most casually confident man Skyler had ever met into a gibbering maniac in mere hours.

Whatever was happening outside, this woman had judged it so dangerous that she'd sedated Skyler to prevent him from rushing outside to help. He would have, too. She'd seen it in him.

Mind reeling, he left the room, which turned out to be a portable unit mounted on a flatbed truck. His aircraft still rested where he'd landed it, under a massive white tent just like those he'd seen in Africa days earlier. They'd sprayed it with something, leaving a milky residue on every surface.

He left it there. The airlock at the edge of the tent lay open, unguarded.

Outside he found bodies. The sun had just risen, and the air was cold. Soldiers and doctors alike lay in the grass. Many had pressed their hands to their heads before succumbing. Those with their necks exposed showed signs of a rash on either side of the spine.

Skyler went to the nearest soldier and took the man's assault rifle.

Lotte's note rattled in his head. He should listen to her. Fly to Abu Dhabi and help if he could.

His eyes were drawn north, though, toward Amsterdam, where his family lived. He couldn't just flee. He had to know if they were like him. Immune, a genetic trait. It was possible, wasn't it?

Somewhere in the darkness a person screamed with inhuman terror. Another sound answered. It could only have been called a roar, yet he knew this to be a human as well.

Both sounds ended abruptly. Then a third, farther off, just at the edge of hearing. Laughter.

If his family shared the immunity, and they were stuck in a city with sixteen million diseased . . .

Skyler stole the nearest truck and drove toward Amsterdam.

The world had fractured.

Fires dotted the landscape. Flames no one fought. Bodies were everywhere. Splayed out on the road or still in the seats of smashed cars run astray.

Not everyone had died, though. The dead outnumbered the living, but the survivors . . . something was horribly wrong with them. Most that Skyler glimpsed were either fleeing, terrified at the sight of his truck, or rushing toward him with snarled features and blood on their clothes.

He swerved away from the aggressive ones at first. But their numbers were too great, and the roads were already crammed with the crumpled husks of vehicles. Eventually he just focused on avoiding the cars.

Each thud of a body against his truck drained a little more of his compassion until he felt cold, almost robotic, in his quest to reach home.

On the outskirts of Amsterdam the expressway became too clogged. He left the truck and moved on foot along a canal. Away from the hellish landscape of the road, his numbness began to fade. He wasn't sure if that was a good thing. The weight of the calamity lurked behind it, anxious to crush his determination. He paused at the bank of a canal and stared at the gentle current.

You may be the only such person . . .

He had no idea what he would do if that were true. It was not, he found, something he wanted to consider. Not something he would accept until he'd searched every corner of the globe for another like him.

A splash in the narrow canal focused his attention. An elderly man crouched on the opposite bank, one hand thrust into the murky water. He had filthy gray hair matched by an unkempt beard. Sores dotted his face and arms. As their eyes met, the ragged man pulled his fist from the water, drew it high over his head, and slammed it down again. The water that splashed into his face did not break his intense, icy gaze.

"It's leaving me!" the old man cried.

"What is?" Skyler asked.

"Everything . . ."

He toppled forward into the lazy current, emerging a heartbeat later in a dog-paddle swim, steel gaze utterly locked on Skyler. The man's lips curled back in a snarl, revealing crooked yellow teeth.

Skyler raised his rifle, then stopped. Despite the malice in the old man's eyes, he swam slowly. He might not even make it across. "Forgive me," Skyler said, and ran north along the bank.

He kept to the canal, relying on his mental map of the city to guide him. The sloped embankments became concrete walls, with a narrow walkway just above the waterline and the occasional stairwell leading up to the streets above.

A riverboat floated by, its lone occupant sprawled face-down on the foredeck. Closer to the city he began to see corpses drifting along in the current, too. At one bridge he saw a city bus, nose in the canal and tail end resting against the concrete span above, clasped by the twisted wreckage of the railing.

Skyler couldn't bring himself to look inside the vehicle. Doing so might force him to acknowledge what his heart already knew: The scope of this, the scale of death and destruction, was absolute. He focused on the narrow passage between the bus and the canal wall, turning sideways to squeeze through.

As he passed the bus a mewing sound came from inside, barely audible, like a wounded animal. Skyler sidled past. Shards of broken glass crunched under his feet. In the shadow of the bridge, darkness enveloped him. He kept going until the sound of glass beneath his boots ended, and then rushed to the far end of the underpass.

The mewing turned into a feral cry. Skyler surged forward, turning back only at the edge of the bridge's shadow. Behind him, a body slid out one of the shattered windows and fell to the concrete with a grunt. He could see only a silhouette. It looked—

Another body slid from the bus, then a third. The trio stood in unison. They all faced him, waiting as if sizing up their prey. There was something primal in the way these diseased behaved. The old man's words came to him then. *It's leaving me! Everything* . . . Everything that made him human?

The trio rushed Skyler together. One ran low, using its hands like two extra legs, an odd way for a person to move, yet somehow it looked natural.

Skyler raised his gun, but thought better of it once again. He'd never shot anyone before. So he turned and fled, racing along the walkway, the sound of baying savages closing behind him. A stairwell ahead. He sidestepped into it and bolted up the steps three at a time. At the top he turned, intending to shoot the lead pursuer and hopefully trip up the other two. A better use of ammo. But his foot caught on a crack in the pavement as he spun, sending his right leg slapping against his left, his body twisting as he fell to the ground in an awkward roll. The gun clattered away, sliding beneath a van.

Skyler crawled to the vehicle. Lying on the asphalt, he reached into the darkness underneath, toward the rifle. The people chasing him were close. He glanced toward the stairs in time to see the leader's head appear above street level. Panic gripped him. His fingers probed for the weapon, his mind caught between the ancient instincts of fight or flight.

His fingers brushed the gun, and in his haste he only pushed it farther away. There were footsteps on the street now, and new grunting sounds coming from somewhere else. Abandoning the rifle, he stood and ran. Across the bridge, dodging slumped bodies, toppled bicycles, abandoned cars. At the end of the bridge he turned and bolted down a narrow walkway that lined the apartments along the canal. Footsteps followed him like unwanted applause. He slipped into an alley, glancing back as he ran. Six followed him. Seven.

At the end of the alley he leapt over a bike that lay on its side, limp rider still on it, hands clasped over the sides of a white helmet. A policewoman, Skyler realized. He skidded to a stop, rushed back, and looked for her holster. Her dead body covered it. Skyler heaved with one arm, grunting with the strain as he fumbled along her belt for the holster. The diseased were silhouettes in the dark alley, racing forward.

His fingers found the gun. Skyler stumbled backward as he hefted it, thumbing the safety as he did so, silently thanking his firearms training. He could barely see the approaching people in the alley, but the space was narrow. Whip-cracks echoed along the passage as he unloaded the clip. The lead pursuer tumbled and rolled, limp. The one behind it went down. The third leapt over the first two, landed in a crouch. It made no effort to dodge the gunfire, as if it had no understanding of the weapon. Skyler shot it in the throat, saw the life vanish from its eyes even before it hit the pavement just a meter away. The realization that he'd killed would only hit him later.

The gun clicked empty on his next trigger pull. In the alley the infected still barreled toward him. And there were more now. Skyler had emerged on a wide avenue, lined with restaurants and boutique shops. Dead bodies were everywhere, part of the landscape. Here and there, though, some moved. They emerged from below shady awnings or from the doors of smashed storefronts, glass crunching beneath their feet.

They're not attacking their own kind, he realized suddenly. *They know I'm different.*

He heard the electric motorcycle before he saw it. The sleek bike burst into view on the sidewalk between Skyler and his pursuers just as the next one emerged from the alley. The rider leaned at the last second, rear tire skidding along the concrete until it slammed into the shin of the diseased person, who lurched backward from the impact, arms flailing, crashing into those behind.

"Get on!" the rider shouted as the skid ended, the bike facing back in the direction it had come from.

Skyler leapt on. He slipped one arm around the rider, his empty pistol pressed awkwardly between them.

The man twisted the accelerator, producing a shrill whine as electricity flowed from the caps to the motor. Skyler almost lost his grip as the motorcycle surged into motion. Immediately the rider swerved left, then hard right, dodging obstacles in the road. The motorcycle barreled through a thick plume of smoke that spilled from a burning shop. Beyond a baby stroller lay on its side, mother and father sprawled behind it. The sight hit Skyler like an enormous weight. Everything he'd seen up until now suddenly became very real. The scope of it all, crashing in. *World's end. Has to be. This is it, and I'm . . . I'm . . .*

He focused on gripping the man's torso as the nightmare blurred by.

The man wore no helmet. His hair, a mess of long dreadlocks, whipped in Skyler's face and smelled of incense and pot. "Name's Skadz!" the man shouted over the roar of wind. He spoke in English, London-accented.

"Skyler!"

"You a cop?"

"Air force. Pilot."

"Good." Skadz made a sharp left, tilting the bike low and accelerating out of the turn into a narrow alley. A stray dog snapped at Skyler's knee as they roared past. The animal had blood on its jaw. Somewhere an alarm wailed.

The bike lurched, flew up a ramp. Darkness engulfed them. Skyler glanced back in time to see a metal gate rolling closed across the entrance to a parking garage before Skadz turned again. He slowed their pace now, rolling between rows of identical sedans parked over wireless charging units. The vehicles were all white, with blue and orange stripes on the side panels. Police cars.

Skadz rolled into an open elevator door, bringing the bike fully inside. He swiped a card through a reader on the wall, then tapped the button for the eighteenth floor. The compartment lurched to life. "I was here when all these blokes started acting strange," he said. "Some were laughing or crying; most were screaming about the headache."

"You're a cop?" Skyler asked.

The man turned to him, an eyebrow raised. Then he chuckled and shook his head. "Never mind what I am. What madness made you enter the city?"

Skyler swung his leg over the seat and stood back as

Skadz dismounted. "My parents live here. I thought they might be . . ."

"Like you?"

"I hoped maybe it was genetic. What about you? No symptoms?"

"Zilch. I feel fine. Well, as good as I can with all this shit going on."

Skyler studied the man. "How'd you know I came from outside the city?"

A chime sounded their arrival. Instead of answering, Skadz rolled the bike out and left it leaning beside the elevator door. He led Skyler down a long hall between cubicles and offices. There were no bodies here, Skyler noted, but things were in disarray. Blood stained the carpet in many places.

At the end of a hall was a door propped open by a roll of toilet paper. A large biometric reader on the wall beside it had been smashed to pieces.

"Holed up here since the madness started," Skadz said, leading the way inside. "Figured it'd be good to get a proper picture of what's going on."

The massive room contained row upon row of dual-screen monitors, laid out auditorium-style with desks in front of each. Again there were no bodies.

On the far wall, which rose ten meters from the floor of the room, was a series of huge sensory-quality displays, already adjusting to provide depth based on Skyler's position in the room.

All of the screens displayed images from around the city. Security and traffic cameras, Skyler realized. "That was smart, coming here," he said, genuinely impressed.

"I'd about given up hope until I saw you walking along that canal. I don't know the city that well so it was something of a bitch to track your path."

Skyler sat, leaned back. "You saved my life out there. Thanks."

The man shrugged. "Had to. You're the first sane person I've seen, Skyler, and I've been watching the city all bloody night."

To that the pilot had no response. If true, and if the disease kept spreading at the rate Skyler had witnessed so far, then he may well be witnessing the world's end. He told the man his story, from the encounter near Alexandria to the doctor who protected him from the initial wave of infection.

"You're a lucky bastard," Skadz said, "and that doctor was wise. The first few hours . . ." He fell silent, shuddered. "Almost everyone just died. Hands clasped around their heads, screaming like you can't imagine. A right fucking mess. The rest, the survivors, are like animals. They flee or fight. Alone or in packs. I watched from here while I could stomach it."

"One spoke to me."

"Yeah," Skadz said. He nodded sadly. "Some can still string a few words together, though that particular skill seems to fade pretty fast. Care for a pint?"

The question caught Skyler off guard. He mumbled agreement and studied the room's monitors as the other man busied himself with a camping cooler stuffed below one of the desks. Every screen seemed to offer a window on death and chaos. Bodies were everywhere, so many the ground itself could barely be seen. The diseased moved among them. A pack perhaps fifty strong roamed the left side of one screen, picking their way through the dead. One pulled a half-eaten pastry from the hand of a woman, sniffing at it as if it had never seen such a thing before, then tentatively took a bite.

Without warning all of the diseased froze, dropping slightly. They glanced off to the right in eerie unison, toward a light-rail station. Then they started to move back.

An automated streetcar rolled into view, pushing aside bodies like a boat through water. The train powered through the corpses with relentless, mechanical drive.

He couldn't look at it, this ocean of death, any longer. He let his eyes drift to the background, to the beloved skyline of the city. A skyline ablaze. He imagined the disease sweeping through, catching millions unaware, and millions more who tried desperately to flee. They'd left food cooking, fireplaces lit. Knocked candles from restaurant tables as they fell. Lost control of cars, spilled down stairwells or from balconies. Airplanes must have fallen like rocks.

Skadz walked over with two bottles of golden liquid,

handed one to Skyler, then sat again. "What part of town are they in? Your parents."

"Off Herenstraat."

The man tapped some controls on one of the screens. A map appeared. "I don't know the city well. Point it out?"

Skyler did. His new friend—possibly his only friend in the world—traced a circle around the area, and the screen zoomed inward. Little camera icons popped up all around the neighborhood. Skyler pointed at one.

While a connection was established, Skyler tried to picture his elderly parents sitting on their balcony or strolling in the garden square behind their simple apartment, oblivious to all this chaos and death. Then he tried to imagine them, immune, fleeing the city. Skyler's gaze flicked to the horrors displayed on every other monitor in the room. He knew in his gut they would not have stood a chance.

An instant later the camera view from a traffic signal on Herenstraat appeared on the screen. Skyler leaned across Skadz, panned, and zoomed along the quaint block of retirement flats until he found the building his parents lived in. The door stood open. Bodies lay on the steps leading to it and on the sidewalk below. He scanned each but none looked like his parents.

After a few minutes of searching the street he found them. They were side by side in the end, in their car a hundred meters down the road, boxed in on all sides by others trying to flee. Skyler zoomed in, and the enlarged picture, though grainy, left no doubt. His father had pulled his mother's face to his chest so she wouldn't have to see. They'd died there, in a traffic jam.

Skyler slumped into a chair and stared at the high-resolution image for a long time. He waited for the grief to come. Craved it. Needed it after everything else. It never came. There was only emptiness. Eventually he reached up and flicked off the display.

"Sorry, man," Skadz said. "Honestly."

"At least they didn't turn into those . . . animals."

Skadz said nothing. The room became very quiet.

"What's your plan?" Skyler asked.

The other man drained his bottle. "Survive," he finally

said. "Haven't thought about it much beyond that. Why? Got a plan?"

Deciding he could trust this man, and not keen on being alone, Skyler told him of the disease-control facility in Abu Dhabi. "I intend to fly there. I think this doctor was right—there might be something about us they can study."

"Us?"

Skyler nodded. "Come with me. You seem resourceful. And, Christ, there might not be anyone else."

The other man stood abruptly. "There's something else you need to see."

He led Skyler to an office a few floors up. Inside he gestured to a wall display. On it, two news anchors sat across a table from Neil Platz, the famed business tycoon. All three looked at once tired and yet hyperalert. There was no sound.

"What's this?" Skyler asked. Then, "Shit, you didn't record them as the infection set in, did you?"

"Nah, man, this is live."

Skyler glanced from the screen to Skadz, then slowly back. "Live? So it hasn't spread that far—"

"It has. No need for sound to tell you what they're talking about. They're saying Darwin is safe. That bloody alien cord, the Elevator, is protecting the city."

"What? You're joking."

"No, I am not."

"But that means . . ." Skyler said, and stopped, the words too ridiculous to voice.

"That means the disease and the space elevator are related," Skadz said for him. "Fucking Builders, man. Mental, isn't it?"

Neither spoke for a long time. The image shifted from the interview with Platz to live scenes shot around the Australian city. The streets were packed like Amsterdam's, but not with the dead or infected. Skyler saw anxious crowds praying in front of a church, then a shaky shot of a running street battle. The camera cut to the now-famous sight of Nightcliff, where the Elevator connected to the ground. A line of riot police stood between the complex and a throng of citizens.

"It's no picnic there, either, mind you," Skadz said, "but if Abu Dhabi doesn't work out you'll want to head there."

Skyler looked away from the screen and regarded the man standing beside him. They couldn't be more different, yet they shared the immunity. "Come with me," Skyler said. "It's possible we can help."

Skadz cracked an unexpected grin. White teeth in stark contrast to his dark skin. "Beats hanging around here, I suppose. But if they want to poke us with needles, I'll volunteer you for the job."

PART 2

Promise of Violence

Chapter 1

HOWARD SPRINGS, AUSTRALIA
15.APR.2278

The rusted shell of the ancient Land Cruiser rang like an enormous bell when the bullet tore through. Another finger-sized hole among the thousands already there, the result of a century or more of target practice.

Samantha lowered the rifle, satisfied. She slipped the butt under her arm and rested the barrel across the crook of her elbow. With her free hand she plucked a bit of orange foam from her ear and looked at her student. "See? It's pretty easy."

The teen removed an earplug as well, copying her counselor. "Doesn't it hurt your shoulder? You know, when it kicks?"

With a shrug Sam stepped behind the girl and, using slow, deliberate movements, helped her get the hunting rifle into a proper hold. With the sound of the gunshot receding into the bush, birds restarted their chatter in the trees around them, as if providing commentary on Sam's aim and the shot to come. Beneath that conversation droned the constant hum of insects and other, nastier things. Sam knew that as long as they were shooting, the crocs would stay away, but that didn't stop her from flinching at every movement in the shadows among the low zamia palms. Under the press of the noon sun, the waist-high trees glowed like jade-green torches below the much higher ironwood canopy.

A whip-crack Sam felt more than heard radiated through the forest, silencing the birds again. A few took flight. Ferns rustled as something small fled through the undergrowth.

"Wasn't quite ready," Sam said, using a pinky to dig at her ringing ear.

The kid, Marni, fifteen and already a dropout, lowered the barrel. "Did I hit it?"

"I didn't see. I wasn't ready." Sam knew she'd missed, though. The Land Cruiser hadn't rung.

"Sorry." Marni spoke too loudly, ears plugged.

Sam stuffed her own plug back in and sighed. "Try again."

The girl fired. Her shot sailed high, making a thin noise as it passed through foliage. "Fuck," Marni said.

"Language."

"Sorry."

"And you don't always have to apologize."

"Sorry! I mean . . . shit. Sorry." Her shoulders heaved as frustration built like a gathering storm.

Sam rested a hand on the girl's back. "Just . . . relax, okay? It's your first try. Take a deep breath this time. Fire at the end of your exhale." Snipers did that, she'd read somewhere. Sam never bothered, but then, she'd never shot at something this big and missed.

Marni fired again. Missed again. She slumped her head forward, blond hair falling across her face. Sam, who had seen this posture before, swallowed. It was the reason they were out here, in the middle of the reserve, shooting things. Bonding. Trying desperately to find something the troubled child was good at. A skill she could wear like a badge. Apparently guns weren't going to fill that void. Probably for the best, really.

Moreover, Sam had been tasked by the camp leaders to teach Marni how to avoid the kind of funk she'd just descended into. Sam knew the feeling well; she'd lived it at the same age, attended the same camp. Anger had been her problem. Violence. Three neighborhood boys ended up in the hospital for trying to get a peek up the only skirt she'd ever worn.

"I'm worthless," Marni said with a tight voice.

Sam took the gun then. Gently, but she took it. She pulled the magazine and stuffed it in her pocket, then emptied the chamber and slung the weapon over one shoulder. Marni just stood there, head down, facing the carcass of the old truck.

Just like me at that age, Sam thought. Same attitude. Same blond hair and sky-blue eyes. A hint of freckles across the cheeks. They could be sisters, except for the difference in height. Marni was a few centimeters shorter than most of the girls at the camp. Sam towered over all of them—even the ranger, Kirk, who would be considered tall except when standing next to Samantha. She had him by half a head.

"Just . . ." Sam paused, considering her words. "We just need to figure out what you're good at."

"And then what?"

Sam shrugged. "Depends on what it is. If it'd been shooting—"

"I don't own a gun."

"If shooting was your thing," Sam said, willing patience, "you'd join a team. Aim for the Olympics, or the police."

Marni folded her arms. "I want to live in orbit."

At that Sam had to suppress a snide reply. Every kid on the planet wanted to get off, and not in the colloquial sense. They wanted to live above, thanks to the constant barrage of info-sensories that Platz Industries released into the airwaves. Wanted to ride the vaunted Darwin Elevator up to gleaming space stations, perhaps see the alien craft firsthand. Such jobs were afforded to a very select few, and none of them were troubled fifteen-year-olds. "They have security guards up there," Sam offered, vaguely remembering that. "They carry guns, I'll bet."

The girl dropped to her knees and curled up. She wrapped her hands around her head and weaved her fingers together, rocking back and forth slightly.

"Look," Sam said, resting a hand on her shoulder. "So you're not good at shooting. So what? There's a million other things—"

Marni let out a soft cry. More of a moan, really.

Oh, for fuck's sake.

Sam's slate chirped from the car, a short distance behind them. She'd left it on the front seat and had ignored similar chirps all morning. It could be only one person: Ranger Kirk. He was the only one allowed to have a comm able to link to the outside nets. Sometimes he'd share news, big important stuff like rugby scores, but otherwise he kept quiet about the wider world. Camp policy. It seemed like a burden lately, too, Sam thought. The man had become withdrawn, even jittery, in recent days. Maybe there'd been a terrorist plot against the Elevator or something. Whatever. He'd refused to talk about it, and Sam didn't much care.

Kirk should know not to interrupt a one-on-one like this. Sam sighed. Now seemed the perfect time to give Marni a little room. Saying nothing, she left the girl where she was and walked to the rugged, mud-splattered vehicle. Behind her Marni moaned again. Sam rolled her eyes and stuffed the rifle behind the driver's seat before picking up her slate.

It vibrated in her hand as she read the screen. Ranger Kirk, who else. Sam answered, pressing the device to her ear for privacy. "In the middle of a tender moment here—"

"Sam! Jesus! Get back . . . fuck. Get back! Get—OH HELL!"

Sounds popped and gargled through the slate, automatically switching to the external speaker when she yanked it away from her ear. The noise temporarily drowned out the queer, hollow moan that Marni was still making.

"Kirk!" Sam tried to shout above the scuffle coming through from his end. One of the kids must be having an episode, Sam thought, and if she wasn't careful Marni might start one of her own any second now. "We're on our way back. Try to—"

A roar came through the device. A sound so loud and savage that Sam jumped, dropping the little slab into the dirt between her feet.

She knelt. The fuck was that noise? A dog or something? It couldn't have been one of the kids. No human being could make a sound like that. "Time to go, Marn!"

The slate had landed facedown, activating the passive screen that covered the back. She'd set the thing up to display a large clock and some other bits of info that might be worth knowing when her alarm went off each morning. The clock read 12:04 P.M. The information below read: 22 MISSED CALLS. 16 NEW MESSAGES.

"What the hell?"

Sam didn't get sixteen messages in a week. Kirk must have really lost his marbles. Then she noticed the little globe in the lower right corner. The outside feed had been restored. Baffled, she plucked the thin slab between two fingers and brushed the mud from it. Then she walked to Marni and hauled the moping girl by her arm to the passenger's seat. The kid never stopped holding her head, and she let out a fearful yelp as Sam thrust her into the vehicle.

Sam barely looked at the girl as they bounced down the dirt trail toward the campsite. Showers of brown water went up from both sides of the vehicle as Sam took the deep puddles without slowing. Marni cowered in her seat as if they might die at any second, a stark contrast to the eager delight she'd shown on the drive out at similar speeds.

"Maybe driving is your thing," Sam said. "Tomorrow you take the wheel, huh?"

No reply. Ahead Sam could see the lodge between the trees.

"Look, we'll find it. Something you're good at, or you love to do. And we'll figure out a plan for you. Okay? Everyone has a niche. You just have to find it and grab on. All right?"

Marni had her legs drawn up, knees touching her chin, arms still clamped around each side of her head.

"Jesus," Sam said, reaching toward the shaking girl with her left hand.

She froze. Marni's neck bore an angry, mottled rash. "Are you sick or something? I'll slow—"

Something thudded against the hood of the car, rolling up and over the windshield, leaving a smear of blood on the glass. Sam stood on the brakes, capacitor-regen whining in response as the car skidded to a halt.

Sam's heart hammered in her chest. "Stay here," she said, and pushed her door open without waiting for the inconsolable girl's response.

Outside Sam's feet landed in an ankle-deep puddle. Mud sucked at her shoes as she worked her way toward the rear. The road was quiet. The birds, the wildlife, silent.

A body lay in the road, ten meters behind. Samantha's

hands went to her mouth as she recognized the uniform even under the dirt and mud. Ranger Kirk.

To her amazement he moved, groaning, and pushed himself up to a half stand. They stared at each other for a few seconds before Sam found the nerve to speak. "I'm so sorry! Are you . . . I mean, are you okay? Jesus Christ, man, what were you doing in the road? I . . ." Sam trailed off.

Kirk's head had tilted to one side, as if he hadn't understood a damn thing she said. And then he coiled, rocking back on his feet, his movements primal, more animal than human.

A car door closed. Sam jumped at the noise, turned. Through the window she could see the empty passenger seat. "Shit. Marni!"

The sound of rustling foliage caught her attention, a dozen meters into the underbrush. Sam raced around the back of the vehicle, half expecting to see a crocodile waddling across the open ground toward the sick teen.

What she saw instead was worse.

The girl was running.

Marni was fifty meters away already, racing between the low palms, oblivious to the fronds that whipped at her legs. And, Sam realized, she was screaming. A high, warbling sound born more of fear than pain.

Sam started after her, then remembered Kirk and turned to where he'd been.

The ranger was two steps away and closing, hands outstretched, face an ugly snarl.

There was no time to think, no time to try to make sense of anything—the spooked girl, the fact that Kirk had been hit by the car and now apparently wanted revenge. Sam just reacted. She ducked under Kirk's hands and drove a shoulder into his midsection.

The older man grunted, whirled, and clawed—fucking clawed—at her face. A clumsy move from a bloke half dazed after getting thrown over the top of a vehicle. Still, one finger ripped across Sam's nose and cheek before she could swing. Her fist took him full in the face. She felt the cheekbone give, heard the sick rattle of teeth grinding.

Kirk staggered, went down on his ass, and then came

again. His arms, she realized, were covered in blood half-way up to the elbows.

"What the fuck is wrong with you?" Sam screamed, stepping back.

He kept at her, spitting blood. She could see redness around his neck for a brief instant, some kind of rash. Then he was on her, hands going for her face again.

"Enough!" Sam yelled, driving her knee up into his groin. He wailed but didn't stop. She swung again, this time not holding back. Her fist lifted him off his feet and sent him down on his back.

He groaned once and went still, a trail of blood running from the corner of his mouth to the reddish brown dirt.

There was no sign of Marni.

Sam glanced ahead. She could see the camp a few hundred meters down the road. And she could hear more sounds. Screaming, a racking cry, and worse, laughter. Insane, maniacal laughter.

Though she couldn't say why, Sam began to jog that way. The fact that she was leaving Kirk in the road never crossed her mind. Chasing Marni into the swamp did, but the girl was already out of sight, and the sonic horror show coming from the direction of camp refused to be ignored.

Ahead the main building came into view. The wooden structure had all the rustic charm one could expect from an Outback Survival School for Troubled Teens, nestled deep in an Australian reserve. Hand-carved driftwood signs served as a guide. Mess hall that way, cabins the other. Big Lodge in the center, an attached garage off to the left.

The normally quaint lodge now had its front door wide open with a body lying across the threshold, coils of intestines and gore trailing inside. One of the boys. The nerves in Sam's gut tightened into a ball of dread. What if one of the kids got to the gun locker? Some kind of rampage? *Oh God.*

She was still a dozen meters from the door when a cold rush of adrenaline finally swept the fear and pain aside. Something terrible had happened, but she might still be able to help. Sam swallowed and tried to see the situation with fresh eyes.

The dirt road widened into an informal parking area in

front of the structure, then branched off east, toward the river, and west, toward civilization. Sam glanced west. Thirty minutes to the highway, another ten to East Palmerston. That's how long it would take for help to arrive. She fished the slate from her pocket and tapped the red emergency-call button. Without the boost of a HocNet her signal was weak, but she still managed to get a connection after a few dreadful seconds. Sam pressed the slab of metal to her ear and waited, feeling suddenly exposed and very, very alone.

A pleasant voice informed her that all addressable channels were in use, and said to try again later.

"Figures," she said to herself, ready to toss the device aside, until she saw the reminder of sixteen messages, only now the count had reached twenty. She skimmed them:

FROM: Mum
MSG: Are you watching the news, dear? It's so horrible.

FROM: Mum
MSG: Don't worry about us. Your dad put up sheets on the windows.

FROM: Mum
MSG: Neighbors arrp4]

"What the fucking hell?" She skipped to the end.

FROM: Chelsea
MSG: Darren safe im driving there plz call

Sam tapped out a reply to the last one, only to get an error that no service was available. *Who the hell is Darren?*

Movement caught her eye, to the right. A girl had burst through the foliage and stopped in the middle of the uneven road. Despite the filth that covered the child, Sam could see the blond ponytail even from here. "Marni! Come to me!"

The teen stayed put. Unlike Kirk, she kept her face turned slightly away from Samantha and her eyes downcast. A submissive posture in stark contrast to the savagery the park ranger had shown. The rest of her body expressed it, too. Hands shaking at her sides, not raised to fight. The toes of one bare foot lightly pressed into the dirt as if she wanted to be able to flee at any moment.

"What happened to you?" Sam asked.

Slowly, achingly so, the girls eyes lifted to meet Sam's. The contact lasted only an instant before the girl flinched and glanced toward the lodge. Sam forced herself to look there, too.

Two people were in the doorway, one hunkered down on all fours, the other standing with his hands grasping the empty frame of the opening. They both had the same expression Kirk wore. Narrow eyes and bared teeth. A simmering promise of violence. Sam swallowed hard. She vaguely recognized both of them as members of the camp. Two kids.

Just kids.

The crouched one moved first. She darted across the planks of the building's front deck and raced toward Marni. The girl, Sam saw, was already running away at incredible speed. A rabbit being chased by a dingo.

Sam turned back. The one in the doorway hadn't moved, but he'd coiled.

"I don't want to hurt you," Sam said, voice wavering. "Please . . ."

The kid rushed forward, closing half the distance before Sam broke and ran for the car. She felt a weight clapping against her thigh as she ran and she remembered the magazine of ammunition in her pocket. The rifle behind the seat.

She'd never make it in time. The deranged teenager was closing fast. And if she did make it, what then? Shoot him?

"No." Sam had to voice the denial to kill the thought. She couldn't hurt one of the kids, no matter what drug or poison had driven them all crazy.

So she ran. She'd find help. If it was a drug they'd all taken, it would wear off.

Sam raced past the knobby-wheeled car and kept going. Tears were streaming from her eyes, and her lungs burned with the exertion. She darted between trees, down a hill, and across a neck-deep stream that on any other day she would have given a wide berth for fear of crocs. And she kept going.

Sometime later she realized she couldn't hear footsteps behind her anymore. Sam slowed to a jog, then a walk. Finally, she collapsed.

Samantha lay in the lumpy mud for a long time, staring at the maze of branches and leaves above her and the blue sky beyond. Shadows crept across her face as the sun made its lazy migration, ever oblivious to the shit mankind got up to.

I have to go back. She mouthed the words to the sky. *It must be tainted dope. One of the little snots must have snuck it in through the garage window, hidden it. They must have spiked Kirk's food, too, before anyone realized it was a bad batch. Damn kids. Goddamn designer drugs.*

"One tiny little flaw in that theory, Sam," she said aloud. With a mighty effort she sat. Then she was up and walking through the bush, hands dangling at her sides as her mind sought answers.

Something had happened, something big, or it wouldn't have garnered messages from her mum down in Perth and Chelsea over in Sydney. What, though? "Marni," Sam whispered to the swaying branches. "Marni was with me. She didn't take any . . . and Mum said they put sheets over the windows. What in the . . ." A chemical spill, or germ warfare? Australia had had plenty of jealous neighbors since that alien cord arrived.

She needed information. Two weeks in the media-free camp had left her—everyone but Kirk, really—isolated. And Kirk had been a sour wreck the last few days. He'd known about this, the bastard. Known and said nothing.

Sam increased her pace despite having no idea what she'd do. At the car she paused. Of Kirk there was no sign. At least, she thought, she hadn't killed him. Carefully Sam pulled the passenger door open. The rifle lay there, tempting, but the thought of shooting at any of the teens, even as a warning, made her stomach churn. She left it and grabbed a remote for the garage door instead, an idea forming.

At the lodge she ran at a crouch around the side to the garage. She removed the unlatched padlock that kept it closed at night and stuffed it in her pocket. No sign of the kids—of anyone—but she heard noises from the lodge. A moan, then a snap-jaw response that left the hair on her neck standing. These were bestial noises, yet she knew they came from human beings. Sam swallowed and went to the rear of the garage, using a conveniently placed log to shimmy into the small high window she knew the kids used to sneak in and out sometimes. She should have reported the broken latch, or moved the log, but hadn't. The idea of catching one of the teens coming in or out seemed useful, another possibility to bond, perhaps. A huge mistake, in hindsight, if tainted pills had been smuggled in here.

As she landed, a jolt of pain shot up through her shins. She stayed on the ground, crouched and listening for ten seconds. Eventually her eyes adjusted. Sam crossed to the interior door that led into the lodge, then fished the key from her pocket and locked it, wincing as it clicked. Then she crept around the edge of the space to where a stepladder hung from a hook on the wall. Taking care not to jostle any of the tools hanging beside it, Sam took the ladder down and moved back to the space below the window. She set it up there and climbed back out the way she'd come.

Outside, the birds were singing. She stood at the edge of the garage for a long time. Listening, watching. Letting her nerves settle. Finally, she walked to the center of the dirt lane in front of the building and cupped her hands over her mouth.

"Is anyone in there?"

Instantly she heard scrambling footsteps, more than one person, and then a noise like a primate's call. Something moved in the trees behind her, too. Sam glanced back and saw one of the boys crawling out from the underbrush, twigs in his hair and a deep cut across his forehead. His eyes were narrow, full of rage.

Sam turned back, swallowing her fear. Four more kids emerged from the front door of the lodge. Another from the far side, opposite the garage. The one who'd chased Marni, she thought.

Sam was surrounded. By all of them, save the girl who'd fled and the ranger she'd decked. Just as she'd hoped.

A moment passed. A pause of primal evaluation. Pack hunters evaluating their prey before some silent signal gives the order to strike.

They came with a ferocity she'd never witnessed, never thought possible, not from people. Sam held her ground, watched them come, reached into her pocket, and pressed the button on the garage remote.

Off to the side, the wide door rattled and squeaked as the old motor pulled it up into the ceiling.

When she could hear the rapid footfalls of the one behind her she took off, angling toward the garage. She pumped her legs until they burned as the six deranged teens fell in behind her, snarling like animals.

Sam ducked under the rising door. She made straight for the stepladder, leapt, and hit the top step as the fingers of her right hand grasped the window ledge. She shoved her left hand, still clutching the garage remote, through the open frame, curling her arm to gain purchase on the wall outside. She pressed the button with her thumb while she pulled, kicking at the same time. Her body slipped through the window as she heard the ladder crash to the ground, a shriek of frustration from one of the kids, and the rattle of the door as it started to close again.

Sam fell to the dirt behind the garage, landing badly on her shoulder and rolling. She bounced up, ignoring the pain. She tossed aside the remote and fetched the padlock from the dirt where she'd left it. She rushed back to the front of the garage just as the door reached the ground. With a grunt she slipped the padlock through the metal hasp at the side of the door and snapped it closed. Locked.

Sam backed away, heaving in breaths, ignoring the freakish howls of anger and frustration coming from behind the door.

These were not sounds people made.

"I'll bring help," she shouted, fighting tears. "I'll come back. Try to . . . try to rest, okay? If you can understand me, sleep it off. I'll find someone who knows what to do."

Whether they could hear her over their wild, frustrated

shrieks, Sam had no idea. She couldn't stay and listen to that sound any longer.

The rugged car had enough cap to reach East Palmerston, just. Someone there could help. Paramedics. Police, too, though that stung.

There was no sign of Ranger Kirk on the road, or Marni. Sam had to force herself not to stop and search for them. The reserve was massive, and Marni at least had fled with shocking speed.

"At least we found your skill, little sprinter," Sam said under her breath.

PART 3

Barrier of Sanity

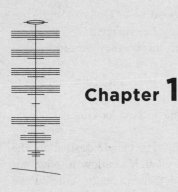

Chapter 1

At the twenty-eighth floor the elevator doors slid open and a handsome young couple entered.

Nigel Proctor flattened himself against the back wall to make room and smiled amicably, despite mild disgust in the woman's gaze and a very obvious sizing-up from her man.

They stood with their backs to Nigel. The man said, "Lobby," same as Nigel's destination, and then slipped an arm protectively around the girl.

Ah, Nigel thought, *the alpha male and his mate. Honeymooners? Perhaps a little tryst?*

The car chimed in acknowledgment and slid quietly back into motion. A speaker on the ceiling doled out "The Girl from Ipanema," as all elevators were apparently hardwired to do. Nigel grinned and hummed along. Idly he wondered if the climbers along Darwin's space elevator followed that universal law and decided probably yes.

After a few seconds Nigel realized Alpha Male was staring at him. A poisonous glance over one shoulder. Nigel stopped humming and cleared his throat. "Here on holiday?"

"Yes," the handsome wag replied, face forward again.

"I'm here to rob the hotel safe," Nigel said.

They both turned their heads. His grip on her arm tightened. The woman's eyes narrowed, jaw falling slightly open.

Nigel did a slight bow, nontrivial in the cramped confines

for a man of his generous proportions. "Only joking! Your reaction is priceless, by the way. Lovely teeth."

Her mouth snapped shut. In unison they turned back to the blank steel door.

"I am here to open a safe, but it's not robbery," Nigel explained. "All perfectly legal. I'm a locksmith."

"Good for you," the man said without looking.

"It is, isn't it?"

The elevator chimed. Lobby. The couple dashed out the instant the opening widened enough to allow it. Nigel allowed himself a second and then, casually, entered the lobby.

He felt good. He was here to do a job, true. Not a tryst, no lovely young thing on his arm, but a job. One that came with obscene pay. Besides, there were worse places to be in the world on that particular day. Africa, for example, which had all but disappeared off the digital map the day before. Total media blackout. Whatever political clusterfuck had started there this time must be pretty nasty indeed. Nigel couldn't bring himself to care much. The nets would return soon enough and there'd be a weeklong media shitstorm, but those were easy to ignore if one was so inclined.

A valet strode past, nose upturned and eyes forward.

"You there," Nigel called. "Direct me to the manager's office."

The man pointed at a corridor off to one side where a bland hallway, almost invisible in the grand lobby of the InterContinental, jutted off. Just then the young couple came back in from the street, she chastising him about forgetting his comm yet again. They stepped back into the elevator. Her eyes settled on Nigel as the door slid shut.

Straightening the lapels of his duster, Nigel crossed the lobby and ducked into the dark hallway. The long leather coat did little to conceal his bulk—if anything it accentuated it—but there was a certain confidence it gave him, the sensation addictive to the point that he wore the heavy thing all the time now, even on a balmy Sydney evening.

A security guard waited at the second-to-last door. The man, South Asian so far as Nigel could tell, inspected Nigel's offered passport with more scrutiny than airport customs had and, finally, opened the door.

Nigel found himself standing in an empty conference room. The walls were windowless. A huge monitor screen, currently off, made up the entire wall opposite him. Resting on the gaudy patterned carpet were six high-backed leather chairs and a large oval table with a green faux-marble texture.

On the table sat a safe. It was square, seventy centimeters on a side and jet-black in coloration save for the large tumbler dial and handle in brass. An antique. Nigel hadn't seen one like it in years.

"He's here," the guard said.

For a moment Nigel thought the man was talking to the safe, of all things, but then another voice emerged from a speaker concealed somewhere in the ceiling.

"Mr. Proctor," the voice said. It was gruff, Australian-accented with a hint of Indian upbringing.

"At your service," replied Nigel. "You must be Mr. Narwan."

"Indeed."

"I thought we'd meet in person. In fact it's a standard procedure—"

"You came here to convince us to upgrade our safe. I happen to be fond of this old mechanical kind and told your boss so. But he assures me you can prove such devices are easily bypassed."

"That's true, but—"

Narwan cut him off. "Open that safe inside ten minutes and we'll talk."

"Why ten minutes?" Nigel asked.

"Any safe can be opened given enough time," the man said. "However, if some nefarious cocksucker had access to my safe for longer than ten minutes, I've got other problems. I'd rather an intruder never made it that far, and fund my security precautions accordingly."

"Fair enough."

"So. Can you do it?"

"Yes," Nigel said.

"Without damaging the safe? Or leaving any evidence of tampering?"

"Yes. But your man has to wait outside, and any cameras or other surveillance gear in here must be turned off. Trade secrets and all that."

A slight pause. "The guard stays, but he'll face the wall. That okay with you, Jimmy?"

"Fine with me," the guard said.

"Mr. Proctor?"

Nigel grimaced but decided not to argue. A secondhand account might actually help add to the mystique his company enjoyed.

"The clock starts now."

Nigel slid his comm from his pocket and glanced at it. "There's still the matter of payment."

"Your fee," Mr. Narwan said, "waits within."

There was a click as the man cut the connection from wherever he was. Probably the office across the hall, Nigel thought, but it mattered little.

"Is he always so dramatic?" Nigel asked the guard.

"Most of the time, yes," Jimmy replied. He wheeled one of the chairs to the corner of the room, plopped into it, and turned himself to face the wall.

"You're going to hear some strange sounds," Nigel said, opening his case.

Jimmy raised one hand and gave a thumbs-up. "No problem, I've got the cricket test on."

Nigel grinned. Everyone had it on. Australia versus New Zealand, first round of the World Cup, live from Pakistan. Nigel didn't care much for sport, but given that he was a Kiwi on enemy turf, so to speak, he hoped the Aussies would do well today and be crushed later on, after Nigel had flown back to Wellington.

Focus, he told himself. Nigel set his heavy case on the conference table and opened it. Opening a safe like this was usually best solved with social engineering, unless one had the proper tool for the job. It just so happened Nigel did.

From his large brown leather case he removed a smaller one with a hard, red plastic shell. He set this to one side and removed his slate, propping it up next to the safe and powering it on. Then he opened the red case and surveyed the contents.

"How's the test?" Nigel asked the guard.

Without turning the man said, "We bowled a naught. Bad start. Wait, are you a Kiwi?"

"I am."

"Your boys are batting now. I think you might have us today."

A silvery bag lay nestled in a foam cavity on one side, barely large enough to hold a sandwich. Attached to one end was a nozzle and a one-meter length of surgical tube, which in turn was capped with a syringe. In another cavity rested a black cylinder that resembled a fountain pen. Nigel removed it and slid it behind one ear. Then he twisted the nozzle at the top of the bag and lifted the syringe.

Now, standing in front of the safe, he loaded the medical imaging software on his slate and prepped it to receive. When the green status came up he delicately slid the syringe into the tiny gap between the combination tumbler and the door of the safe. Nigel slowly plunged the stopper of the syringe down. A thick silvery foam began to flow down the tube and then into the lock mechanism. It was thick stuff and not easy to squeeze through the needlelike apparatus, but after a minute or so a few bubbles began to froth out from the bottom part of the circular gap. Nigel slid the syringe out, set it in the case, and plucked the black pen from behind his ear. He glanced at his slate, confirmed a ready state, and clicked the cap of the "pen." A thin, stiff wire protruded from the tip, barely a centimeter long. Nigel pressed it into the drop of silver goo that clung to the bottom of the lock tumbler and glanced at his slate.

"*No!*" the guard shouted. "Meat-pie bowling motherfu . . ." He trailed off, remembering himself.

"I need to concentrate here," Nigel said evenly.

"Sorry, mate."

A current in the wire activated the goo. The stuff, made for advanced medical imaging, was filled with thousands of tiny sensor packs. Each had a unique ID, and could sense the IDs of those around them in six directions. When the proper current was applied, they transmitted this information over microscopic near-field antennae, which the fluid conducted back into the "pen." The pen then repeated these signals over to the program on the slate. This was Nigel's understanding, anyway. It had been his boss's idea to procure such advanced medical gear for this purpose. Whatever was actually going on inside, within a few seconds the slate translated all this data into a three-dimensional model of the interior of the lock mechanism. Coarse and wobbly, the image nevertheless appeared on the screen. Nigel felt a bead of sweat drip down his brow. He wiped it away. This part was always the hardest. The simple act of understanding just what the hell he was looking at. There were perhaps five thousand sensors in the fluid, but even that quantity resulted only in a model that looked like some kind of avantgarde artwork made of wax drippings. Worse, the image was not of the lock, but of the empty spaces within it. Nigel forced his mind to imagine the inverse of what he was seeing. He spun the blob around slowly by tracing his finger across the screen, then stopped when its orientation matched the physical thing. Up was up, down was down. Good.

"Fucking hell," the guard muttered.

Nigel froze. "What's wrong?"

"Rumble on the pitch. Both teams are at it, plus a bunch of idiots from the stands. Sounds like a real piss-up. God. Even the announcers are at it. Wish I had video."

Rumble on the pitch. Nigel turned the phrase over and over in his head while urging the distraction into one distant corner of his mind and refocused. He gently rolled the tumbler counterclockwise, just one digit over on the dial. On the screen, a second passed without anything happening. He knew that, inside, medical goo had been stirred by that tiny motion. New positional data flowed in and the image updated. The bits that changed were highlighted in red by the software. He went three numbers clockwise and watched the update again, repeating this tiny back-and-forth motion a few times until he had what he wanted: a true mental picture of the mechanism inside.

Four wheels, so only four numbers to the combination. Easy. Nigel did a little jig and set to work.

The guard in the corner whispered, "What the fuck?"

Nigel turned, ready to kill the screen of his slate to pre-serve secrecy. But the man still faced the wall, engrossed in the cricket test. "Now what?" Nigel asked, his desire to ignore the man suddenly outweighed by the sheer astonish-ment behind the words.

"The damn feed's been cut. I mean, it was totally incom-prehensible anyway, just shouts and shit banging into the microphone. But now? Dead air."

"Power loss, probably."

The guard had his own slate out now. He poked at it fran-tically. Probably tapping into the HocNets for news from people at the pitch.

Not my problem, Nigel reminded himself, and focused once again. Hardly anyone used mechanical locks like this anymore. The manager of the hotel probably thought this worked to his advantage. Nigel readied his usual diatribe against the flawed theory of "security through obscurity" as he rolled the wheel slowly to the right. Each second or so the model on the screen updated. Being able to see the interior of the lock made cracking it something even a child could do. He rolled the tumbler until the notch on wheel one caught that of wheel two, then went clockwise until he had wheels three and four. The fence fell into place then. Si-lently. He doubted even with an earpiece he could have heard it. And that was a good thing. He didn't want the guard to turn around expectantly. Nigel tapped in the com-bination on his slate, then inserted a different syringe into the lock. A new signal coursed through the foam, forcing it to slacken. Nigel pulled the plunger back and sucked the modeling fluid out. Vaguely he wondered what the guard would make of the slurping sound. He glanced the man's way just to make sure he wasn't looking, but he was too busy with his slate. "Anything on the Hocs?"

"I don't . . . they seem to be offline. Pakistan, I mean. The whole goddamn place. Just like Africa yesterday."

That gave Nigel serious pause. There'd been no shortage of theories on what was happening in Africa. And yesterday parts of southern Europe had gone dark. And now Pakistan? Whatever it was, it was spreading, and fast. Some kind of

computer virus, that was the theory Nigel subscribed to.
"Well," he said, "worry about it later. Take me to your boss."

The guard turned in his seat, and goggled when he saw
Nigel brandishing the single envelope that had been inside
the safe.

An hour later Nigel was in the bar, keen to drink to his success. Novak & Sons would soon have a contract to supply
the hotel—indeed all eighteen locations in the chain—with
modern safes and the procedures that dictated their proper
use.

"Martini," he said to the bartender. "Shaken or stirred, I
don't give a shit. Very dirty is my only requirement."

The woman leaned against the inside edge of the bar, her
back to the customers, face tilted up and blue-lit by the sensory screen she stared at. She and everyone else, Nigel realized.

He followed her gaze. Three screens were mounted high
on the wall behind the bar. They all showed the same thing:
the wretched scene from Pakistan. The guard had been
right, it was an epic piss-up. RUMBLE ON THE PITCH scrolled
by in big block letters at the bottom of the sensory as perfect, vivid images of the melee were streamed one after
a-gut-wrenching-nother. Nigel looked away as a fist caught
one of the players on an already bloodied mouth.

"Amazing what people are capable of," Nigel said to no
one in particular. "I mean, it's supposed to be a civilized
sport, isn't it? Rumble on the pitch, indeed. Drink, bar-
keep!"

The woman didn't move. The people sitting on either side
of him were still. Nigel glanced back up at the screen. A trio
of evening newscasters was discussing the footage. He'd not
gestured for sound to be beamed his way and heard nothing,
so subtitles appeared in cartoonish bubbles. He caught only
snippets. Things like ". . . mystery ailment sweeps through
Pakistan . . ." and ". . . total information lockdown."

The last, "outbreak of biblical proportions," seemed excessive to the point of irresponsibility.

Nigel's comm bleeped. Not the fancy sensory-grade

model he used for legitimate business, but the throwaway he'd bought upon arrival in case a special assignment arose. The sort of work that required discretion. A little tingle ran up his spine. He fished the thin plastic slab from his duster's inner pocket and pressed it to his ear. No need to check the caller's name; only one person had the number. It took a few seconds for the encrypted link to complete its handshake, then came the sound of labored breathing on the other end. Nigel lowered his voice to a sort of whispered shout. "Boss man! Are you watching this atrocity?"

"Of course I am." This came as a surprise. Novak cared little for sport. The business was his life. "Everyone is. Was. It's unbelievable."

"At least you're not among Aussies." Nigel cast a sidelong glance at the other patrons. "I thought they'd be happier."

Novak spoke again. His breaths came in quick rasps. "Look. Something's come up. Are you in your room?"

"I'm at the bar. Untended!"

"Well get back to your room. Someone will be along to collect you."

Without a drink to finish, Nigel shrugged. "What about the job? We got it, by the way. Just paperwork now."

"Forget it. This one is more important."

In the elevator "The Girl from Ipanema" had given way to a horrendous interpretation of ~/funk's latest megahit, "Orgasm Organism." Even rendered by soulless piano the beat set Nigel shuffling from foot to heavy foot.

The door opened.

A man stood just outside, back to the elevator as if he'd not been waiting, but standing guard. His posture, the suspicious glance backward, his dark comfortable clothes . . . all of it put Nigel on instant alert.

"Mr. Proctor?" the man asked.

A myriad of clever replies flittered through his head. He chose "Yes?"

The man looked him up and down, then tilted his head and pressed one finger against a small black disk adhered to his neck just below the ear. "He's here. Yeah. Understood."

Nigel glanced past the man. Down the hall, standing in a patch of yellow light that spilled from the door of his own room, were two more stiff-backed gentlemen in dark clothing. Presently another pair emerged. The first, a woman, had Nigel's briefcase in one hand and dragged his overnight roller with the other. She looked vaguely familiar, as did the man who emerged behind her. He carried two black trash bags.

The group made their way toward the elevator.

On instinct Nigel moved back into the corner. He watched the approaching people closely, finally realizing where he knew the man and woman from. "Some holiday, eh?"

The woman swept into the waiting elevator first, pressing his briefcase into his chest. He clutched it. Her hand went to her pocket, came back out with a hotel keycard. "Thanks for allowing us into your room, Mr. Proctor."

He took the offered card, realizing belatedly it had been in his front left duster pocket when he'd ridden down. "I have an open-door policy," he said lamely.

The others filed in, cramming the small car. The woman selected the top floor, 83, and within seconds the chime began to count their progress.

Nigel glanced around. "I assume you'll explain who you are and where we're going?"

The woman turned her head slightly. "Were you not contacted?"

"Boss said to wait in my room. That a new job had come up and someone would be by to collect me."

"Which we've just done." She flashed a half smile. "Search him."

Nigel ignored the hands pawing at his duster and pant legs. "Penthouse suite safe, I'm to gather? The jewels of some wealthy dignitary? An executive's datacube, perhaps?"

Her smile ticked wider.

They examined the two locksmithing kits he carried in his coat, showing them to the woman, who gave the slightest of nods at each. Both comms were studied, thumbed alive for a few seconds, then returned along with the kits. "He's clean," one of the men said.

When the doors slid open the woman exited first. She turned left at the penthouse doors and continued down the hallway to a door marked ROOF ACCESS, where she paused and stared up at a discreet bubble camera mounted just above. Nothing happened for a few seconds, then an audible click from somewhere within the wall broke the silence. The woman pushed the door open and powered up a flight of stairs. Nigel followed.

A stiff, chaotic wind brought faint smells of the streets far below. He followed the woman out onto a landing pad. A clunker of an aircraft waited, white surface worn to bare metal in places. Little streams of black scarring trailed from every rivet, and the porthole windows were scratched and yellowed.

Five minutes later the cabin door hissed shut and they were airborne, powering into the sky on the wail of vertical thrusters. Out the window the pin-light jungle of Sydney slid by to the south and east, falling away with every passing second. Nigel shifted in his seat. They'd guided him to the middle row of three. The handsome wag sat in front of him, the woman across the aisle. Neither had spoken since entering the aircraft, their attention held rapt by the glowing screens of their pocket comms. Every now and then they'd glance at each other simultaneously, concerned.

Nigel checked his own devices. The cheap one simply demanded more credit to continue working. He stuffed it into the seatback pocket in front of him, happy to be rid of it. His other device, the high-end model, showed the usual steady connection of the state-run network, plus thirty-seven Hoc-Nets. These he unified into a single river of information and dipped in.

Garbage. Chatter. Kids, speaking a cryptic language anyone over twenty would struggle to understand. As a rule Nigel avoided this kind of shit. Anyone could say anything with as much anonymity as they desired. Information sloshed about, leaked, dried up in a frenetic unreliability that the youth mistook as energy. But in certain situations—an election, a catastrophe—the Hocs were useful. Nigel forced his brain to follow the flow rather than the individual ripples, hoping trends would emerge. The information drifted by, networks falling away as the plane gained altitude and distance, replaced by new ones almost as fast. Almost, but not quite. Steadily the counter dropped until, at cruising altitude and a hundred kilometers from Sydney, the river dried up.

In the blur of messages he'd spotted a few recurring themes that left him cold.

Gone dark.

Lockdown.

Lethal.

Flu?

His mouth tasted faintly of bile. He swallowed with an effort and let his gaze drift to the lone woman in the plane. She sat still. Relaxed, he could even believe, until his eyes slid down to the one hand he could see. Her white-knuckle grip on the end of the armrest painted a different picture.

Nigel became suddenly aware of the handsome wag leaning over him from the forward row, outstretched palmed turned up.

"Your comm," he said.

"What's your name?" Nigel asked.

"Call me Bruce."

Nigel glanced sidelong. "And that's Sheila, I presume?"

"If you like."

He grunted. "What I like is Rebecca, if we're pulling names out of thin air."

"Fine. The comm."

He handed over the device. Bruce passed it to Rebecca, who initiated the shutdown sequence. The man kept his gaze on Nigel, looking him up and down now. "Where's the other? I thought you had two."

"I ditched it. Only good for one use, you know?"

"Okay then." He glanced around at the others in the cabin. "Offline, everybody."

An hour later the aircraft banked. Out the window Nigel's view shifted from horizon to sky, and for a few seconds he saw the strand of winking lights that stretched up until they mingled with the stars. The grandiose sight of the Darwin Elevator eased his frayed nerves somehow.

The window shade came down with a plastic smack.

Bruce's hand lifted away from it, moving to the one immediately forward. Around the cabin, the other shades were drawn closed as the team busied itself with preparations to land.

Going in dark. Comms off. What has Novak gotten me into this time?

A whine started to tickle the edges of his hearing as thrust transferred from cruising vents to those pointed at the ground. Outside the metropolis of Darwin rose up to meet them. The city had a sloppy, haphazard layout born of centuries as a second-rate tourist stop before the explosion of development that followed the arrival of the space elevator. Beach town to metropolis in twelve years flat.

Rebecca turned and looked back at him. "The others will exit first and secure transport."

"You'd think that would soothe me."

She ignored him. "How much time will you need?"

"Somewhere between ten seconds and infinity, given I have no idea what I'll be opening."

The skin between her eyes creased. "Kastensauer. Mark 8."

Nigel's energy drained like air from a birthday balloon. He eased back into his seat and closed his eyes.

"Familiar with it?" Rebecca asked.

He nodded slowly. He knew everything now. "You're here to rob Neil Platz."

Someone in the cabin inhaled sharply.

Nigel sank farther into his chair, as if the gravity of this admission carried with it a physical force.

A few seconds later Rebecca spoke. "How did you—"

"There's only one Mark 8 in Darwin. I know because I installed it. Even if I hadn't, it would not be hard to figure out. Few other than Platz could afford such a . . . capable deterrent."

"How . . ." She faltered. For the first time he heard a crack in her confidence. "How much time?"

Her question barely registered as Nigel thought through the angles. The Mark 8, top of the line, installed at Nightcliff Secure Storage by Novak & Sons out of Wellington, the only authorized installer in this part of the world and one of five worldwide. The Mark 8, requested and paid for by Platz Industries.

The fucking Mark 8, impenetrable.

Not a single recorded breach since first introduced because it could not be breached save for one method: Get someone with access to open it for you.

Which is exactly what these grifters had done. Only . . .

Connections slid into place like the wheels of the safe he'd just cracked, each more quickly than the last until finally he arrived at the obvious conclusion.

This would be his final job.

Try to back out and Rebecca would have him killed. He'd seen their faces. No loose ends on a job of this magnitude. Failure would of course mean arrest, punishment. Perhaps he could claim he'd been coerced, but even if that worked he'd still never get another job in the field.

Success . . . would be just as bad. Once the theft was reported all evidence would point to him, again ending his career. Surely Novak knew this, and yet he'd agreed. Why?

Nigel glanced down at his massive round belly, his long leather duster. He was not the type of man who could vanish. Even if he succeeded and managed to leave the scene alive, he couldn't hide. Not for long.

"How much time?" Rebecca insisted.

Nigel cleared his throat. "To open it? Eight seconds."

She blinked, exchanged glances with her team. Eventually her gaze swiveled back to him, expression fixed somewhere between surprise and skepticism. "Eight seconds?"

"Correct." Eight bloody seconds, followed by an end to this life. Either a bullet to the head or a new career as a yak herder on the Mongolian steppe. No more luxury hotels, triple-diamond sushi restaurants, or Thai masseurs walking on his knotted spine . . .

The aircraft settled onto a landing pad, signaled by a brief chirp as the skids met concrete.

Bruce donned a pair of tactical glasses and moved, the other toughs right on his heels. They leapt out, avoiding the flimsy metal ladder, and disappeared into dim moonlight and a patter of lazy rain.

The cabin became uncomfortably quiet. Rebecca had

barely moved, her gaze on the comm held in both hands. Nigel saw motion on the screen. Sensory feed from Bruce's glasses, no doubt, though he couldn't make out specifics beyond the vague impression of dark hallways and then a stairwell.

Nigel coughed politely. The woman turned her head slightly, waiting. "What's going on, Rebecca?"

"They're securing transport. Once—"

"No," he said. "I mean out there, in the world. The HocNets . . . that cricket match in Pakistan."

"Haven't you been watching the news?"

"I had work to do."

She flinched, amused. The half grin returned.

Nigel squirmed under it. "I'm concerned."

"Why?"

"At best this job will end with me unemployed and on the run. My boss would know this, yet he sent me anyway, which puts him in a sticky situation. Something I know he would avoid unless . . ."

"Unless it was the end of the world," she said, voice flat and suddenly very cold.

Their eyes met and she held the gaze like a mirror.

Nigel faltered first. He glanced down at his hands, at the seatback, at anything other than the truth on her face. "God," he whispered. "What is it? No, don't tell me."

What could be in Neil Platz's safe that was so important it was worth stealing as the world ended?

Rebecca's comm chirped, shattering the moment. She focused on it, muttering commands and acknowledgments in rapid succession. Then she stood. "Come on. Showtime."

She led him down to a maintenance room in the basement. Through a double door, along an unpainted hall laced with exposed pipes, out into a fenced loading area. A large silver van waited, caps whispering readiness. SELBY SYSTEMS was stenciled on the side in large red letters. Nigel had no idea what the outfit did. Infotech, maybe. Rebecca ushered him into the back, where the men from the aircraft waited, dressed now in blue overalls with the same company logo.

Before the door swung shut Nigel glimpsed dark, low buildings and an empty skyline. A warehouse district on Darwin's outskirts, facing away from Nightcliff and the gleaming office towers that surrounded it.

He sat cross-legged on the floor. In the windowless space he felt the vehicle lurch, turn, turn again, then settle into traffic. Even at this hour the city bustled, judging from the sounds. Horns bleated. Foam tires whispered against wet asphalt as cars passed or were passed. Rain drummed on the roof like a thousand nervous fingers.

The van gained speed. The sound outside changed, somehow closer. An alley, perhaps, taken fast. Nigel sensed a sudden tension. He glanced about, found Rebecca staring intently forward. A sharp turn pressed Nigel into the wall. The woman had to thrust her hand to the ceiling to brace against the sudden, clumsy move.

"What's going on up there?" someone shouted.

Ultracapacitors below the van's floor sang to life as power surged into the motors. The van hummed along. Every little bump and pothole sent a jarring thud through the cabin.

"Something's wrong," one of the men said to Rebecca.

"I know."

Another sharp turn, one that dragged on and on, marked by squeals of complaint from the tires. Sudden deceleration threw everyone forward. An elbow dug into Nigel's rib cage.

Somewhere ahead the driver's door opened and slammed shut. Footsteps, someone running. A muffled gunshot, then silence.

Nigel held his breath. Three seconds passed without a noise. " 'Fish in a barrel' mean anything to you blokes?" he asked, jerking his head toward the door.

They glanced at each other, logic beating out surprise. Someone pulled the side door open and the occupants spilled out into some sort of vacant warehouse. People were shouting. There was no coordination to it, no grace. Just panic and adrenaline. Sensing what would happen next Nigel threw himself to the floor.

Gunfire filled the vast room outside.

He pressed his arms over his ears as concussion waves of

sound assaulted them. Hundreds of shots in the span of ten seconds. So many they almost drowned the shouts of rage and extinguished cries of pain. Bullets thudded against the vehicle and clattered around on the floor by his head.

When the shooting stopped he looked up.

Bodies littered the concrete floor outside. Bruce lay among them, faceup, vacant blue eyes staring at the ceiling above. A smoky haze clung to the scene and filled the van with the smell of burned gunpowder. A bit of glass fell and shattered.

Someone in the distance moaned softly like a homesick dog. A single gunshot ended the sound.

"Check the van!" someone shouted. Footsteps followed.

Movement in the van yanked Nigel from his shocked numbness. Rebecca unfolded herself from the far corner of the dark space. She met his gaze and raised a finger to her lips as she moved, quiet as a whisper, to the open door.

Two men in street clothes appeared at the opening, guns trained on Nigel.

Rebecca swung herself out, landing in front of one. Her knee met his groin as a swipe from her arm knocked the barrel of his gun aside. The man fired, bullets spraying high.

Nigel pushed himself to one knee. The second thug had forgotten him, surprised by Rebecca's appearance. Nigel pushed off the back wall of the cabin and launched himself into the man, roaring like a bear. The thug tried to dodge, shifting back on his feet as Nigel's massive frame collided with him. They toppled over, Nigel groping for the gun even as they fell, but the man's grip held. They hit the ground and the man rolled away, coming to a knee in the same motion, raising the gun.

Nigel had no time to dodge or flee. He raised his hands like an idiot and clenched his eyes closed.

The gun clicked. Empty.

"Fuck," the thug said.

Nigel rose, advanced. The thug had time to flip the gun around and swing it like a club. Nigel danced to the side as best he could, taking the blow on his thigh with a meaty smack; so solid was the impact that the gun wrenched free from the bastard's hands.

On equal footing now, Nigel had the advantage. Fists

raised, he stepped in, blocked a poorly aimed punch, threw one of his own. It took the man on the chin, not solid but enough to tip the scales. Nigel followed up with two more strikes on the same spot, each more powerful than the last. The third blow put the man down. Nigel kicked him in the side of the head for good measure, then wheeled about.

Rebecca stood over the other man's body. She was breathing hard and shaking her hands. Nigel glanced at her opponent and saw red marks around his neck where her fingers had dug in. She held a pistol in her hands.

"Job's off?" Nigel asked.

She shook her head and leveled her pistol at him. "Let's get going."

"You can't be serious."

She tilted her head to one side, one eyebrow arched. "Move, now."

"Listen, dear, we only do this sort of work when the money is right and the risk is minimal."

"The money is more than you can imagine. The risk? I'll find somewhere for you to hole up until I can identify another way in."

He grunted. "One that doesn't involve a car wash in bullets?"

"Ideally. Now move, before the backup arrives."

He hobbled along behind her, one hand absently rubbing at the growing bruise on his thigh. Near the exit he detoured to a coatrack. A cane leaned against the side. It had a dark wooden shaft, a brass plug on the bottom, and a fake ivory dragon's head for a top.

Nigel tested it, his fingers wrapping around the serpentine sculpture. He headed for the exit.

Rebecca met him outside the door. Her gaze traveled down to the ornate cane, then back to his face. "You look like a pimp."

He jerked his head toward the murky, warm underbelly of Darwin. "I'll fit right in."

Chapter 2

The decorated officer across the desk threw his slate down in frustration. He ran a hand from brow to chin, normally implacable features contorted in a mixture of fatigue and anger.

An old analog clock on the wall ticked the seconds away. Russell Blackfield kept his hands below the desk, his face carefully controlled. He knew enough to be silent here. No need to remind the lieutenant of the transgressions detailed on the slate's screen.

Disturbing the peace.

Disorderly conduct.

Indecent exposure.

Activity unbecoming an officer.

Best damned round of golf ever, Russell thought. He reined in the smile tugging at the corners of his mouth.

Lieutenant Rockne ground his teeth. A vein at his temple pulsed. The man was career military and looked it: buzzed head, gray at the temples and flat on top. Uniform trim and fit on a thin, muscled body. "I really don't need this right now, Sergeant. I really fucking don't."

"Yes, sir," Russell said.

Rockne leaned in, frowned. "You have no idea. There are things . . . there is something happening in the world, Blackfield, something major, and we're going to get caught up in it soon enough. A week, maybe sooner. I could have orders any minute."

Blackfield said nothing. He'd heard the rumors. A disease

or something. Flu. There might be panic in the streets when news leaks out, and the need for some restoration of calm.

The lieutenant went on. "And, honestly, you do this on the eve of the moon festival? What the fuck were you thinking?"

I was thinking a drunken round of golf cart jousting sounded like a lot more fun than slapping that damn white ball around and pretending to be civilized. Russell shifted in his chair. "I just wanted to entertain our guests. Um, sir."

"It's a miracle none of you ended up in jail. Thankfully I have some pull there."

"Yes, sir."

"Shut up. I don't know why I bothered to intervene. Get out of my sight."

"Yes, sir." Russell stood. The chair scraped on worn hardwood. He made it as far as the door before his superior spoke again.

"If you want any hope of R-and-R for the festival," Rockne began, "then at dawn you're going to take that group of fuckups you call a platoon back to the course, clean it up as best you can, and then march around it until noon. If any of you so much as make a goddamn sound, if I get a single complaint from anyone about noise or exposed genitalia or whatever else, I'll hold you *and only you* responsible. Don't think for a second you'll get leniency twice from me. Is that clear?"

"What about the staff meeting, sir?"

"Oh, right! Your presence will be sorely fucking missed, believe me. I'll send you minutes. Now, are we clear?"

"Very much so."

"I could strip you of your rank for this shit, Blackfield," he said, tapping the discarded slate on the desk. "If that's what you're trying to accomplish, as your behavior lately suggests to me, just say it and it's done. Otherwise, clean up your bloody act. I liked you a lot more when I'd never had reason to see or hear from you."

To this Russell only nodded. He slipped into the hallway and pulled the door closed behind him. He let his feet drag in the hallway and on out into the yard beyond. A cool evening breeze chased the day's heat away. A light rain had left a shine on the ground, a little polish before tomorrow's big party. By the time Russell reached his own barracks he had a spring in his step. *Tomorrow*. A bit of marching in the sun, a chance to discipline his own troops, then, later, the festivities. Weather reports called for clear skies. The girls would be out in tank tops and shorts, dancing under a full moon hanging directly above the Darwin Elevator. It hardly seemed like punishment at all.

Perhaps best of all, he'd done it. He'd lowered the bar. "A low bar is easily leapt," an old con man had once told him. *For a professional liar that old bastard sure was a fountain of truth.* He'd show Rockne, show them all, that he was a man who could take responsibility for his mistakes. And then, more important, transcend them. His turnaround would be the talk of the officer lounge for a year, and grumpy old Rockne would bask in the praise. "I stuck with him early on. I saw the potential within him, sure I did," he'd say. Asshole.

Russell's soldiers tensed when he walked in. Their eyes searched for signs of the verdict on his face and Russell took care to look coddled, even afraid, as he broke the news.

At dawn Blackfield roused his troops and led them back to the scene of yesterday's debauchery. They marched in full combat gear, faces painted camouflage and everything, and they had an audience.

Blackfield expected this. Soldiers from all the other platoons of First Brigade lined the sidewalks around the property. They'd been given leave to taunt, albeit silently, to their heart's content. This was not an opportunity soldiers passed up, and they'd turned out in force despite the hour and the festivities scheduled for the evening to come.

They pointed, laughed, and snickered behind hands held up to shield the sound of taking glee at someone else's punishment. They made rude gestures, pretended to copulate with each other and the trees—really anything, though they were careful not to show any skin. Orders were orders.

Blackfield moved up and down the line as his twenty-four grunts made their first circuit around the perimeter of the course at a brisk, curt march. He called a halt at the seventh green and set them about fixing divots and patching up churned ground where golf carts had made turns entirely too fast the day before. The watchers lining the street threw bits of trash onto the course. Russell would have, too, had he been among them. He wasn't, though, and so he kept his instinctual anger in check. When one of his own shouted an insult at the tormenters, Russell grabbed him by the earlobe and, with nothing more than a glare, set him to the task of fifty push-ups and instructions to catch up once finished.

By the time the sun rose there were citizens along the sidewalks, too. Most were watching; bemused, intrigued. Kids joined in the taunts and shook the perimeter chain-link fence with white-knuckled fists. There were so many now that they formed a human wall around the small course.

For the second circuit Russell drove his soldiers into a jog. Marching chants were only mouthed, as silent as the mocking versions coming from the line of observers. By the third circuit the novelty had worn off, though. The shenanigans of the day before were the stuff of legend by now and all of these bastards had missed it. They wanted a response to their jeers. They wanted a train wreck.

It finally happened when they reached the seventh green again. A group of privates at the rear of Blackfield's line stopped in unison and unleashed a barrage of thrown objects—rocks, clods of dirt, whatever they'd managed to pick up. It might have gone unnoticed, too. Russell had been focused trancelike on the backside of the female soldier he'd put on point. One of the rock throwers slipped, though. Wheeled his arms and flopped backward into the wet grass. A roar of laughter went up from the watchers and the watched alike.

Russell stormed to the back of the line. "What the hell is wrong with you?"

The soldier slipped again before coming to his feet, eliciting another round of muffled laughs from the onlookers along the sidewalk, ten meters away.

"Couldn't take it anymore," the kid said. Briar, by the name on his uniform. Russell barely recognized the spotty turd under the grass and mud splayed across his face.

"You'll take a lot more than that if you don't get your shit together."

"Yes, sir."

"That goes for the lot of you," Russell said. They'd huddled around to hear him. "Push-ups and sit-ups until we're back around."

They mumbled agreement.

"Now!" Blackfield roared. Action, then. They formed a line out of habit and dropped into a series of push-ups. He watched for a few seconds. Kicked a few boot bottoms to correct form.

Satisfied, Russell Blackfield turned away. The others had continued the circuit and were almost to the north side of the property now. It was a shitty course as golf courses went. Nine holes, all short and flat. Easy for the retirees. The course's proximity to the army base made it a likely spot for all sorts of shenanigans when the young recruits mustered up the courage to sneak onto it in the dead of night. Russell strolled across the gently undulating fairways, angling to meet his soldiers directly across from those being punished.

Mushy grass slurped at his boots. Each step left more blades of cut grass on the leather. Flecks of green on polished black. Behind him the crowd noise grew, as if following him, taking on a more and more riotous tone. The sound made his gut feel hollow, despite himself. He tried and failed to laugh the edge of danger away. Something felt wrong.

He glanced back. His troops were still at their push-ups, save one who just lay in the grass.

The crowd behind the fence had swelled, and now churned. Most, he realized with instinctual dread, were not looking at his punished soldiers anymore.

They were turned south, toward the base. He saw fists raised, though in triumph or anger he had no idea. He saw something else then, too. People running, soldiers from the base among them. Lots of soldiers.

"What the hell?"

Kids leapt onto the flimsy fence and climbed desperately for the top. A pair of legs cartwheeled above the heads of those near the back of the crowd.

Whole bodies, then, thrown into the air.

And then he saw the van.

The vehicle cut a path through the crowd at high speed. Even from here Russell could hear the high whine of the strained caps. The van forced its way forward, shoving bodies aside, bouncing as it undoubtedly rolled over others. Some of the onlookers had managed to hold on to the sides. One was even on the roof. A woman in business dress, screaming and clinging to a luggage rack for dear life.

The van slammed into the perimeter fence of the golf course at high speed, bodies sandwiched between. Russell's mouth went dry, positive the damn thing would smash straight through and run right over his exercising soldiers.

Amazingly the fence held. It flexed and then rebounded like a bowstring, throwing the wayward van back a few meters. Lifeless bodies between remained plastered to the fence. Bloody ribbons in diamonds of wire. People were screaming now. Everyone was fucking screaming.

A riot—that was the only word for it—rippled through the onlookers like a shock wave with the van as the epicenter. Some focused on pulling the driver out of the vehicle, presumably to beat the idiot senseless. At least half of them—and there were hundreds now, thousands perhaps—were doubled over in obvious pain, hands clasped around their skulls as if under a barrage of earsplitting sound. Some sort of anti-riot weapon? That was fast.

A gate flung open to Russell's left and people poured through like water through a burst dam. Soldiers from the base made up almost half of the throng.

Blackfield shifted on his feet. He'd been too stunned to move before. Now he just felt trapped. A hundred meters away, his exercising warriors had finally stopped their push-ups. Now most were kneeling in the wet grass, arms clasped about their skulls, anguish visible on their faces even from here. Many of those rushing in through the gate had stopped and taken up the same pose. They were trampled by those crowding in behind. A soldier's boot crushed the head of an old man who writhed in the churned earth.

Russell glanced over his shoulder and felt a chill course down his back and arms.

The chaos along the southern fence of the golf course was contrasted inexplicably by the shocked, frozen reaction of those on the north side. The onlookers there just stared in naked horror. His own troops had stopped, too. Watching. Baffled.

"To me!" Russell shouted at them.

A few raced forward, the fear and confusion on their faces held in check by a more powerful sense of duty. Or, perhaps a sense that some shit was about to go down and they were going to be a part of it. The others hesitated. Most would join when the shock wore off, Russell thought. *They'd better*.

He swung back toward the chaos to the south. Insanity had pushed through Old Downtown like typhoon floodwater.

"Must be that disease," a breathless voice beside him said.

Russell glanced to his right. Schmidt, his second in command, stood there gulping air, rifle held combat-ready.

"Heard it was a flu," Schmidt said. "But, holy fucking hell, look at 'em."

"Get your shit together," Russell snapped. "Can't be a disease. A disease doesn't stop in a line. Look: South side, riot. North side, fine."

"Sir . . . ," the younger man whispered.

"What?"

"Look." Schmidt jerked his chin toward the mass of people pouring in through the south gate of the golf course.

Blackfield followed the man's gaze. Many of those rushing through the gate were fleeing the violence. Citizens and soldiers in almost equal number. Some of those in uniform had spotted Russell and angled toward him.

Behind them were others. These weren't fleeing, they were giving chase. Their faces, every last man and woman and even child, were twisted in a rage so primal they looked like caricatures. One among them stood tall, walking instead of running though his face shared the same anger. Russell knew that face.

Lieutenant Rockne.

Their eyes met and the lieutenant's lips curled back in a snarl. Despite the writhing violence all around he walked in a straight line toward Russell. The city behind was nothing more than a seething mass of death and pain now. Russell heard cars crashing, saw a body burst through a third-story window and fall into the sea of animals below. *Animals, yes.* "They're all animals," he muttered aloud.

Those fleeing rushed straight past the line formed by Russell and his men. Most kept going, but many of the soldiers among them slowed, stopped, and fell into a loose formation.

Lieutenant Rockne came on, leading the pack like a wave toward the north side of the fairway.

"That's far enough!" Russell shouted. The words changed nothing. "I mean it! Don't make us—"

Rockne dropped into a low run. Sort of a half gallop. Those at his back surged along with him. There were so many now, and still they poured from buildings. Bodies lay everywhere, trampled like garbage. Far more dead than alive, Russell thought.

And all south of this spot. It was like he stood at a glass wall, safety on this side and hell on that. Only there was no wall, and when the monsters came . . .

"Move back," Russell said. "Back! Back! Now!"

He turned with his men and ran, the throng of diseased fifty meters behind and closing. A crowd ten-deep had formed along the north edge of the course. Many broke and fled when they saw the soldiers doing so, but a lot of them remained. Frozen by fear or perhaps, perhaps, ready to fight. Maybe they thought they could actually help. Those directly in Russell's path broke and ran when they realized he wasn't stopping. He ignored them all and made for an office complex across the wide street. The front doors of the building were open wide, two janitors standing just within watching the carnage with stunned expressions.

"What are we doing?" Schmidt asked over haggard breaths.

"Moving to a defensible position, what do you think?"

The janitors turned and fled inside as Russell reached the doors. Inside was a bare-bones lobby. Two desks on either side of a hallway leading back. He went behind one desk and flipped it on its side, crouching behind it. His men took up similar positions around him and in the hallway. To his surprise their numbers had swelled. Many of the soldiers fleeing the madness had found their wits, apparently, and fallen in with his squad. Fifty or more to go with his meager eight.

They filled the lobby, pushing back behind the overturned desks or in the hall. Only Russell's men had weapons; the others were all dressed simply. Olive tees and camo pants. Base garb.

A deep rumble began to build from outside the glass doors. Not a second later the stampede hit, smashing into the front of the building like a rogue wave. Floor-to-ceiling panes of glass along the building's façade shattered with the press of bodies, spraying shards across the black tile floor.

Lieutenant Rockne was first through the doors.

Russell Blackfield didn't hesitate. He'd already raised his gun, subconsciously, and now he dipped his head to the sight and fired twice. His superior officer took both rounds to the chest and kept coming. Someone else fired now, clipping him in the shoulder and sending him spinning, sprawling.

Rockne tried to rise, failed, and died.

The room erupted. It was as if the killing had finally made it all real, finally broken through some collective fog within which rules still applied.

Russell shot two more of the less-than-human creatures before the crowd became a confused mess. A writhing sea of clawing fingers and thrown fists. Behavior proved the only way to tell the sides apart. The infected were vicious. Utterly rabid in their desire to inflict damage on those still sane, most of whom were unarmed and cornered. They fought without a shred of dignity or even apprehension, and they were winning.

"Schmidt!" he shouted without looking.

"Sir?"

Russell whirled on him. "See if there's a way out the back."

"What? Leave?"

"Yes."

"But . . . defensible—"

"Fucking *go*."

The man nodded once and bolted down the hallway, staying close to the wall.

Blackfield rose from his crouch and took aim at the nearest savage combatant, firing a bullet into the thing's side just below the armpit. It toppled awkwardly, trampled almost instantly by a replacement. There were too many, and still more poured in.

"Schmidt!"

No response. Russell took aim again, stilled his finger just before shooting as a plain-clothed man tackled the diseased one he'd been about to kill. All around people were screaming and shouting. Some howled, a high, baying sound Russell didn't think could come from human lips.

One of the creatures barreled low into the midsection of the soldier at Russell's right, driving him into the lobby wall. Air rushed from the man in a muffled *hoof* and he went down, screaming. Russell lifted his rifle only for the movement to catch the creature's attention. It leapt off the fallen man and onto Russell in a single motion, driving him backward as they fell together. Its knee met Russell's groin when they hit the floor, filling him with an electric, all-consuming pain. Somehow he'd kept the gun and raised it enough to fire. The earsplitting crack drowned out all other sound for several seconds. His bullet hit the diseased animal in the leg just above the knee, exploding out the back in a splatter of blood that reached the ceiling above. It cried out and took a wild swing at him. Russell turned with the punch, using the momentum to his advantage, throwing his attacker into the shins of someone standing nearby. Russell sat and fired at it again, riddling the thing's back with small red circles.

His balls felt at once on fire and frozen solid. "Fuck this," Blackfield growled. "To the roof!"

Most of his soldiers and a few civilians heeded the call for retreat. By now bodies clogged the entrance to the building, stemming the tide of murderous freaks.

In the middle hallway Russell found a pair of elevator doors closing, the car full of terrified faces staring at him before the two barriers slid together. He kept moving, aware of a growing entourage behind him. The stairwell door pulled open easily. He took the steps two at a time, ignoring the pain from his groin, for three flights. At the end he vaulted a waist-high bar meant to prevent unauthorized wags from reaching the roof.

Outside the sun shone brightly on a gravel-covered roof. Plumes of oily black smoke rose from a dozen fires in Old Downtown. A few people stood about the perimeter, watching the calamity below. They whirled in white-faced terror when Russell pushed through the door, then relaxed upon seeing him.

By evening all the easy prey had fallen to the grinding, animalistic machine of the diseased. The streets below, while still rife with violence, nonetheless became preferable to cowering on a rooftop devoid of resources. "Time to move," Russell said, and ordered the surviving soldiers back down the stairs. They'd march, he decided, until they found answers.

If Russell Blackfield allowed his eyes to defocus, to look beyond the immediate dangers, the city resembled a volcano.

Still distant, the glorious space elevator could just be seen, marked by a few climbers visible between the tiny gap that separated skyscrapers from the clouds they reached for. The huge buildings were tallest near the alien cord's base, and tapered away rapidly. Fires small and large dotted the scene, like the glowing embers spat out by an eruption. Only this eruption was happening in reverse. Violence and destruction had begun at the edges and were creeping ever inward toward the peak.

A long row of sulfur-yellow streetlights marked the road to Nightcliff, wrapped in glowing orbs of smoke from the scattered flames. Flames that no one fought. The two-kilometer stretch of road, when he viewed it at the exclusion of all else, resembled a carnival. Vague human forms gyrating and dancing around the flames, the crackle-chatter of fireworks and celebratory gunfire. Except the people weren't dancing, they were killing each other. They were robbing newcomers and neighbors alike, they were banding together for mutual reasons and turning on each other when those reasons became nothing but well-intentioned dreams.

The sporadic gunfire was anything but celebratory.

Cars clogged the wide street. Every make and model imaginable. Most pointed straight along the path of lights, as every idiot in the north apparently thought when they arrived in Darwin they could just drive up to the Platz mansion and ask for a lift to the safe haven above. They were moths, Russell mused, drawn to a long, thin flame that stretched all the way to the moon.

Not literally, he knew enough to know that. But the moon indeed loomed large above them. That little astronomical event was supposed to have been cause for a party, something the city had been promoting for weeks. "See the great Darwin Elevator silhouetted against the full moon," the Hoc-casts said. *Nothing quite like having your big party canceled due to the end of the fucking world.*

A crash of metal on stone whipped his attention back to the immediate surroundings. Somewhere ahead a delivery truck had barreled out of a side street and slammed into an abandoned city bus. Russell didn't need to see the driver to know he'd lost consciousness in the impact, if not more, for even from here the sound of the horn could be heard above the riot.

Twenty people swarmed out of the same side street and converged on the vehicle, tearing open the back doors. When they swung open Russell saw half of the logo for a popular grocery chain on the door facing him, and understood.

"They're finally getting it," he said, to no one in particular.

All around him the uniformed men who made up the vanguard of the column voiced their agreement. During the first few kilometers of their march they'd all been stunned by the moronic things citizens pulled from shattered store windows.

The food truck drew more looters from the crowd at large, and as the contents began to dwindle the people began to

take from each other. A melee ensued. Russell had thought
he'd seen everything already on this march, but the sur-
prises kept coming. He saw an elderly man punch a teenage
girl in the face as she clawed at the bag of fruit in his arms.
He saw a couple work together to wrest an armful of cereal
boxes from a terrified woman, only to then run off in separate directions as they fled with their prizes. The man noticed the separation first, turned to look for his wife, or
whatever she was to him, and subsequently never saw the
pipe that hit him in the back of the head. Three others fell on
his limp body and tore at the cereal, sending a spray of
golden brown flakes into the air like confetti.

Russell laughed, then, wondering if this mob was really
any better than the savages at the rear of the column.

There were differences, to be sure. The infected didn't
flee at the sound of a gunshot, and they tore for arteries
rather than crunchy bran flakes. What they didn't do—ever,
apparently—was come to their senses.

"Keep moving!" he shouted. "All the way to Nightcliff,
mates!"

Then men hooted their agreement with uncanny unison,
producing a sound the crowd ahead could not ignore. The
deranged mob stopped their street battle and stared at the
approaching soldiers. Russell saw fear first, but then something else. Something more like hope.

They parted. Stood in silence as the column made its way
down the street. The infantry filtered around and over the
abandoned vehicles, not stopping to enforce law or restore
order, but marching with unwavering focus on the brightly
lit tower ahead, and the impossibly long cable that stretched
out from its peak all the way to the sky and beyond.

Russell's radio chirped. "Report," he said into it.

"Starting to quiet down back here," the reply came.
Schmidt, his second, at the back of the line.

"Good, because I need you at the front before we reach
Ryland."

"Copy that. On my way."

Blackfield holstered the radio and glanced ahead. The forest of buildings grew like a stepped pyramid toward the
main attraction. Many of the glass structures, especially

those without their own reactors, were dark. Plumes of smoke rose from dozens of small fires that licked out from broken windows or seeped up from the streets where vehicles, trash cans, and even bodies burned.

He soaked it all in. The whole city reverberated with an energy he'd never dreamed possible. Every last person pushed to one limit or another. Except for his men. They were an ice cube in a pot of boiling water, and Russell knew he needed to reach Nightcliff before it all melted away.

Schmidt arrived a few minutes later. Bags under his eyes matched the color of his buzz-cut black hair. Dots of blood were splattered across his cheeks, brilliant against the pale skin. "You look like shit," Russell said.

The man's eyes were huge saucers, unblinking. "We've developed a following back there."

"How many?"

Schmidt shrugged. "A thousand. More are joining."

Blackfield considered dispersing them, but on second thought decided they'd only make the arrival at Nightcliff seem that much more impressive. "Tell the men to ignore them. We need to keep moving, above all else."

"I did already. Anyway the clingers add a nice buffer between us and the crazies, so no one minds."

Russell nodded. "Casualties?"

The taller man blinked now, one heavy drop and lift of the eyelids. "Lee, Pickens, and Smith. Smith deserted, actually. Said something about finding his girl and ran off."

"He took his equipment?"

"Yeah."

Russell clenched his teeth. "Fucking prick. If he comes back he's shoot-on-sight, understood?"

Schmidt rubbed at his neck before nodding. "Yeah, of course. We all know the rules, sir."

"Good."

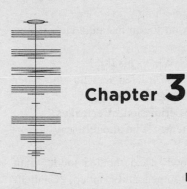

Chapter 3

The crowd in Ryland Square parted in almost biblical fashion at the arrival of one thousand bloodied, battered, angry soldiers.

Despite all the death, despite the waves of infected still worming in through the bizarre safe zone that supposedly circled Darwin, Russell felt his heart swell at the sea of eyes around him. In those stares he saw hope, admiration, fear, and, simplest of all, resignation. A thousand soldiers had drained the fight out of the crowd like a plug pulled from a bath.

Blackfield took care to meet none of those gazes. He kept his eyes locked on the entrance to Nightcliff. There a line of riot police stood, shields covering their bodies from chin to groin. Some held automatic weapons. Most held black truncheons. None held the expressions Blackfield had basked in from the crowd. No, these people were exhausted, hardened, soaked in bloodlust.

Russell aimed for the one in the center and walked right toward her. She was a short woman, a bit plump. A splash of blood across her riot mask hid most of her face from view.

"That's far enough," she said. There was no authority in her voice. She was parroting orders, nothing more.

"Who's in charge?" Russell asked.

"Braithwaite," she said.

"Which one of you is Braithwaite?" Russell barked, glancing left and right along the line of police.

The woman spoke. "He's in the tower."

"Why? He a coward or something?"

The woman's eyes narrowed for an instant. "He's trying to keep the peace."

"He's doing a hell of a job. What's his title?"

"Head of security, and he's ordered that no one enter Nightcliff without his express permission."

"Well go and fucking get permission, sweetcakes."

She ignored the endearment. "Who should I say is asking?"

"The *army,* you blind cow!" He'd shouted louder than he'd intended. The woman jumped as if slapped. "Lieutenant Russell Blackfield in command. That should be enough to get the wag's ear. In fact I want him to come out here and chat. Tell him. Hurry along, love. Double time."

She stumbled back, turned, and ran for the enormous cylindrical tower in the distance.

The crowd, silenced when the troops had arrived, began to whisper among themselves. The whispers grew to conversations. Talk was fine, as long as they weren't rioting.

Russell turned to Schmidt. He grabbed the man by the collar and hauled him close. "Pass word along to the men. Whatever food or booze they looted on the way here, share it. Smile and nod, be friendly. I want this crowd on our side when this bloke arrives. I want it clear that *we* made 'em settle."

"Gave yourself a field promotion, eh?" Schmidt said.

"And why the hell not? You get one, too, come to think of it. Now zip that shit up and spread the orders."

"Understood," Schmidt replied, and turned away. He couldn't have hid his half smile if he'd wanted to.

By the time the thin gray-haired man came up behind the line of riot police, the mood of the crowd had become almost like a celebration. They quieted as if compelled by some sixth sense when Braithwaite reached the perimeter.

Russell looked him up and down. Old, flabby. Tufts of white hair poking out from nostrils and ears. The type of man who liked to sip tea and complain about progress.

"Who are you?" the man demanded.

"I'm your bloody salvation, mate," Russell said.

* * *

They chatted under sulfur-yellow light in the recessed loading dock of a nearby warehouse. Out of sight of the crowd
and the soldiers, Russell felt naked. Braithwaite must feel
the same, and with his flabby old bag-of-bones body Russell
figured he still had the upper hand.

"Right, so what's the score?" Russell asked. "We've heard
damn little from anyone."

"Now just a minute," the old man replied. "I'm in charge
here. If you and your men intend to stay you'll have to take
orders from me."

Russell curled his hands into fists and planted them on his
hips. "Bullshit," he said.

Arthur Braithwaite glanced up, startled. Fear gleamed in
his eyes if only for a second. That was enough. "Excuse
me?"

"Here's how this is going to work," Russell said. "First:
I'm the highest-ranking officer in the army at this moment,
and my troops answer to me and me only."

Braithwaite's jaw gesticulated for a moment, then he managed a single, tiny nod.

"Second," Russell said, "you appoint me head of security.
Give yourself a new title. I'm under you, but in terms of
keeping the riffraff out of this place, that's my job and I'll do
it as I see fit. Agreed?"

"Now wait—"

"Third: I see a hotel over there. Pretty nice one. I don't
care who is in it currently, my men and I will be appropriat-
ing accommodations for ourselves. It's the barracks, for
now."

"Hang on—"

"Look," Russell said, stepping in so close he could smell
the bourbon on the other man's breath, "you need me and
my soldiers if you want to keep this place operational. I hear
the Elevator is the only thing keeping us all from becoming
like those animals out there, so keeping the damned thing
safe is probably a good idea, don't you agree?"

"Of course, but—"

"No buts. Just say 'agreed' and we'll shake hands. No offense, mate, but you look like the sort of man who issues orders via interoffice-fucking-memo. All I'm asking you to do is let me handle the situation on the ground. I'm not much for big-picture stuff anyway, so you can have it."

"Well, how kind of you to allow me the privilege," Braithwaite snarled.

Grinning, Russell clapped him on the shoulder. "There's a bit of backbone! The old man's got some spark left, yet! All right, then. I think we'll get along just fine." He extended his hand.

After several seconds, Braithwaite shook it.

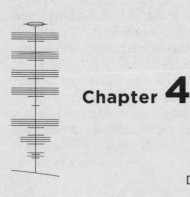

Chapter 4

DARWIN, AUSTRALIA
16.APR.2278

The air clung, indistinguishable from sweat.

Nigel and Rebecca emerged into a maze of low warehouses dotted with the occasional six- or seven-story office complex. Most were dark, unguarded except electronically. A few times Nigel saw armed security doing their rounds, but they paid little attention to the passage of a couple such as this. Rebecca kept to alleys when possible, darker streets when not. She took turns seemingly at random, and once out of the industrial zone she ducked into a massage parlor and pretended to study the menu of services for a while.

He realized belatedly she was studying the screen of her comm, held low in front of her.

Cars and trucks hummed by on the narrow street outside, spraying the remnants of an earlier rain shower into a mist that faded in their wake. People, immigrants mostly, shuffled by with their heads down.

"Shit," Rebecca muttered.

"What now?" he asked.

"No signal, not even Hocs. That's not possible."

"And yet . . ." He studied her, a twinge of sympathy creeping into his thoughts. "Try somewhere else, closer to where the fat cats live."

She shook her head. "I know a place where we can hide out until I can reach Gr—" she stopped herself short of the slip. "My employer."

"This place wouldn't be a luxury hotel by any chance?"

"Parking garage," Rebecca said, walking again. A graceful shadow against the gaudy storefronts.

He fell in step, dragon-headed cane clacking on the damp sidewalk rhythmically. *Rumble on the pitch. Rumble on the pitch.* The phrase had continued to tumble around his head, and now he uttered it internally with each step.

Eventually she turned down a crumbling two-lane road lined with shuttered storefronts, streetlights just branchless concrete trees, broken and useless. Dark forms loomed in shadowed alcoves. Demonic faces lit red-orange by the tips of foul-smelling joints.

Nigel tested his bruised leg. Pain flared with each step, but nothing a tight grimace couldn't keep at bay. Still, he maintained the limp, content to be underestimated.

Eventually Rebecca stopped in front of the barricaded entrance to a parking garage. A long rolling gate blocked the way inside, kept shut by a chain with a combination lock. Despite the darkness she dialed in the code with surprising speed. Unchained, the gate still required the strength of both of them to push aside enough for them to slip through. There'd be motors in the wall somewhere, probably in disrepair. He wondered how long this awful stretch of road would languish before the city's Elevator-fueled prosperity reclaimed it. Darwin's explosion of growth since the alien relic arrived seemed unstoppable. Well, except for the whole end-of-the-world business.

Rebecca locked the gate behind them and led the way down a spiraling concrete ramp. By the end Nigel could see nothing at all. He used the cane as a probe for obstacles, letting her soft footfalls determine the pace.

Three levels belowground she stopped. The air had a bite and smelled of mildew. A loud click preceded the hum of electricity. Weak urine-yellow light crept into the space, cast from a bank of LEDs mounted on a tripod. A new wall had been hastily erected where the driveway should continue on into the parking area. Prefab sections of chain-link fence lay in a stack off to one side.

"What is this place?" Nigel asked, voice echoing in the large room and on up the spiral ramp.

"Heard about it a month back. Two workers, grumbling

about how the local slumlord had hired them to convert a garage into an underground club for drug raves. But the slumlord died. His son fired everyone and fled the country. I found it, cut the gate's power, and added a lock."

"How forward-thinking of you."

She shrugged and moved farther in, stopping to unlock a reinforced door that looked like something yanked from a retro gentlemen's club. Even from a distance Nigel recognized the deadbolt as one he could pop in less than twenty seconds. He filed that knowledge. Rebecca continued into the garage proper: a massive concrete room dotted with square pillars. She flipped on another bank of work lights.

Effort had been made to add flimsy walls between some of the pillars to divide the space, though only a few portions had been painted. In the far corner a room had been built. Rebecca walked inside and lit a camping lantern set on a large oak desk, revealing the beginnings of an office.

"A fine place to run a drug empire," Nigel said.

Rebecca flashed her half smile. "There's some medical supplies in the bathroom. How's your leg?"

"I won't turn down a painkiller or five."

She gestured to a large executive's chair behind the desk. "Get off your feet. I'll be right back."

When she'd gone he sighed and moved to the offered seat. He leaned his cane against the wall and lowered himself into the cushion. The plush leather squeaked against his coat.

Somewhere in the cavernous garage a steady drip of water kept the silence from being absolute. Rhythmic, like his cane on the sidewalk. Like that stupid song in the elevator. Like slow-motion gunfire.

Nigel levered the seat back and closed his eyes. He imagined himself back in Sydney, minutes away from a fat commission and a quick flight home. That outcome felt suddenly more alien than the Builders' great Elevator itself.

An image swam into his mind. The crack of a fist on the jaw of a cricketer, the spray of blood through sputtering lips. "Beginning of the end, that rumble on the pitch . . ." Nigel sang softly, and slept.

* * *

When he woke the lantern had been turned down to a dim glow. A grease-stained bag rested on the desk, the irresistible smell of a meat pie and fries wafting from within. Beside it stood a sweating glass bottle of ginger beer.

Beside that, two red pills.

He levered the seat back up. Something tugged at his arm. A chain rattled as he moved. He eyed it, followed the gray links from a handcuff on his left wrist to another latched to a metal rung on the floor, previously hidden beneath a patch of carpet. "Dammit," he growled. He glanced around, patting without success at the breast of his duster for the locksmithing kits formerly concealed there.

He saw the two kits on the far corner of the desk. Nearby but out of reach. A note rested atop them:

Sorry, but you're my ticket out of this mess.
Back soon.

He took a healthy swig of the beverage, popped the red pills in his mouth, and swallowed. The pie he tore into with ravenous urgency. Sated, he munched thoughtfully on the fries, his gaze absently defocused on the room's only light. The LEDs within the lantern began to blur and swim after a time.

"Drugged," he said. Aloud or not he didn't know. He tried to turn in the chair, the motion that of a flailing drunk. The chain snapped at his wrist, painfully. Something fell to the floor behind him. "Cane!" he bellowed, the word slurring. He groped for it even as the edges of his vision began to darken. Keeping his eyes open became a conscious effort. His fingers brushed the wooden shaft and he coaxed it into his palm.

A tingling sensation began to fill his body. Hurry, he thought. He spun the chair back and patted the cane across the desk until he heard it hit the plastic case of his lock picks. The cane felt like a mallet in his numbing limb as he tried to gently shove the two stacked boxes toward him. Too slow, too slow.

The sound of his own breaths began to drag.

The last thing he heard was the sound of the boxes clattering to the floor.

A hand on his shoulder woke him. He blinked and waited for his eyes to focus. It seemed to take forever. His head felt like a jug of water.

"Wake up," someone said. A man's voice.

Nigel grunted. "When I'm ready." To his own ear he sounded like some drugged-up washout after an all-nighter. He tried to look at the person in front of him and winced in the glare of a flashlight.

"Does he have the rash?" someone asked. A different voice.

"Negative," a third said.

The first man spoke again, his voice nasal and thin, like a weasel in human form. "The woman claims you possess knowledge regarding Nightcliff's safe. True?"

Nigel swallowed. They spoke like police officers, not street thugs. "Who . . . Who's asking?"

"A representative of Nightcliff."

With an effort Nigel rubbed his eyes with his free hand. The room swam into focus. A man leaned over the table in front of him. He had long stringy hair and the kind of eyes that would frighten children. He wore a gray overcoat. The two men standing behind him wore army uniforms, and had compact machine guns drawn and ready. Nigel cleared his throat. "Where is she?"

Weasel-man ignored the question. "Are you capable of entering that safe or not?"

"Not with a gun in my face. Where's Rebecca?"

"Indisposed."

"Dead?"

The man glanced about the room. "She said you ran some kind of empire from here."

"She said that? I . . ." Nigel stopped himself. Possibilities unfolded in his mind. Intending to or not, heard correctly or not, Rebecca had nevertheless given him a gift. This was a new world, and he could make his own identity in it. Willing calm, Nigel spoke carefully. "I'm renovating. Who are you?"

For a moment the man just sat there, sizing Nigel up, as if deciding how much patience he should expend here. "Kip Osmak. Assistant to Chief Constable Arthur Braithwaite, acting commander of Nightcliff."

Nigel leaned forward in the chair, the squeak of his leather duster on the cushion masking the sound of the rattling chain. He glanced upward, groping for clear thoughts, and saw a small black dome attached to the ceiling just inside the door. Security camera. Dead or disconnected most likely, but that wouldn't be common knowledge. "Get all that, Verna?" he said to the dome. *Verna? Sorry, Mum. First name that came to mind.*

Kip turned and followed Nigel's gaze. His friends did the same. Unobserved, Nigel probed around on the floor by his feet until he found the box that contained his implements. He opened it and began to run his fingers across the tiny tools.

The weasel turned back, his façade of confidence drained away.

"Tell me something," Nigel said. Below the table he slid what he hoped was the right tool from its sleeve, resting the case between his legs. "Since when is the army enforcing law in Darwin, anyway?"

Kip licked his lips, tongue darting like a lizard's. "Destroy that camera," he said. One of the soldiers obeyed. He bashed the security camera three times, each swing more zealous than the last. The second blow cracked the glass shell, the third shattered it.

As shards rained down Nigel let the chain fall from his wrist and slipped the lock pick into his sleeve.

Kip turned back, dropping the cane on the desk with a dull thud. "Would one of you please guard the entrance? And the other, search the other floors for this Verna and anyone else? Blackfield was specific. No witnesses."

The two men turned in unison and departed.

"They won't find anything," Nigel said. "Verna is in Dublin, Ireland. That's a remote feed. Can't be too cautious."

Understanding grew across Kip's face. "Ah, I see. You've

been down here all along. You think there's still a world beyond Darwin. Do you have any idea what's going on out there?" He gestured broadly.

"A flu or something."

Kip shook his head. "It's not that simple." He rattled off a story so bizarre Nigel thought it could be nothing other than true. Darwin had become a safe haven against an otherwise all-consuming disease. Billions dead. *Billions.* Millions surviving as some kind of murderous shadow of their former selves. And then there was Darwin, or at least the portion of it closest to the Elevator. The last safe place. An island surrounded by toxic air, under constant assault from the murderous hordes who bore crimson rashes on their necks. An island, Nigel realized, that no cargo ship would ever reach. A new world indeed . . .

The ramifications flooded into his mind faster than he could grasp them. How long would the situation last? What would people eat? Who would maintain law and order?

He glanced at the man across from him with fresh eyes. The army, in charge of Nightcliff.

Suddenly everything that had happened in the last few days made sense. At least he could see a possible explanation. Novak had sent Nigel to Darwin knowing what happened after wouldn't matter. Rebecca, desperate, had sought a new buyer for Nigel's extraordinary knowledge of Nightcliff's vault. Whoever had wanted inside before didn't matter. Outside this garage a great reshuffling was going on, the smart people grabbing what power and resources they could before the dust settled. *Rumble on the pitch.* "Nightcliff Secure Storage," he said carefully.

Kip nodded. "Nightcliff Secure Storage. My boss needs access, and Neil Platz cannot make the trip down just now."

"If I help, I'm guessing your boss might not want me walking around afterwards?"

The man across the table gave the slightest of nods.

"And if I refuse, same thing?"

Again a nod. "Those were my orders."

"What do you do in Nightcliff?" Nigel asked.

"Traffic control. Elevator logistics."

"Hmm. That's interesting."

A hint of surprise flashed across Kip's face, as if this were the first time anyone found his work interesting. "Is it?"

"Absolutely. Look, this city," Nigel said, his thoughts only a short distance ahead of his mouth, "is a powder keg. A time bomb. There's a million people here, not to mention whoever slipped in before the disease hit. I assume some did?"

"Plenty. An avalanche. Please, make your point, I'm due back—"

Nigel held up his hands. "Think about it. Just for a moment. The city is cut off from the world, yes?"

"Yes," he said carefully. "For now."

"What will people eat and drink?"

"Whatever they have?"

Nigel shook his head. "That will only last a week, perhaps two."

Kip pondered that for a moment. "Maybe that'll be enough."

Nigel gave a shrug. "Perhaps. Perhaps not. Suppose for a second this scenario will go on indefinitely."

The other man's brow furrowed. His eyes darted back and forth. For a brief instant he looked like a child who'd just been told that maybe, just maybe, there is no Santa Claus.

"Look," Nigel said. "I'll open the safe for you, no problem. In exchange, you let me live. Given your role in Nightcliff, you'll know what's needed. You'll hear things. I'm a man who can find things and move them. We'd make a great team." Nigel could see his little house of cards growing with every lie he spewed, but if it could buy him a few days to sort things out . . .

The look in Kip's face, though, was priceless. A kid who'd just learned how to perform a magic trick. He was nodding, his beady little weasel eyes suddenly bright and alive. "So . . . you use your connections in the underworld—"

Don't have any. A minor inconvenient detail.

"—and I use my inside position in Nightcliff."

"Exactly," Nigel said.

After a few seconds Kip said, "Clever."

Nigel grinned, and tapped his temple with his index finger. "See? People like us, we need to carve out a new role for ourselves. Make ourselves valuable. So, do we have a deal?"

The weasel of a man extended his hand. "What's your name, anyway?"

"Pr—" Nigel started to say Proctor, Nigel Proctor. But it struck him that his ties to Novak & Sons might be found somehow. Not to mention his total lack of connections to Darwin's underworld. Besides, Nigel Proctor was not the name of a crime lord. At that moment the news screen from the bar in Sydney popped into his head. RUMBLE ON THE PITCH, the headline had been. "Rumble," he said.

"Prumble?"

Sure, why not. "That's me."

"First name?"

"No."

Kip slowly rose to his feet. "Well, then, Mr. Prumble. It's time I took you to Nightcliff."

An hour later, after a harrowing journey through the chaos of Darwin's streets in the back of an armored personnel carrier, Nigel found himself kneeling before the Kastensauer Mark 8 locking mechanism of Nightcliff's vault door.

The room itself was exactly as he remembered it. White tile floor, bare white walls, white-paneled ceiling lined with rows of white LEDs. Sterile as they come. Meant to instill confidence in those who needed to store their belongings here before making an extended trip to the space stations high above. Virtually every megabillionaire in the world had probably stepped through this gigantic door at some point in the last few years, Neil Platz at their side, as they stowed a one-of-a-kind watch or a sensitive datacube for safekeeping while they made their pilgrimage up to see the remnant of the Builders' vessel at Anchor.

Echoing footfalls in the long hallway behind coaxed Nigel out of his semi-trance. It sounded like an entire brigade approached, their boots slapping against the marble tiles like hammer blows.

"Look," he said to Kip, who stood lamely in the corner,

"call me Nigel in front of these people, all right? I'd prefer my, uh, reputation, not precede me."

"Fine," Kip hissed.

At the door all but one of the pairs of boots stopped. Two people entered.

"Is this him?" a gravelly voice asked.

"Yes, Chief Constable," Kip stammered. "His name is Nigel."

Prumble remained facing the lock, pretending to be busy with it. He cast a quick vague glance over his shoulder and saw a gaunt elderly man in a police uniform. The man next to him wore army fatigues, and was powerfully built. Not muscular per se, just . . . hard. Chiseled, the ladies might say. His jaw, his eyes, everything about him said "fuck you."

"G'day," Prumble said. When in Rome, he figured.

"Hello," Braithwaite said. "This is Lieutenant Blackfield, in charge of ground security."

"Tough times ahead for you, eh, mate?" Blackfield asked.

"How do you mean?"

"Maintaining that belly in our little tomb of a city is going to be rough, I wager."

"Hmm," Prumble said. He'd learned over the years that individuals who sought to goad him with comments about his weight were individuals of microscopically small intellect. On any other day he would have devastated the asshole in the way only words can. "I can be resourceful," he replied, instead.

"That's quite enough Mr. Blackfield," Braithwaite said. "Let's talk about the vault."

"Indeed. I assume you'd like to select a new code?"

"Quite," the old man said. "Mr. Platz has asked me to look after affairs here for now, hence the need."

"None of my business, really," Prumble said.

He set about fiddling with the lock, leaning over it to see the digital readout of numbers on a hooded display at the top. He dialed in the installer's code he'd set up years earlier. The wheel spun smoothly under his hand, resisting slightly as the mechanism within used this rotation to generate the electricity needed to operate. It made it difficult to dial the wheel quickly, but Prumble, being used to this sort of thing, still managed to select the proper six-digit sequence on his first try. The dial itself, which was free of any visible numbering, betrayed nothing. Only the digital readout on top indicated what number he'd selected, and whenever he stopped and started turning in the other direction, the display began at a random number. So even memorizing how far he turned the dial each time would not help someone trying to sleuth out the code.

The mechanism made a soft chirp as the installer's code was verified. Prumble let out a long breath and dialed through the maintenance options. "Right," Prumble said. "Use the little screen here and pick your combination. Four numbers between one and a hundred. Your fingertips will be scanned by the dial itself and combined with the code. Your retina will be scanned by a camera behind the readout panel. It will truly be a code that works only for you."

"Why even have the code?"

Prumble shrugged. "The code can be discovered. Your fingerprints can be obtained and replicated, as can your retina. All three combined, however . . ." Again he shrugged, then moved aside as Braithwaite leaned over the dial and began the process. Prumble had been in this very place, three years earlier. An administrator had escorted him then, and he'd been forced to leave the room and wait in a janitor's closet nearby whenever Neil Platz himself had to come in and do this part of the keying. Neil had demanded this conceit, a perfectly normal request when configuring vaults for the rich and powerful.

After ten seconds or so Braithwaite moved away. "Is that it then?"

"That's it. The vault is keyed to you."

"Excellent. Now if you don't mind . . ." To Prumble's surprise, instead of leaving, Braithwaite dialed in his code and opened the vault door. He stepped inside, alone. Seconds passed in total silence before the man emerged again, a datacube in one hand. He snapped his fingers and a guard came forward, holding out an open aluminum case. Braithwaite slipped the cube into a foam support, then took the offered case from the man. "Thank you, everyone. Now if you'll excuse me, I've got a climber to catch."

"Enjoy the ride," Prumble said amicably.

Braithwaite nodded, then cast a second awkward nod at the silent form of Kip Osmak, who stood in the corner of the room, fidgeting. "Kip will see you safely back to . . . well, wherever." Then Braithwaite left, plunging the room into a sudden, uncomfortable silence. Blackfield remained.

"Am I free to go?" Prumble asked the soldier.

Blackfield held up a finger and waited until the sound of Braithwaite's footfalls faded to nothing. "Not exactly. I've got a bit more in mind."

The man laid out his plan. The real reason Kip had sought out Prumble. A pretty simple ruse, but then the best are, aren't they? He wanted the lock rekeyed for Nightcliff's new commander, as was now done, but he also wanted the maintenance access Prumble had just demonstrated for himself, to use "in an emergency."

"What's in it for me?" Prumble asked.

"Your continued existence on this Earth," Blackfield shot back. "I can't exactly let you leave here knowing you can break into our vault."

"That's a good start," Prumble said. It took a force of will to keep the anxiety from his voice.

"Okay, fine. And a willingness on my part, and my boys, to pretend we don't know what sort of work you did before the shit went down. Kip here tells me you had quite the operation going."

"He mentioned that, did he?" Prumble suddenly doubted the wisdom of his chosen persona. Seemed like a good idea at the time. Famous last words if there ever were any.

Blackfield waved the comment away. "The slate's wiped clean, as far as I'm concerned."

"Well . . . I'll need some special equipment to pull off what you're asking for," Prumble said truthfully. Mostly. There was another reason, one he'd only just thought of, but this oily bastard didn't need to know that.

"Special equipment? What the fuck for?"

"Only the 'owner's code,' which I've just configured for Mr. Braithwaite, can be reset without extra gear. To set or reset the maintenance code—what you're asking for—one needs a special transponder box plugged into a recessed port inside the vault itself." *And then I can reset the master code for myself. Everybody wins.*

"You have this box?"

Prumble thought about answering truthfully, then about lying and saying yes. He settled on the in-between option. "I can acquire one."

"Do it," Blackfield said. "Kip, make the arrangements. I want this handled ASAFP."

Kip squirmed in the corner. "Okay. I mean, yes, sir."

Blackfield fixed a nasty stare on the thin man, then spun on his heel and walked out, army boots smacking against the white-tiled floor. His soldiers fell in behind him, obedient as dogs.

A silence stretched to fill the space left by the lieutenant. Prumble glanced at Kip, and found the stringy-haired, dour son of a bitch looking directly back.

"You can actually get this thing, right?" Kip asked.

Prumble shrugged. "Depends. Know anyone who can leave the city?"

PART 4

Distance of Hope

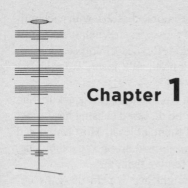

Chapter 1

She sped down the center of the road on a stolen motorcycle. The tach read 100 kph. The wind in her hair felt like a blast furnace. Mounted on the back of the bike, an ancient portable stereo blared Queen's "Another One Bites the Dust."

Sam muttered with the lyrics, leaning the bike into a quick weave around the loping form of something previously human. She shot the creature from only three meters away, a shotgun blast that shredded through the animal's filthy clothes.

Behind her a few dozen of the beasts bellowed anger and grief at the action. They surged, unable to comprehend the fact that they'd never quite catch her. The bike's electric motor churned out its low whine and would continue to do so for days.

The street, bisecting a suburb of Darwin just east of Lyons, was littered with abandoned cars and the bodies of those who fell when the ailment hit. The corpses had shocked her at first. Filled her first with rage and then later a sadness unlike any she'd ever known. So many dead. Everyone she'd ever met.

Now the bodies were just scenery. Not worth thinking about. The formerly human that survived the infection were the only things worth sparing a thought for.

And that thought was *Kill*.

Whatever reservations she'd held back at the lodge about killing the infected died in East Palmerston. Their numbers were staggering, and Sam, lacking the burden of familiarity with any of them, found her remorse dissolve with each pull of the trigger, each swing of the ax, each windpipe crushed by her own two hands. She'd left a sea of corpses behind, and felt no remorse. She'd done them a favor, as far as she was concerned.

Sam ran the gap between a bus and a smashed pickup. She glanced back in time to see the diseased chasing her funnel through the space. A few of them, at least. Most scrambled over the vehicles. Still others fanned around to either side. Persistent bastards, she had to give them that.

Movement to the right caught her eye. In the gaps between a row of two-story condominiums she saw something that made her almost crash.

Standing on top of a row of abandoned cars were people. Normal people. Fifty or more, just standing there. Some held weapons; rifles, shovels, even cricket bats. And all of them, she realized, were cheering. Cheering for her.

There are plenty of ways you can hurt a man, Freddy Mercury crooned from the speaker, *and bring him to the ground.*

"Preach it, brother," Sam said, sighting on another diseased. This one was just standing in the middle of the road, laughing maniacally as some of them were prone to do. Sam's blast took out the former-woman's legs below the knee. She fell forward, still laughing.

Sam leaned again, trailing a line of sparks with the tip of her shotgun. Three rounds left. The line of people—actual sane human-fucking-beings—was still two hundred meters off, across a wide avenue. Sam twisted the accelerator and crouched over the handlebars as the bike surged forward, caps screaming with release. She shot the gap between two buildings. At the far end a wooden fence had been knocked down, forming a natural ramp. She grinned and plowed toward it.

The bike sailed into the air. She lifted the shotgun over her head and let out a triumphant shout to the line of people watching her. They roared in appreciation, a sound that filled her with a strange and sudden joy.

Sam saw the corpse too late.

The body lay just beyond the fence, halfway in the road.

It had been run over by a car, from the look of it, and she was about to add a motorcycle to the poor thing's fate.

Her rear tire landed on the dead man's back and slid out to the left. Sam fought it for an instant and then knew the folly of it. She eased her hands and thighs off the bike and let it fly out from under her, metal screeching on the hot asphalt. Sam hit the ground a split second later, her thigh scraping along the baked hardpan. She slid for a few meters and felt blinding hot pain all along her leg as the road tore through her denim pants, flesh, then muscle. Somehow she managed to turn the slide into a roll. Her shotgun clattered away.

Those along the line to the west emitted a gasp.

The ancient portable radio emitted a few last triumphant notes before shattering as the motorcycle slammed into the burned husk of a taxicab.

Sam could hear the animals now, skittering through the alley and over the wooden slab of fence. Grunting with agony she somehow managed to push herself to a shaky stand. She started to limp toward the line of people. They were across four lanes of road, and none seemed willing to rush to her aid.

"Help me, you pricks!" she shouted, voice cracking from the sting that burned along her leg.

None of them moved. Not a goddamn inch.

"What the fuck is wrong with you?" she shouted. They were shouting back, but with so many voices she could understand none. Their tone implied only one message: *Run.*

She hobbled instead. Sam remembered her pistol then. Taken from a dead policeman outside East Palmerston. She fished it from the holster at her side and aimed behind her. The gun thudded against her palm with each echoing crack of a round fired. The first two creatures over the fallen barricade fell. The third she missed, but it tripped on its fallen packmates and landed awkwardly. Sam took careful aim and put a round in its skull.

More appeared in the alleyway. Still others began to filter through from other passages to either side.

Sam fired until the pistol had no more bullets to offer. She almost threw it, but thought better of the idea and kept it in her grip instead.

Fifty meters now. She tried to run but couldn't. The jog she could manage would never work, she realized with growing fear. Not unless—

The gunfire that erupted from the line of onlookers made her heart sing. Especially given the fact that they weren't shooting at her. "I'm going to make it," she said aloud. "I'm going to make it."

She raised her arms above her head as she moved, eyes skyward, grinning in relief. Far above the fray, she spotted an aircraft soaring, its engines adding to the cacophony of the weapons fire.

A long, worrying silence followed first contact with the tower. Skyler set the aircraft to circle, bleeding altitude instead of fuel. With each trip around he caught a glimpse of the Australian coastline. Somewhere to the east, hidden in a haze of rain, Darwin and its space elevator waited.

Finally the radio crackled. *"Dutch Cargo,* you're clear to approach."

Skadz tapped Skyler's shoulder. *"Dutch Cargo?"*

"That's what our transponder broadcasts on the civilian band."

"Worst name ever, mate. Gotta do something about that."

"Who cares?" Skyler replied. "They're letting us land, that's the important part." He increased power to the engines, simultaneously ending their downward spiral and leveling off. Then he mumbled acknowledgment to the tower at Nightcliff. "Ten minutes until we're down."

Skadz offered a hunk of naan to Skyler and groaned at the refusal before munching loudly on the crust. He chewed thoughtfully for a time as the ocean below drew nearer.

"Valkyrie," Skadz said. "That's a proper name for an aircraft. *Phoenix. Nighthawk.* Fuckin' . . . *Angel of Death.*"

"A bit epic for a Dutch transport," Skyler said.

"Military transport!"

"Still."

Skadz gave a kick to Skyler's chair, a most annoying habit. "C'mon, mate. Anything's an improvement. *Dutch fucking Cargo.* Jesus."

"How about *Melville*?"

The eyebrow, impossibly, rose higher. "What? Are you joking? Have you heard a bloody word I said?"

"It's a fine name," Skyler said. "My grandfather's, after the author—"

"I know who fucking Melville is. People are going to think we're talking about a damned whale."

"She does sort of resemble one." Skyler shifted uncomfortably in his seat. "A winged whale, anyway. It's a fine name. Professional. Respectable. Besides, billions of people have died. I don't think we, as persons immune to this horror, should come riding in on the name 'Angel of Death.'"

Skadz teetered on the verge of a profane rant. "Honestly, mate, I can't tell when you're joking or serious."

A blip appeared on the main nav display. Darwin's liftport, a designated no-fly zone by international agreement, slid onto the screen as a glowing red circle. Skyler nudged the flight stick until the line that marked his predicted path cut right through the center. Warnings about possible use of force lit up the top and bottom of the display, and a high chirp began to quietly ping through the cabin. Skyler ignored it all and locked in the landing option. Seconds later the acknowledgment came back, and the red circle changed to green. He relaxed a bit then. Altitude continued to fall, under a thousand meters now. Whitecaps drifted on the azure ocean beneath him, their intensity growing where they traced the Australian coastline. From this height the world looked pretty normal.

"Last chance, I guess," Skadz said.

"Last chance for what?"

"To have the planet Earth to ourselves. We can go anywhere, mate. The world is literally our fucking oyster."

"We've talked about this. . . ."

"I know, I know. I'm just saying. In case you're having second thoughts."

"I'm not."

Skadz squirmed noisily in his seat, something he did constantly when he was actually in it. He'd spent at least half the flight aft in the cargo bay, pacing. Not much of a copilot, Skyler thought, though of course the man had never been anything more than a civilian passenger on a commercial plane before last week.

The two of them couldn't be more different. Skadz, a Jamaican-born Londoner who described what he did for a living as "a little of this, a little of that" had been in Amsterdam enjoying the coffeehouse culture when SUBS hit. Street-smart and resourceful under the mess of dreadlocks that spilled from his head, he was not exactly the type of person Skyler would have befriended under normal circumstances. But company was company and that counted for a lot right now. Not so much, perhaps, once they landed, though Skyler kept that thought to himself.

Ahead, a line began to manifest along the window. A hairline crack, he thought at first, until he moved his head to get a better look and his brain worked out the perspective. The line was very far away. The space elevator. Despite everything he knew about it, proximity to the alien device still caught the breath in his throat.

It went from the horizon up to the limit of Skyler's view at a ten-degree angle, disorienting in the same way the Leaning Tower in Pisa left visitors off balance. As he stared at the vague, finely drawn line, he could see little blobs along its length. Red lights winked at regular intervals from each.

A minute later the city began to take shape. Skyler saw the densely packed skyscrapers first. Crowded around the base of the cord were gleaming towers of glass, almost all built in the twelve years since the Elevator arrived. Their heights tapered off rapidly from there, giving way to squat warehouses and low-rent apartments, and finally slums. Docu-sensories had been made about the city's explosion of growth resulting in the appearance of the alien artifact, and though Skyler remembered few details he could almost hear the narrator's description of stratification that had occurred. The poor and uneducated living at the edges. Next were the skilled workers who filled factories, warehouses, and modest condominiums. Then came the powerful, the wealthy. Corporate headquarters and surprisingly large embassies. Huge hotels and luxury apartments. Finally, the Platz-owned land around the Elevator itself, marked by modest low buildings that created a buffer between the sentinel high-rise towers and the liftport, which marked the exact point where the Elevator connected to the ground.

He could see it now. A single conical tower matching the cord's off-kilter angle, rising to match the height of the tallest skyscrapers, which surrounded it like a crowd of anxious onlookers. Warning beacons formed orange-red dotted lines along the tower's length and in regular rings around its girth, before giving way to support structures that obscured the very bottom.

As instructed he kept a wide circle around the tower, only tightening his turn once on the eastern side of the city. Suburbs made up the landscape below.

Skyler eased back on the thrust as individual buildings came into view. Motion began to manifest on the ground. Vehicles and then people. For a few seconds it looked normal, like any other city stirring to life with the sunrise.

The western shoreline slid past, off to the right. A smattering of boats were anchored some distance away from the jagged boulders that met the sea. Farther south, a huge messy flotilla crowded the bay. Thousands of boats that must have raced here ahead of the infection. Fires burned on some of them. Skyler shook his head at the chaos and continued his circuit to the eastern part of Darwin, as instructed.

"Look at that," Skadz said. "Below us."

Through the glass footwell, Skyler saw nothing but the antlike movement of people. On this side of the city no rain fell at the moment, and they were out in droves. It took him a second to realize there was a strange abrupt end to the activity, right along the edge of the line of buildings. Hundreds of people were crowded along this invisible border.

As Skyler watched, a lone motorcycle rider raced toward this line. A few dozen people chased the bike, clearly diseased from the primal way they moved. The rider sailed through an alley, took a jump, and landed badly. Skyler winced as the person slid along the ground and tumbled.

"That Sheila might be like us," Skadz observed. "Coming in from the outside."

"Maybe, maybe not," Skyler said. He'd come across a few of the diseased that still seemed capable of intelligent behavior, to an extent, anyway. Riding a motorcycle seemed beyond that aptitude, but who knew for sure? Still, he found some hope in his co-pilot's words.

The scene slid behind them as they entered the central part of the city.

"Holy shit," Skadz whispered.

The streets approaching Nightcliff were packed with vehicles, but few were moving. Most were dark, some just burned-out shells. And people—*Jesus, the people*—were everywhere. Leaning in through broken windows, wrenching away wheels and body panels. They were clustered into gangs; some were visibly embroiled in combat with others or even themselves.

Shadowed forms rushed in and out of broken shop windows, arms full of anything they could carry, backs hunched over at a constant barrage from above. Objects of nearly every shape and size rained down, pelting those on the street below.

"What are they throwing from the windows?" Skyler asked, not really expecting an answer.

"Anything they can't eat, burn, or trade," Skadz replied.

Skyler considered that. "Driving away the refugees."

"That, or just clearing space for 'em. I guess we better hope for that."

They watched in silence as the area called Nightcliff drew near. Skyler could see the landing pad now, blissfully free of looters. The only people he saw within a few hundred meters of it were soldiers and police, many wearing riot gear. Checkpoints marked each intersection, at least the ones Skyler could see, in a rough circle around the Elevator complex. Farther out they became roadblocks. Some were made from portable barricades, others from vehicles stacked on top of each other by nearby loading cranes. A few were simply walls of armed and armored people, looking out instead of in, lit in haunting yellows and oranges by trash fires and the odd road flare.

"I'd call this a nightmare," Skyler said, "but compared to Abu Dhabi . . ."

"Yeah." Skadz shifted in his seat again. "Turf wars, looting, your basic hooligan shit. It's like Birmingham after a right and proper football contest. I call that a welcome change, though I wouldn't mind a little law and order the closer we get to that pad."

Skyler focused on the landing site. The VTOL pads were four concrete disks, arranged in a curved layout around a massive fixed-base loading crane and flanked on either side by caged electrical junctions that no doubt provided capacitor spooling services. Broad, flat warehouses ringed the yard at a safe distance.

He guided the craft along what seemed like a natural path between buildings toward the landing area. Off to his left a sprawling mansion came into view. White and angular, the opulent villa looked wholly out of place next to all the service-oriented buildings.

"Wave to Neil," Skadz said, imparting a mock cheer in his tone.

Skyler kept his hands at the controls.

His co-pilot smirked, the way only a street urchin could at such a display of wealth amid so much ugliness. "Think the old goat is inside, trying to make sense of all this?"

Skyler shook his head. "I'd guess he's up above, riding things out. I would be."

The radio crackled. "*Dutch Cargo,* hold position there, please."

With a slight yank, Skyler leveled the bulky aircraft out into a hover at fifty meters altitude. A high-pitched whine surged from the straining ultracapacitors, loud even against the howling thrust of air being pushed through the craft's massive ducted fans. His eyes danced toward the cap level readout. Just 5 percent remaining; a hover would burn through that in ten minutes. His hands began to sweat, but he kept them firmly on the stick and throttle. "*Dutch Cargo,* holding. What's the problem, Nightcliff?"

"Unidentified ground vehicle approaching," came the reply. "As a precaution we advise you back off to five hundred meters and await further instructions."

Skyler glanced over his shoulder at Skadz. "I don't think we have the cap for it."

"Tell them, mate, not me," Skadz said.

"Nightcliff, we're low on charge. A second approach would be—"

The rapid blinking of muzzle flashes below killed the words in his mouth. Through the footwell window he could see the soldiers swarming toward the south end of the landing area, taking up positions along the main arterial road that approached from the southwest. Vehicles and barricades alike dotted the avenue. How a ground vehicle could "approach" through that mess Skyler had no idea.

Then he saw it, and understood.

Large steel plates had been welded to the front of the thing, forming a wedge. The tires were similarly hidden beneath improvised armor. Whatever the original truck had been, it was clearly powerfully built. As Skyler watched it knocked a streetcar aside like it was no more than a toy. Sparks flew from the plated nose of the thing as the guards' barrage peppered the surface. The bullets did absolutely nothing.

"See that?" Skadz asked.

"Yes," Skyler managed.

"They're not going to stop it."

The same thought had just flitted through Skyler's mind. Whatever the driver's intent . . . on a whim Skyler flipped the radio to the local police band. The cockpit filled with frantic chatter immediately.

". . . Going for the base . . ."

". . . AP ineffective. Repeat, piercing rounds ineffective."

"Conserve ammo, there are civilians—"

"Everyone shut the fuck up!"

Skyler winced, despite himself. That last voice, though shrill, imparted a commander's tone.

The voice went on. "This is Blackfield. We've got grenades ready here. They will not reach the Elevator tower under any circumstances. I don't care if we all need to lie down in front of it. Rally on my position in case any malcontents get out of that thing when it pops."

"Belay that," a new voice said. "This is Chief Constable Braithwaite. If the intruder is packed with explosives and you set it off inside Nightcliff—"

"If we let it get close it will be ten times worse," the one called Blackfield shot back.

"Find another way, that's an order."

Below, Skyler saw a trail of smoke suddenly lance between the line of guards and the oncoming truck. The grenade fell ten meters short, exploding in a brilliant flash of yellow. Shrapnel flew, leaving a thousand little smoke trails in the air.

"Goddammit, that was an order!" Braithwaite shouted through the speaker.

The truck lurched left. Not damaged, just a change of course. It veered ninety degrees and careened down a side street. From his vantage point Skyler could track the vehicle easily. He saw it turn again and barrel down a narrow alley between two warehouses. Then soldiers were scrambling. More shouting came over the radio as chaos won out over order.

"Maybe we should back off," Skadz said. "I don't like this. Not one bit."

The armored truck lurched again, sliding sideways into another street that faced in toward Nightcliff's tower, behind where the guards had set up their final barricade. The vehicle surged forward then, building speed like an enraged bull now that its target, the base of the space elevator, lay directly ahead. There was nothing to block it. Skyler glanced at the soldiers, who were moving that way but far too slow, still unsure where the intruder had gone.

"Hold on to something," Skyler said. He slammed the flight stick forward, tilting the craft's nose nearly straight down. At the same instant he cut power to the engines, dropping the vehicle like a stone.

"What the fuck are you doing?" Skadz roared.

Skyler ignored him. He angled toward the speeding truck, turning to face it as his plane fell toward the ground. Somewhere in the cockpit a collision beacon started to chirp, high and scathingly loud.

"Bloody hell!" Skadz shouted again, gripping his armrests.

The armored truck careened on, oblivious to the aircraft about to meet it. At the last possible instant Skyler slammed the accelerator to pull and yanked back on the stick. The electric motors screamed to life. The whole cockpit shook with the force of it. Something cracked behind Skyler's head. Skadz's knees pressed hard into the seat from behind. Skyler winced, groaning against the sudden reversal of g-forces.

Somehow he managed to keep his eyes open just enough to watch through the footwell window. The driver of the truck hadn't seen them. The vehicle did not slow or turn. It rolled straight into the sudden and massive flow of air being pushed by the aircraft's huge vents. The vehicle's nose lifted. Once the balance tipped it was all over. Heavy plates of armor did nothing against the sheer force of the airflow. The truck flipped upward, its rear sliding underneath from sheer forward momentum. With a massive clang that rattled Skyler's teeth the vehicle slammed down onto its roof and came to rest.

Skyler leveled out and allowed the craft to gain some altitude. Below, a man in a white robe crawled from the driver's-side door, spilling himself out onto the asphalt and crawling away. He tried to get up, tried to run, and then he was shaking violently as little red splotches appeared across his white garment from shoulder to knee. The driver jerked and stumbled before falling flat on his back, dead.

The soldiers moved up and surrounded the truck. They shot into the passenger window a few times. As they flowed around to the back, Skyler lost them from view. He'd seen enough.

A few minutes later, ignoring the angry commands from the controller in the tower, Skyler set down on landing pad four and killed the engines. It took a force of will to release the flight stick, releasing his fingers one by one.

His co-pilot, quiet for the last few minutes, let out a long breath in the newly silent cockpit. "That was brilliant, mate. Mental, but brilliant."

"I thought you'd be angry."

"How do you figure that?"

With a shrug Skyler said, "Risking ourselves just to help these guys out."

"Ah, well," Skadz said, unbuckling his harness, "next

time you put my ass on the line I'd prefer a little heads-up.
As for these blokes, I don't care about them at all, that's a
fact, but the Elevator? Worth the risk if it is really the only
thing keeping the rest of us safe."

With that he extricated himself from the bulky chair and
headed aft. Skyler finished the shutdown sequence, content
to lose himself in the familiar task. He could handle this
process with his eyes closed, but right now shutting out the
world didn't seem like such a bad idea.

The space elevator had changed the world, but that had
been twelve years ago. He'd been a kid, wide-eyed with
dreams of aliens and space travel. Adults wrestled with the
implications of intelligent life beyond Earth, and even as he
came of age he'd always been content to leave such matters
to those wiser than himself. He'd just wanted to be a pilot,
eventually maybe an astronaut.

Now everything had changed again. The boyish dreams
that had guided his ambition were crushed along with everything else he ever knew. Everything save this cockpit,
and the memories he carried of his brief military career. His
family, his instructors, his friends and fellow soldiers . . . everyone he'd ever known, all dead. Or worse, transformed
into a creature that was human only in shape.

He'd shot one of them in Abu Dhabi. Right between the
eyes, from just two meters away. In the time it took the old
man to fall to the ground Skyler had seen the change in his
face. Perhaps it had just been an illusion, something pro-
jected from his own desperate hope, but he'd seen it. The
return, in that crossing between life and death, of the human
within.

Skyler had never shot anyone before this madness. He'd
never done anything worse than punch a man in a drunken
back-alley brawl over a skirt who wanted nothing to do with
either of them. For the hundredth time in a week, Skyler
wondered if he would have been able to pull the trigger on
someone he knew.

Making sense of this world loomed beyond his mental capability. Better to leave solutions to the surviving power
players and focus on what he could do. Let the great Neil
Platz figure it all out. Offer to serve if the opportunity arose.

Voices drifted in from the cargo bay. Skadz and a few others. Skyler's hand went to the harness buckle. He stopped himself, eased back in his chair, and flipped on the intercom.

". . . the right thing to do," Skadz was saying. "We made a snap decision. Sorry if anything was damaged, but from our vantage point—"

"Look, mate," someone said, cutting him off, "you almost got a grenade up your backside. Next time you find yourself in the middle of a security operation you back off and stay the fuck out of it." The voice, a man with a strong Australian accent, spoke in a hushed tone.

The tone of a slighted man, a bruised ego. The idea that someone could be worried about their reputation or jurisdiction given the billions dead or dying across the world just made Skyler sink farther back into his seat. He decided he wouldn't move unless called. Let Skadz deal with it. If he's so anxious to take credit for flipping that truck, he can take the fallout, too.

Boots clanged on the scaffold stairs that led to the aircraft's side door, and a new voice came through the intercom speaker. "Two hundred and fifty kilos," a man said. An older man, Skyler thought. Australian, but a bit more refined than the first speaker.

"Pardon?" Skadz asked.

"Two hundred and fifty kilos of explosives in the back of that truck, the blokes outside are estimating. Religious paraphernalia on the two occupants, who are unfortunately beyond questioning." A pause. "Chief Constable Arthur Braithwaite," the man said then. "We're in your debt."

"Skadz," Skadz replied. "A nickname, and all I'm willing to share if you don't mind," he added at a presumed raised eyebrow.

"Fair enough. Welcome to Darwin."

The slighted man spoke up again. "That grenade was just a warning shot. We could have—"

"That'll be all for now, Mr. Blackfield. Thank you."

"We had them—"

"Thank you."

Silence followed, then boots on the ladder again, receding this time.

"Don't mind him," Braithwaite said. "We're all a bit tense, I suppose. The security situation . . . well, you saw it for yourself. The disease is driving people insane whether they're infected or not. A nasty business."

"We heard Darwin was safe."

Skyler flipped off the intercom and slipped out of his harness. He pulled the last three switches in his shutdown sequence to the off position and sat in the silence of the darkened cockpit. Before him lay a city under siege. The streets, those he could see, were a morass of people silhouetted against trash fires and the headlights of hastily abandoned cars. Everyone seeking shelter or defending it. A giant and lethal game of musical chairs too complex and fluid to wrap the mind around, like a fog that blocked sight of anything beyond the immediate surroundings.

He went back then, and shook Arthur Braithwaite's waiting hand. "Skyler Luiken. Dutch air force. Or was, I guess."

The old man nodded. "Tell me truthfully now, boys. You've really been exposed? No symptoms at all?"

"None," Skyler said.

Skadz nodded. "We put down in Abu Dhabi for a bit, then Diego Garcia after that for almost a day. Before that I ran into Skyler in Amsterdam after everyone else . . . well, you know. We hoped there'd be more like us here."

"Only one or two that I know of, sadly," Braithwaite said, a genuine gloom in his wrinkled features. "The rest of us are confined here. A nine-kilometer radius around the Elevator, unless that changes, too."

"Not a lot of space to work with," Skyler said.

The man studied him for a second, then sighed. "Well, you both look like you could use a hot meal and a pint. I'll take you to the cafeteria and get someone to find you some quarters."

Skyler's stomach growled at the prospect of real food.

"Once you're settled," Braithwaite added, "some doctors will want to examine you. Maybe . . ." He trailed off, a faint twinkle of hope in his blue eyes. "Look, I can't order you to stay close, but if you're really immune . . ."

"We'll help any way we can."

"My thanks." His gaze gravitated to the sealed plastic crates, each labeled with their contents: DUPONT LEVEL-B HAZMAT, QUANTITY 50.

Skadz cleared his throat. "They were just sitting there in Diego Garcia. We thought . . . well, they might be useful, right? And nobody else was around."

The police chief stepped up to one of the yellow boxes and ran a hand along it. "I'm not sure what would constitute a fair payment."

"Well," Skadz said before Skyler could speak, "take a crate now. Gesture of goodwill and all that. You'll want to make sure they work, somehow. We can discuss the others later, once we all know the lay of the land."

Skyler closed his mouth. He'd been ready to say "take them," before Skadz stepped in. His new friend had a different way of thinking. Survival instinct mixed with business acumen. They would need both to thrive here.

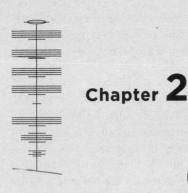

Chapter 2

DARWIN, AUSTRALIA
21.APR.2278

A day later, in a room of white, Skyler sat on a paper-covered bed. He was naked save for a thin blue gown that covered his front. A team of doctors surrounded him, waiting for the vitals harness to complete the basic examination. An array of articulated arms and protrusions extended out from the box, sampling Skyler's pulse, blood pressure, and reflexes. Imaging his eyes, mouth, ears, and nostrils. Foam-padded robotic fingertips probed his scalp, neck, spine, and abdomen.

The machine chirped the conclusion of its examination and rose back into the ceiling. One of the doctors stepped in and began the more delicate work. He took blood—three vials' worth— from Skyler's left arm, and moved on from there. Skin samples, hair samples, a swab of the tongue. On and on it went, all the while the doctors in the room talked quietly among themselves. Occasionally a runner would come in and summon one or more of them in hushed, urgent tones. They'd leave reluctantly, probably off to deal with an actual injury. The city was a mass of terrified, hungry savages, after all, and those were the ones without the disease. But the doctors always came back. They couldn't resist the curiosity that had flown in from beyond the aura.

A thousand questions were asked. Allergies? Medications? Family medical history? Ever dabbled in experimental drugs or designer viruses? Did the Luchtmacht do anything to you? There's no secrets now; you can tell us if they did. On and on it went.

"Lie down, please," one said when the questions finally ended. She was an Indian woman with graying hair and a kind, wrinkled face. "We're going to take you down the hall for an LMRI."

"I can walk," Skyler said.

The woman insisted, so Skyler lay back and allowed the team to escort him through the wide, white hallway outside. Through the door of the next room he caught a glimpse of Skadz undergoing his equally invasive exam. Skadz saw Skyler, too, and flashed a middle finger and a twisted-up face of mock horror. Skyler returned the obscene gesture and lay back, a mild headache nagging at him.

Scans of his brain were taken. So detailed that a datacube had to be fetched to store the three-dimensional imagery. Then he was wheeled to an elevator and taken up twenty stories to a recovery ward. "This floor has been cleared for you and . . . well, the others like you," a nurse explained. Skyler was about to ask what that meant when the young man pushed him into a long room with two rows of beds—twenty at least—along the ubiquitous white walls. Skadz sat on one, still in his exam gown.

Only two other beds were occupied. A man lay in one, studying a personal comm. He glanced over at Skyler's entrance and sat up. Neatly folded on the table next to his bed were military fatigues, though of what nation Skyler couldn't tell.

A few bunks farther down the line lay a woman, one leg wrapped in bandages from ankle to waist. Her eyes were closed. An IV drip line snaked from her wrist to a clear plastic bag hanging from a chrome pole beside her. She had blond hair and an imposing build, tall enough that her feet dangled over the end of the bed.

"Turns out we're not alone," Skadz said. "Skyler, meet Jake."

The man rose to his feet with a soldier's practiced efficiency and shook Skyler's hand.

"Immune, I take it?" Skyler asked.

"Yep," Jake said. His face betrayed nothing.

"You're military?"

He nodded. Again, the lack of expression.

"Who with? What'd you do?"

"Sniper," Jake said flatly. "Australian Army."

Skyler let go of the man's hand. Sniper made sense. The man was calm, precise. His face conveyed, well, not confidence exactly but something between it and boredom.

Turning back to Skadz, Skyler jerked his chin toward the sleeping woman farther into the room.

Skadz only shrugged. "Don't know about her, she's been asleep. Now that we're all here," he said, his voice lowered to a conspiratorial level, "and without our minders hovering, perhaps the three of us could talk."

Jake sat back down on his bed. An answer without answering.

Skyler sat across from him and nodded to Skadz.

"Jake here was just telling me a bit more about what's going on," Skadz started. "Seems the specifics of who's running what around here, and above, are still being settled."

"Makes sense," Skyler said. "The world is suddenly a lot smaller."

"Musical chairs," Jake observed.

Skadz flashed the man a grin, then continued. "Be that as it may, there's talk of putting some kind of militia together. They're testing using hazmat suits as a way to venture out, and if it works they want a few hundred people who know the business end of a gun to go out there and clear the diseased from the land around the Elevator's aura. A purge. Then they're going to barricade us all in and wait for this all to blow over."

"Assuming it ever will," Skyler said.

Jake grunted.

"Stands to reason," Skadz said, "they're going to view us as particularly important in this operation. Maybe even put one of you in charge, with your backgrounds."

"I'm not so sure." At the puzzled expression on Skadz's face, Skyler went on. "We represent a possible cure for, um, this thing."

"SUBS," Skadz said. "They call it SUBS. Synaptic Uncoupling . . . I forget the rest."

Skyler spread his hands. "I think they'll keep us here.

Study us to the atomic level if they have to. We're rare specimens to them, nothing more."

"Well," Skadz said, "I don't know about you two but I can't live like that."

"I'm not sure we have any choice."

"Of course we do."

"You think they'll just let us walk out of here?"

Skadz's face twisted up, dubious. "They can't exactly follow us."

"This again," Skyler said, shaking his head. "Look, do what you want, but this is no time to be selfish."

"Jake?" Skadz asked, turning to the other man.

"Yeah?"

"You're a quiet bastard, aren't you?"

"Mm-hmm."

Skadz grinned, despite himself. "Well, talk, man! What's your take on all this?"

Jake glanced at each of them in turn, then looked down at his hands. "We, our kind, need to stick together."

"Look, you two are military. This life-of-service bullshit is in your bloody genes. But that's not for me, mates. I need something more. I need a life. I need to make my own decisions."

"No one's stopping you," Skyler observed.

"Yeah, well," Skadz said, "that's the thing. Jake here is right. We need to be unified if we're going to control our own destiny. A unified front, right? That shit only works if we're unified."

Jake nodded solemnly.

Skyler shook his head. "I'm not saying you're wrong, I'm just saying I won't leave. We can help these people, in more ways than just as specimens."

"So let's figure out a way to do that," Skadz said, "where we're not caged animals. All right?"

"Can I get in on this?"

The three men turned in unison to the new voice. The woman on the far bunk had woken. She'd propped herself on her elbows and winced as she tried to ease back toward the wall. Jake was up and at her side in an instant, a pillow clutched in his hand. He stuffed it behind her.

"Thanks," she said.

"No problem," Jake replied, returning to his own bunk.

"What's your name?" Skadz asked.

The woman took a moment to let a wave of discomfort pass. "I'm Samantha. Everyone calls me Sam."

"And you have the immunity, too?" Skyler asked.

She looked at each of them in turn before nodding once. Then her face twisted up, concern on her brow. "Wait. Are we it? Just the four of us?"

The group debated ideas for almost an hour, and when one of the nurses finally returned to fetch them, it was Skadz who spoke for them.

Skyler listened to the defiant words, watched the nurse's face pale, and then sat back to wait as Arthur Braithwaite was informed that the patients had revolted.

"I really don't have time for this," Braithwaite said as he strode into the room.

"Well, make some," Skadz shot back. "This is important."

And so the negotiations began, and they lasted until well past sunset. Skyler let Skadz do most of the talking—the man had a gift for it, no denying that—and interjected only when he thought it would cut the palpable tension.

Jake said nothing at all. He seemed content to do whatever Skadz and Skyler wanted, or at least he planned to let them come to a deal and then he would decide if he wanted it or not. Sam voiced strong opinions, always taking Skadz's side. But she lasted only ten minutes before the medications took over and sent her into an uneasy sleep.

In the end Braithwaite agreed. They all agreed, and thanks to some clever wordplay by Skadz, Braithwaite seemed to feel like he'd just brokered peace in the Middle East. The man brought in an assistant to draw up a formal agreement. A sickly-looking, stringy-haired man named Kip. He tapped on a slate as Braithwaite recounted the agreement.

"You'll keep your aircraft," Braithwaite said, "the . . . ?"

"Melville," Skyler said, before Skadz could interject. The Jamaican shot Skyler a somewhat furious glare at that, then somehow turned it into a grin like a schoolboy who'd just been pranked.

Braithwaite went on. "You'll keep the *Melville* in a hangar at the airport, not here in Nightcliff as I'd hoped, on the condition that any excursions outside the known limits of the protective aura be cleared with the tower here. Our needs will take priority, with payment agreed upon ahead of time. Though, I have to warn you gentlemen it's unclear at this point what will serve as currency in Darwin."

"I'm sure we can figure something out," Skadz said.

"Anything else you manage to bring back is of course yours to barter or use; we'll make no claim to any of it. However, we reserve the right to inspect your cargo anytime we deem it necessary to do so. This will be true of anyone else leaving the city."

Skadz perked up. "I thought it was just the four of us?"

"You're the only immunes that we know of," Braithwaite said, "but I was informed just before coming in here that the hazmat suits seem adequate protection against the disease. One does not need to remain near the Elevator, one simply needs to avoid contact with air that has not been scrubbed by it."

"Interesting," Skyler muttered, the ramifications settling like tumblers on a lock. Immunes wouldn't be the only ones who could leave the city, but they could just stay outside longer than anyone else, and with more freedom of movement and use of senses. The news brought a mixture of relief and anxiety.

Samantha stirred. A sound just short of a fearful cry escaped her lips. The sound made them all jump, including her. Her imposing size, obvious even under the hospital blankets, combined with the set of her jaw and the cool look in her eyes, made Skyler morbidly curious as to what she'd been through that would bring her nightmares. The world beyond Darwin could break anyone if it could break her.

"What'd I miss?" Samantha asked, rubbing her eyes.

"We're just talking details," Skadz replied. He motioned

for Braithwaite to continue. "You were saying, about the hazard suits?"

"Yes. Given our success with the outfits, there will be others able to find and recover that which the city needs to function. And, soon, taking the battle beyond our protective field."

Here it comes, Skyler thought.

"You want us," Skadz said, "to lead that effort?"

The police captain sucked in his lower lip and shook his head. "No. Well, maybe. Until the few doctors and scientists we have left finish analyzing the samples you provided today, I think it's best you avoid excessive risk."

"Good," Skadz said.

Skyler glanced between them. "We'll help if needed, of course."

"Of course," Braithwaite replied. "This leads me to one other condition of our deal, however."

"Which is what?" Skadz asked.

The chief constable inhaled deeply. "Until we know if there are more like you, at least one of you should stay behind during any excursion outside. We can't risk losing all four of you at once."

"I can't see how we can function as a team without the four of us," Skadz replied.

"I'm sorry," the man replied, "but this is nonnegotiable."

"It's fine," Samantha said. "I'll stay. I'm not going anywhere with this, am I?" She patted her bandaged leg.

"And when it's healed? What if there's still only us four?" Skadz asked.

Sam could only shrug.

"We'll figure something out," Skyler offered.

"Like what?" Skadz asked.

Skyler thought about it, finally gave a shrug that matched Sam's.

For the first time since Braithwaite entered, Jake spoke up. "Easy," the sniper said. "Priority one: Find more like us."

The airport buzzed with activity. A few dozen aircraft had landed during the chaos of the first days of the disease, adding to an already crowded tarmac. It was an old airport, built long before the ultracap-fueled VTOL revolution. Instead of the modern array of heat-shielded launchpads, it had a three-kilometer-long runway plus all the usual ancillary taxi paths. Grafted on to this maze of concrete were dozens of hangar buildings and retrofitted launchpads. A new terminal to replace the original had been planned but construction had only ever proceeded as far as demolishing the original. Skyler gathered the shift in focus to Nightcliff, along with dozens of private launchpads atop buildings all across the metropolis, had alleviated much of the need for the new structure. Politics had probably gotten in the way.

In the aftermath of the disease the situation in and around the airport was chaotic, to say the least. Skyler once again let Skadz take the lead, this time in navigating the politics of the place. Residents, both old and new, claimed ownership of the various structures along the runway. Things evolved by the hour, with old recreational pilots showing up to claim their hangar and aircraft from squatters, then leaving a short time later with a payment that changed their perspective, or perhaps not leaving at all, having either rousted whoever had tried to claim their property or finding themselves at the wrong end of a gun for their efforts.

This all changed, somewhat, when the immunes arrived. News spread like floodwater, partly because of the rumored capabilities of the three men, and partly because they'd arrived with a sizable military and police escort. The legitimacy of such organizations might be in doubt, but the capability of their weapons no one questioned.

Skadz had a mandate from Nightcliff to pick a hangar, whichever he liked, and Skyler did not envy the task. There was not a place along the entire runway someone hadn't claimed as their own. Whichever one Skadz chose would ultimately require an ousting.

"That one," Skyler suggested, pointing toward a modest hangar. The building had a sign above the massive door that read CROC TOURS!

"Why?" Skadz asked.

"Near the middle, so we don't feel like outsiders here. Plenty of room inside for the *Mel.* And look at the roof."

"What about it?"

"Toward the back. That big flat section, like a sundeck or patio or something. We could grow some food up there."

Skyler kept one last observation to himself. Of all the hangars they'd passed, this one seemed to have only a single occupant: an old sour-faced woman. She stood in front of the hangar door dressed in a dirty shift, arms folded across her chest and a dark scowl on her face. Scowl or not, she stood alone. And through the gap in the door behind her, there was no aircraft.

"The owner doesn't look happy," Skadz observed.

"Yeah, but she's alone and I see no plane inside. Let's talk to her."

The woman resisted at first. Told them to leave, that she wasn't leaving, that she wouldn't sell or be bullied. Skadz proved adept once again in dealing with people. Charm seemed to radiate off the man, and inside five minutes they were sitting inside with the old lady, sipping iced tea, as the escort of soldiers waited outside.

"My husband and I ran this business for twenty-two years," she explained, tears rolling down her cheeks.

"He was out there when . . . ?" Skyler trailed off, silenced by the look in her eyes.

She held his gaze for a moment and then something broke inside her. She began to sob. Skadz moved to sit next to her and put his arm around her. A minute passed before she could speak. "Hal took four students out that day. Made him coffee that morning, and he didn't say thanks. We'd fought the night before. About money, same as always. I never . . . I never thought the last time I'd ever see him we'd be angry at each other. It's not supposed to end like that."

"No, it isn't," Skadz said. The tenderness in his voice was genuine.

"You're a pilot?" the woman said to him, suddenly.

"Nah, I'm just me. He's the pilot." Skadz gestured toward Skyler.

The old woman looked at him, then back to Skadz. "And it's true what they said? You're immune to the disease?"

Skadz nodded.

She gathered herself then. "You want my hangar. The

hangar my husband and I ran our lives out of for so many years."

Skyler held up his hands defensively. It was Skadz who spoke. "We did, but there's no way—"

"It's yours," she said instantly. "On one condition. Bring him back. Bring Hal home so I can bury him."

The rest was details. She needed a place to stay, and though Skadz offered to let her live on in the hangar, her desire to do so had vanished. Safe passage to her sister's house in the Narrows was her request, and Skadz got one of the soldiers to agree to take her there.

Skyler didn't know it then, but the return of remains from beyond the aura would be a constant request in the years to come. One that often led to trouble, and disappointment, and heartbreak. And, eventually, such a request would lead to a mission that changed the world, again.

"First things first," Skadz said. "We need a safe house. Somewhere outside, stocked and secure. A place we can go if the shit goes down."

Skyler shook his head. They'd been at it for hours, all through the afternoon and past a meager dinner. Heavy rain drummed against the thin sheet metal of the hangar roof, almost drowning the distant sounds of gunfire in Darwin's anarchic slums. Almost, but not quite. Part of him wanted to be out there, helping. That part felt shackled, though. Hidden away beneath the shock of everything that had happened, and the distance of hope for what would come. The city was stratifying into the sort of place one would never willingly choose to live, much less thrive. It had become a prison for the last vestiges of humanity. At the airport's lone functioning tavern someone had speculated it would take a few thousand years for humanity to return to its former glory, and that assumed the disease was cured tomorrow. Every day spent trapped here was a day closer to extinction.

The *Melville* rested in the center of the large hangar, her engines exposed, halfway through the laborious cleaning process. She'd be ready to fly in two days, Skyler thought. Whether or not he, Skadz, and Jake would have agreed on a first mission by then remained to be seen, but the chances seemed dim. Everything seemed dim. He felt a bit jealous of Samantha, still lying in that hospital bed. The token stay-behind, waiting for new skin to grow along her leg. Four weeks, the doctors estimated. He hoped they weren't poking and prodding her too much.

"Hmm," Jake managed to say at the safe-house idea. In the man's parlance this constituted a stiff rebuke. Skyler liked Jake a lot.

"From my perspective," Skyler said, leaning back in the folding chair in which he sat, "everything beyond the aura is our safe house. Why settle on one? If things get ugly here, we fly to an island. Somewhere isolated. And wait."

"What if that island has no supplies we can use?"

"Not an issue," Skyler said. "Stock the *Melville* with a week's worth of food for three, and all we need is a place to charge her caps. We can do that just about anywhere."

"Long as the grid remains up," Jake interjected.

"Yeah," Skadz agreed eagerly. "What he said."

"There's mini-thors everywhere. They'll run for decades unattended. Power won't be a problem for us for some time."

Skadz folded his arms across his chest. "I'd still feel better if we had a place to go. Maybe something walking distance from the aura, in case we don't have an aircraft to use someday."

There was some wisdom in that. Skyler couldn't bring himself to outright agree, not after so many hours of arguing, so he said nothing instead.

"Gentlemen, good evening," a new voice suddenly said, from somewhere near the *Melville*.

Skyler fell over in his already-leaning chair. He scrambled to his feet. Skadz and Jake had fanned out to either side of the newcomer. Jake had a pistol in his hand, and stood with the sort of semi-crouch a trained killer used when cornered.

"Who the hell are you?" Skadz demanded. "How'd you get in here?"

"Relax, I am unarmed. My name is Prumble," the man said. He had a mild New Zealander accent and a booming, jovial tone, like a journeyman playactor who never knew when to turn off the stage presence. "As for entry, that was trivial. The locks on this building are pathetic."

"You broke into the wrong place, friend," Skadz said.

"On the contrary," Prumble said, "I didn't *break* anything. The lock—and I use that term loosely—on your back door still functions just fine. In fact even the most astute forensic investigator would never know it had been tampered with. I was a locksmith in my past life, you see."

Skadz, weaponless, glanced somewhat nervously at Jake and then Skyler. The three of them had been pestered endlessly about their unusual status since arriving. A number of people, from curious to downright crazy, had already come calling at the airport gate for them, only to be turned away.

"Be that as it may," Skadz said, "you still came to the wrong place. Piss off."

"I'm exactly where I want to be," Prumble replied. "You're the immunes, are you not?"

"So what if we are," Skyler said. "Why are you here?"

"I'm here to offer my services," Prumble replied. "Everyone is talking about you. And once people realize you're able to move around outside the city they'll never leave you alone."

"Offering your services as a locksmith?"

"For a start." Prumble came to stand between the three of them, his hands splayed out to show their emptiness. He bowed slightly. "I propose a trade."

"What trade?" Skadz asked.

Prumble swiveled his head from speaker to speaker. "I will perform a full upgrade on the security of this building for you. And in exchange, I require something from beyond the aura."

"What exactly do you need?" Skadz asked.

Skyler leaned forward, interest piqued. Lured in by the stage actor voice or the promise of something important, he didn't know, but he already liked where this was going. It was one way to settle the argument as to the nature of the group's first excursion, at least.

"There is a factory," Prumble said, "in Perth, wherein a company called Kastensauer manufactures lock mechanisms. Are you boys up for a little adventure?"